TRIALS  OF THE NEKOMANCER

Book 1

by

⊆・ω・⊇ Dungeon Ducky ⊆・ω・⊇

Table of Contents

Catpurr 1

The Start of a Catventure

Throughout history, necromancers have always faced persecution. They were scorned, hunted, and generally treated unpleasantly, despite being the best class to ever exist.

I mean, who knew that raising the dead and assembling armies of zombies to do your bidding would upset the living? After all, there was an unprecedented amount of free labor to be had by simply animating a few bones.

Murder victims could be raised to find their killers. Skeletons could work the fields, while necromancers could help ease the dead into peace without violently exorcizing them. Any job a living being could do, the undead could do better, with endless stamina and less pay, even the IRS couldn't tax the dead! Why couldn't anyone see that?!

Adam Glow wasn't "anyone."

That's why he pursued the path of a necromancer in hopes of becoming a lich like his teacher.

After all, it was the class that offered all the perks! Immortality, cool animated bones, unfathomable power... What possible downsides could there be to shedding his weak meat suit? Plus, necromancy could help build a utopian society. They just couldn't see it because they lacked vision—lacked ingenuity! The grand leaps in human technological advancement that could be made if only humanity would shed their ignorant ways and embrace the bone!

Sadly, he was alone in his love for the undead. Whenever Adam tried to convince people, he was met with indifference, disgust, or anger—

usually, a combination of all three. This would force him to flee with his only companion, Schrödinger.

Schrödinger was soft, sleek, and aloof, with silky, bone-white fur, and eyes that shone a vivid blood-red, much like the undead under Adam's control. But unlike the walking corpses, Schrödinger was very much alive, and also a cat! The only living thing in the world that Adam truly cared about.

Schrödinger purred in his arms as Adam dodged the thousandth arrow that was fired at him. Despite the jostling around and sounds of explosions going off around him, Schrödinger remained remarkably calm.

Opening his status window, Adam contemplated his escape from his dogged pursuers.

TITLE: ESCAPE ARTIST (+ 5 Luck, Alertness, + 10 Movement Speed)

NAME: Adam F. Glow

LEVEL: 314

MAIN CLASS: Lich Aspirant LVL 145

AUX CLASS 1: Scoundrel LVL 56

AUX CLASS 2: Healer LVL 43

AUX CLASS 3: Punching Bag LVL 70

Familiar: Schrödinger

HP: 1542/15050

MANA: 209/45540

STR: 20(+30)/50

CON: 60(+50)/110

DEX: 60(+70)/130

ARC: 400(+150)550

SEN: 90(+20)/110

EGO: 10(+5)/15

SKILLS: Identify V5, Tongue of Nations V3, Sapping Sting V3, Knife Throw V5, Sneak V3, Deft Hands V4, Pilfer Bones V5, Chill

Touch V5, Cause Fear, Concentration V1, Resurrection V2, Quick Learner V3, EXP Stacker V5, False Life V1, Ray of Sickness V2, Animate Dead V5, Revifivy V3, Speak With Dead V5, Raise Dead V3, Create Undead V5, Eyebite V2, Soul Cage V5, Magic Jar V2, Finger of Death V1, Spirit Shroud V2, Call of Spirits V5, Summon Undead V5, Create Catnip V5, Inflict Wounds V1, Bestow Curse V2, Danse Macabre V5, Vampire Touch V2, Life Transference V3, Blood Rain V2, Shackles of Pain V3, Grasp of the Damned V3, Animate Bone V5, Dodge Danger V5, Animate Flesh V3, Atrophy V2, Soul Bond V5, Blood Pact V3, Healing Hands V2, Brace V4, Absorb Blow V5, Dash V5, Levitate V5, Lightning Bolt V3, Deathly Chill V3, Desecrate Enchantments V5, Gaze of Contempt V4, Life Siphon V2, Putrid Bile V1, Rotting Flesh V2, Death Arrow V2, Soul Barbs V2, Soul Grasp V5, Touch of Agony V3, Wither V2, Death Hold V3, Life Crush V2, Recycle Undead V5, Wave of Darkness V3, Smokebomb V5, Ghost Vision V5, Create Water V5, Summon Deathrider V1, True Teleportation V3, Air Walk V4, Create Bone Levitation V4, Create Soul Reaper V1, Alert V3, Evasion V3, Bone Totem V3, Store Spirits V3, Create Boneyard V3, Summon Army V4, Mana Siphon V4, Harden Flesh V3, Use Magic Device V5, Harvesting V4, Curative Curse V3, Dodging V4, Mend Bone V5, Socially Inept V3, Mass Siphon V1, Iron Maiden V1, New Life V1, Restore Corpse V3, Wraith Form V3, Exorism V2, Scan Mind V2, Spirit Lock V3, Blood Rune V1, Bone Barrier V5, Regenerate V4, Arcane Will V5, Will to Change V5, Shrug Off V2, Identify Undead V5, Mend Flesh V3, Power Speech V3, Damned Messenger V1, Iron Will V2, Cat Lover V5, Tyrant V5, Firebolt v3, Ghostly Flames V4, Shocking Grasp V3, Mind Ward V2, Blood Sword V1, Armor of Flesh V4, Spark V2, Fleeing V5, Hard as Bone V2, Control Undead V5, Dominate Summon V3, Cursed Breath V1, Deft Hands V3, Meditate V5, Poisonous Cloud V3, Summon Death Steed V1, Transfer Summon V2, Summon Cat V5, Corpse Skin V5, Play Dead V5, With V3, Arcane Mark V2, Diagnose Disease V4, Blood Biography V3, Cackling Skull V5, Force Shield V5, Force Armor V2, Death Ward V2, Shadow Walk V3, Ambitions of a Lich V1 (rare), Darken Area V5, Detect Trap V5, Wail of The Banshe V3, One With The Dead V5, Anti-Life Field V2, Soul Bind V3, Portal V5, Lover of Undead V4, Kingslayer V1 (rare), Halt Undead V5, Essence of Doom V2, Store Corpse V5, Undertaker V4, Loved by Undead (unique), Bone Spear V5, Command Army V5, Soulfire V3, Soul Blast V1, Corpse Lance V3, Bone Armor V5, Create Core V5, Muffle Steps V4, Novice Necromancy V5, Apprentice Necromancy V5, Mask Presence V4, Adept Necromancy V5, Expert Necromancy V5, Master Necromancy V3, Ghost Rider V1, Eternal Servitude V1, Demons Of Darkness V1, Shackles of Darkness V3, Swift Harvest V3, Rigor Mortis V5, Final Service V1, Draw Life V2, Transcribe Runes V4, Imbue Death V5, Create Infection V3, Ritual Caster V3, Chanting V5, Wordless Chant V5, Minion Damage Support V4, Summon Swap V3, Darkness Bind V3, Jump V3, Cross Country V5, Wellspring of Mana V5, Mind Shield V5, Poison Spit V1, Bone Daddy V5, Pain Tolerance V5, Grave Desecration V3, Share Sense V4, Locate True Love V4, Spook V5, Create Bone Weapon V2, Scars of Life V5, Good Intentions V5, Rapid Growth (rare) V5, Blessing of Nyx V5 (special), Lost in Translation V3 (curse), Fondness for Cats V5, Doom Scroll V1, Knitting V5, Thermal Sight V3, Fly V5, Cogulate V3, Summon Tentacles V1, Rune Shield V2, Shrink V3, Enlarge V1, Void Storage V5, Multi Hands V3, Fast Reader V3, Transmute V5, Natural Disaster V5 (curse), Analyze Skill V5, Detect Lie V4, Sense V5, Pray V1, Heal Self V5, Reconstitute V3, Arcane Summoning V2, Flesh Sacrifice V1, Regrow V4, Drums Expertise V1, Wade Through Fire V2, Fire Resistance V3, Electric Resistance V2, Holy Resistance V1, Curse Resistance V2, Fate Resistance V3, Blunt Force Resistance V2, Pierce Resistance V5, Slash Resistance V3, V1, Poison Resistance V4, Bone Resistance V5, Fear Resistance V5, Stun Resistance V3, Blind Resistance V4, Arcane Sense V3, Ice Resistance V1, Solar Resistance V1, Dark Resistance V4, Wind Resistance V5, Disease Resistance V5, Nausea Resistance V1, Bite Resistance V1, Acid Resistance V5, Blood Resistance V1, Animal Affinity V1, Combat Casting V3, Duck and Cover V4, From Spell V3, Inhaler V2, Throw Anything V5, Telekinesis V5, Force Grip V3, Toughness V4, Quicken Spell V5, Agile Maneuvers V5, Pick Combat V5, Cooking V2, Warp V2, Combat [illegible]

He was on his last drop of mana—less than half a percent, to be exact—with the other 99.5 percent of it having been used to defend against the overwhelming barrage of the hundreds of spellcasters and bowmen who had led him into a trap.

Though Adam knew better, he couldn't miss the opportunity to snap up an ancient necromancer's artifact—an item he was tipped off about by several paladins gossiping over a campfire, unaware that the person they were hunting was sitting in a nearby tree, observing them as they discussed "heretical activity" and the "Eye of Eli."

Adam had licked his lips, listening intently to the men boast about the artifact being the key to lichhood, the final piece to his puzzle and the answer to all his problems. Of course, there had been many rumors like this in the past, but none quite so... tantalizing.

Despite his skepticism, Adam had arrived to claim the Eye. Unfortunately, the rabid knights and pesky foot soldiers had rigged the temple to explode, causing it to collapse on top of him as he collected his prize. A prize which, much to his soon-to-be-dismay, was actually the *real* artifact. However, before he could warp away from the explosion, a myriad of spells rained down, forcing his auto barrier to activate.

Luckily for him, he had various resistances to the cornucopia of attacks showering upon him. Woefully, he underestimated just how many people had come to kill him and how dedicated they were. Wizards, archers, pegasus riders and their magic-resistant steeds. At one point, Adam thought he spotted a row of trebuchets.

It was only after creating hundreds of spirits and undead within the army's ranks that he was presented with an opportunity to escape. Using **Mass Raise** to summon hundreds of low tier skeletons, and **Summon Swap** to trade places, he was able to break their formation.

Seizing the moment, Adam tried to fly, but something prevented him from doing so, forcing him to resort to brute force. Luckily, he was good at two things: running away and making more undead. He wasn't much of a fighter when it came down to it, but he was always good at dodging and having minions do his bidding.

"Kill that filthy bone-digger!" Goosebumps crawled along Adam's skin as he recognized the voice.

"Ugh! Not this fleshie again!" Adam huffed in annoyance. His notebook flew open, and his notes scattered as he confirmed it with a glance.

It was Junith, a paladin of the Holy Inquisition with whom Adam was well-acquainted. She was unmistakable in her white and gold-trimmed armor. Usually, she held a flaming silver broadsword in her hand, but today she wielded an accursed scorching blade that burned brighter than usual as she charged at him.

Adam grimaced. *Seems she's still furious about that mishap with the king.*

Ever since the complete and *totally* accidental death of a guy that Adam witnessed harassing a woman, the deranged lady and her entourage of holier-than-thou zealots had been baying for his blood.

It wasn't his fault that he couldn't recognize the king from hundreds of meters in the sky, and it was most *definitely not* his fault that the old man died from a heart attack. Granted, his small bolt of electricity meant to stop the harassment may have been the culprit, but from above, it just looked like some old pervert being a lecher!

He had tried apologizing on numerous occasions and had even offered to attempt to resurrect their God King or whatever, but no matter how many times he said he was sorry, the woman always charged at him while screaming something along the lines of "HERETIC!" or "UNCLEAN!" or "PURGE!" or "DIE SCUM!"

Ever since then, they were committed to "exorcizing" him, the Imperial Guard and zealots of the church always on him like flies on a corpse, forcing him to flee.

Adam hugged Schrödinger close to his chest as Junith swiped at him. His passive skill, **Dodge Danger V5,** activated. Boosted by **Evasion,** it caused his knees to buckle, allowing him to effortlessly slide beneath the heavy weapon, dodging the attack.

She hadn't entirely missed, though. Whatever the blade was made of had set off mad alarms in Adam's head as his health bar dropped by a whole 500 points. And it hadn't even touched him! Two more misses like that, and he was dead. He didn't even want to think about what would have happened if he had tried to deflect or guard the attack.

Seeing the expression on Adam's face, the woman smirked, signaling her soldiers to wait.

"You feel that, heretic? This is the Divine Holy Blade of Akalym, forged in the divine fires of our most sacred altar, its divinity so divi— OW!"

Whatever she was going to say, he wasn't going to let her finish. With deft hands, he quickly threw pocket sand laced with mana directly at the jabbering woman and took off, ignoring the accusations of cowardice and swear words from the nearby soldiers.

"I'll gut you like a fish, Heretic!" the angry woman yelled.

Speaking of fish, that does sound good right about now.

All Adam wanted to do was flee with his prize and eat some fish with Schrödinger, but looking at his depleted mana bar and the cavalry on the horizon, it didn't seem likely he would ever eat *anything* with his feline friend again. Whatever array they had used was still draining his mana faster than he could regenerate it, and it kept expanding, covering more ground than he could run. On top of that, it seemed to nullify all the magical enchantments on his armor, making his storage units and special effects useless.

Maybe it's time to see what you can do, Adam thought to himself as he stared at the amulet in his free hand.

Using **Identify**, he tried to read the Eye of Eli, but all it showed was:

Eye of Eli — Legendary Artifact

???

Activation Cost: 100 Mana

"What now?" he wondered.

This was odd, considering his **Identify** skill was at max rank.

Using the skill had cost precious mana, leaving him with less than half a percent of his total mana pool. Looking down at the amulet in his hand, he decided to take his chances with it.

It was usually not a good idea to activate an unknown artifact, especially when one didn't know what it did. But at this point, what did he have to lose? In a matter of seconds, he'd be out of mana and dead anyway.

The deranged woman had recovered and was charging at him with bloodshot eyes, while armored horsemen rode in from the sunset, and Pegasus archers strafed his position with arrows, making Adam grimace.

His only regret was that Schrödinger would probably die here with him.

"Nothing ventured, nothing gained," Adam mused as he used the last remaining bit of mana he had to activate the artifact.

Suddenly, the world around him froze. Arrows stopped mid-flight, and the flaming sword hovered only inches away from his neck. The image of the crazed woman frozen in place would have been hilarious if not for the fact that she was but a mere second away from decapitating him.

An alert abruptly appeared in front of his face, interrupting his introspection. A second later, a voice boomed in his ear, followed by several other voices echoing its message.

THE EYE OF ELI SEES YOU, NECROMANCER. DO YOU PRESENT AN OFFERING?

YES. ←

NO.

With no other choice, Adam willed it to say yes, but what came next surprised him.

CHOOSE WHAT YOU HOLD MOST DEAR TO SACRIFICE TO THE LORD:
YOURSELF (ADAM GLOW) ←
SCHRÖDINGER (FAMILIAR OF ADAM GLOW)

Is this thing serious? Adam thought to himself as his jaw refused to move. He could never sacrifice his only friend. It was preposterous!

There has to be a different option! Cancel… Cancel! Adam willed, but nothing happened. With each agonizing second of internal struggle, the world around him gradually sped up, Junith's blade quivering.

Damn it!

CHOOSE WHAT YOU HOLD MOST DEAR TO SACRIFICE:
YOURSELF (ADAM GLOW) ←
SCHRÖDINGER (FAMILIAR OF ADAM GLOW)

"DAMN IT!" Adam shouted as time continued. He pressed down on the screen just as the flames flicking against his skin began to burn. In the next moment, a massive burst of energy erupted around him, scattering his attackers and leveling the entire landscape, kicking up dust and debris as humans flew, screaming.

"ELI ACCEPTS YOUR GRACIOUS OFFERING, YOUNG NECROMANCER!"

A voice akin to a god bellowed out, shortly before Adam felt a profound fatigue weighing down on him, as if his very soul were being drained.

"YOU HAVE BEEN CHOSEN!"

Strangely, he began to itch all over, a burning sensation creeping along his back as his eyes started to hurt. Checking his status menu, his jaw hit the floor. In fact, he was so stunned he inadvertently dropped Schrödinger, who merely scampered away.

TITLE: Idiot Novice of Eli (???)
NAME: Adam F. Glow
LEVEL: 1
MAIN CLASS: Nekomancer
HP: 10/100
MANA: 0/75
STR: 7
CON: 10
DEX: 12
ARC: 15
SEN: 9
EGO: 10
Buffs: Loved by Undead (unique), Minor Blessing of Eli (unique), Eyes of a Predator V1, Corrupted Blessing of Nyx (unique)
Debuffs: Ha! You Sacrificed Your Stats for a Cat?! V1 (Curse), Catsification V1 (curse)
Skills: Animate Bone V1, Irritating Touch V1, Cat Claws V1, Identify V1, Summon Skeleton V1

"You've gotta..." was all Adam could say before a blue portal suddenly ripped open and dragged him in.

Snapping himself out of his bewilderment, Adam dove and attempted to grab Schrödinger, but it was too late. The spell was already in effect, yanking on his ankles and pulling him through.

The cat looked up, attempting to run towards its master, but was caught by the soot-covered Junith, who now wore a bewildered expression.

"Schrödinger!" Adam screamed in panic as he watched the feline being scooped up by the lady in white armor. Despite racking his brain to figure out how to save his companion, there was nothing he could do.

Nothing at all, as he was thrown helplessly into the unknown abyss.

Catpurr 2
Trial One

Loud screams echoed through the sky as a flailing body plummeted to its death.

"Levitate! Fly! Air Walk! True Teleportation!" Adam rattled off skills as he desperately tried to halt his rapid descent towards the forest below.

Think, Adam! Think!

No matter how hard he tried to rack his brain for a solution, it came up blank. His status screen held no viable skills to save his life.

"No, no, NO! Aaaaaaaah!" Adam screamed, closing his eyes just before he expected to splat into the grassy landscape.

But no impact ever came.

"Huh?" Adam opened his eyes to find himself floating in mid-air, just short of splattering against the ground.

Suddenly, his skill box lit up.

Catsification Curse activated!

Adam's body abruptly spun, reorienting himself with his feet angled towards the ground before he was firmly planted, completely unharmed.

"Hu–whaa?" Adam sputtered, his face contorted with confusion at the events that had transpired as the status screen displayed notifications in front of him.

-1 Life

Curse: Catsification

      Always land on feet. No matter what.

      Nine lives (8/9)

      Weakness to catnip—Irresistible!

> Weakness to milk
> Weakness to chocolate
> Random urge to knock items over
> Weakness to cucumbers
> Weakness to water
> Catsify skills

"What the Nyx is this?!" Adam yelled, his voice coming out at a higher pitch than usual as he stared at the absurdity of the description before him.

He pulled up his system.

BETA SYSTEM v1.01
TITLE: Idiot Novice of Eli (???)
NAME: Adam F. Glow
SPECIES: Nekoboy
LEVEL: 1
MAIN CLASS: Nekomancer
HP: 10/100
MANA: 0/75
STR: 7
CON: 10
DEX: 12
ARC: 15
SEN: 9
EGO: 10
Buffs: Loved by Undead (unique), Minor Blessing of Eli (unique), Eyes of a Predator V1, Corrupted Blessing of Nyx (unique)
Debuffs: Ha! You Sacrificed Your Stats for a Cat?! V1 (curse), Catsification V1 (curse)
Skills: Animate Bone V1, Irritating Touch V1, Cat Claws V1, Identify V1

Everything was wrong! From his stats to his skills, even his species and system interface had been altered.

Suddenly, a message appeared, leaving Adam even more bewildered as he read it.

ConCATulations. This is a pre-recorded message! So uh, don't bother getting mad and yelling at me. Anyway, congratulations on being chosen by Eli! As part of your trial to ascend to lichhood, you've been stripped of your possessions and skills and placed in a foreign land as part of your first trial! So, good luck! Don't die!

Adam's eyes narrowed. For a pre-recorded message, it seemed oddly familiar. However, before he could delve into the fading message, his eyes went wide.

Schrödinger!

He began to panic, looking around for his companion, but his fluffy feline friend was nowhere to be found.

Desperate, Adam started opening and closing his system, repeating to himself that his familiar was still there. But the tab for **Familiar** was missing, and he could no longer feel his pet's special bond.

He collapsed to his knees, stunned beyond all belief.

An absence lingered, like a part of his soul was stolen, a feeling of emptiness that was... indescribable.

Schrödinger...

"SCHRÖDINGER!" Adam screamed in agony, the only reply being the echo of the forest and a flock of fleeing birds.

* * *

After recovering and taking stock of his situation, Adam spent half a day walking through the misty forest in a daze, pondering the facts of his situation.

One—he was short. Incredibly so.

His oversized robes, now devoid of their magic power, served as evidence. His body had regressed to that of a small child, albeit one that was much furrier than he'd been as an adolescent, with a large tuft of red hair on his chest that had never existed before.

Two—his eyes itched. A lot. They wouldn't stop tearing up and kept twitching at nearly every bush and leaf that rustled. Additionally, his ears had been replaced with pointed, furry triangles on his head that quivered when he touched them.

And three—he needed to get back to the Garland continent to find Schrödinger.

Although he couldn't feel his companion anymore, he had the instinctive sense that his feline friend was still alive.

Alive and in danger.

Adam cringed at the thought of the paladins having his one and only friend in their disgusting, meaty clutches.

WELCOME TO TRIAL ONE!
Prove your worth by exterminating the meatbags!

Suddenly, massive, bold words hung in the air above the trees, spelled out in neon-blue lettering.

What the Nyx?

Before he could make sense of the words, his system updated, and a message appeared.

Mandatory quest given!
Exterminate fleshy meatbag creatures that inhabit this area: 0/10

Possible Rewards: Exp, Gold, Pocket Lint, Bottle of Freya's Bath Water, Half-Eaten Cookie
Penalty for Failure: DEATH.

Death? That doesn't seem fair at all!

You have five days to complete the task.
Time Remaining: 119:59:59

Catpurr 3
Eaten By a Duck

"Crap! Crap! Crap!" Adam yelled as he sprinted through the flaming forest, dragging his oversized robes as fast as his little legs could carry him.

Waddling quickly behind, and nearly catching up, was a massive, scaly duck the size of a two-story house, swatting away trees and bushes as it gave chase and quacked hysterically.

Its giant bill opened, spewing red flames as it attempted to run him down. Fortunately, the now nekoboy was a tiny target. The flames had only managed to sear the top tuft of his head, creating a clean bald spot.

MY HAIR! Adam shrieked, frantically patting his red hair, which was caked with smoldering flames.

It had come from nowhere. The moment Adam saw the quest timer, the oversized bird materialized, immediately giving chase with its loud webbed feet smacking the earth.

This is a thousand times unfair! How am I supposed to kill a duckysaur with no attack skills or minions to do my bidding? Adam panicked before spotting a nearby cliff and changing his trajectory, rushing towards the perilous edge.

Gah! If only I had a skeleton!

All he had were **Animate Bone**, **Irritating Touch**, and **Cat Claws**. The latter of which only produced tiny claws from his fingertips, while **Irritating Touch** just made its targets itchy. Nothing that would help against even the smallest cousin of the mighty dragons. At least when he started out as a necromancer, he had the **Animate Minor Skeleton** skill and lots of bones to play with!

Now, he had nothing as he stood on the edge of a cliff, gazing down at the vast expanse below. Adam spun around, his eyes blinking rapidly as they involuntarily dilated at the sight of the white-feathered dragonoid.

Alright! Time to put all my years of running away to the test! Crouching low as the beast quacked in his direction, Adam prepared to evade.

Yet the monster did something strange. It slowed down, adjusting its pace until it reached a brisk stroll and walked right up to the nekoboy.

Adam's new furry ears folded down as he gazed up at the giant creature, which now hovered over his small body with beady, menacing eyes. He had hoped to lure the creature to the edge, making it fall to its death. Contrary to his expectations, the monster wasn't dumb, but rather intelligent! It saw right through the ruse.

It quacked, hitting the nekoboy with its hot breath before opening its yellow bill and revealing a row of sharp teeth that made Adam wince from the stench.

MINOR DRAGON FEAR DETECTED! CONSTITUTION SAVE FAILED! Paralyzation in effect for 20 seconds.

Dragon Fear. Adam knew this skill well, but despite understanding its effects, it did nothing to diminish the fact that he was depowered and incapable of resisting.

Ah. I'm in danger.

Adam closed his eyes. If he were his former self, he'd have had no trouble dealing with a mere Duckysaur. However, now he had nothing. No skills, no passives—nothing that could help him confront the ten-ton duck.

Now he was going to die, and Schrödinger's fate would be left to the gods. A tear rolled down Adam's cheek as he wished he'd never been so greedy for the artifact.

With a loud "*QUACK!*" Adam was snatched up, flames engulfing his body entirely as the Duckysaur roasted and ate him alive.

YOU DIED!

-1 Life

Curse: Catsification

> Always land on feet. No matter what.
>
> Nine lives (7/9)
>
> Weakness to catnip—Irresistible!
>
> Weakness to milk
>
> Weakness to chocolate
>
> Random urge to knock items over
>
> Weakness to cucumbers
>
> Weakness to water
>
> Catsify skills

Reconstituting Body...

Adam opened his eyes, sitting up with a scream while patting his naked, furry body to put out the non-existent flames.

Huffing, he looked down, and realized that his body was no longer burned to a fine crisp, but rather it was healthy and intact, except for the clothes he'd been wearing earlier, of course.

"Stupid flammable flesh! Stupid flammable fur! *Argh!*" Adam scoffed as he stood up and read the message displayed in his system.

He had died.

And by the power of his curse, he had been resurrected, his new default status restored to its max.

However, the timer above was still counting down. Only minutes had passed since Adam had been turned into a charbroiled nekoboy, meaning the **Nine Lives** passive had taken mere moments at best to fully revive him.

Truly, the power of this *Eli* was quite unfathomable. Even at his full strength, it would have taken days for **Resurrection** to take effect, and even then, there were drawbacks and penalties, not just for himself but also for the one being resurrected.

Not that he ever got a chance to succeed; the last time Adam tried, he ended up running out of mana and created an eldritch undead that terrorized the countryside for weeks before he finally managed to bury it under twenty tons of earth. Still, the ability to revive someone so quickly was nothing short of godlike in any necromancer's eyes, a testament that perhaps he hadn't chosen poorly.

"QUACK!"

"Wha—"

At the sound of the familiar squawk, Adam snapped out of his admiration for the lich. Eyes wide, he tried to dodge, but was immediately snatched up and devoured by the oversized duck.

"QUACK, QUACK!"

YOU DIED!
-1 Life
Nine Lives (6/9)

Adam woke, screaming once more, the feeling of the duck's stomach acid burning him alive still haunting his thoughts as he immediately willed his body to stand and move.

He took no chances. Considering how the duck had materialized from thin air at the beginning of the quest and then reappeared to swallow him whole, the beast had to be connected to the quest, or at the very least, a part of it.

And he was right. The instant he dashed towards the tree line, the Duckysaur reappeared, materializing out of thin air to gobble Adam up.

Catpurr 4

Curiosity Killed the Cat

Adam woke again, lying in the dirt. Rolling over, he immediately took off, first running on all fours before standing upright and darting for the trees.

He was on his sixth life, with only three remaining. The Duckysaur had hunted him down thrice already since the first time, when it burnt away his clothes.

In one life, he had run into a tree and gotten flattened.

In another, he had encountered a goblin creature and was beaten to death before the Duckysaur incinerated them both.

And finally, in the last life, he attempted to flee, but before he could gain enough distance, the massive duck descended from above, turning Adam into paste.

However, there was a silver lining to all these deaths. Adam had found the way to complete his objective. He pulled up his quest menu, eyeing the 1/10 that was now displayed instead of zero.

The answer to completing his quest had been revealed when the goblin was incinerated along with Adam.

If he couldn't physically kill or hunt anything because of the giant half duck-dragonoid chasing him around, then all he had to do was have it kill things for him.

A simple solution.

As long as he was the cause of something else's death, even indirectly, it counted. Or at least, that was the running theory as Adam scampered for his life. However, part of the problem was that despite being a forest, there was hardly any life to be found.

"QUACK! QUACK!"

He clenched his jaw, furry ears perking up at the horrendous war cry. It was coming, and fast.

Fortunately, his last life had been excellent for testing this theory as he frantically ran, searching high and low for lifeforms to kill. Eventually, he stumbled upon a goblin encampment before being flattened.

Thankfully, this respawn had put him in a nearby zone, the landmarks of destroyed trees, pulverized stone, and burnt logs from one of his earlier lives already visible.

He was on the right track.

All Adam had to do was keep running for his life and locate the goblins.

"QUACK! QUACK! QUACK!"

Despite the Duckysaur's cries, Adam kept his head straight, learning from his previous life what would happen if he turned around. Normally, he had skills to help him navigate dense trees and forests, but not this time.

This time, all he had were his little tiny legs and his fleshy arms to part the sea of green foliage. But he could feel it; the creature was close—*too* close—each step shaking the earth as its obnoxious quacks reverberated through the air.

However, Adam's worries didn't last for too long. His eyes picked up light, not in a beam or anything like that, but from a torch that was lit nearby.

Despite it being daytime, the goblins had lit torches around their camp, perhaps in a bid to ward off predators. Whatever the reason, Adam smiled as he changed direction and sprinted towards their walls. And then, he spotted it. The monster ahead of him was some cousin to the standard goblin. Green skin, pointy ears, wearing rags with beady yellow eyes adorning its skull. But unlike regular goblins, these monsters had tusks and a small bump at the base of their spine where a tail seemed to be growing.

The first goblin to spot him immediately began shouting, grabbing what looked like a makeshift spear and charging Adam as he raced towards their encampment.

However, its advance was short-lived. The moment the Duckysaur burst from the trees, the goblin went wide-eyed, squawked, and fled.

Oh no you don't! Do not flee from me, my sacrificial lamb!

The green-skinned creature immediately attempted to dash into its encampment to close the wooden gate, even going so far as to shoo Adam away. But the nekoboy was quick and dove into the camp filled with goblins just as the gate shut.

He hit the ground and tucked into a roll, landing on his tiny feet as angry gibberish erupted all around him.

Adam kept running, with no time to gawk or stare at the goblins, as the Duckysaur rammed through the wooden fortification, sending debris and splinters in every direction.

"SCREEE!"

The goblins screamed, fleeing in terror as the duck began spewing hot flames, roasting anything that moved with rapid *quack, quacks.*

[2/10]

[3/10]

[4/10]

[5/10]

[6/10]

[7/10]

Adam laughed, his kill counter finally shooting up as he made his way to a cave to seek shelter from the chaos outside.

This was it; he'd finally complete this quest. And if the Duckysaur was part of the quest, then he'd finally be free of it as well.

Out of curiosity, Adam turned his head to watch the spectacle, only to feel a pressure on his shoulders before a loud boom resounded, and everything went dark.

Eh?

Adam's vision spun, literally, or so it felt. He didn't know what had happened, but he couldn't feel his legs. Nyx, he couldn't even feel his body anymore as he suddenly found himself rolling on the floor, smooth dirt hitting his cheeks.

He looked around, realizing that he was inside the cave, but everything was dark, almost as if someone had closed a door.

Then it occurred to him! He'd been—

YOU DIED!

Nine Lives [2/9]

[Reconstituting Body...]

Sitting up, breathing heavily and wide eyed, Adam clutched his neck, his eyes twitching as he realized he'd been decapitated.

This testing area is absurd!

"QUACK! QUACK! QUACK!"

With no time to lament or process his sudden death, Adam was once again on the move, the magical enraged duck already hot on his tail.

Catpurr 5

Excalipurr

"How's the test going?"

"Oh, pretty swell. He's died seven times already."

"SEVEN?! Maybe scale it back a little? I thought you wanted a successor, why are you punishing him for your mistake?"

"My mistake? You're the one who set the touch screen sensitivity too high, giving him five days to complete the test instead of five hours! The Duckysaur is just to even things out a bit."

"By killing him over and over again?"

Silence hung in the air for a while.

"Well?"

"I am a strange and magnanimous god, my methods shrouded in mystery even to the shrewdest of bein—Ow! That's my eye socket! Freya! Freya! That's my eye socket you're sticking your claws into!"

"You can't feel pain! Why are you complaining?! You literally see through the skull on your staff! And spare me that mysterious god shtick! Be nice to the poor humanoid!"

"But it's *my* experiment! How will he be prepared for the tower if I coddle—"

"ELI!"

"Fine. Consider yourself lucky that I don't have a tongue or glands to spit at you. Actually, wait. Let me grow some."

***

"I... I can't," Adam wheezed, utterly breathless after hours of nonstop running. Clutching his chest, he leaned against a large spruce as the quacks closed in.

"I'm going to die again. I've been running for four hours straight, and I'm going to die again!" Adam lamented, his heart racing within his chest.

[System Error Detected!]

Huh?

Adam eyed his screen, looking at the abundance of *error* messages that displayed over his system interface before it abruptly changed, warping to reveal that his quest timer had been adjusted from five days to a mere three hours.

Seriously?! Seriously! As if it was kicking him while he was down, the quest timer had shortened, making Adam's eyes go wide.

He was screwed.

But he wouldn't give up, not when Schrödinger was waiting for Adam to rescue him.

There was still a chance.

Strengthening his resolve, Adam pushed off the spruce and took off, determined to find something—anything—in this near empty forest to kill in order to complete his quest, hopefully ridding himself of the Duckysaur.

However, despite his willing mind, his body proved too weak, causing Adam to let out a slight wheeze and hiccup before stumbling over a tree root.

Oh crapbask— "Eh?!"

Adam face-planted, hitting the hard, trembling ground, his hands scraping against the soil.

Okay. I've reached my limit. Eat me. I'm ready to respawn, he thought.

Adam groaned, completely out of stamina, bleeding into the dirt.

"QUACK! QUACK!"

The thumping continued, this time accompanied by quacks as the Duckysaur spotted him. Adam tensed up and closed his eyes, bracing himself to be devoured.

A moment passed.

Then another.

Before finally...

Nothing happened.

"Huh?"

Adam opened his eyes, realizing he was still alive. He immediately turned, glancing over his shoulder to find that the Duckysaur, which had tormented him ceaselessly since his awakening in this hell, had suddenly vanished.

"Huh..."

Adam looked around, taking in the sight of pulverized trees, crushed stone, and enormous duck prints in the earth, a pair of which were imprinted only a few feet away from him.

"Huh..." Adam muttered for the third time, hypothesizing that the disappearance of the Duckysaur had something to do with his system glitching out.

However, this respite was short-lived as a *"SHCREE!"* pierced the air, the unmistakable cry of a goblin.

Adam spun, narrowly evading the naked creature as it swung its club at him.

"Tsk! **Grasp Heart!**" Adam instinctively said. He extended his hand outwards to activate his skill, only for nothing to happen.

Crap!

Adam retracted his hand, retreating just in time to avoid the club's swoop. Without hesitation, he lunged to the side into the green foliage, creating distance between himself and the goblin.

"I need a weapon! Something... Anything!" he cried, eyes frantically darting as he searched for a stick or rock to defend himself with.

Suddenly, something shiny fell from above, its edge slamming into the ground, launching Adam through the air amid a storm of dirt and debris.

Stuck in a tree, he opened his eyes, spotting what appeared to be an ornate golden longsword with a blue hilt buried in the earth.

Not questioning it, Adam bolted for the weapon as he observed the goblin. The creature was dazed, but swiftly recovered in the dirt nearby.

Latching his little hands around the sword's hilt, Adam pulled, attempting to wield the weapon. However, the moment he grasped it, his system lit up with a worrying message.

[The Holy Sword Excalibur rejects you! Stat requirements not met.]

"Wha—This is useless!"

Adam's ears twitched, warning him just in time of the goblin as it charged at him from behind, forcing him to abandon the majestic weapon and flee.

* * *

Elsewhere, at the same time.

"Ah... Oops. I forgot it has a stat requirement. Hmmm... Something that doesn't require stats... This list is too long. Ahh, I know!"

* * *

Picking up a branch, Adam spun just in time to use the tree limb as a shield, deflecting the club swinging at him to the side.

However, it wasn't enough to deter the goblin; it immediately advanced, transitioning into an overhead swing. Adam dug in his heels and raised his branch to catch the attack.

The tree limb cracked but held firm, a testament to the material's durability. Seeing its attack blocked, the goblin opened up its pasty green maw and let out a scream, revealing a long, forked tongue and razor-sharp teeth stained with green muck.

Grimacing, Adam stepped back, raising his impromptu weapon in both hands to show the monster he wouldn't back down.

The goblin snarled once more before its jaw formed into a wicked grin as it licked its lips.

The two locked eyes, catlike pupils dilating as the boy's vision seemed to narrow in on his assailant.

However, before the two could come to blows, the sky suddenly lit up, casting iridescent golden light upon Adam and the goblin.

"Huh?"

"Scree?"

The duo looked upward, eyeing what appeared to be dozens—no—*hundreds* of gold summoning circles in the sky, various weapons emerging from each.

Oh... Oh, but... Why?!

The circles disappeared, releasing hundreds of weapons. Metal weaponry plummeted, creating a hailstorm of projectiles that pounded the earth, causing Adam to scream and dodge frantically to avoid death as explosions tore the area apart.

"SCREEEEE!"

"STOP TYEING TWE KHLL ME!" Adam screamed as he and the goblin ran, sprinting through the killzone of the falling weapons-turned-projectiles.

* * *

Elsewhere...

A slap rang out, followed by a high-pitched cry of "OW!"

Catpurr 6
Weapons Galore

Standing amidst a field of iron flowers, Adam rested his hands on his knees, panting as he took a moment to recover from the fact that he just survived nearly being impaled by hundreds of falling weapons.

The goblin that had been chasing him wasn't as fortunate. Adam spotted its twitching, headless corpse beneath a massive iron hammer. Sadly, the monster's death didn't count towards his kill counter, but at the very least, he now had something to wear. He walked over and stripped the body of its thin rags.

Covering his unmentionables, he walked around, surveying the landscape littered with weapons embedded in trees, stones, and earth.

Admittedly, Adam wasn't much of a fighter, typically leaving all the menial tasks such as combat and battle to his summons. He preferred to run away, or to cast spells as he fled.

Unfortunately, luck wasn't on his side this time. Only two hours remained on his timer, and time was ticking. He needed to pick a weapon and start slaying if he was going to complete this quest.

Ironically, despite the abundance of metal weapons strewn about, he instead grabbed the goblin's club. It was much lighter and came with a strap looped through it, allowing him to wear it on his back for easy carrying.

Moreover, unlike the heavy metal weapons that surrounded him, the goblin's club was a better fit for his size, enabling him to properly wield it as a bashing tool for his needs.

"Ah, if only I had armo—" Adam paused, his gaze immediately shifting skywards, hoping to avoid triggering another downpour of heavy metals.

When nothing happened, he huffed, the tension visibly draining from his shoulders.

Acting swiftly and with purpose, he sifted through the array of weapons before him. However, besides being heavy and made of iron, there was nothing noteworthy or special about them, unlike the golden longsword. It was almost as if someone had mass-produced these weapons, only to dump them all on top of him.

Picking up a short spear, he eyed the dead goblin, bones jutting out of its green carcass, before an idea struck him and he went to search for a dagger.

Eventually finding one in a tree, he freed it and immediately cut open the still-warm body and scoured it for bones. For most, this would have been a sickening act of desecrating a corpse, but for Adam, this was simply a routine occurrence.

"Hmmm..." he furrowed his brow, ripping off bits from his newfound rags to secure the goblin's fresh phalanges to his weapons' hilts.

Rising to his feet, Adam walked away and pointed at the iron dagger he'd left behind, activating **Animate Bones** and designating the bone material as its intended recipient.

[1/2 Animated Bones capacity]

"Come here!" Adam willed, expending his mana.

Instantly, the weapon jolted, flying from the ground and nearly impaling its master. He sidestepped to avoid it, and the weapon hovered in the air where he once stood.

Ah, I forgot how finicky these low-level skills are. Come to my palm! The floating weapon obeyed, and flew towards Adam, who caught it in with a now-sinister gleam in his eye.

"Ehehehehehehe," Adam mused, his eyes narrowing to crescents. At last, after being hunted for hours on end, it was finally time for the hunted to become the hunter.

Don't worry, Schrödinger! I'll survive and find you.

* * *

After scurrying through the forest with renewed vigor, Adam spent some time scanning the area for signs of life. An idea occurred to him: climb a tree to search for smoke.

As dusk approached, the twin moons peaked above the horizon and the sun began to cast shifting shadows in the forest, enveloping the shrouded areas beneath the trees in near darkness.

Oddly, despite lacking night vision or any eye-enhancing skill, Adam's eyesight remained unaffected by the shifting light, allowing him to see unimpeded.

Scanning the horizon, Adam searched for traces of activity. Having visited the goblin camp twice over and encountered them this far out, there was a chance they had a base nearby. With only an hour and fifty minutes remaining, he'd need to find the camp and find it fast.

Luckily, the gods seemed to be smiling down upon him as he spotted the reflective orange glow of flames not too far from him.

* * *

Elsewhere, at the same time...

"Alright! We've got a camp going, what's for dinner?" Rochester asked, the dirty blonde rogue stretching as she laid down in the grass beside a middle-aged elf who was busy stirring a pot with a scowl.

"I don't know. Take a guess? Yesterday was stew, the day before that was stew, and the day before that one was also, hey! Wouldn't ya know it, stew," Locke quipped as the green-haired elf lifted the ladle to take a taste test.

"Ehk. Meat," Locke retorted sarcastically.

"And yet you still eat it," Hyde said, the spearman leaning over to inspect the bubbling orange goop.

"What? Do you expect me to starve?"

"You could just… eat around the meat, or ya know… eat the vegetables?" Rochester suggested, gazing up at the setting sun.

Locke scoffed. "So you want me to cook two meals instead of one?"

"Well, you're the one complaining. I'm just trying to make conversation."

"I'm also the one cooking, and if you don't want me to poison your meal, you'll hush so I can concentrate."

"On what? Stirring?" Hyde quipped.

The old elf closed his eyes and sighed.

"*Please* go feed the boars, one of you. I can't deal with both of you pestering me at the same time," Locke said before his eyes narrowed at the sound of nearby rustling leaves.

An enemy attack.

Catpurr 7
The Ninth Death

Crapbaskets.

Adam's eyes widened. After spending time tracking the smoke and heat source, he had finally found his target. The only problem was, they weren't goblins, but rather sapient beings—seasoned adventurers by the looks of their armor, wagon, and the pile of goblin bodies.

This was bad, real bad. He only had forty-five minutes left on his timer, and he had hoped to use the cover of darkness to ambush his targets, swiftly killing them as he'd been taught in his youth.

Yet now he stood, well, *crouched* in the shadows of green leaves, eyeing the elf and two humans arguing about their spilled stew in their wrecked camp, debating on what to do.

From the bow on the woman's back, she appeared to be the designated pathfinder. The man in purple armor, brandishing a green-bloodied spear, seemed to be a warrior. Lastly, the elf, Adam surmised, was a mage of some kind, as he held no weapon in his hand. Traces of permafrost coated the treeline, a completely frozen goblin standing off to the side.

Despite lacking any particular qualms about killing people, Adam did try to avoid harming innocents whenever possible. Now, though, he was faced with a moral dilemma: ambush these tired warriors and end his quest, or move on and hopefully find something else to fulfill his quest requirements.

However, considering that he had encountered zero lifeforms getting here, it was extremely doubtful that the latter option would work. This meant that it was either kill, or be killed for failing his test.

And he didn't want to die; that was why he'd chosen the path of undeath with the ultimate goal of immortality. A perfectly reasonable dream for any sapient brain piloting their meat suit.

Crapbaskets...

He gripped the iron dagger by the blade, the weapon feeling heavier than when he'd first picked it up, and adjusted it in his childish grip.

00:41:07

Forty-one minutes. That was all he had.

It was a no-brainer. From the way the spearman was limping, it was evident that he was injured. But he was confident he could take the man out with one throw. From there, using the ensuing confusion, he could—

"OINK!"

He froze, his eyes turning towards the sound of the ranger opening a door on their rickety carriage and releasing two large pig-like creatures wearing leather harnesses that connected them to the cart.

Oh... How convenient, Adam thought, his eyes shifting targets.

Using the cover of the shadows, he moved quickly. It was evident that after the goblin raid, the survivors were taking no chances and were beginning to pack up and move. If Adam were to strike, he needed to do it now.

Observing the trio move to board their cart, he formulated a plan and waited until the oversized pigs were repositioned in front of the wagon before making his move.

Sorry, he thought.

With deft hands, he threw his dagger, a sense of déjà vu washing over him, reminiscent of his childhood as he watched the weapon spin through the air towards his victim.

[9/10]

The blow was precise, striking the pinkish-brown boar in the skull and killing it instantly. Now came the hard part. Steeling himself, Adam picked up his iron spear, its haft wrapped in tattered rags, and charged out of the underbrush towards the last remaining pig.

Immediately, an arrow found its mark, piercing Adam's throat. His eyes widened as he stumbled backwards, collapsing to his knees. He dropped his spear, just a few paces shy of the frantically squealing boar.

"Uhk?! Uuuuuh," Adam gurgled, his body shaking as he clutched at the arrow in his throat, choking on his own blood. He watched as his HP rapidly began to deplete.

Crap! Crap!

"Oh, fennic!" the ranger shrieked, lowering her bow as she dismounted the wagon and raced towards Adam with shock and dismay in her eyes. She collapsed beside the dying boy's body, drawing him close.

"Oh, God! OhGodohGodohGodohGod—OH... GOD! What have I done?! I'm so sorry! I am *SO* sorry!" the ranger cried, clutching him as she wailed and panicked.

"A *kid*?! You shot a *kid*! What the fennic is a kid doing out here?!" the spearman yelled, his hands on his head as he joined the crying archer.

"Oh, fennic, we are screwed! We are so screwed! They're gonna lock us away forever!"

Suddenly, the face of a middle-aged elf appeared in Adam's dimming view. He shoved the ranger away and applied pressure around Adam's throat.

"Hey kid! Kid! Stay with me!"

Oh, great. I'm being choked now.

"OH, GOD! Oh, *God!* Locke, do something!" the ranger yelled.

"I'm trying!"

Despite the flurry of panic and crying, and his HP bar draining with his blood, Adam kept his eyes focused on the pig with his hand outstretched.

Immediately, the ranger leaned down, taking Adam's bloody hand in hers.

"I'm sorry! I'm sorry I'm sorry!"

Ignoring her frantic apologies, Adam eyed his spear on the ground, the weapon still angled towards the boar.

Float up fifteen centimeters. Then shoot forwards, he commanded, his last thought before his vision went dark, and he died in the elf's arms.

YOU DIED!

* * *

"Oh God! I d-d-didn't!" Rochester choked, her shaking hands clutching her face in disbelief as the feral boy's body went limp in Locke's arms.

"He... He's dead," the elf said sadly, removing his hands from the child's body and standing up, attempting to put distance between himself and the oddly furry corpse.

"It's okay. You didn't know. No one would blame you," Hyde said, the blonde spearman crouching down to comfort the distraught Rochester as she cried. "I mean, who expects there to be kids randomly roaming around in the woods? I thought he was a goblin and was about to throw my spear at him!"

"B-But I shot him!"

Suddenly, a glow illuminated their surroundings, causing everyone, even the hysterical archer, to pause. The boy's lifeless body abruptly began to levitate and emit light.

"Oh... Oh, he's going to heaven! He's ascending!" Hyde said, attempting to reassure Rochester as she choked back a sob.

Immediately, Locke fell to his knees, the agnostic elf making holy gestures and joining the duo in awe as they watched the boy's body ascend into the heavens.

"Look, he's going to a better place," Hyde assured, hugging Rochester close, the woman genuinely hoping that was true.

The boy began to shine brightly, incredibly so, until suddenly, a loud explosion forced the trio to shut their eyes and look away as a cornucopia of colorful confetti momentarily banished all nearby shadows.

The trio opened their eyes, their entire bodies and the surrounding area now coated in colorful dust that reflected the light of the twin moons and the glare of their wagon's torches.

Stunned at what had occurred, none of the adventurers moved until finally Hyde looked down, inspecting the glitter on his arm, which was oddly... cat-shaped.

"Okay... What the Nyx just happened?

Catpurr 8
Quest Catpletion

Nine Lives [1/9]
[Reconstituting Body...]

Adam blinked, as he awoke nude in a field of white flowers under the cover of darkness, devoid of his weapons and rags.

Clutching his neck, he sat up, eyes wide as he checked his timer and quest tracker.

[00:36:00]
[9/10] Meatbags Eliminated

WHAT?!

Panic overtook him as he rose, questioning how it was possible that the quest wasn't complete.

"No, no, no, no, no, no, no! I killed it! I totally killed it!" Adam lamented, pulling at his red hair in confusion as he recalled the events of his last life.

He had killed it; he *had* to! That pig had to be dead, unless somehow the adventurers had stopped it or he had missed! There was no wa—

[10/10]

Oh. What?

[CONCATULATIONS! QUEST COMPLETE!]

Immediately Adam was bombarded with a wave of notifications, his system screen suddenly erupting in ephemeral sparks, celebrating with a digital skeleton giving him a thumbs up.

[Rolling rewards...]

Suddenly, his screen transformed into an ephemeral slot machine, displaying various types of rewards on the side: a jar, a cookie, XP, gold, and what appeared to be a clump of dust that Adam could only assume was pocket lint.

His eyes widened, and his ears twitched, wondering what he would get. Given his recent streak of bad luck, he half-expected to receive the half-eaten cookie.

He fell to his knees and closed his eyes, almost praying as he begged for the XP to finally level up and acquire some attack skills to defend himself.

As a long-range fighter, Adam hated getting his hands dirty. After all, the whole point of being a necromancer was so that he could have minions to do all his work for him.

Yet, all his current skills were physical in nature!

[Ding!]

At the beep, Adam opened his eyes, hoping for the XP, but what he received surprised him.

[Reward obtained! Freya's Bath Water!]

NOOOOOOOOOOOOOO!
Suddenly, a blue crystal jar materialized, ejected from the system, landing in his tiny hands.

"What am I supposed to do with bathwater?" Adam lamented, the sloshing jar of water, which was oddly warm as he clutched it.

Okay, hold on. Maybe there's something special to this! Remembering he had an inspect skill, he activated it. However, upon doing so, he frowned.

[Freya's Holy Bath Water]
Item Description: *Bath Water stolen from the Goddess Freya as she was relaxing during her routine bubble bath.*]
[???]
[???]
[???]
[Holy Imbue effect if consumed or applied on weapons.]

Wha—

A cold chill swept through the air, causing every hair on Adam's skin to stand on end as everything around him seemed to freeze, including himself.

I can't move? Panic rose within him, struggling futilely against the tremendous pressure bearing down on him.

Suddenly, a green-robed figure with pale skin stood before him, her beauty literally taking Adam's breath away as his body failed to breathe under her gaze.

She approached, her emerald eyes furious as she yanked the jar away.

Then, as abruptly as she had appeared, she vanished, the pressure dissipating and leaving Adam all alone under the starry sky.

"M-M-My reward!" Adam screamed upon finally being able to move. All that effort, and his reward was stolen! He fell to his knees, raising one little fist to the cruel heavens. *"MY REWARD!"*

[Rerolling rewards...]
[Reward obtained! Half-Eaten Cookie!]

At the notification, a cookie materialized, landing at Adam's knees and plopping into the dirt.

He stared at the dirt-covered cookie filled with little chocolate dimples and a massive chomp mark on it.

Several moments passed until finally, he picked it up.

"At least it's not pocket lint..." Adam sighed.

Inspect.

[Half-Eaten Holy Ambrosia Chocolate Chip Cookie of the Gods]
Item Description: *A half-eaten cookie stolen from the mouth of the goddess, Islandr. Still has remnants of her saliva on it from when it was yanked out of her mouth.*

Wha—

Adam's eyes widened at the list of several potential buffs.

THIS COOKIE IS INSANE!

Despite the dirt, Adam immediately opened his mouth to take a bite, yet the moment he tried, time froze again.

What?! No! Not again!

Suddenly, a short brown-haired, green-skinned woman appeared, standing at the same height as Adam, her glowing golden eyes glaring at the little cat boy as overwhelming pressure flooded the area.

"A mortal such as yourself shouldn't possess this," the goblin-like girl growled before prying the item from Adam's frozen fingers.

My reward! Stop! Why?

The green-skinned woman disappeared, leaving him alone once again in the grassland, shuddering in the cold, naked as the wind blew.

Adam sat on the ground, his shoulders slumping, unsure how to process what had transpired.

I miss my cat...

[Rerolling rewards…]

Little furry ears perked up, twitching as the system rerolled his reward.

[+500 Experience Obtained!]
[Level Up!]

YES! Adam's ears wiggled, his mood immediately spiking.

[Skill selection available!]

Wait, what?

[Please select a starter skill from the Nekomancer skill tree!]
    Summon Minor Skeleton
    Locate Bones
    Drain Mana
    Mana Bolt
    Mana Claws
    Double Jump
    Mana Dash
    Upgrade Cat Claws
    Upgrade Eyes of the Predator

"This system sucks!" Adam yelled. Compared to his old system, this one severely nerfed his class and the skills obtained. Instead of leveling up a class and gaining several skills and stats like he was used to, he was now presented with a system that forced him to choose one, *ONE,* skill as a level up reward.

Yet, despite how different and nerfed this system was compared to his previous one, Adam cast his disbelief aside, immediately knowing which skill he would choose.

Catpurr 9

Under the Moonlight

[SKILL, SUMMON MINOR SKELETON SELECTED!]
[Expend 100 mana to summon forth bones to do thy bidding]

Immediately, Adam chose **Summon Minor Skeleton**, the skill appearing beneath his skill list as his system updated, displaying five free points to spend.

[LOVED BY UNDEAD DETECTED! SKILL SUMMON MINOR SKELETON BUFFED TO SUMMON SKELETON V1!]

Oh, thank you! Thankfully, Adam's passive ability registered, buffing his summon. A skill he'd possessed since childhood, this passive trait boosted all related skeleton-based skills by a factor of one, allowing him to summon creatures and command those he otherwise wouldn't be able to. He smiled at his stat sheet. Since each point of arcana provided him five points of mana, if he dumped all his points, he'd be able to use the skill.

"Finally!" Adam rejoiced, eagerly pressing the screen to allocate all of his points into arcana for the mana recovery, excited about summoning a minion.

However, the moment his tiny little finger touched the screen to add the point, his body suddenly exploded, showering the area with cat-shaped confetti and glitter.

***

Elsewhere...

"Ah... Whoops. Perhaps I should ask Bastet to help properly tune this."

* * *

"HU—WHA?!" Adam screamed as his vision returned, his hands rapidly patting his naked body as he tried to make sense of what just occurred.

Did... Did I just explode?! But why?

He pulled up his system, wondering what had happened.

BETA SYSTEM v1.02
TITLE: IDIOT NOVICE OF ELI (???)
NAME: Adam F. Glow
SPECIES: Nekoboy
LEVEL: 2
MAIN CLASS: Nekomancer
HP: 100/100
MANA: 75/75
Free Points: 5
STR: 7
CON: 10
DEX: 12
ARC: 15
SEN: 9
EGO: 10
Buffs: Loved by Undead (unique), Minor Blessing of Eli (unique), Eyes of a Predator V1, Corrupted Blessing of Nyx (unique)
Debuffs: Ha! You Sacrificed Your Stats for a Cat?! V1 (curse), Catsification V1 (curse)
Skills: Animate Bone V1, Irritating Touch V1, Cat Claws V1, Identify V1, Summon Skeleton V1

He found the 1.01 had been updated to 1.02, perhaps a direct consequence of his previous explosion.

The free points seemed to call to him, and he immediately wanted to spend them, yet he refrained, the memory of his innards going in a hundred different directions still fresh in his mind.

Seeing as his catsification curse hadn't triggered, he still had a life to spare, meaning that whomever was running this little experiment was at least benevolent.

"Nothing ventured..." Adam said, before squeezing his eyes shut and tapping the screen. Instantly, a surge of power coursed through his veins, his body's mana circuits reconfiguring to enhance his mana storage and flow.

[ARCANA STAT 20 REACHED!]
[Mana Recovery BUFF ACQUIRED!]
[Natural Mana Recovery Enabled]
[1 MP per Hour]

Oh, well that's... low, Adam groaned, his fluffy ears drooping as his head bowed. Although he was pleased he'd unlocked **Mana Recovery**, he'd completely forgotten how long it took to recover mana at a low level.

Sinking into the cold grass, he sighed and gazed at the stars, observing the constellations.

Considering that the stars above mirrored those he'd seen during the countless nights he'd been on the run, it was safe to assume he was still on the same world. The only difference, however, was the absence of his furry feline friend.

Well...

That and the fact that he'd lost all his skills, levels, items, artifacts, and even the clothes on his back. But none of that stung as much as losing his soul-bond.

For all his life, he had Schrödinger, his first and only friend, a gift from his Master, before she disappeared following the path of lichhood.

As an orphan exploited by the thieves' guild, Adam had the fortunate luck to try and steal from a lady in expensive robes, resulting in perhaps the best mistake Adam had ever made.

That had seemed a lifetime ago, and all he retained from those serene days of learning with his teacher was Schrödinger.

Fortunately, the cat was soulbound to Adam, extending its life. However, now that they were apart and his skills were wiped, he couldn't help but worry as his mind feared the worst.

"I'm coming, Schrödinger..." he whispered, hand raised to the green and red moons above.

[WELCOME TO TRIAL TWO!]
[Prepare to be teleported!]

Bruh... Son of a—

A portal suddenly opened beneath Adam, hurling the nekoboy into unknown space at warp speed. He screamed before he was ejected and collided with a hard surface.

"UHK!" he exclaimed, his face sliding off the hard substance he'd been face-planted into.

"Errrr." Shakily picking himself off the dirt floor, he found his face dotted with splinters from his collision with what Adam now recognized as an upright log wall.

Steadying himself, he leaned against the wall, taking a moment to recover from the abrupt teleportation before he—

"BLEH." Adam retched, staining the wall with... rainbows?

What the Hel? Why is my vomit glowing?!

[Mandatory quest given!]

Oh, come on!

Adam blinked, his head already throbbing with a headache.

[Collect a batch of cookies from Rosemjre Bakery]
[0/20]
[Possible Rewards; EXP, Gold, Pebble of Smiting, Fire Stone, Thunder Stone, Shadow Stone, Ring of Holding, Divine Catnip.]
[Failure: DEATH.]

Oh great... This again.

[You have three days to complete the task.]

Just great.

Catpurr 10
Errand Cat

[Collect a batch of cookies from Rosemjre Bakery]
[0/20]
[Possible Rewards; EXP, Gold, Pebble of Smiting, Fire Stone, Thunder Stone, Shadow Stone, Ring of Holding, Divine Catnip]
[Failure: DEATH.]
[You have three days to complete the task.]
[71:59:55]

Am I being used as an errand boy? Adam narrowed his eyes, processing the quest he'd been given.

* * *

Elsewhere...
"Oh, can you update it so it's milk chocolate chip?"
"Yeah, yeah, then you stop bothering me and my experiment, right?"
"For now."

* * *

[QUEST UPDATED!]
[Collect a batch of Milk Chocolate Chip cookies from Rosemjre Bakery]

I'm totally being used as someone's errand boy! Adam's eyes widened, furious at the indignity of being used as a divine being's cookie procurer.

[**71:59:10**]

Sigh...

He looked to the left, then to the right, wondering where exactly he was. Judging from the wall he'd unceremoniously face-planted into, the glow of fire behind it, and the fact he was tasked with a quest to find cookies from a bakery, he was likely just outside of a village or town. But why did everything smell so smokey?

Moving swiftly, Adam kept one hand on the wall, while the other shifted away foliage as he crept along the town palisade in search of the entrance.

Finally he could make out the faint orange-red glow of torches illuminating a small clearing with a dirt road. The only hitch was, he didn't spot any sentries or gate guardians. It had been a while since he last used a town entrance, but Adam was fairly certain there should have been at least one guard.

Then he saw it, the actual gate. Or, what remained of it, in the form of splinters, wood chips, and shattered planks.

Alarm bells ringing in his mind, he hunkered low and edged towards the entrance where he peeked around the corner of the broken-down gate, only for his jaw to drop at the sight that lay before him.

Oh you gotta be kidding me! Why is everything on fire?!

From the building that read ***O.R.P.H.A.N.A.G.E*** in big bold letters to the shop that read ***Rosemjre Bakery***, everything was consumed by orange flames!

"HOW AM I SUPPOSED TO GET COOKIES IF THE BAKERY IS BURNING DOWN?!" Adam screamed, clutching at his red hair.

He closed his eyes. Judging from the lack of people, monsters, or screams, and the intensity of the flames dying down, he quickly formulated a plan of action.

Alright, Adam, the bakery hasn't burned down all the way just yet! There has to be some cookies remaining, right? Right?! Otherwise, why would they give you an impossible quest?

Stepping over the splinters, he made his way across the dirt field towards the burning bakery. Despite the roof being ablaze and the smoke billowing from its upper windows, the building seemed strangely intact. He quickly reached for the bronze door handle and turned it.

[-1HP]

"YOINK!" Adam yelped, all the hairs on his body standing on end as he involuntarily leaped backwards, his hand scalded just from touching the doorknob.

"Ow! Ow! Ow!" He waved his hand around, the usually pale appendage now bright red from the burn wound.

The fist clenched; he was no stranger to pain, but without the **Pain Tolerance** skill, everything seemed to hurt so much more. Suddenly, a part of the building fell away, dropping the sign that swung on one axle and nearly decapitated Adam. He ducked at the last second.

Seriously?! Can't I catch a break?!

* * *

Elsewhere.

"Hehehe. No."

* * *

Ah, this is so stupid! Adam thought, before taking a deep breath and charging at the door, throwing his shoulder against it as the timer ticked down.

Ow.

Ow!

OW!

WHAT IS THIS DOOR MADE OUT OF?! ADAMANTIUM?!

Once, twice, three times he threw himself against what he had *assumed* was a simple wooden door. Yet, it wouldn't give.

Adam calmed himself, taking a moment before he walked back across the field, nearly reaching the village entrance. He then took a breath.

"AAAAAAAAAAGH!" he screamed, sprinting back across the village and crashing into the door. Finally, the wooden barricade gave way, and he entered the storefront of the bakery where he was greeted by the heat of the flames. Everything on the ground floor of the bakery seemed to be relatively undamaged. Except for the ceiling, which was engulfed in flames, everything else was fine.

But despite successfully breaking the door, there was just one problem.

Oh... Oh, you've gotta be kidding me!

Adam was stuck, his charge having propelled his upper half into the bakery, leaving his back end sticking out.

"Gah! GAAAAAAH! WHAT DID I DO TO DESERVE THIS?!" he screamed in frustration, wiggling to and fro as he tried to pry himself free of the wooden door.

Suddenly, a burning support beam from above crashed into the storefront, kicking up debris and flames that rapidly expanded, covering nearly every inch of the storefront in fire.

Adam remained motionless with a blank expression, taking in the scene of hell that had spontaneously erupted around him.

He closed his eyes.

"This is fine."

Despite the intrusive urge to let the flames consume him to end this nonsensical string of events, he gritted his teeth and pushed, using every bit of his forearm strength to pop himself free from the door.

"Huk!" At last, he landed with a thud, his hands hitting the warm wooden floor.

Quickly, the little nekoboy made his way through the bakery, avoiding the flames and frantically scanning for his quest objectives.

Cookies! Cookies! Adam searched high and low, sifting through cabinets, containers, and unburnt boxes that were yet to be touched by the encroaching flames.

"Cough! Cough!"

Sweating heavily, he spotted a door behind the counter, no doubt leading to the kitchen. Luckily, unlike the front entrance, it wasn't locked and had been left slightly ajar, allowing Adam to enter the backroom which was filled with jars, boxes, bags, and masonry ovens.

Then, he saw it. A clear jar filled with cookies, speckled with gooey black pieces. No doubt, the chocolate chip cookies he'd been sent to find.

Finally.

Adam grinned, his luck looking up for once. Without wasting a second, he bolted and vaulted over the center table used for cooking, and grabbed the container just as the fire began to intensify around him.

Making a beeline to a nearby window, he lightly tossed the jar into the dirt before leaping out, and scooped up his prize, eager to complete the trial and be rewarded.

Suddenly, a loud snap resounded just as he got clear of the bakery. He turned to watch as the roof of the building buckled under the strain of the flames, caving in and finally bringing down the bakery.

"Crapbaskets!" Adam exclaimed, falling to the ground to avoid the shower of debris and splinters sent in all directions by the bakery's collapse.

Huffing, he got to his feet, prize fortunately still intact.

"Great... Now what do I do?" he said aloud, exhaling heavily as he tried to catch his breath and checked his timer which was still ticking down.

After several moments of sitting in the field and eyeing his timer, Adam began to grow worried, wondering if there was a trick or something involved with the quest description.

Out of curiosity, Adam opened the jar, wondering what made the cookies so special. However, the moment he took a cookie out and inspected it, he short-circuited.

Raisins...

The cookies he'd salvaged weren't chocolate chip but actually raisin cookies!

"No! No! Nooooo!!" he wailed, standing up and smashing the jar into the ground out of desperate fury.

"WHY DO YOU INSIST ON HURTING ME?!" the boy screamed, falling to his knees with his hands raised to the heavens.

There had to be some trick, maybe a gimmick, or some clever ploy. There was no way he was just going to die because he had grabbed raisin cookies instead of chocolate chip, right? *Right?*

Suddenly, a droplet of water hit Adam's skin, followed by a second, a third, and a fourth.

It was raining.

[CATSIFICATION CURSE ACTIVATED!]
[YOU ARE WET!]
[-20% to all stats until dried!]
STATS CHANGED!
STR: 7 > 6
CON: 10 > 8
DEX: 12 > 9
ARC: 20 > 16
SEN: 9 > 7
EGO: 10 > 8

[WARNING: ARCANA BELOW STAT POINT THRESHOLD! MANA RECOVERY BUFF LOST!]

Immediately, he was struck by a wave of fatigue, his body struggling under the curse's debuff.

It just keeps getting better, doesn't it... Adam sighed, then trudged his way towards the ruins of the bakery, hoping to find a batch of chocolate chip cookies for his quest.

Catpurr 11

Summon Skeleton

Adam groaned, his eyes fluttering open, hit by the disgusting stench of the outhouse in which he had taken shelter. He was no stranger to the odor of death and decay, but the reek of fermenting urine and feces was an entirely different matter. Wincing, he stretched to alleviate the kinks of sleeping on the hardwood floor. Still, he was dry now, even if the smell seemed to cling to him as he pushed open the wooden door to the freedom of fresh air outside.

"Ugh..." Adam winced, the harsh golden rays of sunlight beaming down upon him from above, already ruining his day.

[60:23:44]

Adam glanced at his timer; it was time to get to work.

Following last night's escapade, the nekoboy had spent hours sifting through the rubble in the rain, hoping beyond hope to find his quest objective. From what he knew from his brief stint as a thief, bakeries of all kinds had some form of storage room for storing extra food and materials throughout the season, away from prying eyes. And he was right, fortunately. His tenacity paid off, revealing a hatch in the kitchen buried under ash and other large debris. Unfortunately, he didn't possess the strength, tools, or minions to clear the obstruction, forcing him to abandon his efforts and seek shelter from the rain.

Scanning the remnants of the burned-down town and the lack of fleshies, Adam decided to go on a stroll, searching for materials he could use. After all, there had to be something he could use to clear the rubble. Not to mention... he was growing tired of being naked.

[57:59:24]

After spending a couple of hours combing through the town, it became apparent just how barren the place really was. Apart from one building with multiple bunks and scattered linens, none of the places seemed to be even remotely lived in. It was almost as if someone had decided to just burn down an empty ghost town.

Although he was curious about the circumstances surrounding the town, the fire, and the complete lack of any sign of life, he ignored these questions, and instead focused on finding items he could salvage as his timer ticked down.

He found some bundles of rope, a partially charred greenish floral robe, a burnt kitchen knife, a cast iron shovel, and finally, and probably the most important items that left him with the most questions, several gold coins.

The currency was different from anything he'd seen before, and was engraved in a language he didn't understand. But a gold coin was still a gold coin, no matter the nation or world. Still, it helped him confirm that he was in an unexplored region.

Wearing the robe and fastening it to his body with the shortest length of rope, Adam walked back to the bakery carrying the cast iron shovel. Standing amidst the wreckage of the store, he eyed the large beam that blocked the hatch and a nearby tree, formulating a plan.

Rope+Tree+Skeleton+Iron Shovel+Leverage=Mission Clear, Adam surmised, already leveraging the shovel to raise the beam, just enough to tie a bit of rope to the tip of the rubble.

Now, it was time for the next step: summoning his minion.

Moving to the back end of the orphanage, Adam now stood in front of several graves, preparing his skill.

After everything he'd gone through so far, he felt a bit nervous. In the past, the system he had used was efficient, easy to understand, and easy to exploit. All he had to do was hang around battlefields, earning XP as the fleshies killed one another, and then use the fresh corpses to deal with monsters drawn by the stench of death, earning him even more experience.

It was a useful system, one that benefited everyone involved. Adam got to level up, the meatbags got to slaughter one another, and then the necromancer would provide a monster cleanup service for free, protecting nearby towns and other areas that would otherwise be ravaged by hordes of monsters seeking fresh meat.

This new system didn't earn him any experience from killing, it seemed. That, or his XP multiplier was incredibly nerfed with heavy restrictions imposed on him. There was also no telling what exactly the *catsification* curse did in terms of skill usage.

Adam opened his menu, reading over the curse, wondering what exactly Catsify skills meant, as it had done nothing to **Animate Bone**. At least, nothing he had noticed.

Sighing, he decided to take a chance and raised his little arm, palm outstretched. In his current form, he was just too weak to lift debris of that caliber, and he needed help. But with an activation cost of a hundred mana, he knew he would only get one chance at this.

"Sorry for this, but I need your help. Summon," the boy whispered tensely, feeling the mana in his little body twisting and churning as it left his body to create a blue summoning circle on the ground beside the grave.

[SUMMON SKELETON [½]

He could feel it—his power and energy condensing as the earth parted, releasing magical steam from the sigil as the forces of arcana bent to his will, conjuring a servant of bone to do his bidding. But something was amiss. The sigil grew excessively bright, actually becoming blinding, and took the shape of a grinning cat.

[CATSIFICATION CURSE ACTIVATED!]
[SKILL CATSIFIED!]

Oh crapbaskets!

Adam shielded his eyes as the cat-faced sigil exploded, releasing steam, dirt, and ash everywhere, forcing Adam backwards, away from the sigil.

Blinking and now covered in soot, he opened his eyes while coughing. The dust dissipated to reveal nothing in the spot where a humanoid skeleton should have been.

Impossible! Where is the skeleton? I can feel the connection! Adam looked around frantically, trying to search for the being he had used all his mana to summon. He needed it!

Finally, he looked down, spotting his summon.

Ah... Why am I not surprised...

His teeth clenched, before he slowly lifted his head upwards towards the blue skies above.

"WHY?!"

Instead of a full-sized humanoid skeleton that could help him clear the debris to complete his quest, what had appeared was a miniaturized skeleton, tiny bones arranged in the shape of a small house cat. It looked up, gazing at its master with ghastly yellow eyes before, suddenly and without warning, it flopped onto its bony side.

Catpurr 12
Purrpose

With the rope wrapped around a large spruce and one end tied to the fallen beam, Adam clenched his teeth as he wrapped the other end around his hands and made another attempt.

"Ugh," he groaned, the rope immediately biting into his soft skin as he dug his feet into the ashen grass. "C'mon! C'mon!" he internally screamed, his small stature and limited strength working against him. "AAAAAAGH!"

Adam tumbled to the ground, panting heavily, releasing the rope and inspecting his bloody hands, marred by the rope burns.

Sigh... Why is life so difficult...

Not one to sit around moping for too long, Adam stood up, gripping the rope once more despite his injuries. As he did so, he spotted his summon, the little skeleton cat, carrying a piece of debris in its rickety, clattering mandible.

Heh.

It wasn't much, but at least the skeleton *was* helping. As a low-level minion, it couldn't do much in the way of, well, anything.

Beyond basic commands like 'attack target', 'defend', 'follow', 'guard', and 'stop,' low-level skeletons completely relied on their masters to constantly provide them with orders. Fortunately, his unique ability, **Loved by Undead,** remained with him and buffed his skelekitty and all its functions, allowing the monster some autonomy from its master.

He watched the creature work, the little skeleton forming a small, helpful pile in the corner.

Noticing its master observing, the skelecat stopped, its eerie yellow eyes shifting to peer at the nekoboy.

"*Chitchitchit.*" It opened its mouth, clacking its mandibles at its master while pawing at its pile, almost as if to say, "*Look at what I've done.*"

In a way, it was adorable, but it still couldn't compare to Schrödinger.

Adam felt a pang in his chest at the thought. He sighed, folding into himself as he hugged his knees close, missing his friend.

"*Chitchitchit.*" The skelecat clattered, approaching its master and rubbing its bleach-white skull against Adam's ankles.

He reached out, petting the smooth skull out of habit, yet the act brought him no comfort.

Sitting in the dewy grass, the nekoboy suddenly found himself reminiscing about the day he met his best friend.

It was a day much like this one, in a scorched town that mirrored this settlement in its desolation and ruin. But, unlike the wooden husks surrounding him whose flames were now extinguished, the town in his memory had been engulfed in an undying green fire that persisted even through heavy downpours of rain.

A nameless village, fallen victim to monsters after another "Holy" skirmish had swept through the countryside. Even now, he could recall his teacher's words, the sorrow in her voice as she looked at him with her only functional eye.

"Why do you want to be a lich, Adam?" the raven-haired woman asked, her emerald eye gleaming with power as the green flames reflected upon her bone-pale skin. She stood at six-three, a tall woman even without her golden heels, wearing clothes that exposed nearly every inch of her tattooed skin, save for her neck concealed by a spiked choker, her breasts veiled in velvet, and the gold waistband that held the sheets of long purple cloth obscuring her thighs, except for the areas covered by stockings.

"For immortality, of course. I don't want to die. Plus, undead are cool!" young Adam had responded absentmindedly, his hands poking at the floating spirits of the deceased as they drifted by.

"And then what? What would you do if you gained eternity? What would be your purpose?" Master Razalia asked as she reached down into the rubble to pick up a carcass of a small, soot-covered animal. She lifted her gaze upwards, the triangular tattoo beneath her eye glinting as the air around them came to life with power.

"Spread your teachings to everyone around the world so that everyone will know how awesome necromancers are!"

A childish answer that brought a gentle smile to his teacher's lips as her blackened hands hummed with heavy power.

"Adam. There will come a day when I'll ask you this question again," the woman said, turning to her protegé and kneeling to meet him at eye level. Her golden eyepatch opened to reveal her ghostly spiritual eye, a replacement for the one she had sacrificed for power. "And when that day comes, I hope you'll have found a purpose that's your own."

Confused, the boy opened his mouth to reply, but a sudden cough and the subsequent cry of a baby kitten interrupted him.

Resurrection—a miracle wrought by his teacher—left Adam in awe. This, this was the power he wanted, the power to defy death!

"*Meow. Meeeow!*" the kitten cried, frightened and angry at being wet and held in some stranger's hand.

"Here," Master Razalia said, handing the little furball to the boy.

"Huh? W-what? What am I supposed to do with this thing?" he asked, reluctantly extending his hands, his face twisted with visible disgust.

"Nourish it. Care for it. And although it may appear as if I've burdened you, one day, you'll come to see this as a gift," Razalia said as she patted the young Adam on his head.

The sound of a creak made his tearful eyes snap open. Unbeknownst to him, he had fallen asleep, but the shifting of wood startled him to his feet, his heart racing.

First he peered to the left, then to the right, his eyes rapidly scanning the town in search of possible threats.

Oddly, there were none. Instead, what he saw was something that made his eyes widen.

His skelecat was tugging on the rope, gradually lifting the fallen beam off the hatch using the pulley system Adam had created.

What?

Without hesitation, the nekomancer sprang into action, grabbing the shovel and thrusting it beneath the pillar.

"Keep pulling! Keep pulling!" he commanded, positioning his hand beneath the beam to help shift it as the skeleton continued to lift it.

"That's it! That's it! Come on!" he laughed maniacally as he placed himself under the pillar, using his body to free the hatch. "Ahahahahaha! Yes! Yes! Yes! Yes!"

Suddenly, a snap sounded out, and the weight of the beam bore down on the boy.

"NO! NO! NO! NO!" Adam shrieked.

The pillar began to fall, perilously close to crushing him, but he acted swiftly, sending a command to his skelecat. The creature sprinted to its master and headbutted him free from the collapsing column just as his strength gave way.

He landed in the dirt, his hand breaking his fall as the pillar sent dust and debris flying. The nekomancer was safe, but his summon was not so fortunate.

Adam immediately sprang up and dashed towards the fallen log as his connection with his companion was severed. Similar to the feeling he had experienced during his transformation into this... size.

No, no, no! He dug through the debris beside the log, reaching for the lifeless animal skull that was coated in dirt.

The skull he found was just large enough to fit inside his palm, the image of Schrödinger's white fluffy face overlapping with it.

Adam tossed it aside, looking away before he cradled his head in his hands, trying to collect himself from the flood of emotions coursing through him.

"Purpose..."

Catpurr 13

A Goddess Gets Her Cookies

"So now the last evolutionary bit on our list... Tail, or no tail?"

"Well, he's a cat. He should have a tail, no?"

"It's not that simple, since he's a biped. If we make that a possible evolution, he'll have to grow a caudal vertebrae or a prehensile tail."

"What is it the humans of Earth say? *Dealer's choice?* I'm too old to think of everything these days."

Sigh.

"Eli, this is important. What you've done is create an entirely new form of life, and Nyx is unhappy you corrupted one of her Blessed to do so. The least you can do is be a bit more serious while we try and calibrate their system."

—The Goddess Bastet speaking with Eli about Overhauling a Species System

* * *

Coughing from all the ash in the air, Adam walked across the ruined basement, moving until he found himself amidst a collection of soot-covered jars.

He crouched down, digging through the dirt until he brushed a jar, activating his system.

[1/1]

[CONC*A*TULATIONS! QUEST COMPLETE!]

Immediately, the jar disappeared, vanishing into a golden glimmer. *Ah. That was easier than I thought.*

[Rolling rewards…]
[DING!]
[Reward obtained! Soul-Bound Ring of Holding!]

His screen popped up, immediately spitting out a silver ring that fell into his hand, sending a tingling sensation up Adam's spine, making him flinch.

He held it up, using his **Inspect** skill to examine the silver band, which lacked any discernible features, save for a cat face etched into it.

Adam groaned as he reviewed the ring's information. *Seriously? Why is everything cat-themed?*

[Lvl 1 Ring of Holding/SOUL-BOUND!]
[Item Description: *A shard of a mythical item forged in the heart of a neutron star on the brink of becoming a black hole. The original source is said to have been created to contain all the universes' woes and illnesses, and was thus dubbed the Prolific Source of All Troubles. This shard has been repurposed as a storage device and can hold up to five inanimate objects weighing up to 200 pounds. For every available slot, there is a chance to generate one random item per slot per day.*]
[Storage Space 1/5]
[View stored items]

Prolific source of all troubles… Adam laughed bitterly. "How about, no."

He flung the ring, discarding it into the ashen pile before him, and turned to leave the basement.

I have enough of a headache worrying abou—

Just as his hand touched the ladder, he suddenly felt the cold iron return, this time wrapped around his finger.

Ah, soul-bound... Right... Great.

He closed his eyes, sighing. *Well, might as well see what's in it.*

[**Slot 1:** *1600oz Block of Cesium.*]

What's cesium? Adam moved to retrieve the item from the storage unit to inspect it. But just before he could, a loud growl echoed through the basement, freezing him in his tracks.

What the Hel was that?! Adam panicked as he hunched down, scanning for threats.

"*Grrrrrrrrrrrrrrrr.*"

It happened again, but this time, he was paying attention, noting that his stomach was the culprit of the noise.

Great. That's right... I need to eat, Adam inwardly sighed.

Apart from cooking fish for Schrödinger and sharing a meal with his friend, he didn't like eating. In fact, he loathed it and found it disgusting, preferring instead to use a Ring of Sustenance to take care of all his bodily needs. There was something about ingesting flesh and living substances that made him... uncomfortable. Unfortunately, he no longer possessed that ring, which meant he was now just as frail and vulnerable to hunger as everyone else.

[WELCOME TO TRIAL THREE!]

Oh my God.

[Prepare to be teleported!]

"Please... Just let me re—" His plea was cut off as a cat-shaped portal opened up and sucked him through.

* * *

Same time, elsewhere...

"YOU &*$%@#&! I WANTED CHOCOLATE CHIP COOKIES! WHAT THE &^%4@# IS THIS &^%$($@ PIECE OF %#^% &$@#?!" an irate, green-skinned shortstack yelled as she waved an ash-covered jar around at a hunched-over skeleton in a pink bathrobe and shower cap.

"You asked for a batch of chocolate-chip milk cookies. My successor accomplished the test, giving you exactly what you wanted," Eli replied, ignoring the Goddess of War as he disrobed and reclined on a black slab massage table that had been set up in a damp underground swamp.

"THIS?!" Islandr shattered the jar in her coarse green hands, revealing a massive glob of melded dough and chocolate chips. "THIS IS NOT WHAT I WANTED! DOES THIS LOOK LIKE COOKIES TO YOU?!"

"Eh, tomato, potato. Same thing, right? They all go to the same place with you ingestors," Eli replied as one of his heavily armored death knights appeared, delicately placing sliced cucumbers on its master's exposed eye sockets.

"WHAT ARE YOU DOING?! WHY AREN'T YOU FIXING THIS?! I WANT MY COOKIES, DAMN YOU!" Islandr raged, infusing her voice with godly mana to shout at the skeleton before her.

"It's called a spa day. Very popular with mortals on a world called *Eeerth*," Eli slurred out, unperturbed at the War Master's display of power as a grim reaper began massaging his skeletal toes. "Huhuhu, that tickles, stop it!"

"GAH! I HATE YOU! I'LL GET YOU BACK FOR THIS! I SWEAR IT! I SWEAR!" the goblin screamed before turning and running away, leaving the dank underground through a flight of stone stairs.

"Gah, what are you, one eon old? I swear, kids these days," Eli sighed after several moments of silence, removing the shriveled cucumbers from his bleached skull. With his mood soured and his spa day ruined, he got up, waving his minions off, and placed his skeletal toes into a pair of pink bunny slippers laid out for him before he accessed his display. Pulling up a screen, Eli let out an "*Oh,*" upon spying Adam spinning wildly through a portal as he spewed rainbow-colored vomit. "Whoops, I forgot about you. Hmm... Maybe a break would be good for him as well."

Catpurr 14

System Update!

"AAAAHH!" Adam spun wildly through a rift in the fabric of reality while vomiting rainbow-colored goop.

"AAAHHH... OOOF!" The nekoboy suddenly found himself ejected from the purplish-gray void, landing into a pile of muck that he splatted into, despite putting his arms out to break his fall.

[-12 HP]

He groaned, releasing bubbles into the pool of goo, carrying his sighs to the world beyond.

Wearily he raised his head from the murky liquid, wiping his eyes clean. As he glanced up, the sight of vibrant flowers, a brilliant sun, and a smoothly paved stone road cutting through a sea of green pines greeted him. Fortunately, he had landed in the one area where there was mud, which broke his fall.

Unfortunately, he was now coated from head to toe in muck that clung to his hair and was quickly drying against his skin.

"Oh... What fresh Nyx is this?" He quickly resigned himself to wallowing in the muck. "More Duckysaurs? Goblins, perhaps? Maybe a flaming meteorite this time? Or, even worse, perhaps Junith will teleport here to finish the job with her stupid blade of Aka*LAME*."

* * *

Elsewhere, in the Holy City of Faith

"ACHOO!" Junith sneezed, the heavily scratched paladin suddenly overtaken by sneezing fits, interrupting her session of moodily gazing out the yellow-tinged glass window that overlooked The Holy City of Faith.

"Blessings be upon thee, Sister Junith. Are you perhaps unwell?" a woman dressed in the white robes of the nunnery inquired as she passed by, leading a coven of other sisters of the Order.

"No, Sister Estia. However, I sense a disturbance, as if someone speaks ill of me..."

"Good Heavens! Who could possibly sully a warrior as virtuous as yourself?!" Sister Estia exclaimed in shock.

* * *

With Adam

"—with her stupid fleshy skin, stupid gold armor, and stupid god—" Adam ranted, recalling the woman's grotesquely twisted face. "—and most of all, her stupid giant, meaty hands!"

* * *

With Junith

Junith squinted, her blood boiling as she sensed it, *HERESY!*

"No, I sense it! Someone is out there, tarnishing our order's Holy Patron! WE MUST PURGE THE UNCLEAN!"

"UNCLEAN!" a chorus of zealous battle nuns chanted in unison, echoing Junith's words.

* * *

With Adam

"Gah! Stupid! Stupid! Stupid!" he spat, flinging mud to the side as a noise pricked his ears.

"Ho, kool ta taht! A fres yob lla eht yaw tou ereh! T'ndluohs eh eb gnikrow eht sdleif?!" Weird words sounded out, drawing his attention away from the mud and towards a fancy, horse-drawn carriage, covered in gleaming gold plating. On top of the carriage sat an open box instead of an enclosed compartment, revealing four elegantly dressed individuals having a picnic.

What truly caught Adam's attention, however, was the procession of fully armored knights, each one sheathed in steel with royal blue capes, guarding the ornate wagon.

Oh crap.

Alarm bells rang in his mind. He didn't need to be a High Alchemist to know these were royals. For some reason, he just had a terrible track record when it came to nobility.

Apart from the Emperor, there had been a run-in with a nobleman's daughter in the woods, a Duke he had polymorphed into a chicken, and a count's son who had warned Adam about courting death, only for the brat to later die in a magic casting contest that had gone horribly wrong, by way of a massive explosion.

All these events that had disastrous outcomes were, of course, not in any way Adam's fault. That would be ridiculous.

Except the Duke. That one... That one was definitely my fault, he acquiesced, wondering if the spell had been removed now that he had transformed.

Watching the quickly approaching convoy, Adam did the only thing he could think of.

He smiled and waved.

No sudden movements.

"Ylrettu cirabrab," exclaimed a man in extravagant robes with long, snow-white hair and a goatee, nearly giving Adam a heart attack as he stood up on the wagon and pointed in his direction. However, the subsequent laughter and taunts from the other well-dressed occupants of the carriage reassured him that they were just mocking him and weren't ordering the soldiers to attack.

The carriage passed by, ignoring the grubby nekoboy as he sat there in the mud, watching them in turn. One soldier approached, tossing a shiny object that made Adam's hand lash out, instinctively catching it. He hadn't meant to, but something compelled him to catch it.

Opening his palm, he found what appeared to be a coin.

Huh, I guess they think I'm just some homeless brat playing in the mud, Adam surmised, waiting until the last of the knights were out of sight before he got up and stepped onto the paved road.

Considering the absence of supplies onboard, the flaunting of their wealth, and their leisurely pace, they must be near a town or city. And he was right, as the next passing second confirmed his conjecture and presented him with a new quest, as well.

[WELCOME TO TRIAL 3]
[MANDATORY Quest given!]
[Visit The Human City; Vilenciel]
[Possible Rewards: EXP 500, Copper Pieces x50, Cicero's Gacha Coin x1, Minor Health Potion x1, Minor Mana Potion x1]
[Failure: EXP Drain 1000]
[You have three days to complete the task.]
[71:59:58]

Huh?

Eyeing the rewards, Adam realized that something was wrong. It was too... reasonable, too *safe* for the task assigned. He couldn't be certain of the consequences of failing the assignment, especially the EXP drain, but one thing was clear—it was far better than death.

Adam opened his system. Apparently it had updated again.

BETA SYSTEM v1.03
TITLE: IDIOT NOVICE OF ELI (?????)
NAME: Adam F. Glow
SPECIES: Nekoboy
LEVEL: 2
EXP BAR: 500/1000
MAIN CLASS: Nekomancer
HP: 88/100
MANA: 100/100
[SEALED FUNCTION]
[SEALED FUNCION]
Free Points: 0
STR: 7
CON: 10
DEX: 12
ARC: 20
SEN: 9
EGO: 10
Buffs: Loved by Undead (unique), Minor Blessing of Eli (unique), Eyes of a Predator V1, Corrupted Blessing of Nyx (unique)
Debuffs: Ha! You Sacrificed Your Stats for a Cat?! V1 (curse), Catsification V1 (curse)
Skills: Animate Bone V1, Irritating Touch V1, Cat Claws V1, Identify V1, Summon Skeleton V1

[VIEW SKILL DETAILS→]
[VIEW QUESTS →]
[VIEW ????/ ACCESS DENIED!]

Well, that's quite an update, he thought, noting the sealed functions, the experience bar, and the general lack of death threats. It was almost as if someone had taken the time to refine the system to make it more user-friendly.

Adam sighed. This was going to be a long and challenging journey, one that, though painful thus far, was at a much different pace than the constant running from inquisitors.

With slumped shoulders, a lowered head, and mud-caked attire, the mud-soaked nekomancer pushed himself off the ground and followed the same path the nobles had taken.

Catpurr 15

Catnapped

Walking behind the wagon of nobles, Adam soon found himself standing before a tall gate—well, hidden in the bushes before a tall gate, to be more exact.

Many guards dispersed the crowd outside the iron gate, ensuring a path for the nobles to pass through.

Adam observed them, noting how the men in steel armor tossed luggage aside, forcefully shoving people clear of the road. It seemed that regardless of the nation or world, the treatment of the lower class was still the same.

As he stared at the wagon disappearing behind the iron gate and masonry, he finally decided to step out, joining the line of people clamoring to enter the city.

"Lacipyt selbon, ta siht etar ll'ew eb etal!" exclaimed a scrawny, sleep-deprived man in leathers, carrying what seemed to be a coffin on his back and kicking the dirt in frustration.

"I dlot ouy ton ot pots dna yrt ot llup eht drows tuo," retorted a heavily endowed woman wearing a bonnet and the scant attire of a mage. She yawned as she scratched her green hair. "Sa fi ouy dluow eb yhtrow fo a yardnegel drows ekil Excalibur."

Catlike ears twitched. He didn't understand the words being said, but he did recognize the word Excalibur. Were the pair talking about the sword he had left behind?

Man... I sure do wish I had my tongue of nations still... Adam silently lamented, curious about the conversation. The man seemed offended by the woman's words, leading to a heated exchange between them.

As the line moved, Adam attempted to walk past them, only for the couple to immediately stop what they were doing and turn to him mid-sentence, alike in their expressions of shock.

"A imed-dlihc?!" the woman exclaimed in disbelief. Her eyes darted left and right before she motioned to the man, who quickly pulled out a brown hat, forcing it on Adam's head despite his protests.

"Tahw era uoy gniod tuo ereh?!" she hissed, leaning in close with plain panic in her eyes. "Erehw era ruoy stnerap?!"

Huh? To the nekoboy the woman was speaking nonsense, but considering the pair's reaction upon seeing him and subsequently covering of his cat ears, the dots were simple to connect.

The city was hostile to demi-humans, and these adventurers were trying to protect him. At least, that seemed to be the case, as the woman gestured for him to leave and yelled at him in her weird language. Discrimination wasn't a new experience for him, but he didn't mind. After all, he didn't need to interact with any of the locals. He just had to enter the city and complete his quest.

"I t'nod kniht eh sdmatsrednu su," the man replied, grimacing as he noticed a guard patrolling down the line and nearing their location.

Alright. Time to walk away very slowly, Adam thought, already taking a step back from the hysterical woman. Her slender arm slapped down on his shoulder.

Alright, time to run!

With fearful eyes, he tried to yell and bolt, but the woman clamped her soft hands on his mouth as it opened, muffling his cries.

CAT CLAWS!

Immediately, his fingernails grew, revealing claws. Despite scratching at the woman and flailing about, Adam was pulled in by the lady's gargantuan strength, forcing him inside the scrawny man's coffin despite his protests.

"Hey! WHAT THE NYX?!" he yelled as the door slammed shut on the wooden coffin, sealing him in darkness.

* * *

"Is everything alright here?" a guardsman asked upon reaching the pair of suspicious adventurers.

"Yup! All good here, officer! No smuggling or kidnapping kids here!" Sehn replied nervously. The guard glared dubiously at the scratch marks on Titania.

Oh great! We're going to be sent to the gallows for smuggling a demi-child, Titania bemoaned.

"Sir, ma'am, would you two mind stepping out of line for me?"

"Sehn, you idiot," Titania groaned, questioning why she had to be paired with this idiot when she was perfectly capable of questing alone.

"Guild ID and passport registration please," the guard requested. The two complied, brandishing their credentials.

"Rank C Geomancer, Rank B...?"

The guard stopped, his head cocking sideways at Sehn with confusion and doubt.

"Yes! Yup! I know it doesn't look like he's a B-Ranked Warrior, but he is. You can run our licenses with the local guild if you don't believe us," Titania interjected before Sehn could run his mouth again, fully aware that the soldier wouldn't believe Sehn based on his withered body alone.

"Uh huh," the soldier said, handing them back their passes. "Would you mind showing me what's in the coffin?"

The two exchanged a look.

When neither moved for a second, the guard placed his hand on the pommel of the blade hanging on his waist.

Oh, uh. Titania frowned, eyeing the other guards that were approaching.

"Is there a problem?"

"Nope! No problem!" Sehn hastily responded, too quickly. Titania cringed.

Holding her breath, she watched as Sehn undid the straps of his coffin, setting it down on the paved road where he slowly opened it to reveal its contents.

"An empty coffin?" the soldier asked, brow raised. "I hope you two aren't planning to leave here with a body."

"Haha! No officer! Not at all, this is just a quest item for Lady Velinora," Sehn explained, quickly producing a quest writ with a royal stamp on it from his jacket pocket. The officer raised a brow, leaning over to inspect the writ before peering down into the empty sarcophagus.

"Don't cause any trouble," the soldier said before going back up the line. "And put in a word for me with the noble, eh?"

"Yup! No problem," Titania said, all smiles as the man walked off.

* * *

After passing through the iron gates with the rest of the crowd, the pair strolled down the bustling, brightly lit streets of the stately city for some time before eventually losing their composure.

"Oh, God! Why did you throw him in there?! We just kidnapped a demi-child!" Sehn hissed, pulling Titania into an alley and tapping the magic coffin on his back. Fortunately, the guard hadn't looked too deeply or reached into the coffin; otherwise, he would have realized that it was a storage device and not just some plain old sarcophagus.

"What else was I supposed to do?! Kick him into the fields?! The guards would have seen him!" Titania shot back. "How much oxygen is in there?"

"Enough. I think? It's not like it was made to store living things," Sehn replied, visibly sweating. "What do we do?! We can't keep him in there. And we can't just take him out; the Purists will root him out like a bloodhound!"

Titania's eyes darted over to some pedestrians looking at them, but they quickly averted their gazes upon meeting hers. She sighed. "See the guild master. She'll know what to do."

Sehn grimaced, his eyes wincing with pain.

"Oh man, I *just* got back to B-Rank; we're gonna get in *SO* much trouble!" Sehn whined, pulling at his red hair and letting out a quiet scream.

Catpurr 16
The Adventurer's Guild

In a void filled with weapons, snacks, and random knick-knacks, Adam floated—a prisoner inside of the storage box that he'd been abruptly stuffed into.

Is this what it feels like to be a jellyfish? Adam wondered as his body drifted in the seemingly endless expanse. He had always pondered what the inside of a storage unit looked like, but he just never imagined it to be so... spacious.

And so stale-smelling.

[CONCATULATIONS! QUEST COMPLETE!]

The familiar words appeared before Adam's eyes.
Huh, I guess they brought me into the city.

[Rolling rewards...]
[Ding!]
[Mana Potion x1 obtained!]

Suddenly, a purple vial appeared in his hands. Although small, it oozed with power, piquing his curiosity.

At a glance, it clearly wasn't just any Mana Potion, but rather something absurd, much like all the other items he'd obtained.

Inspect.

[Deluxe Mana Potion of Impeccable Magical Restoration: Restore 100% of the User's Mana]

"Oops. I must have loaded the wrong item in the dispenser."

Incredible! A potion of this caliber was virtually unheard of! Ten, twenty, maybe even a fifty percent boost to natural recovery he understood; those were the kinds of potions he knew of. But a mana potion that could fully restore the user's magical capacity?! It boggled his mind.

Immediately, he began envisioning all of the applications for an item of this caliber.

Tsk. If only I had a potion like this during Junith's attack! Adam grimaced, his face heating as the scenario began to replay in his mind—the mistakes, the obvious signs of a trap, and most importantly, the last time he'd seen his friend.

His eyes fell shut.

He had been greedy, too greedy. His ambition in pursuit of his dream had cost him everything he held dear—his items, his skills, and his friend. He could see that. But was he wrong?

No.

Of course not! Adam's eyes snapped open. It was the world that was wrong!

They just didn't understand! The masses couldn't comprehend the utopia that could be created if they just embraced the purity of the bone! After all, humanity's ultimate form was death. All he aspired to do was recycle and reuse.

Adam sighed, picturing all he could accomplish, all the lives he could save if the world just allowed him and Schrödinger to simply be. Instead they feared progress, stuck in their ignorant ways.

He clutched the vial for a moment before activating the metal band on his finger, stashing the potion. Like all storage units, a vorpal pool materialized, drawing in his potion and presenting a System screen of the item being slotted inside.

Now… I wonder if they'll le—

Before he could finish his train of thought, blinding light flooded his senses.

One moment he floated aimlessly in the void, and the next, he found himself in a dimly lit room with five pairs of eyeballs staring at him. Two were familiar—the green-haired woman and the brown-haired man who'd catnapped him earlier at the gate—but the three others were new.

A blonde, burly man with a menacing face and handlebar mustache.

A red-haired woman wearing glasses in a maid outfit.

And finally, perhaps the most menacing out of the group, a raven-haired woman wearing a black suit, sat with her legs crossed. Despite her glaring purple eyes, frowning black lips, and obviously annoyed attitude, what truly worried Adam was the red whip laid across her lap.

Ah. I'm being sold into slavery.

No one uttered a word, giving the boy time to survey the scattering of wooden chairs, red tapestry, and crates that surrounded him. The room seemed to resemble a hideout of some kind. If he had to guess, he was underground, judging from the stone walls and flat wooden ceiling.

"Uh. Hello? Please don't kill me."

At Adam's words, the group of people turned to each other.

"Elttil yob," the massive man said gently, his muscles barely contained beneath his white button-up shirt. Looking up at him, the giant seemed to take up half the room with his size alone, blocking the exit that lay behind him. "Od uoy kaeps Naillegir? Erehw era ruoy stnerap?"

Adam blinked at the gargantuan outstretched hand holding a cookie. It was warm, still fresh, and perhaps worse of all, emanating a scent that awakened his hunger.

"Ees? I dlot ouy eh t'nseod kaeps ruo egaugnal. Roop gniht si ylbaborp gnivrats," the mage said as Adam took the cookie, ravenously devouring it in three bites. As soon as he was finished, the giant handed him another. "S'ti a eugnot ev'I reven draeh erofeb."

Adam cocked his head to the side, not understanding a word of what was being said. Instead, he was more focused on the crumbs, licking the chocolate chi—*Oh no!*

[CATSIFICATION CURSE ACTIVATED!]
[WEAKNESS TO CHOCOLATE!]
[You are being acutely poisoned! -8% HP per second]

Ah, crapbaskets.

Suddenly, Adam seized up, foaming at the mouth as his entire body spasmed and he fell to the floor.

* * *

"OH, EARTH MOTHER!" Titania screamed as the boy suddenly had a seizure and collapsed to the ground. Without wasting a second, she rushed beside the pale boy, attempting to figure out what was wrong as the child wiggled frantically. "OH, EARTH MOTHER! OH, EARTH MOTHER!"

"He's been poisoned! He's allergic to something in the cookie!" Ruebella yelled. The receptionist had used her scan skill to swiftly diagnose the flailing demi-child.

"STAND BACK!" Arnold bellowed, the titan of a man suddenly tearing away his shirt to reveal his massive pectorals and chiseled abs. "THE PURITY OF MUSCLE SHALL REVITALIZE HIM!"

In an instant, the blonde musclehead was beside her, grabbing the boy out of her arms and enveloping him with his muscles. Arnold then began to glow, his skill, **Healing Hearth** activating and restoring the complexion of the little demi-child's body.

"BE HEALED, LITTLE BOY! BE HEALED!" Arnold cried, squeezing the boy with his biceps so hard he let out a high-pitched squeak that silenced the whole room.

"Did you break him?! Be gentle, big guy, you're crushing him!" Sehn yelled, moving to pry the boy from the man's embrace.

The child suddenly coughed, expelling black spittle all over the man's arms. "Huuur! Huuuuuhah!" the boy wheezed as he began violently squirming, trying to escape from the titan's grip.

"Haa! Tel em og, uoy dezisrevo gabtaem!" the boy screamed in his odd tongue.

"It's okay! It's okay! You are safe, child!" Arnold cooed, gently setting the boy down, prompting him to run off to the edge of the room with his fluffy ears pressed downwards.

"I t'nod dnatsrednu uoy!" the boy yelled, clutching his chest in panic as everyone collectively tried to comfort him.

"Enough!"

At the word, the room suddenly fell silent as the guild master cracked her whip, striking the air with a crisp *snap*.

Every eye in the basement shifted to the guild leader, in return the woman glared at everyone present.

"Can't you brain-damaged idiots tell you're crowding him? Give him some space before I start handing out pay cuts," Valentine growled, the no-nonsense guild master clearly unhappy with the events transpiring. "Ruebella," she said, snapping her fingers to summon the receptionist to her side.

"Y-Yes, mistress?"

"Bring me a skill jewel of linguistics. Lowest tier we have."

The receptionist stiffened for a moment.

"B-But..." Ruebella began, before her voice turned into a whisper. "The lowest one we have is a C tier and costs two gold coins. Are you—"

"It's fine," Valentine snapped, her icy eyes settling on Titania and Sehn. "These two will repay the guild in full, plus a fee."

"Very well, mistress," Ruebella said before disappearing.

At the woman's words, Sehn and Titania stiffened, their minds involuntarily short-circuiting as the price hit them.

"Whaaa?! But that's like forty thousand coppers!" Sehn cried, the warrior already on his knees and groveling. "Please, you can't do this to us! I just got out of a mountain of debt!"

"Sehn," the raven-haired woman said, placing the tip of her heel beneath Sehn's chin.

"Y-Yes?"

"What did I say about stirring the pot?"

"N-Not to?"

"And do you think bringing a demi-child into a city run by Purists is indicative of *not* stirring the pot?" Valentine said, her icy tone radiating tranquil fury as her eyes sparked with power.

"I—I—"

"It was my fault; I panicked," Titania interjected, coming to Sehn's rescue. "The kid was trying to enter the city, and I had to hide him before a guard noticed us."

"Yes. You've explained this already," Valentine sighed as she nudged Sehn away. "Yet the problem still remains that you've endangered our entire guild through your actions."

"We're very sorry, mistress. But we couldn't leave a child, demi or not, to wander alone," Titania said, her voice firm, and her gaze met the guild leader's.

"Tsk. Whatever," Valentine replied, holding out a hand as Ruebella returned, the skill crystal in hand. "Time to see where this boy's parents are, so we can get him out of here."

Catpurr 17
A Good Night's Rest

"You want him to participate in the trials?"

"Yes, yes, I said this twice already, haven't I?"

"It's just... once this starts, Eli, there's no going back. Not for any of us. Are you sure this is what you want? Once Voltrain and the others find out, they won't be happy."

"Pah! Do you know what the biggest problem with immortality is, Freya?"

"Everything gets boring after a thousand years?"

"It's having a song stuck in your spiritron from the eleventh millennium and being unable to get it out because you're the only one in *existence* that remembers the song but you can't recall how it ends."

"I don't understand your point."

"The point *is*, I'm tired, Freya. I'm truly tired."

***

"Dloh mih nwod ylthgit!"

"M'I gniyrt!"

"T'ond truh mih!"

"GAH! LET ME GO! FLESHBAGS!" Adam squealed, writhing as the group of catnappers struggled to hold him down.

"Er'uoy gniracs mih!" another woman yelled.

"Hguone." Suddenly, the raven-haired woman rose from her chair, briskly walking over and seizing Adam by the face to direct his golden eyes to her purple ones.

Observing her, there was a certain familiarity to her facial features that reassured the boy, reminding him of his teacher as she glared at him.

"Eb llits."

[PARALYTIC SKILL DETECTED! EYE OF MEDUSA!]
[VITALITY CHECK FAILED! YOU ARE BEING PARALYZED!]

NOT THIS AGAIN!

All of his muscles seized up, rendering his body unresponsive as he slumped and sprawled on the floor.

"Od ti," the woman commanded, releasing his face as she walked away, her heels clicking against the wooden floor.

Suddenly, the interface lit up, a system message offering him a choice.

[Compatible skill crystal detected!]
[Jewel of Linguistics {Rigellian}]
Gain the ability to understand and mimic common tongues native to this region
[Accept Skill? Y/N?]

Well that's new, Adam thought. It was the first time he had come across skill crystals, or even the Rigellian language, for that matter.

Accept.

Immediately, his screen updated, displaying **Artificial Linguistics {Rigellian}** under his 'New Skills' list.

"S'ti enog! Did it work? The crystal disappeared," the green-haired woman asked.

"Well it's hard to tell 'cuz the boss paralyzed him," her coffin-toting companion replied.

I can understand them!

"Try blowing on his ears," the man suggested.

"What's that supposed to do?" asked the woman.

"I don't know; I'm just spitballing ideas here."

"Well, go be an idiot elsewhere, Sehn. Do we have a room to place him, Ruebella?" she huffed, turning to the red-haired maid.

The woman in the maid uniform straightened at being addressed. "E-Every room is b-booked. I—I can take him into mine—"

"Say no more, Ruebella!" said the blonde giant. "I shall accompany this youth for the night and warm his puny body with my majestic pectorals!"

Please, no, Adam inwardly groaned, his face still planted into the floor.

"*Or,* we could just leave him in the basement," said the green-haired woman.

"Y-You mean l-lock him in here?" asked the maid.

"Well, it beats him wandering around, and someone stumbling across him. Let's just keep him down here for the night until Medusa's Glare wears off."

Adam was rolled onto his back, positioned where four pairs of eyes peered down at him.

"Hello, can you understand?" inquired the green-haired woman.

"You ask, knowing he's still paralyzed, and I'M the idiot," retorted the man in leathers before being punched in his shoulder.

"He can still hear ya, dingus," the mage said, before turning back to Adam with a gentle smile. "If you can understand me, please know that we're doing this for your safety and ours. We're going to keep you in here for the night until the skill wears off, and then return. But I promise you, we don't mean to harm you. We only want to help."

Adam lay there, eyes fixed on the green-haired woman, still unable to move.

"It's going to be okay."

Easy for you to say. You're not the one paralyzed and surrounded by strangers!

Before long, the group dispersed, leaving Adam alone, gazing at the ceiling where a glass fixture spilled light.

This sucks, he groaned. None of his captors had the foresight to move his head away from the light.

Fortunately, after a few moments, the light within the glass fixture thankfully dimmed, causing him to wonder about the technology of this foreign nation.

The light source wasn't flammable, that much was certain, as evidenced by the absence of the resin scent typical of torches. Instead, it emitted a glow, albeit an exceedingly bright one that irritated the nekoboy's sensitive eyes.

If he had to guess, it was some form of electricity—a technology his master had experimented with as an early concept for illumination and power.

Sadly, it never materialized, due to technical challenges coupled with the Inquisitors hounding them made it nigh impossible to proceed...

But it was still heartening to see humanity progressing.

Suddenly, the sound of a hatch being unlocked and opened grabbed Adam's attention.

"H-Hello, I brought a blanket and pillow for you," the red-haired maid said, leaning over Adam and draping a light blue blanket over his body.

How thoughtful...

"I, uhm... Sorry about Lady Valentine. She's a really n-nice person, just under a lot of stress," the maid apologized, then introduced herself. "I-I'm Ruebella Antoniette, the chief receptionist of the Vilenciel Branch Guild Office. In a couple of hours, the effect of the Mistress' skill will wear off. Until then, j-just bear with it, okay?"

Okay, he thought, even though the woman couldn't hear him. She fluffed a pillow, carefully lifting his head to place it beneath him. Despite his entire body being numb, the item was clearly soft, and oddly, emanated a fragrance like lilacs.

"T-there you go." The maid smiled, patting the boy on the head, creating a strange feeling in the pits of his stomach. Kindness, that's what Adam experienced for the first time in a long while.

And it was strange. He mentally short circuited.

"W-We'll figure o-out accommodations for you tomorrow," shen said, flashing a smile and heading towards the entrance.

"T-Thank!" Adam suddenly groaned, making the woman pause. She pivoted, the frills of her dress spinning as she turned back with wide eyes.

"Thank you," he spat out, causing the woman to smile.

"Relax, we'll sort everything in the morning," Ruebella said while leaning over her charge. "If you need anything, just knock on the hatch, okay?"

"O...keh," he slurred as Ruebella finally left.

With the sound of the hatch closing, Adam blinked. The effects of the paralytic skill had begun wearing off.

An eternity seemed to pass before the lights finally dimmed, granting him some comfort.

"Ugggh..." he groaned as his eyes darted across the now-dark room.

His fingers wiggled stiffly as sensation returned to his body. Attempting to massage his sore eyes, he managed to slap his face, his coordination still lacking.

[WELCOME TO TRIAL 4!]
[MANDATORY QUEST GIVEN!]

"Grreaat... Moah sufhering..." Adam moaned.

Catpurr 18

Testing the Curse

Opening his eyes, golden eyes fluttered open to meet blue eyes and bulging muscles, barely contained by an apron that read *Meat Connoisseur*.

Scrambling, Adam immediately backed into the room's far corner, shifting away from the mass of flexing muscle.

"YOU'RE AWAKE! GOOD MORNING, LITTLE BOY!" the man bellowed. Catlike ears twitched and pressed downwards from the giant's enthusiasm. "I brought ham!"

Suddenly, an oversized hunk of meat on a bone, the size of the nekoboy's head, materialized in the man's giant hands and was placed in front of Adam.

"Uh…" he replied, unsure of what to make of the situation as his eyes focused on the piece of meat.

"If you prefer something else, I have steaks, chicken, lamb, T-bones, pork, and fish!" the man recited with enthusiasm. With each item listed, another piece of meat dropped onto an enormous silver platter.

Hungry as he was, Adam was tempted, but restrained himself from taking a bite as the basement hatch opened and several people scrambled down.

"Arnold! You're frightening him!" The green-haired woman barged in, pulling Arnold back as he attempted to shower his charge in meat.

"NONSENSE! HE JUST NEEDS A LITTLE BIT OF PROTEIN!"

This is a little bit? Adam thought, eyeing the towering pile of food.

Ruebella appeared, laying out a serving of orange juice, bread, and vegetables. "G-Good morning. Remember me?"

"Ruebella Antoniette," Adam replied, meeting her gaze and reciting the woman's name aloud.

"V-Very good." She smiled warmly. "We weren't sure what food your kind ate, so we got a l-little bit of everything h-here for you. J-Just knock on the hatch when you've finished."

"Thank you," Adam replied after a pause, looking down at the linens.

The maid left, taking with her the green-haired woman and the jovial titan of pure muscle, leaving Adam alone with a massive pile of food.

The moment the hatch closed, he instinctively leapt at the food, unable to withstand his rumbling stomach and hunger pangs. He quickly and uncouthly devoured as much as his sharp little teeth allowed, ripping and tearing. For reasons unknown, an abyssal hunger had awakened in him, turning him into a ravenous machine whose sole purpose was to consume.

Once two whole trays had been licked clean, leaving only bones, he fell over with a loud belch, expelling cat-shaped confetti that glittered before dissipating.

Seriously... How does that even work? he wondered.

Composing himself, Adam sat cross-legged for a moment, before finally standing up and making his way towards the hatch.

He banged on it. A moment later, Ruebella appeared and asked if he was finished.

When he nodded, she left briefly, returning with a large brown hat to cover his ears. With express instructions to do as he was told, the demi-human was finally let out of the basement guided by Ruebella through a long hallway marked by a series of numbered wooden doors.

He glanced left and right at the flanking doors engraved with inscrutable words. It seemed, despite the skill crystal granting him comprehension of the spoken language, it didn't give him the ability to read or write it.

"H-Here we are," Ruebella said, stopping before an open door in the middle of the hallway. Inside the room was a tub filled with hot water from which steam rose.

Oh no.

Ruebella picked up a set of clothes and handed them to him—a brown tunic, trousers, and a cloak.

"T-There are f-fresh clothes, and a cloak. When you are done, please ring this bell." She handed Adam a small bell, continuing, "It is dangerous for you to walk around uncovered. So please wear the hat or the cloak. O-Okay?"

"Okay," Adam acquiesced. After all, there wasn't exactly much he could do in this situation.

Sighing, he entered the bathroom as Ruebella closed the door, enclosing the nekoboy inside with the steam.

Passing through, he turned, spotting a fogged-up mirror flanking his side. With one hand, he set his clothes aside and wiped away the condensation, revealing a soiled image of himself peering back.

Crapbaskets, I REALLY AM A CHILD?! Adam inwardly exclaimed, finally getting a good look at himself. Besides being caked in mud and sporting muddy, cat-like ears, he looked exactly as he did twenty years ago. Clad in his rags, he was hit with nostalgia, recalling his time in the orphanage and his struggle to survive. The freezing nights begging, starving, and weeping—nights long behind him as he grew in power thanks to Master Razalia.

He touched his face, his now golden eyes which appeared tinged red in his reflection.

That's new, he mused before opening his mouth to notice his enlarged canine teeth, much bigger than an average child's.

Taking full inventory of himself, he exhaled, touching the red tuft of fur on his chest.

This really happened. A new lease on life.

Albeit without his furry friend.

Adam peered at the bathtub, considering the foamy water before sighing and stripping.

"Well... let's get this over with," Adam grumbled, when an idea struck him.

Seeing an opportunity to test the effects of his curse, Adam slowly dipped his hand into the water, the heat making his body swelter. Yet, despite submerging his entire forearm, the curse didn't activate.

He went further, dipping his whole shoulder into the water. When that failed to trigger his curse, next both arms, before retrieving the appendages and fully stepping into the tub.

Adam shivered as the heat of the bath made his hairs stand on end. It'd been some time since he had properly bathed, usually relying on his skills to dispel odors. Still, despite the water reaching his knees, his curse hadn't activated.

Hmmm...

Gripping the edges of the tub, he lowered himself, gradually descending until finally, an alert appeared on his interface.

[CATSIFICATION CURSE ACTIVATED!]
[YOU ARE WET!]
[-20% To all stats UNTIL DRIED!]

There it is, he thought before abruptly losing all strength, collapsing fully into the water.

Well... at least there's a threshold, Adam considered as his body floated upwards.

Catpurr 19

Guild Master Valentine

"Heave! Heave! Use your forearm strength!"

"I'm trying!"

"Well try harder!"

"GAAAAAAH!"

"Ladies and gentlemen! *Another* failure! Excalibur remains sealed in stone! Come one! Come all, test your strength for only ONE silver and get a free HOLY sword if you can free it from the earth!"

—Adventurer Rochester, hosting a strongman competition to see who is worthy of the mysterious blade from the Heavens.

***

Drying himself with the towel that had been laid out, Adam's catsification curse finally dispelled, restoring his stats back to normal.

Inspecting the clothes, he realized they seemed to fit perfectly, almost as if someone had measured him when he had been sleeping. Which was impossible, considering every time Ruebella came to check up on him throughout the night he had woken up, noting the woman peeking down at him.

Still, it didn't change the fact that his clothes fit nicely. Reaching over, he donned the final article—the black cloak, ensuring his furry ears were covered as he eyed himself in the mirror.

So this is me now...

Looking away from his reflection, Adam summoned his quest menu, perusing the next trial.

[Trial 4]
[MANDATORY QUEST!]
[Receive the Ticket of The Abyssal Tower!]
[Possible Rewards: EXP 500, Copper Pieces x50, Cicero's Gacha Coin x1, Minor Health Potion x1, Minor Mana Potion x1]
[Failure: DEATH.]
[You have seven days to complete the task!]
[159:56:20]

It drew from him a sigh, facing yet another life-or-death quest. He wasn't quite sure what the Abyssal Tower was or where he'd get a ticket, but he would soon find out, one way or another.

Reaching over, Adam grabbed the gilded bell Ruebella had left on the bathroom counter.

Ringing it twice, he stood by the wooden door, patiently waiting until the receptionist appeared, signaling for him to approach. She fidgeted with his hood, ensuring his ears were properly covered.

Adam nodded at her instructions to stay close, intertwining his fingers with hers.

Satisfied with the response, she guided him through the guild halls. They passed through a spruce-covered corridor and a flight of stairs before entering through a door that led into the main foyer.

As the door swung open, Adam was instantly overwhelmed by noise, light, and the pungent aroma of alcohol and cigarettes. Dozens of people—nearly a hundred—donned various suits of armor and clothing. Mages, warriors, rangers, and rogues drank merrily, gambling, or congregating in front of a large bulletin board displaying dozens of fliers.

Scattered around the room were several maids dressed just like Ruebella, six of them by Adam's count. They bustled about, serving food, handling paperwork, and even handing out goods and inspecting materials brought in by adventurers.

Feeling oddly claustrophobic from the multitude of faces in such close quarters, Adam froze. Ruebella urged him towards a stairwell marked **"STAFF ONLY!"**

Regaining his composure, the boy followed along, making his way up the stairs and going through a red, rugged hallway. At the end of the corridor loomed a large golden door.

"T-The guild master will ask you q-questions. Just a-answer t-them truthfully, o-ok?" Ruebella advised. He nodded, and as she opened the door, he stepped through, immediately drawing the attention of three pairs of eyes: the scrawny man with the coffin on his back, the green-haired mage, and finally, the muscular man flexing his biceps before a large, rounded mirror.

"Take a seat," the raven-haired woman instructed, not bothering to look up from the mountain of paperwork heaped upon her ornate desk.

Adam glanced at Ruebella, who gestured towards the leather chair that sat parallel to the woman who appeared to be the guild master.

As he shuffled over to the chair, the raven-haired woman handed a piece of paper to the green-haired woman beside her—the same one who had catnapped him. Reading the script, she frowned, while the scrawny man beside her began to openly weep.

"Child, where are your parents?" the guild master inquired, finally lifting her gaze to meet Adam's, her purple irises glowing.

[The Gaze of Truth sees through your lies.]

Adam tensed momentarily, feeling the effects of a skill and its message wash over him. Yet strangely, nothing immediately happened.

"I'm an orphan," he replied truthfully, meeting the woman's dark eyes with his own.

"Where did you come from?" she continued.

"I don't know."

"Are you lying?"

"No."

At Adam's words, the woman's gaze darkened further. "How did you get here?"

"I don't—" Before he could claim ignorance, his words abruptly twisted, and he blurted out, "I came out of a portal!"

"The skill forces me to speak the truth?!" Adam began to inwardly panic, his breathing becoming uneven, and strangely he started to sweat. The group exchanged looks and fixed their gaze on him.

"Who sent you?" the guild master asked, her fingers twirling the pen she used to write.

"I..." Adam huffed, uncertain of what to say. He couldn't openly admit that some being bordering on divinity had dropped him here on a whim.

"I don't know," he finally replied, technically, a truth. He had no idea who had teleported him; for all he knew, Eli was outsourcing everything to a minion who was screwing with him.

"Why are you here?" she asked, and Adam felt as though he were burning up.

"Mistress Valentine, maybe we shouldn't press him so hard? He's just a child," the green-haired woman suggested. Arnold chimed in, "Dearie, I concur with Titania, he is just a boy."

"Silence," Valentine said, raising a hand as she repeated her question.

Unable to resist her skill, Adam truthfully answered, "I'm here to grab a ticket to the Abyssal Tower."

At his words the guild master froze, dropping her pen on the desk, and everyone around her went wide-eyed with horrified looks.

"Why are you here?" Valentine repeated yet again, this time with furrowed brows and plain skepticism as she leaned forwards.

Adam repeated his reply, causing the Ruebella to lift her hand to her mouth. Even Arnold deflated.

"Boy," Valentine whispered. "Do you even know what you're looking for?"

"No." Adam dry-swallowed, the escalating heat becoming nearly unbearable.

"Do you know what the Abyssal Tower is?"

"No."

"Why do you want a ticket?"

"Because I have to; otherwise, I'll die and won't be able to save my friend!" he cried, his head hung low, unable to take the heat of the woman's skill. At his confession, the sensation stopped, accompanied by the click, click of approaching heels.

The guild master crouched down, cupping the boy's face, guiding his eyes to meet hers. "Who told you about the tower?"

"N-N-No one. I have a quest..." Adam whispered.

At his response, Valentine moved swiftly, yanking his shirt off. Too weak to react, he was exposed to Valentine's clinical scrutiny, her expression quickly becoming one of bewilderment as they fixated on the circular sigil on his shoulder blade. He had not noticed it until just then.

"Impossible... No..." Valentine backed away, until her expression shifted to sudden outrage. "Out! Everyone OUT! Now! Ruebella!"

"Y-Yes ma'am!"

"Find him a room, I don't care who you have to kick out. Do it. Titania, Sehn. Since you brought him here, you'll be responsible for him," Valentine said, sitting back at her desk and going over her paperwork. "Ensure he knows exactly what he's seeking and the consequences of what he wants."

"Yes ma'am," the duo beside her replied, promptly moving towards Adam.

"C'mon lad. Let's go," Sehn said, escorting a confused Adam away with Titania in tow.

* * *

Watching the group leave, Valentine sighed, and Arnold began massaging her shoulders. She reached over, touching the man's massive, comforting hand.

"A child this time," Valentine said as her expression twisted. "Why are the gods so cruel?"

"I'll ensure he's as comfortable as possible, dear," Arnold said, embracing his wife.

"Please do," Valentine whispered, kissing his hand before he left. As the door closed, she reached down, opening a drawer to reveal a purple slip. Retrieving it, she stared at the paper emblazoned with a seal shaped like a burning star, marked by three dozen tiny hole punches.

Her abyssal ticket. Notched at floor thirty-six. Besides herself, she could only count on two hands the number of people who had reached that far, two of whom were in her employ.

She closed her eyes, reflecting on all the "Chosen" who had passed through. All the lives she would never see again. From the moment she saw him, she suspected the boy was one of them. Being a demi-human so distant from any known tribe and unfamiliar with the local language could only mean one thing.

Either he was an escaped slave from Lady Vilenciel's menagerie, or he was another soul compelled by the threat of death to seek the Abyss. Both scenarios spelled trouble. The latter for the boy, and the former for the guild.

Although slavery was illegal, it was no secret what the daughter of the Duchess did in her free time to demi-humans. With Purist ideologies spreading, many preferred to turn a blind eye to avoid the fury of the doting Duchess.

Valentine hung her head low, a headache forming.

"Maybe it's a good thing I didn't ask for his name." She sighed, wondering if she should have taken a closer look at his tattoo to figure out which god could be so callous.

Catpurr 20
Pep Talk

This is going to suck, Adam thought, reflecting on the events of the meeting with the guild master.

Sitting in a room adorned with a wooden dresser and a bed spacious enough for an adult, the nekoboy waited, peering through the pink-tinted glass window that offered a view of the massive gilded city outside.

Observing the pedestrians from his vantage point on the fourth floor, he watched as the citizens carried on with their day. Looking down, the city resembled any other he'd flown over, but one stark difference stuck out to him.

The streets were walked only by humans.

No delvers, no lizardfolk, and no elves—just humans. This sight seemed especially peculiar, considering he was from a place teeming with a variety of species.

It had been the same within the tavern. Every being he had come across had been human.

This might be a problem, he realized, considering his escape as he pulled his hood further down.

Adam was no stranger to discrimination, after all. He had been pursued throughout his life just based on his class alone. He could easily imagine the troubles he'd get into as a young demi-child wandering these streets.

A knock at the wooden door diverted his attention from a family strolling hand in hand.

"Hello?" the familiar mage with green hair said, poking her head in to look at her guild's guest.

"Hello," he replied, as the duo known as Titania and Sehn crowded into his recently acquired living quarters.

"I'm Titania Nobora, and this is Sehn. We're adventurers for the guild. Do you have a name?" Titania introduced herself, while Sehn struggled to make his coffin backpack fit inside the room.

"I'm Adam," he replied, glimpsing the swift movement of a white-haired maid peeking into his room. Making eye contact, the dark-eyed woman vanished, allowing Ruebella to enter, holding a box.

"Adam," Titania said, adjusting her dress as she sat down beside him. "Do you know where you are?"

"Uh, no," he truthfully admitted, feeling uneasy as the scantily clad woman leaned in and put a hand on his lap. Adam never had much of an interest in the meatsuits of others, yet as he sat there his eyes began to unconsciously drift downwards, causing him concern as he refocused.

"You're in Vilenciel, the imperial fortress city of the Western Alinora Plains."

"Okay," he replied, with absolutely no idea where that was or its significance. The only discernible aspect was that he was in a Fortress City, indicating a high military presence, or a capital of some kind.

"You have no idea where any of that is, do you?" Titania remarked, noticing his blank stare.

"Nope."

She sighed. "And you have no idea what the Abyssal Tower is either, do you?"

Looking off to the side, Adam checked his interface, reviewing the quest marker in case there was any information he had missed.

"Nope," he responded.

Titania looked down for a moment.

"The Abyssal Tower is... a bad place," she explained.

Sehn snorted. "That's an understatement," he interjected, folding his arms as he leaned against the wall. Titania shot him a look.

"Kid, the Abyssal Tower is a hellscape designed to kill you," Sehn continued.

As I thought, Adam sighed to himself.

"SEHN!" Titania snapped.

"What? You can't pamper him if you expect him to survive," the leather-armored warrior retorted, shedding his nervous demeanor as he undid his coffin, letting it drop to the floor with a loud *thunk*. He crouched beside Adam. "How much time do you have, lad?"

Taken aback by the man's intense focus, the boy took a moment before responding.

[159:36:20]

"Six days." Adam grimaced, realizing the gravity of the situation from Sehn's tone. Judging by everyone's earlier expressions in the guild room, he knew he was in for a rough time. This, however, was the last nail in the coffin, so to speak.

"Then we have some time. Listen, the Abyssal Tower is a twisted game show the gods put on for their own amusement. They offer rewards, skills, abilities, and promises of power," Sehn explained, producing a purple slip of paper adorned with a symbol of a sword and shield, punctured by a dozen holes. "To enter, you need one of these—an abyssal ticket."

Seeing his quest objective, Adam's pupils dilated. He lunged, attempting to snatch the item to complete his quest. But Sehn had already anticipated this, yanking his arm back almost immediately.

"Not so fast!" Sehn yelled, catching Adam by the head one-handed as the nekoboy reached for the paper Sehn held aloft. "Each ticket is unique to its owner and soul-bonded, meaning you can't have mine!"

At his words, Adam deflated, stopping his assault. "So where do I get one?" The pair exchanged glances, both looking serious.

"Do you understand what we're saying?" Sehn asked, his jaw clenched.

"I do. I am prepared," Adam declared resolutely. "Either I do it and I die, or I don't, and I die."

Sehn blinked, the boy's words catching him off guard.

"At the Temple of the Six Gods. That's where all tickets are issued," Titania butted in as she presented her own ticket, depicting a symbol of a tree with five holes punched.

Great. More gods, Adam sighed to himself, lamenting all the woes he'd already endured.

"So, once I get this ticket, all I have to do is complete trials, right?" he asked, examining Titania's ticket as she extended it. Upon touching it, he could sense it was magical in nature. The item was akin to silk in his hand as he inspected the light gold engraving of the tree on it.

"It's not that simple, lad," Sehn replied, as Ruebella started unpacking what looked like bits of leather and metal armor. "The trials are challenging, even for someone as good-looking as me. Fortunately for most, you only have to ascend to the fifth floor to negate the death penalty."

So even after I get a ticket, there will be a compulsory death penalty, Adam thought, absorbing all the information and forming his own conclusions.

"Sadly, most don't make it past the first floor," Titania sighed, and Ruebella signaled for Adam to stand.

"P-Pardon me," Ruebella said as Adam rose, and she began outfitting him with leather straps and pieces of metal.

"What's this for?" the boy inquired, curious about why he was suddenly being armored up.

Sehn's expression swiftly changed, his lips curving into a devious smile.

Oh, no.

"Why, training, of course!" Sehn exclaimed, patting Adam on the back. "We don't want you dying immediately! Uncle Sehn is going to teach you how to fight!"

Catpurr 21

I Want to Be an Adventurer

Entering through a side door, Adam found himself in a room constructed with circular walls, surrounding a massive sand pit in its center.

Inside, he passed a couple of men sporting iron badges on their collars as they left, sparking another question in him.

His eyes scanned the now vacant room, taking note of the weapons on the racks lining the walls before Sehn ushered him inside.

"All right, kid. First things first, what's your class?"

Oh crap. Adam froze, uncertain whether to lie or tell the truth. His past experiences taught him that telling people he was a necromancer usually resulted in torches, screams, and demands for his blood.

"What? If I'm gonna help you survive, it's best I know your class and your starting skills," Sehn insisted, dropping his coffin on the floor and kicking it open.

"I'm a rogue," the boy finally replied, lying through his teeth.

"What skills do you have?" Sehn asked, producing a pair of wooden daggers from the coffin.

"None. I, uh... rolled poorly on my starter skills," Adam nervously claimed, hoping that Sehn would buy his lie.

The man frowned, studying the boy before shaking his head. "Yeah, well, that's pretty common, sadly."

Oh good, he bought it, he sighed. Being a demi-human was bad enough, but adding the fact that he was a necromancer to the mix? It was a recipe for disaster.

He wasn't sure how Sehn would react, so he kept that information to himself as he picked up the small buckler Sehn had laid out. As the man scrutinized him, Adam did the same, noticing the small emerald badge tucked into the inner part of his collar.

"What's that badge you're all wearing?" he asked, trying to engage in the dreaded small talk to glean some information.

"This?" Sehn raised a brow, pointing at the emblem. "It's our guild rank emblem, lad."

"And you're Emerald-Ranked?"

"Yup. B-Ranked Emerald," Sehn replied proudly, before boasting, "comes with tons of privileges and perks."

Catlike ears twitched at the mention of perks. After all, if there was anything at all he could use to his advantage, he would take it.

"Such as?"

"Ah, how about we focus on training first?"

"Is it possible for me to get a badge?"

Sehn's face twisted. "Errr, let's—"

"If you can earn it, sure," the guild master interjected, materializing suddenly from a flurry of shadows along with a stocky figure in a maid outfit. On closer inspection, Adam realized it wasn't a man, but a very muscular, dark-skinned woman with blonde pigtails, rivaling Arnold in size. "Thank you, Lunafreya."

"Of course, mistress." The maid posed before vanishing in another flurry of shadows.

"So you're interested in a guild pin, are you?" Valentine said, her heels clicking on the smooth tile as she circled the massive sand pit and approached the pair.

"Depends on the perks and what the guild can offer me," Adam replied immediately.

Valentine crossed her arms, wearing a small smirk.

"For a child, you're very articulate."

Oh crapbaskets! Adam silently panicked, realizing he'd been talking to them as if he would with any other meatsuit.

"Oh… I'm a very quick study," he replied sheepishly, hoping the woman wouldn't use her truth gaze again.

"Is that so?" she asked rhetorically, pinning Adam with her purple gaze. "The perks include discounted room rates, contracts, a secure spatial storage space, discounted item and material processing, and access to our guild's contacts for adventuring needs and gear—all at a guild discount," she finished.

Well, that would certainly be useful. Especially if they're making me stick around for these trial things, Adam thought, analyzing the potential benefits.

"So, what do I need for a badge?"

In response to Adam's inquiry, Sehn seemed to muster some courage and raised his voice. "He's just a kid; isn't there an age limit?!"

"That is something determined by me, the guild master," Valentine asserted, folding her arms while glaring at Sehn. He promptly retreated as she returned her gaze to Adam. "Simply pass a brief five-minute combat test, and I'll admit you as a bronze tab adventurer. You'll get a spatial storage unit here and a room, backed by the guild. Of course, you'll have to pay a small guild tax, assuming you survive your contracts."

After a moment of contemplation, it seemed like a no brainer to Adam.

"Sounds like a good deal," he said, extending his hand to seal the pact as his teacher had taught him to do. "When do we start?"

Valentine blinked, displaying an expression of momentary surprise before lightly smiling and shaking his hand—a rare expression from her, one not of exasperation.

"Oh boy," Sehn huffed, a look of concern on his face as Adam turned to him. Ruebella had entered through the door they had used, with a frying pan in hand.

Shaking his head, Sehn stepped away, dragging his coffin behind him, uttering a weak "Good luck" as he abandoned Adam to his fate.

"Now," Valentine replied, releasing the boy's hand. "Temperance, engage."

What?

At the guild master's command, Ruebella's expression abruptly shifted. Her eyes widened before narrowing again into furrowed, angry slits.

Oh, crapbaskets.

He swiftly ducked, anticipating the maid's arm movement, and evaded the frying pan that came flying at his head.

ARE YOU INSANE! Adam wanted to cry out as another frying pan forced him to jump, abandoning his previous position to avoid becoming debris on the pulverized tile floor.

Twisting midair, he landed on all fours in the dirt, ears folded, eyes wide. His heart was pounding in his chest as his vision pulsed.

The dust settled, revealing a glaring, red-eyed Ruebella. The shy and nervous girl from before was nowhere to be seen, and had transformed into a furious battle maiden, her arm outstretched, directing a dozen floating frying pans, all aimed at him.

Oh... Oh crap.

Catpurr 22

Ruebella the Destroyer

"STOP! I surrender! I yield, I YIELD!" Adam screamed, vaulting into the air to evade the projectile that detonated the earth beneath his feet, propelling him through the air.

"Three minutes! You got this, lad! Just hang on!" Sehn yelled as the boy hit the ground and tucked into a roll, narrowly avoiding another cast iron pan that nearly claimed his life.

Teeth clenched together and his ears folded as he glared up at Ruebella. The maid was positioned in the far corner of the sand pit surrounded by her arsenal of floating frying pans.

Lifting her hand, Ruebella retrieved her spent weapons, which whirled through the dirt, boomeranging back to rejoin the rest of the metallic arsenal.

"This is ridiculous!" Adam moaned as another barrage of iron hurtled his way.

Drawing upon his twenty-five years of dodging experience, Adam ducked, dove, and weaved, attempting to evade the onslaught of frying pans that narrowly missed his lithe frame by mere millimeters.

Unfortunately, while his mind knew what he wanted to do, his unfamiliar body did not, failing at a crucial moment to cooperate. Adam was struck on the metal plate covering his chest.

[-15HP]

"OOOF!" he cried out. He went sprawling, nearly landing on his back. However, just as he was about to touch the ground, his curse activated, spinning his body and burying his face in the sand as his hands made contact with the earth. He lifted his face, spitting out a mouthful of gritty brown grains.

"Two minutes left!" Titania declared, redirecting his attention towards her and the two maids flanking her—a blue-haired woman and a pink-haired one. The two exchanged coins with a smile, as a grinning Sehn accompanied them.

ARE THEY MAKING BETS?!

Suddenly, a whoosh echoed, prompting the boy to press his face into the dirt as a frying pan whizzed overhead. Wasting no time, he swiftly rose, scrambling to his feet and darting away, throwing himself back into his precarious dance with death.

"Temperance, escalate the difficulty," Guild Master Valentine instructed, sitting cross-legged in a chair that had mysteriously materialized in the room.

"What?" Adam spun, his eyes locking onto her. *WHAT DO YOU MEAN UP THE DIFFICU—*

Before his train of thought could finish, Ruebella drew back her fist, thrusting it into the sand, generating a massive ripple that formed a nearly twenty-foot-tall wave of sand.

"Oh... crapbaskets," he murmured, his ears pressing back as his eyes went wide. His jaw dropped at the sight of the looming sand tsunami.

This isn't fair at all!

In desperation, Adam turned and sprinted, abandoning his position. But despite how his tiny legs propelled him with all their might, he was swiftly overtaken and buried beneath the earth.

OXYGEN! OXYGEN! The boy wiggled anxiously, his heart racing as he found himself trapped in constricting pitch darkness. *Don't panic, hold your breath and calm down. You've been buried before.*

In his youth, part of his training to earn the necromancer class had involved being buried multiple times to understand the undead he raised. Granted, it had been in a coffin, not sand, but the fundamental principles still applied, right? He immediately began to work, wriggling until his hand broke through into open air. He moved frantically, scrambling at the dirt.

I'm near the surface, Adam surmised, quickly shifting his body to displace the sand that enveloped him.

A moment passed, then another. Finally, the boy clawed his way out, spitting out sand as he gasped for air. He shook his red hair, dispersing the sand particles, and used his free arm to try and dig himself completely free.

However, as he struggled, a shadow fell over him, and he paused.

Oh no.

It was Ruebella. The woman glared down at him, another frying pan in hand.

"W-Wait! No! Please!" Adam cried, putting his hand up to shield himself as Ruebella swung down.

"HALT!"

At Valentine's command, Ruebella stopped, her frying pan a mere two millimeters from Adam's face, just brushing his hair.

"Temperance, stand down," Valentine ordered. The red glow in Ruebella's irises faded back to her usual brown.

"S-S-sorry!" Ruebella cried, the girl returning to her normal state as she tossed her weapon aside and knelt in the sand, immediately dusting the boy off.

Okay. What just happened? he wondered as his head spun. The woman seemed to have a split personality, or something, controlled by the guild master's words.

Valentine materialized beside Adam, who remained mostly buried in the sand with only his arm and head sticking out.

"You passed," Valentine declared, dropping a piece of copper into his free hand. "Ruebella, have his information filled out and tidy him up. But keep his ears covered, we don't want our guests asking too many questions. Afterwards, take him to the temple to get his ticket."

"Y-Yes, mistress," Ruebella stammered, while the pink-haired maid in the distance laughed.

"Pay up, bitches! Ahahahaha!" the short, pink-haired maid screamed jubilantly, leaping into the air. "I told you the guild master wouldn't let her kill him!"

Sehn and the blue-haired maid reluctantly opened their pouches, depositing several coppers into the woman's outstretched, gloved hand.

"Lunafreya," Valentine snapped her fingers, summoning a murder of crows that coalesced into the familiar, muscular maid.

"You called, mistress?" the dark-skinned woman said, flexing her titanic biceps.

"Bring me to my office."

"As you will, mistress." Lunafreya bowed, and shadowed crows whisked the two away in an instant.

"C-Come with m-me," Ruebella said, extending her hand. Although hesitant from the earlier encounter, Adam eventually relented, taking the woman's outstretched hand.

She plucked him from the sand like a ridge carrot, dusting his body free of sand and debris.

She stuttered out yet another apology as he set the boy down, where he adjusted his hood to conceal his ears.

* * *

It didn't take long to input his information. After filling out a simple questionnaire with Ruebella and turning in the copper tab, Adam was finally handed a small copper badge engraved with words.

Standing at the receptionist's desk, the clamor of the crowd badgering his concealed ears, Adam examined the tab in his hand.

[Adam F. Glow] [#692023]

[Tax bracket: 1]
[Title: Idiot Novice of Eli]
[Bronze Rank-D]
[Class: Rogue]
[Tower Floors Cleared: 0]
[Certified at The Vilenciel Guild Office. If found, please return to your nearest Guilder establishment for a reward!]

"Idiot novice of Eli," Titania murmured, leaning over to scrutinize the title. Adam hadn't intended to reveal it, but when inquired about his title, he unintentionally echoed the words, causing his interface to display to those gathered that he possessed one—an ability he was unaware he had.

"Who's Eli? Is that the one who brought you here?" Sehn asked noisily from his right, Titania at attention on his left. The two adventurers crowded him, creating a confining space.

"I don't know," Adam groaned, wanting to be left alone. With so much contact with the fleshies, his social battery was draining rapidly, and his tolerance for the surrounding cacophony, confusion, and violence grated on his nerves.

"Well! Welcome to the guild, lad!" Sehn laughed, patting the young adventurer roughly on the back, causing him to lurch. "Let's get some grub, and then we'll take you to the church to get your ticket."

Adam sighed, dreading his imminent visit to the religious establishment. After all, it was the fault of a bunch of religious wackos that he was in his current predicament in the first place.

Everything for you, Schrödinger. To the ends of the world.

Catpurr 23

Temple of the Gods

After sitting through lunch with Sehn and Titania in the guild's back office, Adam was eventually guided out of the building through a backdoor that led to a damp alley behind the office. Stepping outside, he was greeted by the bustling activity of crowds, people engaged in conversation, the sounds of haggling, and merchants advertising their wares.

"Once we get you certified with the temple, we'll bring you back here for some more training," Sehn said, making the boy tense up.

"Please, no," he unintentionally squeaked, making Titania and Sehn laugh at his reaction.

Titania leaned down, adjusting his hood, pulling it up to better conceal his ears. "Remember, we can't allow anyone to see your ears until we reach the temple."

"And remember," Sehn added, eyeing the ring on Adam's finger, "clench your fist when walking through a crowd; it makes it harder for pickpockets to steal from you."

"Yeah. Got it," Adam replied.

"Take my hand so we don't lose each other, the city is quite big," Titania offered.

Seeing her outstretched hand, Adam froze, his teacher's image suddenly overlapping with Titania's, stirring up memories that were both fond and painful.

"Adam?" his teacher whispered, only for her form to dissolve, replaced by Titania, as she smiled at him with concern and repeated his name.

He took her hand, the rough texture of her calloused palm a far cry from what he remembered a human hand as feeling like.

Come to think of it, the guild master's hand was rough as well, he pondered, wondering if he had misjudged Titania and her class.

The trio walked, emerging from the cramped alley to join the flow of pedestrians.

"Gabbages! Get your gabbages here!"

"Roho fruit! Guaranteed to improve performance in bed!"

"Tired of sticky feet?! Get Medic Schol's anti-aging, anti-stink foot cream!"

Adam strolled through, observing the peddlers vigorously advertising their wares, shouting nonstop.

"Hey, lass! Cute kid! How about a stuffed toy for your youngin'?!" a bearded man yelled, blocking their way.

"No thanks," Titania smiled, attempting to walk by politely, but the man persisted, obstructing their path. "No, sorry we're very busy."

"C'mon! Everyone likes toys! You won't deny your child a gift."

"We really *are* busy, sorry, no."

I guess we would look like a family on a stroll, Adam thought, feeling awkward as Sehn muttered, "Take a hint, lad."

"Only fifty coppers! Nay! I'll drop it down to thirty, just for you!" the man insisted, attempting to force the doll into Titania's hand.

This was a mistake.

"I SAID NO!" Titania snapped, engulfing her hand in sizzling green flames. Several onlookers stopped, gawking at the scene, but no one said anything. The man's eyes went wide as saucers as he dropped the toy and immediately fled.

"Tsk. They never understand when to piss off," Titania groaned, picking up the abandoned stuffed teddy bear.

"Here you go," Titania said, handing Adam the toy.

"Isn't this stealing?" he questioned. Sehn playfully tousled the boy's hair over his hood.

"Think of it as compensation for the bother," the man replied, and the trio resumed their journey.

It didn't take long before they stood before an ornate building, adorned with red flowers, ocean-blue tiles, and pillars carved from bone-white marble. Serene waterfalls cascaded into expansive, aquamarine pools.

"Ah, the Rip-Off Temple. It never ceases to amaze me how much they manage to get away with," Sehn commented, hands on his hips as he spied a group of heavily armored paladins marching up the stairway into the church.

"Why do you call it the Rip-Off Temple?" Adam asked, prodding for information.

"Oh, you'll see, lad," Sehn scoffed, gesturing for them to proceed. As they approached the gate a paladin caught sight of them, and immediately scowled.

"Sehn! Come to pay me what you owe?"

"Doesn't the church preach temperance and patience?" Sehn retorted, causing the paladin's expression to tighten.

"We also stress honoring one's word and paying our debts," he growled, knuckles whitening as he gripped his halberd.

"Relax, Howard, I'm good for it. You know I always settle my debts."

"Yes, but only *after* cornering you behind Oharra's and beating you until you can barely stand. Who's the runt?" the guard asked, agitated gaze landing onAdam.

"Who, him? My son," Sehn laughed. The guard remained unamused.

"Bull. Not only are you poor, but you're also ugly, both physically and spiritually. I refuse to believe anyone would willingly have a child with you."

Adam winced on Sehn's behalf. *Ouch.*

"That's hurtful. I thought we were friends."

"No."

"Frenemies?"

"*No.*"

"Colleagues? Can we settle on colleagues?" Sehn clasped his hands together in supplication.

"Absolutely not."

Titania stepped forwards. "He's with me, he's my nephew. I just want to introduce him to Coco."

"Hmmm... If you vouch for him, fine. But no funny business," the man grunted before extending his hand.

Sehn sighed, and he and Titania each handed the guard a silver coin.

"*Ahem,*" the man coughed, shaking his hand when the trio tried to pass.

"What? Him too?! Don't kids eat free or something?" Sehn exclaimed, prompting the man to point at a sign nearby.

"Five hundred coppers?!" Sehn yelled, reading the sign adorned with coin illustrations and unfamiliar words that Adam didn't understand.

"If you don't like it, leave the runt."

"It's fine, I got it," Titania sighed, producing what seemed to be a hard plastic square and tapping it against the guard's outstretched wrist.

A moment passed, then another, before finally Howard nodded, stepping aside to allow them entry.

"See? Complete rip-off," Sehn said to Adam as the trio entered the temple.

"Sorry. I'll pay you back," Adam offered, but Titania waved him off.

"Don't worry about it," she said, while Sehn muttered something about debts.

Ascending the stairs, Adam marveled at the spaciousness and grandeur of the temple, estimating the manpower and funds required for the construction and upkeep of such an impressive feat of architecture.

Wouldn't be a problem if they used the undead, he mused, dismissing the thought as the trio navigated through crowds of knights, warriors, and clergy cloaked in elaborate religious robes.

The boy shrunk into himself, recalling his last unpleasant encounter with religious zealots.

At least I'm not branded anymore.

"You'll be ok; just follow me," Titania assured him as they passed through an elaborate grand marble archway that brought them into a vast, circular room with no roof, exposing them to the open sky.

In the center of the room, a massive runic engraving adorned the floor. Initially, it seemed simple—a circle within a circle, with interconnected rings pointing in each cardinal direction. However, upon closer inspection, it proved anything but. Each line of the etching consisted of dozens of smaller symbols, minute and challenging to discern for anyone lacking Adam's familiarity with runes.

Incredible. Wonder what it does, he thought, pausing to appreciate the time and dedication invested into crafting such an elaborate and complex rune. *Only zealots could be so committed.*

"Adam? What's wrong?" Titania inquired, noticing his gaze fixed on the floor, absorbed in the runecraft.

"Oh, uh... Sorry, spaced out," the boy replied before following along, eyeing the six pillars ahead, each adorned with unique emblems—two of which he recognized from Titania and Sehn's abyssal tickets.

Must be altars or something, he speculated, observing the distinct features of each pillar. One was covered in vines, another festooned with swords, and one bedazzled with fairy-like lights, marking each column as distinct.

However, what really caught Adam's eye was the central feature among the columns—a square tub, filled with steaming water, occupied by a scantily clad *priestess* lounging on the pool's edge, her arm and leg dipping into the crystal clear water.

"Oh, hi Sehn. Hi Titania," the white-haired woman purred, her tone flirtatious as she greeted the two adventurers. "And hello, Adam Fenix Glow."

At the mention of his name, Adam froze, inadvertently dropping the doll, causing the two beside him to frown. He had never told anyone his middle name; in fact, the only person who knew it was Master Razalia, and that was because she had been the one to give it to him.

"Welcome to the Temple of the Six Gods."

Catpurr 24
The Seventh God

Upon hearing his name, Adam stood frozen, uncertain of how to respond as the priestess raised her hand, beckoning him forwards.

"Don't be scared," the woman giggled, observing the boy's hesitation. "I'm a prophet, I foresaw our meeting ages ago lul. Although, in that future, you were way taller."

"Lul?" Adam repeated, confused by the unfamiliar term, but more intrigued by the mention of the word *future*.

"Ah, sorry. My ability is a bit wonky. Sometimes I see things from random futures and mix up words. Don't be shy, I don't bite."

He glanced at Sehn and Titania, both nodding in reassurance.

"It's alright. You can trust her," Titania assured.

"Just not with your money," Sehn added with a wry grin.

Reluctantly, he approached, shuffling across the black tile floor as the woman, known as Coco, left the pool, droplets of water trailing behind her wet body. She was short, standing at about five feet and three inches, just a tad taller than the nekoboy, with icy blue eyes.

"Your hood. Please remove it, I want to see what you look like," Coco instructed. For just a moment, Adam froze in hesitation

"Does that mean she doesn't know what I look like in her vision?" he pondered.

After everything he had heard so far, it didn't seem like the best course of action to reveal himself, especially in a temple filled with zealots. But when he turned back to Titania for reassurance, she nodded, giving Adam her approval

And so he sighed and complied, causing Coco to gasp and widen her eyes.

Oh boy. Here we go.

Standing before him, the priestess of the gods gazed at him intently, slowly raising her hand.

The necromancer tensed; was this it? Was he about to die again? Where would he even respawn this time? Would he find himself naked in the city? What—

The woman reverently placed her hand on the boy's head, touching his ears.

"O...M...G," she uttered slowly, her eyes captivated as her other hand began prodding at his catlike ears, pinching them.

Wha—

"Ow!" he hissed, stepping back and clutching his ears. "Why did you pinch me?!"

"Oops. Sorry," she giggled. "I just had to check if they're real!"

Adam scowled at her, perturbed by her audacity. But soon his anger dissipated, replaced instead with disgust and confusion as the woman's expression transformed into zealous fascination.

Danger! His legs twitched in preparation to flee but he found himself caught, lifted off the ground by the woman's embrace, her enthusiasm cracking his spine.

His body involuntarily squeaked, and Coco gasped in glee, hugging him even tighter.

[-10 HP]

"UGK!"

"YOU'RE SO CUTE! DO YOU WANT TO JOIN THE CHURCH?! I CAN MAKE YOU MY PERSONAL ASSISTANT!"

"Let me go! Let me go!" he screamed, his back popping again as it squeaked a second time. *WHAT THE NYX? WHY IS MY BODY A SQUEAKY TOY?*

"ACK!" Instantly, his cat claws emerged, scratching at the woman's face, only to screech against her skin like metal on metal.

The grating sound reverberated, making Adam cringe as every fiber of his being shuddered.

"Oh! Don't do that! You'll activate my divine protections!" Coco laughed, maintaining her crushing grip. "I could just eat you up; you're so adorable!"

"H-Help! Help me!" the boy cried, struggling, as the priestess giggled and his breathing became shallow.

This is how I die. I knew I shouldn't have come here.

"AHEM!" Titania coughed, finally interrupting Coco.

Released from her embrace, Adam collapsed onto the ground, his mouth foaming.

"Oops," Coco said, crouching down to poke at Adam's crumpled form. "Are you okay?"

"Please... I just want my ticket..." he groaned.

"For the Abyss? Sure! That's what everyone comes for. All you've gotta do is strip!" Coco giggled, her expression abruptly shifting, horrifying him further. "W-What?!"

"Take off your shirt. I need to see your mark to confirm your status," Coco insisted, poking his tiny nose. "Heh, I booped your snoot."

Reluctantly undressing, Adam removed his cloak, revealing the mark on his back.

"Is this a joke?" Coco asked, running a cold hand over the etching seared into his back. She spun, staring hard at the duo of adventurers.

"You know forging a divine insignia is punishable by the stockades, don't you? I knew you two were always getting into trouble and having money issues," the priestess hissed, her eyes twisting in fury as she began to radiate energy, "but to involve a child? I'll incinerate your bodies until your bones become turned into ash."

"W-What! We didn't do that! He said he needed an abyssal ticket, so we brought him here!" Sehn cried, the floor beneath his and Titania's feet humming to life with golden particles as the temple responded to the priestess' anger.

"It's true! We'd never hurt a child!" Titania exclaimed, a mix of outrage and fear in her voice as the temple shook. A wall of energy suddenly blazed, encircling the inner sanctum of the temple. The two turned to run, but chains of spectral light erupted from the ground, binding them in place.

Seeing the misunderstanding, Adam acted quickly to save his benefactors as mana condensed around Coco.

"I need a ticket!" the boy bellowed, standing defiantly before the priestess to block the attack she was preparing.

"Stand to the side, I'll protect you. They won't be able to hurt you anymore," Coco reassured, raising her other hand and effortlessly lifting the child into the air, displacing him as her orb of power grew and—

"I HAVE A QUEST!" Adam screamed, prompting a shift in the woman's expression, and the oppressive energy swiftly dissipated.

"A quest?" Coco echoed, blinking as she gently set him beside her, gazing down at him.

"You have a quest?" she repeated.

"Yes. I need a ticket, or I'll die. I swear it," he insisted. Coco's mouth twitched, her expression dubious.

She doesn't believe me.

"I swear," Adam reiterated.

"If you're saying this out of fear that they'll hurt you, I can protect you." With her power, he believed it, but...

"My system says I need an abyssal ticket. Please," he stressed again.

A moment passed, then another, before she finally turned away.

"I'll humor you, then. Stand in the center of the circle," Coco instructed as she walked back to the pool of water.

Crossing her legs, she sat on the black slab's edge, and Adam assumed the position on the central symbol on the floor.

"Stay still," she advised before the engraving came to life with blue energy.

Suddenly, he felt an intense pressure, as though dozens of hands were poking and prodding him.

"Gah!" he exclaimed, his tattoo glowing, unleashing an ethereal shadow that swiftly enveloped him with flickering, undulating darkness.

"I-Impossible!" Coco cried. The shadows rose off him, twisting into an expansive, glowing glyph that hung in the air.

A symbol of an ouroboros, a serpent devouring itself.

Adam screamed. His body was fracturing as his HP dwindled, each passing second costing him precious health points.

"A—A *seventh*? A seventh god?!" Coco gawked, frozen in place as the boy's eyes rolled to the back of his head, and he passed out.

Catpurr 25

Day of the Dead

Emerging from a portal made of bones, Eli shuffled into his crypt sporting a sombrero, a black-armored knight closely trailing behind. Draped across the knight's arms were half a dozen bags, each bulging with festive trinkets shaped like skulls and marigold flowers.

"Eli? Oh goodness, you've returned! Where have you been?!" Freya, the Goddess of Life, exclaimed, turning towards the hunched skeleton.

Swapping his black coat for a pink bathrobe from a minion T-posing to serve as a coat rack, Eli seemed to freeze, pausing for a moment before addressing the goddess.

"Visitando un lugar llamado Tierra para el día de muertos," Eli replied, prompting Freya to tilt her head.

"Is that Spanish?"

"Si, a festival on Earth. Very kind, those Mexicans," Eli explained.

"You went to Gaia?" Freya said, with worry in her voice. "This is the first time you've left your sanctum in two eras."

"So?"

"This is big news, Eli!" Freya exclaimed, her joy short-lived as a commanding voice resonated.

"**Eli!? ELI!**" a divine voice echoed, shaking the large, underground sanctum that the Primordial God called home. "ELI, YOU OLD SKULL! ANSWER ME! WHERE ARE YOU?"

"What did you do?!" Freya hissed, the bricked chamber trembling. This was too sudden—what had *he* learned? He shouldn't know anything yet.

"Nothing?" Eli replied casually, switching skulls with the skeleton serving as a coat rack.

Suddenly, the ceiling collapsed, allowing sunlight to flood the crypt.

"Voltrain?!" Freya cried, wafting away the dust in the air as a figure clad in golden armor brandishing wings of radiant light descended.

Freya frowned, wondering whether the god was more knowledgeable than she had originally thought.

"WHERE IS HE?!" the divine being of Light and Creation demanded, radiating holy energy that dispelled the darkness around them.

"Hello," the skeleton wearing Eli's bathrobe greeted. "What can I do for you today?"

"Don't play coy with me!" Voltrain barked, pointing with a golden gauntlet. "WHAT DID YOU DO?!"

Worried, Freya turned her gaze back to Eli, the real Eli now masquerading as a coat rack. Had Voltrain already caught wind of his schemes?

"I have no idea what you're talking about," Eli's doppelganger retorted as a gaggle of skeletons emerged, grabbing the coat rack and retreating into a tunnel nearby.

Freya grinned, seeing Eli making a clean getaway as Voltrain bore down on his sacrificial pawn.

"You buffoon! An eon of seclusion, and you go out and do this?!" the golden god berated. He revealed a small sphere in his palm, broadcasting images of a chaotic scene of skeletons and zombies rising from the earth, causing havoc among humans.

"What? The children asked to see their grandparents and loved ones, so that's exactly what I did," *Eli* replied, shrugging as the black-armored knight, better known as the Angel of Death, removed the sombrero from his bony head and vanished.

"So you travel to a world without a system and proceed to use magic?! Your little act of 'KINDNESS' just exposed their world to mana! Now there are system users on Earth cropping up way ahead of schedule, with no administrator in place!"

At the words of the chief guardian of the gods, Freya's somber expression became one of utter shock.

It seems he isn't aware of Eli's plan. Was this a diversion?

"Oops," *Eli* replied.

"*Oops*?! YOU EXPOSE A WORLD TO MANA, AND ALL YOU HAVE TO SAY IS OOPS?!" Voltrain roared, sparks emanating from his body as a burning blade materialized in his hand. "It took us two millennia of scrubbing to isolate that planet for redistribution!"

"Volt—" Freya began, about to tell the god he was talking to a doppelganger. But before she could, the irate god interrupted her, pointing with a gloved hand.

"NO! No defending him, Freya! I've tolerated his antics because he's kept them contained within the Ithenasphere and doesn't make any claims for territory!" Voltrain turned back to *Eli*, pointing his shining blade at the skeleton. "What do you have to say for yourself?!"

"Sorry?"

At the skeleton's unconvincing apology, Voltrain stiffened, his eyes widening before narrowing again with fury.

"Hold on. You aren't Eli!"

"Uh... No, I am not. I'm Bob, the coat rack," the doppelganger said, before being abruptly incinerated by Voltrain's divine light, leaving behind only a smoldering mark on the ground.

"ELI!" Voltrain screamed, prompting Freya to shield her eyes as he exploded into a blinding flash.

As the brilliance faded, a ringing persisted in Freya's ears as she reopened her eyes.

"Oh boy. Just wait until he finds out about Adam," Freya sighed, already imagining the impending headache on the horizon.

* * *

The nekoboy in question awoke, his golden eyes fixed on the black tile floor.

I'm alive?

It didn't take long for him to realize he was elevated, laying on his stomach on a slab, shirtless, a pair of bare feet pacing within his field of vision.

"Ugggh," he groaned, pushing himself up and flipping over.

"Boop Snoot," Coco chimed, suddenly appearing with cat ears on her head and poking his nose. "Oh good. You're awake."

"What happened?" he asked, ignoring the headband with ears made to imitate his own. He pulled up his interface, checking his status, but found nothing amiss.

"A little complication," Coco explained as the boy sat up, rubbing his back that suddenly itched while the rest of his body ached.

"Complication? How long have I been out?"

"Uhm." She looked away sheepishly, her two pointer fingers connected. "Two days?"

T-TWO?! That was two days he could have been making progress!

"MY TICKET?!" Adam yelled, immediately pushing himself off the slab to stand on his feet. He touched the floor, yet his legs refused to support his weight, buckling and sending him face-first into the ground.

"The good news is that we have your ticket issue sorted out," Coco said, poking him.

"Really? That's swell," the boy groaned, still laying on the cool tile. *Wait, why does it sound like she's about to say 'but'?*

"But—"

Oh, there it is.

"—there are implications and concerns that I have regarding your mark."

Of course.

"Who is Eli?" the priestess asked, crouching beside him.

"I have no idea," Adam replied, tilting his head to look up at the priestess' icy blue eyes. "All I know is that I was chosen."

The two sat there in silence for a moment, neither uttering a word.

"You know what's fascinating? I've spent the last two days in our archives, delving into old tomes and grimoires, yet I never came across a god named Eli," Coco remarked. "In fact, no one has. There's no mention of anyone by the name of Eli, except for a baker who lives three blocks away from here."

Oh... crapbaskets. If Eli was a divine entity, and the Church of the *Six* Gods hadn't heard of him, either Eli wasn't a god, or Adam was committing heresy against their religion by introducing a seventh god to their six.

"Yet, you bear a divine insignia that resonates with the temple. One that can't be imitated due to its unique divine mana signature," Coco said, tapping her chin. "Quite fascinating."

She seems oddly calm, considering this bombshell, Adam considered, before asking aloud, "So, what happens now?"

"Nothing much," Coco replied with a smile. "I give you your ticket, and you go about your way. However, should you survive the first floor and make it out, I want you to report your findings to me."

"Findings?"

"Yes, for most, the first floor trial follows a standard pattern. But a chosen few will encounter very unique trials, things that range from being dropped into an ocean, to landing in a desolate snowfield. There was even an adventurer who was disintegrated in lava. So all data is good data."

"L-Lava?!" Adam exclaimed, recalling the torment of being consumed alive by the Duckysaur's stomach acid.

"Oh yes, the only reason we know about that one is because his teammate possessed a ring of flight, successfully completed the trial and provided a detailed account," Cocoa explained casually.

"Teammate? Does that mean one can enter with others?" It was easy to shift his focus from the gruesome death to gathering information for survival.

"Yes, but only if they belong to your divine house or have a pass issued by the gods. Many opt out of it as each participant increases the difficulty of the trial, but the rewards also scale based on the party's strength," the priestess said, prompting him to nod in understanding.

"Let me guess, Eli doesn't have a noble house?"

"That would be correct. You're the first to ever have her brand."

His head tilted, ears pricking inquisitively. "Her? How do you know Eli is a 'her'?"

"I don't!" Coco exclaimed, the cat ear prop falling off as she quivered with excitement. "I'm the only one that's heard of this god!"

So I'd be going it alone. He grimaced, ignoring the woman's antics as she fiddled with her dislodged headband. For a moment there, he had hope that he'd be able to receive help, but it seemed such a thing was no longer an option. He was not overly bothered by it, but considering he had no minions at his disposal, besides his skelly cat, or even any offensive skills, it seemed clear he was in for a tough time.

"I *am* the only one that knows about this, right?" Coco asked.

"I think so?" he replied, returning to his thoughts. *At least I still have a spare life,* he sighed, remembering his catsification curse. "So, is that it? No burning me at the stake? No drowning me to cleanse my sins, or having me hung for heresy?"

Coco giggled. "Of course not, silly! We're an organization that promotes peace and prosperity."

Riiight. The kind that requires armed paladins at your temple, Adam said silently.

"Although it would be best if you didn't publicize your god's name or mention it to anyone but me, okay?"

Right. Aloud, he said, "You seem oddly calm for a priestess that just found out about a potential seventh god," making Coco smile.

"Oh, if only you could only see what I see," Coco replied vaguely, her left eye twitching.

Unbeknownst to Adam, Coco's eyes saw not only the nekoboy as he was now, but several divergences. His body moved in various directions, symbolizing the different paths he could take. If she squinted, she could even see a larger shadow, an adult version adorned with bone shackles, standing over him in silence, weeping.

It represented a hidden trauma of some kind, one that hung over him like a cloud, revealing his true appearance. Moreover, now that the seal had been triggered, Coco could distinctly see the symbol of a god—an emblem of a serpent devouring itself.

Coco smiled, gazing at the 'boy' who sat upright with a furrowed brow, lost in thought.

This must be a test from the gods, the priestess reasoned, offering a hand out to guide him to where he would receive his ticket.

"Come on, let's get you dressed to receive your ticket. Titania and one of the maids from the guild are waiting for you," Coco urged, and Adam hesitated before taking her hand.

Catpurr 26
Abyssal Ticket

Standing before an altar adorned with six emblems, the Chosen of the newly revealed seventh deity furrowed his brow.

"How exactly is this supposed to work if my divinity is a seventh being?" he silently pondered, lips pursed. Coco, now wearing a new cat-eared headband, stood beside him, humming softly.

"Hold out your hand. If my theory is correct, the altar will respond," she instructed.

Adam complied, reaching his palm towards the circular monument.

Suddenly, he sensed a connection forming, his interface forcefully opening with a cascade of error messages. He barely avoided staggering backwards in shock, when bold blue words appeared:

[CONNECTION ESTABLISHED!]

"Incredible," Coco whispered, eyeing the slender tendril of divine, golden energy extending from the nekomancer to the altar.

It coalesced, swirling into a small energy sphere in front of the glowing monument. Hovering briefly, it solidified into a solid sphere before abruptly shattering, releasing a floating purple slip of paper.

My ticket, Adam thought, grabbing the item, while his system quest tracker promptly updated.

[Ticket of the Abyss (Eli) Obtained!]
[CON*CAT*ULATIONS! QUEST COMPLETE!]
[Rolling Rewards…]

[Ding!]
[+500 Experience Obtained!]
[Level Up!]

Yes!

[Please Select a Starter Skill from the Nekomancer Skill Tree!]
—Upgrade Summon Minor Skeleton
—Locate Bones
—Drain Mana
—Mana Claws
—Double Jump
—Mana Dash
—Mana Bolt
—Upgrade Cat Claws
—Upgrade Eyes of the Predator

His gaze lingered on the new options available.

Well, this is new. Maybe I can get an upgrade to get a human skeleton instead of a cat, he mused.

While the young chosen was looking through the list, Coco remained silent, standing to the side. Instead, she observed the ticket in his hand, marked with a serpent devouring itself.

As he went through each skill on the list, Adam tapped the screen to read the ability descriptions.

"May I see your ticket?" Coco asked. He turned, handing her the item. She examined the symbol, running her fingers over the purple slip.

"Incredible," she whispered, studying the ticket. "Just so ya know, while an abyssal ticket cannot be destroyed, it *can* be stolen. So make sure not to be so willy-nilly with your ticket. Without it, entering the Abyss is impossible."

"Oh, I see," he said. *Yeah, that could definitely be a problem. I wonder if I can store it in my ring.*

"Here, take it," Coco said, returning the ticket. However, as Adam reached for it, a problem arose.

"Uh... Coco?"

"Yes?"

"You can let go of the ticket now," Adam asked, tugging at the divine material held firmly in Coco's grasp.

"Yes, of course, of course."

"You're still not letting go."

"In a bit," the priestess replied, a hint of manic excitement in her eyes as she resisted.

"Coco, aren't the others waiting for me? I should go."

"Just let me see it for a bit longer!"

"Coco, give me my ticket!"

"Just let me hold onto it a bit longer!"

* * *

After an hour of arguing with the priestess and agreeing to certain terms set by her, Adam finally exited from the chamber, returning to the main temple where the pillars of the gods stoically kept watch.

"Adam! So good to see you're safe!" Titania exclaimed. Ruebella waved shyly from beside her. "We were so worried when you suddenly collapsed."

"I'm okay," he assured them, finding an unusual smile forming as he glanced at the abyssal ticket looped around his wrist. He proudly displayed it to the two concerned women.

Heh, having someone care about me isn't so bad.

"I see you've got your ticket. Have you gotten a quest update yet?" Titania inquired as the trio walked out of the temple. She furrowed her brow at the seemingly blank ticket, a magical concealment activated by

Coco to shield it from prying eyes. The ticket could also be securely locked to his wrist, preventing anyone from taking it, unless they removed his arm.

"Uh, no. Not yet," he replied as they walked side by side.

Exiting through the main foyer, and out the temple, Adam spotted what appeared to be Howard, the gate paladin, sporting a fresh black eye with a busted, bleeding nose.

I wonder what happened to him, he wondered, dismissing the thought as quickly as it came. *Not my problem.*

"Yo!"

Ah, Adam thought , quickly putting two and two together from Sehn's battered appearance as the man climbed the stairs. Much like Howard, Sehn had a busted nose, black eye, and a split lip, but unlike the paladin his injuries emitted steam, smoke rising from his cuts and wounds.

"Sehn?! What happened to you?" Titania cried, grabbing the man's bleeding chin in concern.

"Ah, you know you're so cute when you're worried about me," Sehn grinned, instantly erasing any sympathy Titania felt, her expression transforming.

"Gross." She shoved him, sending the adventurer tumbling down the flight of marble stairs he had just climbed.

"Are you crazy?! You could have killed me!" he yelled, sitting upright as the trio passed him. Howard chuckled haughtily from above.

"But did you die, though?" Titania retorted, disregarding the man as even more smoke rose from underneath his clothes.

"No! But you *could* have!" Sehn argued, picking himself up and following the group as they headed back to the guild hall. "Hey, do you think I could borrow a couple of silvers?"

"Uh? No."

"Oh c'mon, ya know I'm good for it."

The green-haired mage crossed her arms, launching into a lecture. "No you aren't. You can barely settle your current debts as is, owing me a silver would just collapse the mountain of debt you already have."

"Ruebella?" Sehn wandered around the group, poking his head in front of the maid.

"Y-Yes?"

"How about it? One silver? I promise to pay you back! I just need to buy some food."

"O-Okay," the maid replied, reaching between her breasts. Titania intervened, grabbing the woman's wrist.

"No ya don't. If you give in to his demands, he'll keep asking you for loans."

"O-Okay," Ruebella acquiesced. Adam took the chance to observe her mannerisms, noting the differences between this version of her and her combat mode.

Maybe it's a mental command or something.

"Look! I promise to pay you back, Rueb! Honest! At the end of the day, a man's word is all he has," the coffin carrier pleaded, until Titania stepped in.

"Don't listen to him, he barely counts as a man. Even Adam here is more manly than you, and he's a child."

Thanks? But is that really a compliment?

"Eeeeh. Uhm," Ruebella squeaked, appearing flustered as the duo stopped and began arguing. "I, uhm. P-Please don't a-argue."

While the trio meandered, Adam decided to pull up his skill list, opening up the upgrade paths for the abilities he had.

[Upgrade Summon Minor Skeleton]
[Available Upgrades]
—Upgrade skill to Summon Skeleton V1
—Remove Corpse Requirement (+20% Mana REQ.)
—Increase Minion Capacity+1

—**Optimize Mana Requirements (-20% REQ.)**
—**Strengthen Summon V1 (+10% To skeleton stats)**

Glancing at the list, he was surprised at how many augmentations were at his disposal. His old system relied on earning passives and boosts with each level he gained, stacking skills without allowing him to pick and choose abilities. This resulted in dozens of unused skills bloating his interface. Here, it seemed he could best optimize what he wanted more efficiently.

In a way it was a downgrade but it wasn't so bad a trade-off.

He browsed his other upgradable skills, keeping his options open.

[Upgrade Cat Claws]
[Available Upgrades]
—**Integrate Mana Circuits.**
—**Durability Increase. (+10% Increase to claw durability)**
—**Sharpen Claws. (+10% to claw sharpness)**
[Upgrade Eyes of the Predator]
[Available Upgrades]
—**Integrate Mana Circuits**
—**Improve Night Vision(+10% Night Vision)**

Integrate mana circuits? Are my eyes and claws not connected to the rest of my mana circuits? Will it give me more upgrades if I do so? the nekoboy pondered the skills and their implications. Unfortunately, in his current state, his skill points were too precious to waste testing theories.

Reviewing the list, the *remove corpse requirement* stood out to him. Although it would bump the cost of his summon skill to one hundred and twenty, he could offset the negative by dumping his newly obtained stat points into Arcana, raising his overall mana to one hundred and twenty-five.

A no-brainer.

After all, in a trial where he might struggle to find a corpse, the ability to summon one would be the difference between being able to use his skill and not.

[Remove Corpse Requirement selected!]

He confirmed, immediately tapping the screen to dump all his free points into Arcana, his body trembling with energy.

"Hmm?" Sehn paused mid-argument with Titania, turning towards Adam. Ruebella shifted her attention as well. "Did you level up, lad?"

"Uh, yeah." *They sensed that?* Adam thought to himself, realizing there was more to these people than he initially thought.

"Lad," Sehn said, crouching down. "In the future, you should let us know first so we can help you choose a skill and plan your stats accordingly. What skill did you pick?"

Oh crap. Adam froze, uncertain of how to reply.

Catpurr 27
Lying Through My Fangs

"Priestess."

"Yes?"

"As per your request, the investigation into the individual or entity known as Eli has yielded no results. My deepest apologies. Would you like me to submit a request to the Grand Bishopess for a more thorough inquiry?"

"No. It is fine. Carry on."

—Priestess Coco Viviane Velfett of the Six Pillar Church, speaking with a nun regarding her search query.

***

"Magic Optimization?" Sehn repeated with a puzzled expression. "For a base rogue class?"

"Maybe it's because of his species. There's a lot we don't know about demi-humans," Titania suggested. The three were now back at the guild office, standing in the middle of an isolated training room—the same one Ruebella had pulverized before. The place had been restored to its original state, all traces of Adam's bullying at the hands of Ruebella's frying pans erased. Even the black tile had been repaired.

Sehn sighed. "Please kid, just tell me why you picked **Magic Optimization?**"

"Uhm, because magic is cool?" he responded immediately, thinking of an excuse to cover the lie he had told regarding his sudden increase in mana capacity.

"And you put all your stat points into Arcana, didn't you?"

"Yup."

Sehn sighed even harder. "It's fine, this is salvageable. You're only level one, right?"

"Yes," Adam lied once again.

"Good. Ruebella, Tilith, and Lunafreya are capturing monsters for you to earn experience. Actually, you haven't met Tilith, have you?"

Capturing monsters? Like bringing them here? "Uh, no, I haven't," Adam replied aloud, turning as a murder of shadowed crows suddenly appeared, depositing three figures in maid outfits.

Ruebella and Lunafreya were familiar to him. The buff woman was carrying a massive iron cage tightly packed with goblins, screaming and wriggling in outrage.

The last maid, presumably Tilith, he didn't recognize. She had rainbow-colored hair, dark blue eyes, and held an umbrella to shade her from the light.

"HELLO!" the woman greeted with jubilance, waving at those already gathered.

"One cage filled with goblins, as requested," Lunafreya grunted, the colossal woman approaching and placing the packed cage of green bodies on the ground with a loud thud. "Fifty heads, each a hundred coppers, minus guild discount. Grand total is forty silver."

What? Adam frowned, observing as Titania dropped a handful of small coins into the buff woman's giant palm. Strangely, a sense of unease, similar to guilt, crept over him as he watched Sehn fish out a coin from his boot, handing it to Ruebella as payment for the bag in her hands.

The boy was aware of the pair's financial troubles, and witnessing the lengths they were going to help him, he felt bad about the lies he had told.

But I can't risk them ostracizing me, he rationalized. After all, he had been persecuted and mistreated throughout his life; first as an orphan and then as a necromancer. Who's to say their opinion wouldn't change when they realized he could raise the dead? It had happened before.

No...

It had to remain a secret. Just like his god, a topic they had, thankfully, yet oddly, not questioned until now. Right now he was too weak to expose himself; his priority at the moment was staying beneath everyone's notice.

Secrecy would be his key to victory. It would ensure his survival, at least until he could rescue Schrödinger and get revenge on the fanatical church that had set him on this path.

"Alright, lad," Sehn said, placing the bag on the ground. "We're going to run through some exercises before introducing you to combat."

"Okay?" Adam said, raising his brow.

"Pretend I'm trying to kill you. How would you fight back or escape?"

"You want me to attack you?" Adam said skeptically.

"Yeah lad, go ahead. Come on," Sehn beckoned, adopting a wide stance and crouching low in front of him, almost as if poised to pounce. With his tall, broad frame, shouldering his bulky coffin, he loomed over the childlike demi-human.

"Are you sure?" Adam asked, all eyes on him.

"Yup. Go for it."

"Uh. Okay." The cat-eared boy proceeded to kick Sehn in the crotch.

"HULP!" the man wheezed, his body spasming before crumpling into the sand with a thud.

"Oh, my."

"Oh dear."

"O-Oh!"

The three maids exclaimed in unison, as Titania erupted into a burst of uncontrollable laughter.

"Haaaah," Sehn squeaked, out of breath and in the fetal position as he clutched his nethers. "Haaaaaaaaah."

"Sorry?" Adam said, gazing down at the man struggling to breath.

"N-No. No, no. Y-You did good, lad," Sehn moaned, his body still shaking. "You did... really... good."

* * *

After composing himself, Sehn opened the bag he'd bought from Ruebella, revealing a compact set of leather armor perfectly tailored for Adam's small frame.

As the nekoboy donned the armor, he tugged at the collar, feeling the leather cling to his undershirt, making him sweat.

"From this moment onwards, you will eat, sleep, and train in this armor daily," Sehn declared, pulling the leather hood attached to the armor over the boy's head. "You haven't received your quest update yet, so there's still time to train. We'll make use of every second until it's time for your trial. Understand, lad?"

"Uh, yeah," Adam replied as Sehn guided him away from the cage.

Yawning, Tilith approached the iron cage, strolling around it with her umbrella lightly brushing against the metal. Squinting, Adam could make out what seemed to be spores leaving her hands and flooding the cage, causing the squirming monsters within to calm.

Titania joined in, opening the metal cage and seizing a drowsy goblin by the scruff of its neck, bringing it towards him.

"Alright," Sehn said, extracting a metal dagger from the coffin laid out on the floor. "This part is crucial, Adam. So, pay attention. This is for your safety, and your survival, lad."

Suddenly, the man thrust the dagger into the creature. It woke and began to scream.

"These are monsters, specifically goblins—a species whose sole purpose is to terrorize and annihilate sentient life. They breed by capturing adventurers and forming raiding parties," Sehn explained, the monster's green blood seeping onto the sand. "If you want to survive the trials, it's crucial that you learn how to take a life, and not hesitate when the time comes.”

“Uh... Okay,” the boy said, motionlessly observing as Sehn adjusted the knife in his hand, before stabbing the squealing monster repeatedly. Adam was no stranger to violence; he had, after all, used hordes of skeletons to eradicate countless monster waves in the past.

But Sehn didn’t need to know that. Instead, he stood there, playing the part of a clueless student learning from his master.

“Alright, you’ve seen how it’s done. Now, it’s your turn,” the man said, offering the dagger to Adam while Lunafreya summoned her crows, making the corpse vanish in a flurry of shadows.

Titania opened the cage, grabbing another ‘*subject*’ and bringing it towards them. The creature hissed as it eyed the boy, now wielding a knife.

“It’s okay. You can do this,” Sehn assured him.

Standing there, Adam frowned, eyeing the monster and recalling when one of them had bashed him over the head.

Suppressing the lingering rage from his previous death, he swiftly stabbed the monster in its heart, putting it out of its misery.

[+ 100 Exp!]

[100/2,000 EXP]

Suddenly, a notification flashed in front of him, his experience bar rising.

At least earning experience is the same. Now, all I need to do is find some secluded field and perform last rites, he plotted to himself, staring blankly into space. *I’ll have to test my skelecat’s combat ability.*

“A-Adam?”

Hmmm... Maybe my next upgrade should focus on optimization. If I dump all my next level-up points into Arcana, I should—

"Adam?" Titania interrupted, resting a hand on his shoulder and diverting him away from his line of thought, her gaze on the blade still embedded in the goblin's chest cavity. "Adam, are you okay? Give me the dagger."

"Hmm? Oh. Here," the boy said, removing his hand off the dagger as Titania hugged him.

"I'm sorry we're making you do this," she said.

"It's fine. Let's just finish this," he replied, oblivious to the woman's concern as a notification appeared on his interface, giving him a new quest. "Every bit helps."

Catpurr 28

Silk the Doll Maker

"Just bob and weave! Bob and weave! Stay on your toes and dance around him!" Sehn yelled as Adam caught Arnold's fist with his face, sending him tumbling through the sand.

As a healer whose abilities were channeled through skin contact, Arnold proved to be the perfect sparring partner. Each punch that connected not only inflicted injuries on his charge but also healed him, counteracting the damage.

However, this didn't mean Adam wasn't getting hurt.

Because he was.

A *lot*.

With each blow he received, a valuable lesson was ingrained in the fiber of his being, reinforcing the idea of not getting hit.

"I'm very sorry for this, little boy!" Arnold bellowed, leaping into the air and slamming his fists downwards.

Crapbaskets!

Adam rolled away, narrowly avoiding the attack, and swiftly rose to his feet as dust choked the air.

Now at level three, the child huffed, raising his palm to unleash a bolt of mana, his newly acquired and sole offensive skill. A neutral ability chosen in order to keep up appearances.

"**Mana Bolt!**"

At his command, a bolt of blue magic in the shape of a cat's face whirled in his palm, shooting through the smoke and striking Arnold, who came barreling out of the sand cloud.

The attack splattered against the titan's skin, the ability proving ineffective against the oncoming wall of pure muscle.

Fortunately the purpose of the attack wasn't to inflict damage but to connect with his target, demonstrating that Adam could hit his foe—the whole point of this training.

With feline grace he leapt to the side as Arnold's fist came crashing down, creating a crater in the ground. In response, Adam hurled one of his weighted wooden daggers, hitting Arnold squarely in the head.

Another hit!

"That's good, lad! Just a few more hits!" Sehn's encouragement resounded.

"You got this, Adam!" Titania cried out, joined by several maids who cheered and made bets. The blue-haired Ravi, Sinclair with her short, pink hair, and the twin maids all engaged in betting with Sehn, while Tilith lay curled up at their feet, nestled into Lunafreya's giant, muscular lap.

Spurred by their cries, Adam felt invigorated.

I can do this! Just three more an—

Distracted, the boy took a blow to his side, sending him flying and tumbling through the dirt.

He spun, rolling several times before his curse kicked in, slamming him face down with his hands in the sand.

"No time for distractions, child!" Arnold bellowed, continuing his assault as Adam clutched his rib and rose to his feet.

He pivoted, eyes widening as Arnold's clenched fists narrowly missed his head.

Wasting no time Adam bolted, going low and gripping his remaining dagger at an outward angle. He lifted it up, 'slicing' Arnold's external abdominal oblique before spinning and slashing the man's latissimus dorsi. Two muscle groups, two hits.

One more, he huffed, backing away as the titan spun.

"Very good, Adam," Arnold acknowledged, his muscles bulging beneath his thin white shirt. "BUT LET US SEE HOW YOU HANDLE *THIS!*"

Oh, no.

Arnold flexed, striking a pose that emitted an irritating pulse of bright, vibrating energy, resonating outwards with the man as its epicenter.

[-10 HP]

Adam crossed his arms as the impact set his innards quivering. His small stature lifted a few inches into the air.

He landed on his feet, kicking up dust as he slid across the ground, bracing himself for Arnold's rapid succession of poses. Another pulse hit, and the nekoboy tried to race forwards, but the same thing happened, forcing him back.

I need a different approach, he grimaced, tightly clutching his wooden dagger as each wave of energy knocked him backwards. Formulating a plan, Adam waited for Arnold to flex, anticipating the next pulse of energy.

This time, the boy leapt backwards, allowing the wave to catch him and send him flying. Tumbling through the sand with some theatrical flair, he hit the ground, face in the dirt, immediately going limp.

"HMP! A good try, Adam!" Arnold spoke, his expression soon shifting to one of panic as he observed the unmoving boy covered in sand. "Oh? Oh *no!* SWEET CHILD, ARE YOU OK?!"

He raced over, hastily dusting the sand off Adam as everyone anxiously approached, various faces filled with concern. Arnold began to hug the boy's seemingly lifeless body.

"BE HEALED, LITTLE BOY! BE HEALED!" Arnold cried, only to get smacked in the face with Adam's remaining dagger.

"Ten hits," he declared, flashing a smile before being abruptly engulfed by Arnold's massive biceps. "ARRGH!"

* * *

"Good job, lad," Sehn commended, arms folded as he guided Adam through the wooden halls of the Vilenciel Guild Office. "But there's much room for improvement, like with your dagger throw."

"I thought it was a good throw." The boy frowned, picking sand out of his red hair.

"The problem with throwing a weapon is that once you let it go, it becomes something you've lost," Sehn explained. "Sure, in some situations it might be beneficial, say, if your blade was coated in poison. But more often than not, the damage a knife throw inflicts is non-lethal, unless it hits the face or throat."

"I see," he said as Sehn opened a wooden door leading into a workshop. Inside, the entire facility was filled with spinning machines, hundreds of spiders and cobwebs weaving in and out within the shop.

Above them hung a sign that read *"Follow the path markers, please."* On the floor were clearly marked arrows, directing foot traffic away from the bug-infested machines.

"Moral of the lesson is, once you've thrown a weapon, you've basically given it to your enemy to reuse. Otherwise, it was a good session all around, especially that last maneuver you pulled," Sehn said as a short, white-haired maid holding a doll with an eerie resemblance to its owner approached—the same girl who had spied on Adam during his first day at the guild.

"Hi, Silk. We're here for the pick-up," Sehn greeted the white-haired seamstress, as a tiny spider crawling along the girl's chest caught Adam's attention. He had a sudden inclination to swipe at the bug, but restrained himself upon seeing the thousands of spiders scuttling about in the vicinity.

"Hello, Sehn," the doll in the girl's hand replied, addressing the coffin bearer. "Your order is done. That will be five silvers."

Adam frowned, watching him hand over the payment, unfazed that the doll had just spoken.

"I'll pay you back for your help," the boy blurted out, realizing he hadn't thanked Sehn or Titania for all they had done.

Sehn turned, his usually slanted eyes widening before settling into a smile. "No problem, lad."

With payment exchanged, Silk spun around, revealing a hidden door behind a wall. Beyond it were dozens—no, *hundreds*—of tiny dolls, each unique in its own way, lining the walls within the vault. Some wore armor, others various styles of clothes, and a few were even nude, a couple appearing splattered with what looked like blood. What really caught Adam's attention, however, was the doll in the far corner shaped like him, complete with cat ears.

Weird, he thought to himself as Silk returned, this time with a fur-lined black cloak.

"Come here, kid," Sehn beckoned, positioning Adam in front of Silk, who draped the cloak over his shoulders. "Normally, I'd say capes are tacky, but this looks good, lad."

[C-Grade Luminweave Cloak of Protection+2]
[Item Description: *Synthetic fabric that hardens in response to physical trauma, offering physical protection against blunt and slashing forces. Manufactured by Silk, the Voice of Thousands.*]

The moment the cloak touched his shoulders, a notification lit up in front of him, displaying pertinent information about the enchanted item he now wore.

Voice of Thousands? His eyes flickered towards Silk, the little girl shuffling away and vanishing into the cobwebs.

"So? How is it?" Sehn asked, already ushering Adam out the door.

"Fits nicely," he responded, which it indeed did. After all, the woman who had designed all the armor and clothes he had been wearing was the little girl who had just left.

"Good, we'll try to get you a few more things before you leave tomorrow," Sehn said, the pair exiting the workspace and returning to the hallway.

He paused, facing the man.

"Thanks, Sehn. I really mean it."

The warrior smiled. "Just come back alive, kid. That'll be thanks enough."

"Yeah, sure," he sighed, pulling up his quest tracker.

[PROVE YOUR WORTH!]
[ENTER THE ABYSSAL TOWER]
[Possible Rewards: EXP 500, Copper Pieces x500, Cicero's Gacha Coin x1, Minor Health Potion x1, Minor Mana Potion x1]
[Time Remaining 22:46:18]

Less than a day. That was all the time he had before he would be forced to enter the Tower for his trials.

Catpurr 29
Schrödinger

[**Time Remaining: 19:20:01**]

Less than a day. Adam sighed as he lay on his small cot, eyeing his timer. Now that he was finally alone, he rubbed his finger, summoning the interface to distract himself from his nervous and wayward thoughts.

He still held a hundred pounds of cesium, whatever that was, in his ring—an item he had wanted to inspect, but hadn't due to its assumed massive size. The best place to take a look at it would have to be within the trials.

Shifting his eyes, he glanced over the third, fourth, and fifth slots, filled with random objects after he had forgotten to use placeholders in the ring's slots.

[Orb of Slope Finding x 1]
[Ring of Invisibility x 1]
[Crona's Amulet of Time Travel x 1]

T-TIME TRAVEL?! Immediately, he pulled the item from the ring, summoning it forth from the void. He used **Identify** to inspect the gold and silver necklace, a clear white gem embedded in its center.

[Crona's Amulet of Time Travel]
[Item Description: *A prototype amulet made by the Goddess Crona. Has the ability to teleport the user one second into the future or one second into the*

past. Requires a charge time of one second to activate. User is also affected and reset along with everything else.]

"THIS IS USELESS!" he yelled, throwing the gleaming necklace away before turning his attention to the other two items.

[Ring of Invisibility]
[Item Description: *When worn, this ring turns invisible. That's it, it doesn't affect the user.*]

Useless.

[Orb of Slope Finding]
[Item Description: *A round marble. When placed on a surface, it will attempt to find the nearest slope.*]

"Useless! This is just a marble!" Adam groaned, holding the tiny blue ball and metal band in his hands. Besides being shiny, the items were utterly and unequivocally useless.

Maybe I can pawn these for money, he thought, plopping down on his cot. If he had his old skills, he could probably deconstruct them, and just resell them as goods or even augment them.

However, in his current state, they were all just useless trinkets.

I wonder how Schrödinger is doing, Adam sighed, rolling over and attempting to sleep.

* * *

Faith, the Capital of the Volbrook Theocracy

"Report," Junith commanded, the paladin's back turned from the invited guests as her gaze remained fixed on the partially destroyed Holy Sanctum of Voltrain below.

"Sis—Sister Junith," a bald man dressed as a church scribe stammered, his robes scorched, numerous bright-red scratches standing out against his pasty face. "I regret to inform you that we have had little success in our efforts to investigate the feline abomination."

"And why is that?" Junith inquired, her eyes shifting to a torn tapestry below them, now engulfed in flames.

"Well, as you may be aware, we aren't capable of *seeing* the cat. Every attempt to observe it directly results in the feline teleporting, causing complete destruction of the surrounding area within a one-foot radius. All attempts at eliminating the abomination have ended in failure, with even the Spear of Righteous Light proving ineffective against the beast. The best we can do is trapping it within the Sanctum using the cathedral's security measures. There is also the issue of its fire-breathing abilities."

As the scribe spoke, a twenty-foot torrent of flames erupted, casting light on the devastated church beneath.

"Have you tried corralling it into a secure containment chamber?" Junith asked, her fingers tracing a scar on her cheek from where the necromancer cat's claws had nicked her.

"We have, but only the Sanctum's enchantments are powerful enough to contain its devilish magic. The Bishop expresses great displeasure at present circumstances."

Junith sighed. It was as she feared. The necromancer's beast was untouchable, nay *indestructible*. For the brief moment she had held the cat, her interface had categorized the creature as an indestructible item, leaving even her holy sword incapable of taking its head.

When she tried to dispose of the beast, it began manifesting powers, forcing the army to confine the fire-breathing cat within the enchanted prison originally crafted for its master. A prison that was fueled by the life force of hundreds of believers.

This solution, however, was temporary at best. Even though it was for the sacred act of purging heresy, the toll of so many lives burdened Junith's conscience heavily.

Hopefully studying the creature might reveal a link to its master, Junith thought, furrowing her brow as she thought of the portal, and the day the necromancer filth had vanished without a trace. Her hand tightened around her sword as she mentally replayed the encounter with the coward who had thrown sand into her eyes.

Suddenly, a knock at the onyx double doors diverted her attention.

"Come in," Junith commanded, and a black-robed girl entered.

"Sister Junith, the Duchess of Volbrook has arrived with her father."

"I see. Bring them in," Junith replied, dismissing the scribe by ordering him to continue his investigation.

As the nun and scribe departed, it didn't take long before a displeased, white-haired girl emerged, clutching a golden box in her hand.

"JUNITH!" Rosetta barked, the little brat bursting through the doors and immediately demanding answers. "WHERE IS HE?! WHERE IS THAT FILTHY, DISGUSTING NECROMANCER?!"

"Currently beyond our reach. The seers are attempting—" Junith began, only to be cut off by the little girl's tantrum. She turned her wrath to a nearby golden table, flipping it.

"YOU PROMISED ME! YOU SWORE YOU WOULD KILL HIM! THAT THE CURSE WOULD LIFT ONCE YOU DID!" Rosetta wailed, anger resonating in her voice as she wreaked havoc on the room. "I GAVE YOU MONEY! MERCENARIES! FOOD! *EVERYTHING* YOU REQUIRED!"

Junith sighed. "We are making every available move we can to deal with the heretic—"

"LIAR! While you stand here, my father remains a frog!" Rosetta cried, thrusting the box forwards and revealing a lush terrarium within, a large, fat toad seated in the center.

Junith arched a brow, surveying the creature. "My lady, that is a toad, not a frog."

"What? They're the same thing," the interim duchess said, looking down at the box with furrowed brows.

"A toad is bulkier, more squat, with rougher skin and a dry appearance, whereas a frog is more lithe, agile, with moist skin," Junith pointed out. The girl seemed unaware that the box contained not her father, but rather a common toad.

"Nonsense! This is my father! He's just gained a little bit of weight from overeating, that's all," Rosetta argued, holding the box at eye level. "Isn't that right, father?"

A moment passed, then another. Silence descended on the room as the duchess stared at the toad and waited for a response.

When the 'frog' didn't respond, Rosetta went wide-eyed, abruptly dropping the box and running through the double doors, screaming, "FATHER! FATHER!"

Seeing the brat run off, Junith turned her gaze to the toad crawling on the ground. A moment passed, then another before she approached it, positioning her armored boot over the creature.

"Filth," Junith uttered before crushing the creature.

* * *

Elsewhere.

Beneath a large oak-like tree, beside a splendid mansion of gold and silver, sat a large green frog as it ribbited silently in fear. A solitary tear fell from its eye as it hid, evading the flock of aerial predators swirling above, biding their time for their chance to feast on his portly amphibian body.

Rosetta! Please save your Papa!

Catpurr 30
Final Day of Rest

Waking up to the soft light filtering through his bedroom window, Adam twitched, blinking rapidly as he smacked his face with his palm.

"Why does the sun keep rising?" he complained, pulling up his interface to check how much time he had left.

[11:12:07]

"Today's the day." He sighed, pushing Tilith's face off his chest. Groggily, he rose to his feet, sweeping the useless trinkets onto the floor beneath his bed. If he survived the trials, he'd hav—

"Eh?"

Adam spun around, his gaze locking onto Tilith, her rainbow-hued hair sprawled across his bedsheets. *The Nyx*—He squinted, wondering what the woman was doing in his bed. "Hey. What are you doing in my room?"

When the woman didn't respond, he poked her. "Hey! Get out of my room so I can change!"

Still met with silence, he shook her, hoping to elicit some reaction. Nothing.

"HEY!" he barked, slapping the woman on the head. Finally reacting, a pale hand shot out, seizing his wrist and pulling him into a warm embrace.

"What the Nyx?! Hey! Let me go!" he protested, struggling to break free as she squeezed him like a teddy bear, bringing his face to her cleavage. "Ow! Ow! OW! STOP! LET ME GO! RELEASE ME, MEATBAG! I DENY THEE, HARLOT! I DENY THEE!"

"Mmm, cuddly," moaned Tilith, just as the door to his room burst open.

"Adam!" Titania exclaimed, her eyes darting between Adam and Tilith, who was still squeezing him tight.

"Help me!" the nekoboy yelled, his face being buried in cleavage as his hand reached for his savior.

* * *

It took some effort, but after about thirty minutes, Adam was finally wrested from her clutches.

"Noooo. My teddy!" Tilith wailed, as the sleepy girl was dragged out by her arms, firmly held by the twin maid sisters Sinclair and Ravi.

"Adam, are you okay?" Titania asked, the displeased nekoboy sitting cross-armed, hair tousled from the assault.

"Let's just get some breakfast."

* * *

Sitting at a wooden table in the kitchen of the guild office, Adam waited as the scent of food filled the interior of the building and wafted out into the reception area. A typical tactic the guild used to make adventurers hungry and part them from their hard-earned coin.

"Here you go, little Adam! A nice steak with celery and asparagus! Make sure to eat your greens; they're important for your body to grow big and strong!" Arnold said, giving a hearty laugh as he laid out food for the other staff members.

"Hey, how come he gets the full-on T-bone while we get sirloins and strips?" Ravi complained, as the pink-haired munchkin maid stabbed at her food with a dagger, before lifting it to her mouth to munch.

"Because he is a growing boy. And has room to grow, unlike you," Lunafreya replied, taking a seat beside Adam.

"Are you calling me short?!" Ravi cried, her voice almost offended. "I'm not short! I'm *compact!*"

"Settle down, or you'll give yourself an aneurysm," Lunafreya cautioned, as the muscular lady leaned over the boy's smaller frame with a grin. His eyes widened as a large butcher knife suddenly appeared in front of him, which began slicing his T-bone for him.

Despite the surprise, Adam sat patiently and said nothing. Ruebella gracefully poured him a glass of green colored juice, while Titania placed a small bowl of piping-hot grits by his side.

"Lucky bastard," Sehn grumbled, his jealous tone reaching Adam's ears. He cast a brief glance towards the man seated in the distant corner of the kitchen, shrouded in shadows, nursing a small bowl of porridge.

"Today's the big day, Adam. How are you feeling?" Titania asked, taking a seat beside him. The whole kitchen was focused on him. Lifting his gaze from his meal, he prepared to respond, but then suddenly, it hit him.

Sitting there, surrounded by people who seemed to care for his well being, Adam's jaw tightened. An overwhelming surge of emotion, a desire to cry, gripped him as they anticipated his reply. The years of isolation, the fugitive life, with Schrödinger as his only friend—memories of persecution drowned him. He found it hard to breath, his eyes welling up as struggled to maintain composure. A sensation had reawakened in him, one that he hadn't felt in a long time.

Happiness emerged, intertwined with guilt at lying. They didn't know that he wasn't a child. All the hospitality he received was a product of deceit.

"A-Adam, are you okay?" Titania asked, the entire table moving to console the nekoboy as he hung his head low and used his hands to stifle unexpected tears.

* * *

"I think we overwhelmed him," Titania said, wearing a frown as she stood outside Adam's room, the hallway now congested with concerned onlookers.

"Poor lad," Arnold cried. "Purrhaps a fresh meal will soothe his troubled heart. I SHALL DO SO POSTHASTE!"

"Uh. I don't think that's going to help," Titania said, but Arnold had already disappeared, accompanied by Lunafreya, who trailed behind with a butcher's blade in hand.

"W-What should w-we d-do?" Ruebella asked.

"Maybe we should give him some space," Titania suggested. "There's not much we can do if he wants to stay locked up in his room."

"His trials are today. Maybe he's scared?" Sinclair offered, twisting the abyssal ticket on her own wrist.

"Pfft, if he's gonna be a wuss about it, he might not stand a chance," Ravi scoffed, only to be clocked on the head by Sinclair.

"OW! Wutz *tat* for! You made me bith mi tong, you ore!"

"I can't believe I'm related to you. Have some tact, idiot."

"Im noh an idgit!"

Suddenly, the click of heels on wooden boards made everyone stiffen up.

"We are opening in less than an hour. Why are you all standing around instead of DOING. YOUR. JOBS?!" guild master Victoria Valentine's voice boomed, her purple gaze swiftly dispersing the group of maids.

"Titania, Sehn!"

"YES, MA'AM!" The duo snapped to attention.

"Stop using the Repentas for your pet project. While they are on the clock, they must fulfill their obligations as contracted servants to the guild," the guild master declared, arms folded, as her frown deepened. "Understood?"

"Y-Yes, ma'am!" Sehn replied. Titania hesitated for a moment before following suit.

"Good," Victoria sighed, her shoulders relaxing a bit. "How is he?"

"Today is his day, so... emotional," Titania replied.

"I would be too if I thought I was going to die," Sehn quipped, earning an elbow from Titania.

"That can be arranged," she hissed.

"I see," Victoria said. "Get him whatever you think he needs to survive. But don't go overboard. I'd hate for money to be wasted."

Suddenly, the door swung open, revealing Adam, clad in his leather armor, cape, and metal daggers gifted to him by Sehn.

"I'm ready for the trials," he declared, his eyes reflecting resolution and determination. "Where do I need to go to enter?"

Catpurr 31
The Twilight Plaza Incident

On a brisk afternoon, in a white-tiled plaza teeming with adventurers, Adam stood, just another face in the crowd of people milling about, entering their trials or assembling raiding parties.

"Are you ready?" Sehn asked, adjusting the hood over Adam's face as the boy sweltered under the sun's heat.

"As ready as I can be," he huffed. *Time to be inconspicuous.*

After nearly an hour of walking, the trio of adventurers had navigated through the bustling city, traversing bridges and gates leading to a central plaza that was designated the main tower entrance.

Officially it was named Twilight Square, but guild members like Sehn and Titania called it the Plaza of Departure. It bustled with adventurers, merchants, and entertainers, the focal point for those challenging the tower, separated into two: the Labyrinth and the Abyssal Tower.

The Labyrinth welcomed those not chosen by gods to explore its depths, while the Abyssal Tower was a place only those with tickets, like Adam, could venture. Both places were dangerous, the Tower doubly so. But for those not chosen, at least the Labyrinth offered them a chance to earn rewards by hunting monsters and gathering materials.

The others had wanted to see their young ward off as well, but between the flood of adventurers, hungry patrons, and customers placing orders, the guild staff were swamped.

"Okay. Remember, all you need to do is approach the waystone and then brandish your ticket," Titania instructed, pointing towards an obelisk in the distance where several people took turns entering portals that materialized every few seconds.

"You got everything, lad?" Sehn asked, and Adam ran a quick inventory. Four vials of mana regeneration, three vials of HP regeneration, ration cubes, and his two daggers on his waist. Between his leather armor, cloak, basic adventurer tools, and hidden mana potion, he was as ready as he could ever be, considering the circumstances.

"Yeah," he replied, adjusting the small buckler on his leather-clad forearm.

Sehn nodded, the trio advancing towards the lines, drawing the attention of onlookers.

"Bit short to be entering."

"Is that a kid?"

"No way."

"Take your kid to work day?"

"Maybe it's a filthy dwarf?"

"I've never seen a dwarf; aren't they shorter?"

"You're thinking of gnomes; dwarves are about ten feet tall at least."

"Wait, what? That doesn't sound right."

"Why do you think they're called dwarves? Cuz they *dwarf* you."

A cacophony of voices overlapped, many making little effort to conceal the focus of their discussion.

Just keep moving, Adam urged himself, flanked by Sehn and Titania, who acted as honor guards, guiding him through the crowd.

The trio paused, standing in front of the white pillar etched with various runic encryptions.

"Thank you, Sehn, Titania. For everything," Adam said sincerely, extending his wrist towards the white obelisk before him. Immediately, it glowed.

"Bloody hell."

"No way."

"Seriously?!"

"I wonder which god chose him." The onlookers murmured, openly speculating.

"The best thanks you can give is getting out alive, lad." Sehn smiled, gripping the leather strap of the coffin on his shoulder. "Just do what you need to do to survive."

"I can do that," Adam assured, his ticket glowing in response to the obelisk.

Suddenly a purple rift tore open mid-air, its magical energy creating a large gust of wind that pushed the crowd back and nearly removed the nekoboy's hood, saved only by his quick reflexes.

So much for being inconspicuous!

The energy in the air swirled, rotating and expanding before reshaping into a door. Bones formed a door frame, which was quickly filled in by a purple door etched with a serpent devouring itself in the center. Unlike the circular portals that were common all around him, Adam's was square, corporeal, with a handlebar seemingly crafted from an outstretched, skeletal hand, apparently reaching out to shake his own.

The door landed with a resounding thud, and the once-lively city square fell silent. Not a word, not a sound, not even the birds or merchants dared to break the hush.

"WHAT KIND OF PORTAL IS THAT?!" a man cried out, before the crowd surged, shifting and racing towards Adam's position, eager to witness the unfolding phenomenon.

"MY GABBAGES!" a merchant cried out in the chaos, as a stampede formed.

OH, CRAPBASKETS! Adam thought, wide-eyed, as a tidal wave of adventurers rushed him, eager to catch a glimpse of his 'portal.'

"Crap! This is bad!" Sehn pivoted, hurling his coffin at a group trying to rush over, tripping them. Titania punched her fists together, releasing a blast of green energy that pushed another group back.

"Adam! Into your portal, now! Don't let them see you!" Sehn urged, as an adventurer leapt over the crowd, only to be intercepted by a murder of crows that appeared suddenly, carrying the man away, screaming.

Lunafreya?!

Suddenly, a woman's massive figure landed in the square, slamming a metal chair into the ground. Seated upon it was the Vilenciel Guild Master herself. The woman stood up, her heels clicking against the concrete. She swept her raven hair to the side and bellowed out:

"BE STILL!"

[You have been designated as an unintended target of the skill: Voice of Command]
[Skill effect resisted!]

As a notification flashed on his interface, Adam spun around, witnessing the entire frenzied crowd freezing, with only a few stragglers still in motion.

Victoria Valentine turned, wearing an odd expression before she pointed at the door. "Go. Now. This will only delay them for a few moments."

In the heat of the moment, Adam didn't need to be told twice. He swiftly spun, reaching out and grasping the outstretched boney hand. With a forceful pull, he swung open the door, and was immediately greeted by several skeletal appendages that pulled him in.

[CONCA*TU*LATIONS! QUEST COMPLETE!]

* * *

Upon return to the guild hall, Sehn and Titania camped out in Victoria's office, awaiting her reaction as she paced around.

"Okay. What the hell was that?" the guild master demanded, turning to face the window overlooking clamoring adventurers, church officials, and nobles seeking answers regarding the incident in the plaza.

Titania and Sehn exchanged glances, before addressing their guild master.

"We have no idea," Titania replied, while Sehn removed the ice pack from his black eye, affirming Titania's response. "Maybe... Maybe it has something to do with him being a demi?"

Victoria pinched her nose, wondering how she would explain this. She could already sense the lengths which the research institute, and nobles and church officials would go to for an explanation.

"Get in contact with Coco; see if she can offer any insight into the boy's portal," Victoria sighed before snapping her fingers. "Lunafreya."

"Yes, mistress." The gargantuan woman emerged from the shadows, bowing.

"Find Leona and have her release a statement that the abilities and information of our members is confidential. And that we will be taking no questions. From the church or otherwise," Victoria instructed.

"As you command, madam," Lunafreya said, disappearing in a murder of summoned crows as Sehn and Titania promptly left to fulfill their own tasks.

"Trouble is brewing," Victoria frowned, a headache blossoming in her mind as she stared out the window towards the castle in the distance.

Catpurr 32

Undine's Temple

The moment Adam stepped through the portal, he was immediately and without warning teleported to a new location. No long-winded tunnels in the fabric of reality. No spinning for hours, doing cartwheels and vomiting. No shenanigans.

This time, he was immediately transmitted to a different place, a far cry from where he had just been.

"HULP!" he exclaimed as he tumbled out of the skeletal hands' embrace, landing on a smooth, marble platform.

The portal closed, taking the skeletal appendages with it, leaving Adam alone. Rising to his feet, he quickly assessed his surroundings. His hands gripped his daggers as he scanned the slick cavern walls, illuminated by the flickering blue torches hanging beside the portal.

"Well at least it's not lava..." he muttered, eyeing the underground cavern dotted with large pools of water.

Just my luck. Of course, I'd be surrounded by water...

Alone, he pulled up his system, examining the notification that was waiting for him to dismiss it.

[CON*CAT*ULATIONS! QUEST COMPLETE!]
[Rolling Rewards...]
[Ding!]
[Cicero's Gacha coin!]

Suddenly, a coin ejected from his screen, and Adam caught the gold metal object. He squinted at the golden coin, rimmed with pink and depicting a smiling clown.

Inspect.

[Cicero's Gacha Coin[Unique] x 1]

[**Item Description:** *A consumable item bound to the Nekomancer Adam Glow. Allows one roll at the system gacha interface for a random Reward.*]

Gacha? What the Nyx is a gacha? His brow creased in thought.

He held the coin aloft, wondering how to use it. Judging from the last sentence of the description, it must have been part of his system.

TITLE: IDIOT NOVICE OF ELI (?????)
NAME: Adam F. Glow
SPECIES: Nekoboy
LEVEL: 4
EXP BAR: 100/2,000
MAIN CLASS: Nekomancer
HP: 100/100
MANA: 125/125
[SEALED FUNCTION]
[SEALED FUNCTION]
Free Points: 5
STR: 7
CON: 10
DEX: 12
ARC: 25
SEN: 9
EGO: 10

If he had to guess, the coin likely had something to do with the sealed functions. But what?

Lifting the coin, he placed it onto his system, where it immediately began to react, sparks of mana touching the coin. However, just as it seemed the coin was about to disappear into his system, an error message appeared.

[ERROR! Requirements not met to unseal Gacha System!]
—Level 5 Required!
—20 Constitution Required!
—20 Arcana Required!

"Tsk." He pocketed the coin, stowing it in one of his armor's pockets.

Hmmm. Maybe I should distribute my skill points, he thought, leering at the water. He had kept his free points after farming the goblins, not wanting to arouse suspicion from Sehn or the other maids who could detect mana.

The initial plan was to dump the points into Arcana upon entering the Tower, but now, looking at the water, Adam had other ideas.

STR: 7 → 10
CON: 10 → 12
HP: 100 → 110

Survive. Adapt. Overcome.

While he was intrigued by the reward system, he wasn't in much of a rush to access a system that would give out random rewards. No, purrhaps what he needed to do was to make a more even spread, rather than concentrating everything into Arcana. Especially since he'd be operating with reduced stats in this dungeon.

After allocating the stat points, the difference was immediately felt, particularly in his Strength.

"At least this way, when I get debuffed, I won't be completely screwed," he muttered, observing the smooth cavern that was utterly devoid of any entrances, escapes, or tunnels, except for the glowing water encircling the platform he stood on.

He took a step forwards, peering over the edge, when suddenly a notification hit his face.

[Welcome to Floor One! The Water Temple of Undine!]
[Mandatory quest given!]
[Find Pirate King Laffy's Treasure! 0/1]
[Eons ago, a pirate band known as the Golden Hats were led by Pirate King Laffy on an expedition for the Water Spirit Undine's divine protection. Here a deal was struck between Laffy and Undine, wherein the Pirate King left his most precious treasure behind.]
[Optional Sub Quest 1: Exterminate Crabs 0/25]
[Optional Sub Quest 2: Exterminate Crabs 0/100]
[Optional Sub Quest 3: Exterminate Crabs 0/1,000]
[Optional Sub Quest 4: Exterminate Crabs 0/10,000]

Treasure? A fetch quest then. Examining the area again, the nekoboy's daze was drawn towards the rocks in the rippling water that emitted a faint glow, gently illuminating the underground.

"At least I can see," Adam mused. If the temple was underwater, he'd have to figure out a way to explore. He wasn't a bad swimmer; even with his debuff, he was confident he could navigate the water with relative ease. No, the bigger concern was the potential lack of oxygen, or the risk of getting trapped underwater. It was easy to lose track of time and become lost when traversing tunnels, and this was doubly true underwater. There was no guarantee that there would be any light further on.

Adam's brow furrowed as he examined the sub quests and the escalation between each task.

Ten thousand... *This... This might be a problem.*

Fortunately, this quest didn't seem to have a timer, meaning he had all the time he needed to complete it.

He reached down, grabbing a small pot and matches from his waist as a cat-shaped summon sigil appeared.

It was time to go hunting.

Catpurr 33

Researching the Water Temple

"Ugh. If only I had Share Sense still," Adam groaned, seated on the platform as his skelekitty emerged from the water, using its phalanges to pull itself up onto the smooth marble.

"Alright. About five meters." The new calculation was added in charcoal to the parchment map, spread out on the temple ground and illuminated by a nearby fire.

Six days had passed since entering the dungeon, and during that time, Adam had been scheming, strategizing, and exploring the watery tunnels below.

Well, his skeleton had.

The nekomancer had come up with a relatively straightforward system using his skeleton.

As a non-breathing, non-living entity, his cat would dive into the waters, exploring the tunnels on its master's behalf. When encountering a turn or a split, it would return, tapping on icons he had fashioned using pebbles to denote the nature of the tunnel.

L for left, R for right, U for up, and D for down.

Additional rock symbols were used to represent the paths, indicating curves, straight shots, or crossroads. By calculating Skittles' swim distance with time elapsed, Adam was able to map out a small labyrinth in the underwater temple, even identifying pockets of air and rooms occupied by monsters.

Adam frowned, picking up a small blue glowing crystal and placing it in his mouth.

The glowing crystals scattered throughout the underwater cave helped to adsorb oxygen, but also released it, oxidizing the water for the plant life and fish swimming below him.

The crystal in Adam's mouth began to dim, its oxygen depleting. He continued sucking, removing the air until the crystal lost its blue sheen and went clear.

Dropping it on the platform, the rock immediately began to glow again as it absorbed oxygen once more.

These findings were recorded in the third slot of his storage device, using a journal Ruebella had gifted him, something he could use to pass the time.

"Rate of re-oxygenation, less than half a second," Adam jotted down.

He glanced over the last few pages, each filled with drawings of fish, crystals, and images of the various items he had discovered during his stay on the floor: *Lora fish, glow jellies, Dyrid seaweed, shard of Dios marble.*

Keeping notes was important, not just for his sanity, but to document his findings.

Inspect, Adam said to himself as he lifted a piece of marble etched with golden engravings recovered during his exploration.

[Shard of Undine's Temple]

[**Item Description:** *A remnant of Undine's Temple. After the war of gods broke out, Undine abstained, choosing instead to be a shelter for those lost and displaced by the war. For her actions, she was revered and praised. Sadly, with her increase of worship, her divinity grew, making her a target of scorn. This fragment is all that remains of her legacy.*]

"No good deed ever goes unpunished," he reflected as he closed his leather-bound journal. He took one final glance at the map, studying it, before rolling up the parchment and brushing away the residue of dead fish. The items returned to the storage ring, including one fish bone for later.

The boy sighed. It was time to get to work. Checking his pockets filled with the glowing crystals one last time, he walked to the platform's edge, pulled up his interface, and reviewed his skills as Skittles went ahead.

Once he hit the water, he'd have no mana left, unless he dispelled Skittles.

"Nothing ventured. Nothing gained," he repeated, motivating himself as his leather-clad foot hovered above the water's surface.

Taking a moment to collect himself, he stuck a glowing crystal into his mouth and clamped down.

Then he dropped, falling into the water with a splash.

[CATSIFICATION CURSE ACTIVATED! YOU ARE WET!]
[-20% to all stats!]

Dismissing the notification, Adam acted quickly, dragging one hand after the other and swimming through the water towards a distant tunnel, where Skittles was waiting.

Blinking repeatedly to acclimate his eyes to the water, the boy latched onto his skeletal companion, allowing it to tow him forwards, conserving his energy.

Five meters left, Adam counted down, visualizing the map in his mind. Releasing his skeleton, he followed in its wake as the pair entered the next chamber, teeming with colorful fish.

Already the crystal in his mouth was dimming, but luckily this chamber held an air pocket.

Breaking the water's surface, he extracted the crystal from his mouth and took a deep breath. Holding the rock aloft, it quickly regained its glow, adding its light to the rest of the cave.

Alright. Let's get back to it.

Adam dove back down, swimming through the water to enter the next section.

Cave after cave, he swam, sometimes holding onto Skittles to propel him forwards, occasionally stopping to examine faded glyphs and ancient golden inscriptions on the cavern walls. However, fatigue set in after the sixth tunnel, his eyes stinging from prolonged exposure to the water.

Fortunately, the next checkpoint had an air pocket, granting him a brief respite.

He hit the surface, and inhaled deeply, surveying his surroundings.

There was nothing but stones. Rocks were scattered everywhere, the ceiling adorned by a few glowing crystals, like false-stars.

Noticing an outcrop of stone he could rest on, he swam to the edge. Pulling himself up, gripping the ground, he freed himself from the water. As he did so a glint caught his eye, and he rolled just in time to avoid the projectile that came hurtling at him.

Scrambling to his feet, Adam's daggers were drawn, his eyes narrowing as he stared into the darkness.

"Pt-*Oh!*" A sound echoed, followed by a projectile that nearly struck him, saved only by quickly deflecting the rock with his dagger.

Adam stepped back, stumbling from the force of the attack. Taking the glowing rock from his mouth, he threw it towards the shadows, only to reveal something that made him frown.

It was a crab.

An *excessively large* crab.

A very large crustacean that *didn't* appreciate being brought into the light. Its rocky gray legs shifted, massive pincers clamping as its crusty, gray back opened up to reveal dozens of wiggling tentacles

"Oh… crapbaskets," he muttered as the creature shot off the ground and charged towards him.

Catpurr 34
Crabby vs Nekomancer

"CRAP!" Adam exclaimed as he hastily retreated, narrowly dodging the massive claw striking the ground.

With daggers in hand, he skillfully sliced through the pursuing pink tentacles hellbent on catching him.

Inspect!

[**Giant Morian Crab of Undine's Temple**]
[**Monster Description:** *A highly territorial decapod crustacean, capable of growing up to seven feet tall. Primarily dormant during its life cycle and hibernates once pregnant, awakening only to feed and confront intruders in its lair. Once its offspring hatch, the crab sacrifices its body for nourishment, ensuring their survival in the waters.*]
[**Strengths:** *Durable exoskeleton shell, ???, ???, ???*]
[**Weaknesses:** *???, ???*]

"*Great! Not very useful!*" he internally complained, swiftly ducking as the crab's large claw slammed against the slippery cavern walls, narrowly missing him. Fortunately for Adam, with the crab's body tilted sideways, it had a hard time catching him. *Un*fortunately, he couldn't do much to hurt the monster, as his daggers clanged uselessly against the monster's chitinous shell.

The monster turned, hurling its massive appendage towards the nekoboy, who raised his cape. The black fabric reacted, solidifying just in time to deflect the blow and send him crashing backwards through the cave.

"ARGHH!" he groaned in frustration, eyes narrowing as adrenaline pumped through his veins, preventing his weary body from succumbing to exhaustion.

Taking a deep breath, Adam sprinted, putting as much distance as he could between himself and his foe, moving to the far edges of the outcropping.

After spending a moment observing the creature, two things became apparent.

One, this was a completely unfair boss encounter.

Two, the thing was *too massive!*

The creature snapped its chitinous pincers, its eye stalks suddenly glowing, causing every hair on the boy's body to stand on end.

AN ATTACK!

He swiftly dove to the left, narrowly avoiding a searing blast of mana that obliterated the spot he had just occupied.

"Laser eyes?! IT HAS LASER EYES?!" Adam shouted internally as the crab suddenly unleashed a barrage of **Mana Bolts** from each eye.

"SCREW TIIIS!" he yelled to himself, abruptly changing direction, attempting to dive back into the water. Given its size compared to the width of the caves, there was no way it could follow him.

[-20 HP!]

"GAH!" Adam spun in midair from a **Mana Bolt** before splashing into the water.

Don't pass out! Don't pass out! he chanted, clutching his side in agony as the bloodied water around him exploded from the crab's relentless mana bolts. *Skittles! Come!*

Suddenly, something tugged at his cape, dragging him away from the attacks as he hastily stuck a breathing crystal into his mouth.

* * *

"Gaaaaugh!" The boy gasped for air, spitting out the blue crystal as Skittles helped to drag him back to dry land.

He slumped onto the ground, breathing heavily as he bled profusely from his side. With each passing second, his HP dwindled, leaving him with only thirty remaining.

Conducting a swift scan, he surveyed the cave, searching for any signs of threats. Finding none, he rolled onto his back, letting out a pained groan.

Pain tolerance. Would be so *nice right now...*

Adam reached for the right side of his waist, grabbing a vial. Swiftly uncorking it, he shakily emptied the contents of the red potion into his mouth.

"Aaaaaaaaah," he groaned, skin sizzling and releasing steam as the tincture rapidly regenerated his body. He huffed, taking in a cold, deep breath and sucked in air through his teeth.

"Breathe in... Breathe out," he recited, his eyelids fluttering as exhaustion overwhelmed him, forcing them shut.

* * *

Adam found himself floating, weightless, drifting in a void.

"Adam... Adam... ADAM!"

His eyes snapped open, at the sound of a woman's velvety voice as she nudged his ribs.

"M-Master?"

The woman with the golden eyepatch peered down at him, brow raised as she folded her arms against the backdrop of an open blue sky emphasizing her pale complexion.

"Yes. Why do you look so surprised? Get up; we're moving," Razalia declared, adjusting her wide brimmed hat to shield her from the beating sun, casting her shadow across the forest floor.

"Five more minutes," the boy groaned, wrapping himself in a green blanket and turning over to cuddle a baby Schrödinger.

Suddenly, the blanket was yanked away, pulled into the earth by a skeletal hand that magically emerged from the ground.

"Get up, Adam, or I'll leave you here. Inquisitors are nearby; they have our scent."

"RAZALIA!"

At the sound of her name, the woman's expression became serious. "Oh, she's closer than I thought."

"HERETIC!" a voice yelled, followed by a massive boom that shook the nearby forest. Adam flinched, closing his eyes at the unexpected attack. When he opened them a moment later, a green shield had sprung to life around him.

"Hello, sister," Razalia Des'heart said, smiling sadly. The barrier shuddered once, then again, as a silver hammer struck it repeatedly. On the other side of that hammer was a paladin in golden armor, borne aloft by burning wings.

"TRAITOR! HERETIC! FILTHY BONE LOVER!" the blonde paladin raged, making Adam flinch as unfathomable power poured into the head of her weapon before it struck once more. "DIE, SCUM!"

"I missed you too, sister." Razalia smiled as her barrier flickered, but held firm. She glanced down at her fingers, picking dirt out of them, while various men and women dressed in white and gold robes emerged from the bushes, each adorned with emblems of Voltrain etched on their shoulders.

Adam swiftly leaped to his feet, cradling the meowing feline against his chest while conjuring a ball of green mana in his hands, as he prepared for combat.

"I have no sister!" the paladin barked, stepping back and radiating an irritating golden light, mirrored by the surrounding inquisitors.

Razalia sighed.

"Douglas. Gawain. Come out and play, but don't rough up my baby sister too much. Do whatever you wish to the others."

At the woman's command, the tattoos of a knight and a skeleton on her arm animated, transforming into inky shadows that materialized a black-armored knight engulfed in blue flames and a hulking skeletal monstrosity wielding a bone axe. The Bonemass and the Living Armor, two high-ranking necromantic creatures bound to Adam's master.

"Purge them!" the blonde paladin roared, only for Razalia to turn to Adam, her palm outstretched, hand ablaze with green fire.

"Wake up, Adam," she said, strolling towards him as her monsters decimated the inquisitors.

"What?" he asked, confused by his master's actions.

"Wake UP."

Suddenly, Adam was lifted into the air, his body tingling with a burning sensation as the world around him distorted.

He blinked, fear in his eyes, as the woman he trusted the most raised her hand engulfed by raging, necromantic flames and blasted him, setting him ablaze. Razalia only cackled.

He screamed, Schrödinger releasing a wretched meow as it crumbled into dust in his hands. "WAKE UP! WAKE UP WAKE UP! *WAKE UP!*"

At last he awoke, escaping the nightmare with a scream, only to find himself surrounded by dozens, maybe hundreds, of tiny insects pinching at his skin.

"WHAT THE NYX?!" Adam cried, rolling on the rough ground to squash the bugs crawling all over him. *GET OFF GET OFF GET OFF!*

Around the crumbling walls of the ruined sanctuary, a scream of "WHY CAN'T I JUST CATCH A BREAK!" echoed, as tiny bugs entered the nekoboy's mouth.

Catpurr 35
CRABS! CRABS! CRABS!

"AAAAAHH!" Adam screamed, frantically brushing his arms, now coated with tiny bugs, and stomping on them as they hit the ground.

[Optional Sub Quest 1: Exterminate Crabs 12/25]

WHAT?!

A notification abruptly appeared on his screen, diverting his attention from the pinching and burning. Looking down, he fumbled with a glowing crystal from one of his pouches, inspecting the bottom of his boot as he lifted it.

"Seriously?! BABY CRABS?"

The revelation stunned the boy for a moment, but his stupor lasted only a second as the persistent pinching continued, making him shake and pat his body all over.

"AAAAHHHHHHHH!"

***

After an hour of swearing and smashing tiny baby crabs, the swarm had finally been beaten back, allowing him to plop onto the ground and take a breath.

[Optional Sub Quest 1: Exterminate Crabs 25/25]
[Optional Sub Quest 2: Exterminate Crabs 100/100]
[Optional Sub Quest 3: Exterminate Crabs 235/1,000]

[Optional Sub Quest 4: Exterminate Crabs 235/10,000]

He pulled up his quest list, reviewing the subquest and finally realized why the quest requirements were so high.

"Damn crabs," he huffed, wiping his sweating brow. His eyes darted towards what he had at first assumed was a large boulder, only to discover it was the carcass of an adult Morian Crab, filled with hundreds of tiny babies.

He turned his gaze away from the corpse, focusing instead on his skellie cat, busy hopping around and crushing little crabs as they tried to flee, contributing to Adam's crustacean genocide.

*If only I had **Summon Undead**,* he sighed, imagining using the Morian's corpse to fight the still-living, massive crab just a few caverns away.

"Oh, how simple life would be if I just had my skills..."

Standing up, he paced around, occasionally stepping on tiny crabs as he contemplated his next move.

"Resting on land is too risky. Can't keep swimming; I'll get tired, and I'm already vulnerable underwater with the curse," he paused, hand instinctively moving to the hole in his leather armor.

He needed a way to offset the curse, or at the very least defend himself.

Fighting underwater was tantamount to suicide, especially against amphibian monsters.

Suddenly, Adam paused as his foot crushed a tiny crab. His gaze shifted, focusing on the side where a tiny **+5 XP** in the periphery of his vision.

Huh.

He pulled up his system, observing the half-filled experience bar.

EXP BAR: [1275/2000]

Interesting, he murmured to himself, realizing that each crab contributed to his experience bar.

An evil gleam materialized in his eyes as they shifted towards the crab carcass, swarming with baby Morians.

"Perhaps my diet could use a bit more crab," he mused, giggling wickedly as he approached the carcass.

* * *

Dropping the large rock now stained with crab guts, Adam wiped his brow and stared at the message that filled the interface.

"Note to self. Next time, grab a club," he grumbled, plopping down onto the slick cavern floor after hours of crab smashing.

[Level Up!]

[**CON*CAT*ULATIONS! Level 5 reached! System functions unlocked!**]

[**Titles can now be swapped out!**]

[**Median level reached! +5 bonus stat points**]

[**Passive Ability: *Adherent of Death* obtained!**]

[**Ability Description:** *You are a practitioner of Death. As a necromancer, you deal in undeath—not just by raising the damned, but also by sending others to their graves. Through violently and ruthlessly ending the lives of at least a hundred living beings, you have demonstrated your prowess to not only give life, but take it. +20% potency to all Necromantic related skills. Living creatures will be more wary of you.*]

[**Please select two skills from the Nekomancer Skill Tree!**]
[**Upgrade Summon Minor Skeleton**]
—**Locate Bones**
[**Upgrade Animate Bone**]

—**Elemental Affinity**
—**Necro Heal**
—**Drain Mana**
—**Mana Claws**
—**Double Jump**
—**Mana Dash**
[**Upgrade Mana Bolt**]
[**Upgrade Cat Claws**]
[**Upgrade Eyes of the Predator**]

Observing the notifications, Adam grinned. This was definitely the boost he needed. His smile broadened even more when he realized he had received ten bonus points to spend, which was twice what he had expected.

Tapping his interface, he brought up the upgrade path for **Summon Skeleton** and immediately selected mana optimization.

Upon confirming his choice, the tension in his shoulder visibility eased. Eyeing his available mana, which had changed from 000/100 to 20/100, Adam now had the ability to launch two **Mana Bolts**.

With one skill point remaining, he considered the **Mana Bolt** upgrades, scrolling through a list of available enhancements for his ability.

[**Upgrade Mana Bolt**]
[**Available Upgrades**]
—**Upgrade Mana Bolt to Mana Bolt V2**
—**Empower Mana Bolt (+20% Damage +50% Mana cost)**
—**Optimize Mana Requirements (-20% REQ)**
—**Extend Range (+50% Effective Range)**
—**Shorten Cast Time (Reduce cast time by 50%)**
—**Add Multi-shot (-20% Damage +1 Projectile)**
—**Increase Projectile Speed (+50% speed, adds impact damage)**

—**Imbue Available Elemental Affinity. (Change mana structure to empower with available elemental affinity)**

Adam stood there for a moment, pondering before making a decision.

[Upgrade Increase Projectile Speed selected!]

Opting for the projectile speed augment, he chose it because, after having tested the ability in water during his first day in the cave, he had found that it suffered a velocity penalty when traveling underwater. Now though, with a fifty percent upgrade, he hoped it would at least be able to hit something.

Next, he pulled up his interface, examining his stats.

BETA SYSTEM v1.03
TITLE: IDIOT NOVICE OF ELI (?????)
NAME: Adam F. Glow
SPECIES: Nekoboy
LEVEL: 5
EXP BAR: 00015/4,000
MAIN CLASS: Nekomancer
HP: 110/110
MANA: 020/(100)125
[SEALED FUNCION]
Free Points: 10
STR: (8)10
CON: (10)12
DEX: (10)12
ARC: (20)25
SEN: (7)9
EGO: (8)10

Buffs: Loved by Undead (unique), Minor Blessing of Eli (unique), Eyes of a Predator V1, Corrupted Blessing of Nyx (unique), Adherent of Death.

Debuffs: Ha! You Sacrificed Your Stats for a Cat?! V1 (curse), Catsification V1 (curse), Wet (Catsification)

Skills: Animate Bone V1, Irritating Touch V1, Cat Claws V1, Identify V1

Summon Skeleton V1 (++), Mana Bolt V1 (+), Artificial Linguistics {Rigellian}

[Main Quest: Find Pirate King Laffy's Treasure! 0/1]
[Optional Sub Quest 3: Exterminate Crabs 380/1,000]

Initially, Adam wanted to dump all of his points into mana. However, as he fished out the gold and pink coin, he hesitated. With his ten points, he could dump them all into Constitution and unlock the Gacha System. Whatever *that* was. But he didn't, choosing instead to spread out his stats so that he could stand a better chance at surviving.

STR: 10→12
CON: 12→ 14
ARC: 25→ 30
SEN: 9→10

With his mana now at 120, courtesy of his curse, and coupled with the optimization, Adam could unleash four bolts.

As he sighed, his gaze fell upon several baby crabs still scuttling around. An idea blossomed in his mind as he observed the oversized crab carcass.

If there was one dead giant crab, there were probably dozens of other dead giant crabs. Although that also meant there were probably crabs of various sizes skirting around, Adam decided to take the risk. After all, if he could find another colony of baby crabs… he'd have another source of free XP.

A murderous glint flickered in his golden eyes, bordering on mania. Turning, he gathered the various oxygen crystals on the ground before hovering his foot over the edge.

It was time to go crab hunting.

Catpurr 36

Destruction of a Goddesses' Property

Ascending to the surface of the water with a crystal in his mouth, Adam slowly peeked out, scanning the dim cavern for his prey. Approaching the water's edge, he tread water just short of the landmass before him.

From a pocket on his armor, he retrieved one of the glowing crystals, exchanging it with the one in his mouth.

Tossing the old crystal onto the outcrop, it bounced several times on the slick floor before settling near what seemed to be simply a large rock. A large rock that wasn't actually a rock, but rather a Morian crab.

Almost immediately, the creature reacted, rocky carapace shifting as its stalky eyes glowed red.

TIME TO GO!

Adam swiftly plunged back into the water, evading the red bolts of mana that pulverized the land, one striking the water's surface.

On to the next one.

Skittles, augmented through its master's new passive, pulled him underwater, tugging on his cape and helping position him safely away from the magic attacks.

The duo swam, retracing their path through the tunnel they used to enter the cavern until they reached a specific wall lined with dozens of crystals—Adam's marker.

Breaking the water's surface, the nekoboy swam towards the land.

A safe zone.

He took the crystal out his mouth, tossing it into the water where the rest of the glowing pile lay.

Taking a seat beside the canvas he had left behind, he pulled up his quest menu and experience bar.

[Optional Sub Quest 1: Exterminate Crabs 25/25]
[Optional Sub Quest 1: Exterminate Crabs 100/100]
[Optional Sub Quest 3: Exterminate Crabs 881/1,000]
[Optional Sub Quest 4: Exterminate Crabs 881/10,000]
EXP BAR: 3230/4000

Adam had kept busy moving to and fro, scouring caverns for the remains of deceased Morians. He had sought out the carcasses of mother crabs, systematically eradicating their offspring.

Soon, he thought to himself, marking the new location on the canvas. A few hundred more baby crabs, and he would hit level six.

In the eighth cavern, he laid down, taking a moment to rest. Almost every cave had a Morian—some dead, some alive. Two had half-dead Morians slowly being eaten alive by their young, but still spry enough to launch **Mana Bolts** towards him.

Sighing, he retrieved the firestarter kit to ignite the bundled driftwood and rocks, forming a makeshift campfire.

He sat up, striking the magnesium striker to create sparks. A fire to dry him and provide warmth was a necessity before he turned in for the day.

His skeleton cat clambered up and out of the water, its jaws clacking as it approached its master. Skittles shook itself, water spraying everywhere before settling beside Adam, resting its mandible on his lap, its eerie, glowing eyes looking up at him.

Unconsciously, the boy rested his hand on its axis, stroking the skeleton's backbone. In response, Skittles purred. Well, clacked. Its mandibles were making a *chick-chick* sound as its master petted it.

At the noise, he frowned, gazing down at Skittles, the image of Schrödinger overlapping with the skeleton.

Adam sighed.

"Maybe I should finally see what this cesium thing is," he said out loud, removing his hand from Skittles and rubbing the ring on his finger as he eyed the spacious cavern around him.

Rubbing the ring, he activated the interface, pointing his storage unit to the open space beside him. Immediately a small portal opened up, depositing a large sil—

Suddenly, everything went dark.

[YOU DIED!]

* * *

Elsewhere, in a distant realm.

"All I'm saying is that if they were going to explore our territory, maybe they should use materials that can actually withstand the pressure of the depths. And maybe not using a knockoff game controller to steer would have helped," remarked a blue-haired, tanned woman clad in a light blue blouse with a trident-shaped pendant, as she read from her golden electronic tablet.

"You shouldn't speak ill of the dead, Triteia," responded Unidine, as the blue-haired goddess sipped from her cup of mocha macchiato. A fireball whizzed over her shoulder, obliterating the very coffee shop where she had ordered her beverage.

Despite the chaotic scene and the panicked screams of humans fleeing, the two sea goddesses remained unfazed, casually seated amidst all of it.

"I'm just saying," Triteia sighed, grabbing a sugar packet for her drink, "after teaching orcas to hunt their ships, you'd think they'd get the memo that the sea isn't meant for them. But what are you gonna do? And what's the deal with using a mermaid as their cup logo? A dangerous creature luring humans to their deaths doesn't seem fitting for a coffee brand."

"Beats me. No matter which realm I go to, humans still make questionable choices," Unidine commented, watching as several men in matching blue attire known as 'police officers' pulled out their firearms and engaged the horde of goblins pouring out of a green portal.

"Focus on the one casting the fireballs!" yelled an officer holding a shotgun, directing the others. Amidst the chaos, a goblin lunged at him from behind a car with a cleaver, but he swiftly countered, striking the monster with the butt of his weapon before stomping on it and unleashing a barrage of gunfire at the horde with both hands.

Unidine observed him, wondering if she'd found her Chosen.

"Him?" Triteia asked, tracing Unidine's line of sight. "Is he the one we've been waiting for?"

"Mmhm. His pet goldfish says nice things about him, and he volunteers at an aquarium for endangered species," Unidine replied, taking another sip of her coffee when a notification suddenly appeared in her line of sight.

"PSSSSSSSSSSSSSSSSSST!" Unidine's eyes widened, inadvertently spitting out her coffee all over Triteia.

"HEY! WHAT'S THE BIG IDEA?! MY HOST JUST GOT THIS DRESS!" the woman across from her shouted before her expression rapidly shifted from anger to concern. "What? What happened?! What's wrong?!"

"MY MOTHER'S TEMPLE JUST EXPLODED!" Unidine screamed, looking at the message that revealed that a consecrated ground belonging to her domain had suddenly disappeared.

Catpurr 37

I... Have Become Death, Destroyer of Crabs

[YOU DIED!]
[Subquest Complete!]
[Hidden Subquests Complete!]
[Rewards Obtainable! View Quest Log to view and accept!]

Adam's eyes fluttered open, a cascade of notifications assaulting his vision as his body, naked except for the ticket bound to his wrist, floated in the churning water.

But... why?

In a state of shock from the recent events, the boy floated on his back, vacant gaze fixed on the sapphire sky above. This was it—no more spare lives.

All he could recall before everything faded to black was taking out the cesium to inspect it, and then, suddenly, everything erupted into white. A mystery, one there was time to dwell on as the gravity of his situation sank in.

Taking just a moment to recover from his abrupt and sudden death, he twisted, shifting from his back to scan his surroundings. He paddled in the water to keep himself afloat, a frown etched on his face.

Everywhere he looked was water, an endless expanse of blue, nothing but the small nekoboy to disrupt its vastness.

Oh. I'm dead-dead.

Adam took a deep breath flipping back on his back to tread water, muttering a sarcastic "Great..."

He opened his interface, scouring the system to take a peek at the rewards he had earned from his abrupt death.

[Subquest Complete!! 10,000 Crabs Slain! Rewards Available!]
[Hidden Subquest Complete! 100,000 Crabs Slain! Rewards Available!]
[Pending Rewards!]

He raised a sodden hand, reaching for the interface displaying pending rewards, only to be bombarded by a flurry of notifications that made him go wide eyed.

[Passive Obtained: Heat Resistance V1 (Common)]
[Passive Description: *You have been burned, yet survived. Whether from standing too close to a fire, or prolonged exposure to scorching sunlight, you now possess resistance to heat and its combustible effects.* **+5% Fire resistance, reduced flammability by 5%]**
[Passive Obtained: Explosive Renaissance V1 (SR)]
[Passive Description: *Whether by (mis)fortune or intentional ingenuity, you've triggered an explosion claiming the lives of thousands of beings. All skills with an AoE or Splash effect will have its effective radius increased to, at will, a maximum of 20%.* **+10% To AoE skill potency. +10% MP cost of AoE skills.** *Toggleable.***]**

[TITLE OBTAINED: Bane of All Crabkind (UR)]!
[Title Description: *Your insatiable bloodlust has led to the extermination of hundreds of thousands of crabs, wiping out an entire species. You see crab, you kill crab. In your mind, the only good crab is a dead crab. No crustacean is safe. Your actions instill fear, and every crab will dread your name in the shadows.* **+5 STR, +5 CON, +5 DEX, +150% Damage against Crustaceans.]**

[TITLE OBTAINED: Desecrator of Grand Temples (SSR)]!
[Title Description: *Through your actions, you have desecrated and annihilated a sanctuary belonging to a powerful divine being. This being is extremely angry. You should run.* **Passive:** *Chosen and sentient beings of faith will be more wary of you.* **+10 ARCANA, +10 EGO. +10% damage against those chosen by the divine.]**

[SKILL OBTAINED: Genocidal Aura (SSR)]!
[Skill Description: *You're a monster. A singular being hellbent on the destruction of an entire species. Your actions in exterminating at least 50% of a species allow you to emit killing intent so vile that many will fear you merely by being in close proximity. Fear effect. Scales with* **EGO** *stat.* **Passive:** *living creatures will be more wary of you.*]

[Subquest Reward! Choose an item.]
—Pendant of the Mermaid's Lover
—Aquamarine Ender Pearl
—Trident of the Nameless Soldier

"Oh... oh no," Adam whispered to himself, swiftly connecting the dots. Whatever it was, the cesium had set off a massive explosion, obliterating the temple and every living creature within it. On one hand, Adam was happy that he'd never have to deal with crabs again. On the other hand...

HOW AM I SUPPOSED TO COMPLETE THE QUEST IF I BLEW IT UP?!

His jaw clenched, as the boy did his utmost not to scream as he stared blankly at the three suns overhead. *Wait. Three suns? Where the Nyx even am I?!*

Time passed. Aimlessly Adam floated in the endless sea, reflecting on his life and the choices that led him to this point.

Finally, he surrendered, sinking beneath the waves as the weight of his actions sank in. Merging with the sea, he became just another naked fish in the ocean of drifting waves, soon to be erased from this world, with no troubles and nothing to worry about ever again.

This is nice, he mused, floating, until suddenly his body's need for oxygen kicked in, jolting him back to reality and forcing him to paddle to the surface.

"GAH!" Breaking the surface, he inhaled deeply before letting out a scream, voice laced with pent-up frustration and anger at the absurdity of it all.

"IT'S NOT FAIR! IT'S NOT FAIR! *IT'S NOT FAIR!*" he raged, flailing wildly. "GAAAAAAAAAAAAAAAAAAH!"

Yet, despite the nekoboy's tantrum, it accomplished nothing, only draining him of his already diminishing stamina.

He lay back down, treading water on his back, and remembered the subquest reward screen.

Then he pulled up the interface, examining each item.

[Pendant of the Mermaid's Lover (SSR)]

[Item Description: *A pendant originally crafted and* intended *to be bestowed upon a human prince, beloved by a mermaid princess. Because of rising tensions between the oceanic merfolk of Lurkulk and the land-based inhabitants of Treshtov, their relationship was deemed taboo. However, seeing the agony of the lovers separated by war, a compassionate merfolk crafter named Gijii took pity on them and crafted an amulet that would allow the two to escape together. Sadly, like the rest of the world, they were swept away by the War of the Gods.* +2 ARC, *Grants the* **Water Breathing** *Ability when worn.*]

[Aquamarine Ender Pearl (SSR)]

[**Item Description:** *An extremely durable and highly conductive pearl capable of channeling immense mana. A product of an extinct species, the clams that once birthed these massive pearls were sadly hunted to extinction. Now a highly sought-after research material, sorcerers and wizards alike clamor to use it in enchanting, staff creation, or various magical trinkets. It has a lovely golden sheen to it. Can also be used as a bludgeoning tool.*]

[Trident of the Nameless Soldier (UR)]

[**Item Description:** *An ornate trident as blue as the ocean that birthed it, entwined with magical golden vines pulsing with power. Last wielded by a human refugee who courageously picked up the fallen weapon to stand against the forces of Yashwa, the God of War. Through his sacrifice, many merfolk were able to escape. Although his name remains unknown, merfolk revere and honor him during their day of remembrance.* **+12 STR, +3 CON, +13 DEX, +5 ARC, + 6 SEN, +5 EGO.** *Merfolk who witness this weapon in your embrace will question their behavior towards you. Confers the* **Blessing of Undine** *when held.*]

"Oh, you've gotta be kidding me," he groaned, looking over the potential rewards. Despite his heart and soul clamoring for the trident's impressive stats and the pearl's future utility, both would be useless so long as the pendant was crucial to his survival.

However long that survival might last remained uncertain. The salty taste and stinging sensation in his eyes indicated he was now in saltwater. And now, without his survival gear, he had no way to distill the saltwater into drinkable water.

"Well... Dying of dehydration is better than drowning," Adam muttered, selecting his reward. "I think."

Plus, I'll need it to search for the ruins... or whatever remains of them...

His interface spat out an amulet, an aquamarine piece of jewelry crafted with what seemed to be metal seaweed twisted into a band, adorned with various crystals Adam recognized from the temple he had been exploring.

He donned the amulet, immediately sensing a peculiar surge of energy as his mana increased, and his body adapted to the item's effects, his system showing the **Water Breathing** skill.

He studied the skill, brow furrowing. To activate the breathing, he'd have to fully inhale water...

Meaning... he'd have to drown himself.

Lovely.

It didn't take long before the boy clicked his teeth, annoyance etched on his face.

Time to test it. He closed his eyes and slipped below the waves, into the water's salty embrace. There he lingered for a moment, floating, mustering the courage to drown himself.

Nothing ventured. Nothing gained!

He parted his lips, and water rushed in, his eyes snapping open as his lungs strained and burned.

Just breathe! Adam forced a breath, his lungs completely filling with salt water.

"UCK! ARGH! ACK!" Despite it all he endured, spasming as bubbles escaped his mouth.

Ah. I guess I misunderstood. Crapbaskets.

This was Adam's last thought, as he started losing consciousness, his eyes rolling to the back of his head.

Suddenly, he inhaled, breathing returning to normal as the amulet around his neck glowed.

"OILY CRHP!" he yelled underwater, his voice muffled by the curtain of blue as his vitality returned.

He began to paddle, stabilizing himself from his downward drift. Blinking to acclimate to the saltwater, it was time to get to work. He swam upwards, attempting to establish a focal point between his current position, the three suns, and anything discernible as a landmass before he began his search.

These next three days would most likely be his last, but he wouldn't go down without at least *trying*, even if the world seemed out to get him. However, as he swam, he noticed something floating in the water—a chest of sorts—making Adam go wide-eyed.

Oh, you've got to be kidding me.

Catpurr 38
The Super Crab

On a cool evening, as delvers and merchants went about their business, Titania sat on a bench in Twilight Plaza. Her hand was extended, offering bird feed to a flock of sparrow jays that routinely visited.

"Here you are," Sehn said as he came up from behind, taking a seat on the marbled furnishing. "Another day of waiting, huh?"

"Nothing better to do," Titania replied. "Once he gets out, he'll need someone to help him."

"As much as I appreciate your enthusiasm, it's been over a week, almost two now," Sehn said, fiddling with the strap of his coffin. "We gotta accept he didn't make it."

Titania sighed, her brow furrowing. "No. He'll make it."

Sehn looked at her, curious about her confidence. "How can you be so sure?"

"Do you remember what Coco said when she met Adam?" the mage asked, making the man purse his lips. " 'In that future, you were way taller.' "

"Oh, c'mon. You know her visions aren't always accurate. Remember when she said I'd die on floor five? Or that we'd have a kid? Nonsense," Sehn dismissed, waving his hand. "Look, I'm here because we've got a new job. Our debts won't pay themselves."

"Yeah, I know."

Sehn placed a hand on her shoulder. "We did all we could. I'll be waiting at the gate. But this is a time-sensitive quest."

"Okay."

Sehn stood up, scratching his head as he walked away. Just as he did so, a brilliant light erupted, illuminating the nearby surroundings.

"The hell?" He turned around, his jaw dropping, mirroring Titania's utter shock as a large blue portal opened up, spilling water across the smooth plaza floor.

Riding the wave of water, a small naked figure wearing what appeared to be a straw hat emerged, hitting the concrete floor and rolling several times before quickly scrambling to his feet.

"Adam!" Titania called out with excitement, waving to the boy as he sprinted towards them.

Sehn narrowed his eyes; something was wrong.

"Adam?" Titania called, this time in confusion, her expression shifting as the naked child approached, face consumed with panic.

"Adam, what's wro—" Titania began, moving to intercept him as he slipped under her embrace before dashing directly into the city.

"CANTTALKRUN!" Adam yelled, his words fading with his tiny fleeing body.

"What?" both asked, bewildered, as they watched Adam streaking naked into the city. Yet their confusion was short-lived as screams, followed by a loud monstrous roar, echoed.

"Oh shit!" Sehn spat, eyes widening, swiftly unslinging his coffin from his back as a massive red crab materialized, its colossal, chitinous legs cracking the plaza floor as it emerged from the massive portal.

"DUNGEON BREAK!" a man yelled, and multiple blasts of mana and skills erupted as dozens adventurers, previously milling about, sprung into action, reacting instantly to the sudden appearance of the Super Crab.

Sehn reached into his coffin, grasping about for a weapon as the numerous eyestalks on the monster began to glow, rendering the crab impervious to the humans' assault.

Crap!

Titania and Sehn separated, dodging as a tidal wave of mana sundered the earth where they had just stood.

In response to the adventurers' attacks, the crab opened fire, its six glowing eyes converging to produce a massive beam of blue energy that began to destroy the city square.

"MY GABBAGES!"

"FORM UP!"

"Alert the watchmen!"

"Decapitate the eyes to stop its assault!"

The adventurers mobilized, a group already forming to deal with the colossal crab while merchants scattered in retreat.

Titania raced forwards, hands glowing with verdant energy, and leaped into the air. However, just before she could strike, the crab vaulted into the air, blatantly disregarding the adventurers—as well as the laws of physics.

It latched onto a building, racing across the massive tower before leaping from building to building, stirring debris as it raced deeper into the city.

The direction?

Adam's frantic flight.

* * *

"Crap, crap, crap, crap, crap!" Adam panted, eyeing the notification on his interface that ticked down.

[Mandatory quest given!]
[SURVIVE! 0:09:15]

[THIEF! You have stolen the Pirate King's treasure! You have been marked for death by Sebastian, the Royal Abyssal Crustacean. He will not stop. He will not rest. Not until either you die, or he does. Should

you lose the Pirate King's treasure within the allotted time, your quest will fail. Survive until divine intervention!]

Everything happened in an instant. The moment he dove and opened the floating chest underwater, grabbing the yellow straw hat, the Super Crab had appeared.

Its massive body, a distant silhouette initially, swiftly closed in with lethal intent aimed at the nekoboy.

Fortunately, a portal had opened up, sucking him through. *Un*fortunately, the crab had tagged along, both riding through a vortex that deposited them back at Vilenciel.

"Oh my stars! A nude child!"

"Halt, boy! Cover yourself!"

Adam ignored these bystanders, and continued streaking through the streets in the nude, a firm grip on his straw hat.

"Ten minutes. That's all I need!" he silently implored in desperation to the heavens above, flinching as a loud explosion resounded.

Involuntarily, he turned his head, eyes widening as the colossal crab bounced from building to building.

"OH, COME ON!" he yelled. "WHY?!"

The crab's eyestalks glowed, unleashing bursts of mana that splattered around its tiny target. Merchant stalls, residences, and even people fell victim as it relentlessly pursued him.

Bastard! Adam gritted his teeth, the screams of bystanders assaulting his ears.

He stopped, darting into an alley, aiming to divert the giant crab away from the pedestrians.

Gah! What street was this?! He glanced about at his surroundings, stopping just in time to avoid the massive claw descending towards him.

"CRAP!" He dove away, landing on his butt as the crustacean's limb snapped and smashed into pavement.

An eye swiveled around, the bulbous stalk lighting up in preparation for the familiar attack.

"**MANA BOLT!**" he yelled, hand outstretched, releasing a magical, cat-shaped bolt of energy. It struck the crab's eye, knocking it away just as it fired.

Debris showered down as he crawled away. He tried to run past, but the claw blocked his path, forcing him back into the retreating crowd.

"Sorry, sorry, sorry, sorry!" Adam repeated, weaving through the fleeing masses.

He banked left, then right, navigating through the people, a bloodcurdling roar resounding, followed by the massive crab landing before him.

It shattered the ground, pincers clamping as its remaining eyes pressed together and began condensing mana.

"Crapbaskets," he muttered, ears folding back as the crab opened fire.

Catpurr 39
Floor One Cleared

"Crapbaskets," he spat as the crab unleashed its attack. He shut his eyes, fully aware that he couldn't dodge, not at this range, not with the overwhelming amount of mana gathering.

I'm going to die to a stupid, oversized crab.

Yet oblivion never arrived. Instead, a massive clang echoed, prompting him to open his eyes.

His jaw dropped as a knight appeared—the woman was clad head to toe in expensive purple armor, standing firm with her enormous golden tower shield raised.

The bulwark intercepted the attack, dispersing the blast widely as she held her ground against the crab.

"NOW!" a gruff voice commanded from within the helmet.

Suddenly, two figures emerged from the nearby rooftop—maids, one with pink hair, the other with blue. Both were wielding massive weapons.

Ravi landed on the crustacean's carapace, slashing with her massive pink greatsword, slicing through the monster's eye stalks and disrupting the beam attack.

In response, the Super Crab convulsed, attempting to shake its uninvited guest. The short woman pivoted her greatsword into the air for an overhead swing.

Sinclair, however, had other ideas. As the giant crab attempted to leap, two large hammers appeared. Hammers that would have looked like ordinary home working tools, if not for their size and the fact that iron chains bound them to Sinclair, who swung them around with ease.

The hammers soared, burying themselves in the crab's rocky shell as it ascended.

Sinclair stomped her feet, cracking the ground as she grabbed the chains and pulled, sending the crab crashing back to the road. Ravi emitted a manic laugh and slashed at the monster's face.

The crab shook violently, slashing with wild abandon as a crack appeared in its shell. Sinclair evaded left and right, occasionally ducking the monster's attempts to free itself from her chains.

Seeing his chance, Adam turned and fled, putting distance between himself and the crab as he watched the spectacle unfold. He'd leave it to the experts. After all, he knew when he was outclassed.

"Cordon off the area! Seal its escape and shield the civilians!" Valentine's voice echoed, capturing Adam's attention as the guild master appeared on a nearby rooftop. Beside her stood Lunafreya, along with Arnold and Silk, the latter two clad in battle gear, joining the fight alongside dozens of soldiers.

Silk's back suddenly opened, revealing a number of mechanical spidery legs. She leapt off the building, rushing past Adam, still clutching her doll. Upon landing, webs shot from her silver appendages, binding and immobilizing the massive crab as it slashed at Sinclair, only to be thwarted by Ravi's oversized sword.

Adam felt guilty about abandoning the maids to deal with the mess he had made, but what exactly was he supposed to do? All his mana blast did was turn its eye stalk red.

Suddenly, he was grabbed, pulled into Titania's arms as she covered him with a cloak.

"Adam!"

"T-Titania?!"

"Oh, thank the Earth Mother, you're alright!" she exclaimed, embracing the boy in her arms. "Let's get you somewhere safe!"

Adam complied, attempting to follow her, but hesitated as a notification hit his screen.

[YOU HAVE BEEN LOCKED ON!]

His eyes widened, mirroring Titania's. She swiftly pulled him behind her as an explosion reverberated.

In the moment he was spun, he saw it—the massive crab, its shell marred with dozens of cracks, spilling blue blood as various weapons protruded from it. Ravi clutched a large, severed claw. However, it wasn't the crab's state that left him in shock; it was its actions. The enemy had somehow broken free of Silk's webs, its body glowing green as it charged through the soldiers, barreling directly towards Adam, indifferent to everything in its pursuit of his life.

Suddenly, something smashed into the crab, sending it careening sideways into a building. A massive crack appeared in its shell, rupturing its protective armor. Yet somehow, despite being covered in injuries with a wooden coffin embedded deep in its shell, the crustacean still staggered forwards. Its remaining claw reached out, snapping towards Titania, who shielded him with her body.

Just before it reached the duo, Sehn descended from above, a golden spear in hand, piercing the monster where its eyestalks once were and pinning it to the ground.

[CON*CA*TULATIONS! You've defeated a great foe!]
[TRIAL ONE CLEARED!]
[*ELI IS PLEASED WITH YOUR INGENUITY OF USING OTHERS*]
[You have earned the recognition of your Patron!]
[Favor of the Gods +1]
[Title Upgrade! Idiot Novice of Eli → The Primordial Eli's Chosen]
[Buff Upgrade! Minor Blessing of Eli → Blessing of Eli!]
[Rolling Rewards...]
[ERROR! Come back later!]
[Time Remaining until next Abyssal Trial: 671:59:54]

Ignoring the notifications, Adam heaved a sigh of relief, his body trembling as it came off its adrenaline high. He pulled the robe tight, his entire body suddenly cold as the straw hat on his head disintegrated abruptly.

Sehn leapt off the crab, his spear dissolving into a flurry of golden particles that wafted towards him, reintegrating into his body.

"Took you long enough," Titania said, her shoulders slumping as a crowd began to gather—soldiers and adventurers eager to get a glimpse of the now-motionless Super Crab. Noticing the boy's ears were fully exposed, Titania acted swiftly, pulling the cloak up towards his head to shield him as the crowd closed in.

"Hey lad, are you okay?" Sehn asked, approaching Adam. The latter opened his mouth to respond, but found himself unable to.

His vision warped, teeth clattering. Then his knees buckled, and Adam unceremoniously lost consciousness.

* * *

As everyone gathered around the child, no one seemed to notice a tiny dot in motion—one with six legs and a small, chitinous shell, scurrying away from the deceased Super Crab. It observed Adam for a moment, watching carefully as they carried him elsewhere, before it took the chance to scurry away into the sewers.

Catpurr 40
Day Back

"HE DID WHAT?! TO *WHAT?!* ELI! ELLLLLLLLLLLLLLLLLLLLLLLLLLLLLLLLLLLLLLLLLLI!"

—The Primordial God Voltrain upon learning of Adam's existence and the loss of Undine's Water Memorial.

* * *

Sunlight streamed through a nearby window, casting an annoyingly warm glow directly into Adam's eyes. His ears twitched, face scrunched up in annoyance as he involuntarily groaned before waking with a sigh.

His eyes fluttered open to the sight of the familiar wooden roof of his bedroom in the Vilenciel Guild Office.

"And here I was hoping it was all just a dream," he muttered, turning over to find himself face to face with Tilith, her colorful hair sprawled on his pillow, drooling.

Adam lay there for a moment, taking in a deep breath.

"Of course."

Slowly moving his leg, he pressed it against her abdomen before swiftly kicking her off his bed.

She landed with a thud, emitting a slight groan that echoed in the room for a moment, before it went silent again.

The boy peered over, frowning with an arched brow as he observed Tilith splayed out on the floor, still sound asleep.

"Huh... Weird."

He lay back down, opening his interface to check his pending notifications while rubbing his new necklace.

[Level Up!]
[Level Up!]
[Level Up!]
[Rewards Available!]
[Time Remaining until next Abyssal Trial: 665:45:24]

Three levels? Adam's brow furrowed. It made sense that he gained so many levels from the crab dying, but now when he thought about it, he wondered why he hadn't gained any experience from blowing up the temple. A hundred thousand crabs had died, which should have easily sent his levels skyrocketing.

The creases in his forehead deepened further.

Maybe it's because I died before I could absorb the experience, he surmised. After all, he *was* at the center of the explosion, in addition to being its cause.

He tapped his screen, pulling up the rewards section. *At least not everything was a bust.*

[Temple of Undine's Reward List!]
[Please select a reward!]
[C Skill: Water Infusion]
[C Skill: Aqua Shot]
[R Skill: Water Shroud]
[R Skill: Water Breathing]
[SR Skill: Waterfall]
[SSR Skill: Summon Morian Crab]
[SSR Ski—

Adam's hand immediately slammed on the interface for the Morian Crab.

[Reward selected! Skill: Summon Morian Crab acquired!]

A tingling sensation coursed through his body, making him involuntarily twitch as his internal mana circuits shifted.

He opened his skills list, a smile playing on his face as he read the skill.

[Summon Morian Crab]

[Skill Description: *Summon a loyal Morian crustacean that will imprint on you upon being called forth. It will follow and defend you, even giving its life if need be. Permanent summon until dispelled. Only one may be active at a time.*

Cooldown: *Three Days* **— 200MP]**

So little mana, too! Adam immediately opened his stat page, swiping hurriedly to get to it with an evil grin on his face, as he imagined unleashing a giant crab upon unsuspecting foes.

BETA SYSTEM v1.03

TITLE: The Primordial Eli's Chosen (+20% Mana recovery, +5 Arcana. Undead Favorability)

NAME: Adam F. Glow

SPECIES: Nekoboy

LEVEL: 8

EXP BAR: 0000/10000

MAIN CLASS: Nekomancer

HP: 140/140

MANA: 185/185

[SEALED FUNCTION]

Free Points: 15
STR: 12
CON: 14
DEX: 12
ARC: 30(37)+5+2 (**EQ**)
SEN: 10
EGO: 10
[RESISTANCES]: Fire (5%)
Buffs: Loved by Undead (unique), Blessing of Eli (unique), Eyes of a Predator V1, Corrupted Blessing of Nyx (unique), Adherent of Death V1, Explosive Renaissance V1
Debuffs: Ha! You Sacrificed Your Stats for a Cat?! V1 (curse), Catsification V1 (curse), Wet (Catsification)
Skills: Animate Bone V1, Irritating Touch V1, Cat Claws V1, Identify V1, Summon Skeleton V1 (++), Mana Bolt V1 (+), Artificial Linguistics {Rigellian}, Genocidal Aura

Catlike eyes widened upon discovering that his title had been upgraded, giving him a passive boost to mana recovery as well as Arcana. He looked at his Con stat and free points, immediately allocating the points.

CON: 14 → 20

ARC: 30 → 36

[GACHA UNLOCKED!]

He let out a low chuckle. However, his amusement was short-lived as he realized his coin was missing.

"Crapbaskets." Adam furrowed his brow. Fortunately, his concern was alleviated when a new interface appeared—an image of a jester holding a box with a counter that showed his available coins.

[Cicero's Gacha Coins x 01]
[Daily attempts left: x 03]
[Tier 1 Box Prize Pool: 24 items]
[View Pool]

An eyebrow arched, as it occurred to him that this was basically a lottery system of some kind. He lifted his hand, attempting to tap on his screen when, out of the blue, a knock at his door distracted him.

"Adam? Are you awake?" called Titania.

He dismissed his system, opening his mouth and telling her he was as he rose from bed.

The door swung open, the green haired woman entered but promptly averted her gaze as she let out a yelp. "ADAM!"

Wide-eyed, he flinched, wondering if he had done something wrong.

"Put some clothes on!" she hissed, turning her back to him and shutting the door.

Oh. Adam looked down, realizing that, aside from the amulet and cloak on his back, he was still nude.

Rolling his eyes at the absurdity of being offended by some nudity, he walked over to a dresser where a heap of fresh clothes lay. A white tunic and black trousers, coupled with a black cloak.

He quickly got dressed, stepping over the unconscious Tilith as he pulled up his hood.

"How are you feeling, Adam?" Titania inquired, scrutinizing the boy with a furrowed brow as he exited the room.

"I'm okay," he replied before finding himself enveloped in a sudden hug.

"Oooooh, I was so worried!" Titania exclaimed, squeezing her charge so hard his body made that irritating squeak it did when he was compressed. Initially tensing at the touch, he attempted to back away, yet for some reason he didn't. In fact, it was oddly comforting to be held by her.

"Oops! Sorry!" Titania apologized, releasing him. Her eyes almost lingered, as if she perceived something different about him. "Are you hungry? Breakfast is almost ready."

His stomach growled in response.

"I'll take that as a yes."

"I suppose I am," he replied.

* * *

Sitting there tearing through a steak in the back of the guild office, Adam couldn't help but wonder why everyone was staring at him. The maids kept a distance, and even Arnold, amidst his cooking duties, was looking directly at him, almost as if expecting him to attack.

"Ahem." Titania cleared her throat, apparently nominated by the staff to address the boy.

He looked up, eyeing the woman who seemed nervous all of a sudden, as she made her way around the table to sit beside him.

"What?" he asked, putting his utensils down.

Titania bit her inner lip before finally asking the question that was on everyone's mind.

"Adam. Who is Eli?"

"What?" he repeated, oblivious to the fact that just above him, suspended over his head, was a visible symbol of a snake devouring itself, flickering with colorful lights, all pointing down at a title that read: [**The Primordial Eli's Chosen**].

Catpurr 41

Catlateral Damage

Adam furrowed his brow, tilting his head with a quizzical expression as Titania explained that his title was on display.

He looked up, his eyes shifting to eye the edges of a neon sign that spelled it out.

OFF! OFF! The boy's expression twisted into an irritated scowl, willing the title to disappear. But the damage had already been done. Now there were too many questions, and answers that the gathered members of the Vilenciel office wanted as they stared at Adam. Coco had informed him that Sehn and Titania were bound by secrecy, with geasses preventing them from discussing it with those unaware of Eli.

However, it seemed the cat was now out of the bag, as Titania seized the opportunity to ask the question she had harbored since leaving the temple.

"I don't know," he replied, returning to his breakfast. "All I know is that he sucks."

At his words, Sehn laughed.

"Don't tell anyone from the church your god sucks," the man advised, apparently the sole individual in the room who seemed uninterested in Adam's title.

"Do you want to talk about what happened in the Tower?" Titania asked, her face filled with worried questions. "Or about the bone portal and the giant crab?"

"Sorry. I don't know anything about it. All I know is that I was in an underwater temple."

Everyone's expressions shifted at that, odd looks appearing as Titania pressed for more details.

"Underwater? Can you elaborate?"

"Uh, sure," Adam replied, before he began regaling them with his underwater escapade. He recounted how he had taken notes, explored, and spent the week harvesting crabs while avoiding the broodmothers. Of course, he omitted the part where his skeleton had done most of the work and the fact that he had exploded the temple. Actually, when he began to think about it, a sinking feeling gnawed at his stomach.

What if I had tried to inspect the item here?

That thought was swiftly dismissed. Adam didn't want the potential deaths of his benefactors weighing on his mind.

Suddenly, as he was in the midst of fabricating how he'd '*found*' the straw hat, a familiar clicking of heels striking hardwood reached his ears.

"Why are you all standing around again?" Valentine whispered, her voice carrying a chill air of disapproval as her glare invaded the room, scattering the maids. Arnold finally attended to the charred slab of meat on his iron stove. "You! Boy! Come with me!"

Adam looked like cornered prey, as the guild master pointed directly at him.

Uh oh. He recognized that tone, the same his master used when he had messed up, or was about to be reprimanded. He shrank into himself, glancing towards Titania, who suddenly found other tasks, notably tying the shoelaces on her laceless boots.

He sighed before getting up, quickly walking with his head down, as Sehn muttered, "Good luck."

***

It didn't take long for Adam to find himself sitting across from Valentine in her office, the two enveloped in a heavy silence that stretched for what felt like an eternity.

He was in trouble, this he knew. The extent of that trouble was less clear, but recalling the Super Crab attack on the city, he glimpsed the gravity of the situation.

"Uhm... I'm sorry?" he offered, but the woman's purple irises remained hard as stone as she glared at him, hands folded in front of her face.

"Super sorry?"

Still no response.

"Who are you?" Valentine inquired, her voice icy, her eyes glowing as they focused on Adam.

[THE GAZE OF TRUTH SEES THROUGH YOUR LIES!]

Crap! This again!

"A child," he immediately replied, a half-truth.

"Who is Eli?"

"I don't know." Another half-truth. He *technically* didn't know. All he had was conjecture.

Valentine narrowed her eyes as the boy began to shiver.

"Are you an other-worlder?"

"No?" he replied, uncertain. Considering the moons were the same, for all he knew, he was still in his home world of Eloisa.

"Did you come from another realm?"

"I don't know," he replied, his eyes blinking rapidly as his body started to sweat.

The woman leaned forwards, scrutinizing her quarry for a moment. "What class do you have?"

Adam's heart skipped a beat. This was it, a question he couldn't trick...

Or maybe he could?

"Nekomancer," he replied, observing the woman's reaction.

Valentine blinked twice rapidly before her head tilted to the side, and her brow furrowed. "Did you say necromancer?"

"No. *Neko*mancer," he clarified, noting her reaction.

"Ne-ko-mancer?" she pronounced, pursing her lips.

"Yes."

"What does the class do?"

The moment of truth.

A moment passed before finally, he felt a compulsion, ordering him to speak.

"Allows me to summon cats," Adam replied, deadpan.

The two sat there for some time, motionless, until finally, Valentine dispelled her ability, burying her head in her hands.

"Do you understand the headache you've caused me?" she exclaimed, abruptly rising and slamming her palms on the wooden desk. "Destroyed property, mass panic, inquisitors breathing down my neck, Clocktower watchmen asking questions, and perhaps worst of all—WORST of all, is that I have NO answers to give them."

"I—"

"Hush, child!" Valentine snapped. "Adding to this mess, you are a demi-child in a city filled with Purists, chosen by an unknown being to participate in the Abyss. An additional god to an already established order of worship," she ranted, her back to the boy, peeking out the velvet curtain to look through the tan-tinted window. "First and foremost, as a member of our guild, our office is partially responsible for your mishap. And as such, must pay restitution on behalf of the damages sustained during the dungeon break. A grand total of two hundred gold."

Adam frowned; he had no idea how much that was in this country's currency. "I don't kn—"

"I'm not finished. And it won't be coming from my pockets, but yours." At her words, Adam's mind went blank.

She began to circle around the desk, hands clasped behind her back. "Do you understand? You will work day in and day out to pay your debt. Seeing as you've survived your modified trial, I have more than enough faith you'll repay us," Valentine, now positioned behind Adam, grasped his shoulders firmly. Leaning down, her breath grazed his ears as she whispered, "*in full*, compensating for the headache, time, and predicaments you've caused me. Do I make myself clear?"

"Y-Yes," he replied, a chilly pressure sending every hair on his body standing.

"Good. Now get out of my office, and make sure you stay covered," Valentine said before releasing him and walking to her desk where stacks of paperwork awaited her. "Titania and Sehn will fill you in on how things are done around here. However, one more problem, and there will be consequences."

With his clearance to leave, Adam wasted no time, donning his hood and swiftly exiting. Or, he tried to, but froze as the guild master snapped her fingers, the sound echoing preternaturally loud.

"Push in your chair. Leave the office cleaner than you found it," Valentine scolded. Adam did as told before fleeing.

***

As the door slammed shut, Valentine's forehead pressed against her desk with a low groan. She delved into a drawer with her free hand, revealing an old tome with a blue cover.

She sighed, sitting upright and flipping to where she left off—a page depicting a warrior emerging from a peculiarly shaped portal. One crafted from a mass of bones, as various skeletal appendages pushed him out.

Catpurr 42
Working for a Living

"Are you saying I can't reward him?"

"That's not what we're saying at all! We're saying you can't steal our bathwater, food, and godly weapons to send down to *some mortal!* It disrupts the balance and systems we have in place! Do you know the damage you could have caused if he had drunk my bathwater?!"

"No, but I am curious to find out."

"NO, ELI! NO! DO *NOT* OPEN THAT PORTAL!"

—Eli and Freya arguing over rewards to include in Adam's System.

* * *

"This is a copper coin, this is a silver coin, and this is a gold coin," Titania explained, arranging the metal currency on a wooden table. "Now, can you tell me the value of each coin?"

Adam glanced down, the pair seated in the bustling lobby of the Adventurers' Guild. People shuffled around as they took jobs, accepted rewards, and loudly carried on discussions, bustling to and fro.

"A copper is a copper. One silver is a hundred coppers, and a gold is two hundred silvers, or twenty thousand coppers," he replied as Sehn appeared.

"Nice, lad. We'll make an adventurer out of you yet. Smart, aren't ya?" Sehn said, placing two pints on the table as he sat. He ruffled the boy's head with one hand while the other slinked towards the gold coin.

It was quickly batted away, as Titania scowled before pocketing the coin within her bra.

"Nice try," she spat, flipping the copper his way before turning back to Adam. "Anyway, as a new adventurer, normally we'd get you started on E-Rank quests. Something soft to start you off."

"But you're a bonafide Abyss Walker now," Sehn butted in, cracking a sly smile. "That's child's stuff; we're bumping you up to play with the big boys."

"Okay?" Adam replied, eyes shifting from the man towards a group of adventurers huddled in the corner of the room, staring at him.

Titania rolled her eyes. "What he means is that we can get you higher paying jobs, better quests, and take you along with us on quests as our journeyman."

"Journeyman?" Adam echoed, noticing that a man kept looking at him as he exited the guild hall.

He didn't know why, but it gave him a bad feeling.

"Our apprentice. We'll take you on jobs with us to earn money and rewards. As an Abyss Walker, all you'll need to do is show them your punched ticket and you'll be more accepted," Titania explained, displaying her ticket before gesturing towards the bulletin board Ruebella was restocking with various fliers. "However, for our first job together, how about you pick something for us?"

"Me?"

"Yup! After all, thanks to the Super Crab destroying our contractor's shop, he can't pay us for what he needs," Sehn said, reclining in his chair and sipping the orange beverage.

"Any quest?" Adam asked as he stood up, eyeing the crowd gathering towards the bulletin board.

"Sure, lad. Just keep it C or below. And nothing too dull, like picking flowers."

"Ignore him," Titania said. "Picking flowers would be perfect for a starting quest."

Adam shuffled his way across the guild hall, passing Sinclair as she cleaned a table, to stand beside Ruebella, who flashed a smile as the crowd around the board parted for their youngest recruit.

He neared it, scanning the sheets of stationary tacked to the walls, when suddenly he frowned.

He turned around, shuffling back towards the pair waiting for him.

"What's wrong?" Titania asked, furrowing her brow as she sipped from her pint.

"I can't read," Adam said, prompting Titania to choke on her drink.

"Huh, that's right. You didn't originally know our language, huh," Sehn remarked, rubbing his chin. "I suppose kids your age would be in school, or studying at the Clocktower. Reading and writing are fundamental skills for any adventurer. It's kind of a moot point taking you out, if you don't even understand how to read a food menu."

"Wait, you said you took notes on the Water Temple," Titania interjected, slamming her pint on the table. "Adam, you know how to read and write, don't you? Just not in our language, right?"

"Uh... Yeah," he replied.

"Can I see your notes?"

Adam hesitated for a moment, then reached into his cloak, pretending to shuffle around underneath it before summoning the journal out of his ring.

Sehn arched a brow, scrutinizing the leather-bound item as he placed it on the table.

"Fascinating," Titania remarked, inspecting Adam's sketches and little notes of each item he had recorded. "Have you ever seen a language like this?"

She presented the notebook to Sehn, who shook his head.

"Ya know, the Clocktower might be willing to compensate you for these notes. They're always interested in other languages," Titania suggested, suddenly excited. "We can even enroll you in some reading classes or such at their library."

At the mention of a library, Adam's ears twitched, his curiosity piqued. "Library?"

"Yes! The Clocktower is an organization of mages and researchers. They possess the largest collection of tomes and magical research notes on the continent."

Adam's heart quickened, his eyes widening as Titania detailed the functions of the organization, ranging from excavations, to research, dungeon delving, and even paying adventurers for materials acquired from the Abyss.

"I also heard they had an index for classes and class paths. But that's just a rumor I've heard," Titania added.

"Let's go."

"Huh?"

"Let's go! I want to go to the Clocktower," Adam declared, slamming his palm on the table. This sounded like the perfect opportunity to learn more about the world.

The two adventurers exchanged glances before turning back to Adam.

"I'm game. Let's do it," Sehn said, lifting his coffin off the floor.

"To the Clocktower it is, then," Titania said, rising from her seat.

* * *

As the trio departed, a dark-haired man clad in a casual white tunic observed them. He waited several moments, allowing Adam and his companions to leave, before rising and exiting through the double doors behind them. He wasn't alone. Several others joined him, forming a group that spilled into the bustling street, their eyes fixed on the departing trio.

"Twilight, Selen, Blueno, Rolo. Pleasure seeing you all here," the agent belonging to the Six God Church said, lighting a small white stick of tobacco using a metal device that produced a small flame. "It's always fun when our respective organizations send us out for a stroll together. So, same deal as usual? Stay out of each other's way, no foul play, and refrain from murdering each other. Assuming, of course, that this is all just data gathering."

"Works for me," grunted Blueno, the dark-haired Merchant Guild Agent, as he folded his arms and walked off, the other spies following suit.

"As long as you stay out of my way," Twilight added, the government agent under a new guise already as he vanished into an alley.

"Ditto," Rolo said, the teenager suddenly vanishing, almost as if he'd teleported.

And finally, Selen. The woman pecked Donny on the cheek before snatching his cigarette.

"I'd hate for a handsome man such as yourself to die from black lung," the Clocktower mage said coyly, teasing Don as she grazed his chin with her fingers before sashaying off.

"I'd wife you up if you'd just join the church," Don teased, as the woman returned, "Never in a thousand lifetimes!"

Don sighed, taking out another stick from his pocket.

Well, Adam. Let's see who you are.

Capturr 43
Clocktower

"Eli."

"Voltrain?"

"Eli!"

"Voltrain!"

"ELI!"

"Oh, you're *angry*."

"ELLLLLLLLLLLLLLLIIIIII!"

***

Standing before a grandiose tower adorned with a clock on its edifice, Adam frowned. The building would have been imposing and magnificent, if not for all of the moss, mold, and crumbling bricks that marred its façade.

"This... Is the Clocktower?" he asked, turning to face Titania, who seemed genuinely excited.

"What? Isn't it amazing? Golden walls, magnificent inscriptions, lovely plants?" she exclaimed, prompting Adam to look around. Instead, he noticed empty garden pots, a cracked paved path, and a row of withered, thorny bushes.

"Uhm... Sure," he responded, quickly looking away as a brief flash of color darting past, catching his eye.

He squinted, blinking a few times, occasionally glimpsing specks of gold fading in and out of existence. A sign of some magic being done? *Huh...*

It became clear Titania was seeing an illusion of some kind, one that didn't affect him. It seemed Sehn saw the same thing as his adventuring companion, since he didn't bother to correct her.

"Shall we?" Titania suggested, walking towards the double doors at the base of the tower.

The trio lingered, waiting for a response. Suddenly, a beam of light descended upon them, as dozens of what appeared to be tiny walking mushrooms of various sizes came hobbling into view.

"Welcome to the Clocktower. How may we be of assistance?" a voice emanated from one of the mushroom creatures. The three largest mushrooms scrambled to stack on top of each other, the one acting as the head swaddled by a large cloak.

"We're here to acquire a quota for some research materials we have, as well as enlisting my nephew in basic reading and writing courses," Titania announced, displaying her wrist adorned with the abyssal ticket.

"We're sorry, we're currently closed right now, and are not accepting new..." the mushroom man began to respond, but trailed off as he noticed Adam. The boy wasn't looking at him; instead, his gaze was fixed on the tiny mushroom people bustling around

Interesting. Adam activated **Identify**, attempting to examine the unfamiliar creatures.

[**Mush Folk**]

[**Monster Description:** *A generally peaceful race of humanoid mushroom-like beings from a distant realm. They come in various colors, each possessing distinct abilities. When threatened, they can communicate via telepathy to create illusions, deterring potential threats. They reproduce asexually and can thrive in various environments, though they prefer damp and warm climates.*]

[**Strengths:** *Illusion Magic, ???, ???, ???*]

[**Weaknesses:** *Highly Flammable, ???, ???, ???, ???*]

Several of the polka-dotted mushroom people looked up, realizing they had been identified, and locked eyes with Adam.

The two groups stared at each other until suddenly, the tiny Mush Folk surrounding the three giant mushrooms in a cloak collectively hopped, fleeing in blind panic. A few of them stumbled into each other as they scrambled out of his golden gaze.

"Ahem! We may have an opening. Come on in," the stack of Mush Folk said, abruptly taking an entirely different tone as the ancient wooden door creaked open.

Titania walked forwards, taking Adam's hand, and entered the main foyer.

Inside a spacious entryway sprawled out before them, far larger than the building's exterior had suggested.

Spatial distortion of some kind, he concluded, taking in the barren walls and the various students milling about.

"Welcome to the Clocktower!" a voice suddenly rang out. Adam's eyes were drawn to a half-naked woman, wearing a wide-brim hat and smoking a pipe.

She floated down the stairs, reclining on her back on a magical cloud, assessing the trio with an air of disdain.

"How may we be of service today?" she asked, flipping over as her emerald eyes flickered towards Adam and the Abyssal ticket on his wrist for a moment, before returning to Titania and Sehn.

"We'd like to enroll my nephew here in reading and writing courses, if those are still available," Titania said, indicating Adam.

The woman looked down, cocking her head as she took a puff from her pipe.

"I heard there were research materials that needed appraisal?" she asked, ignoring the earlier request.

"Oh, yes. Adam?" Titania coaxed.

He held out the journal. Rather than taking it, the woman twisted her hand, and the item floated towards her on a bubble of mana.

She opened the journal, glancing over each page with indifference. "What language is this?"

"It's an encrypted code. Something only I understand," Adam chimed in, drawing those emerald eyes once more.

"Ah. You must be the little boy responsible for the enlarged crustacean attacking our city."

"That... would be me, yes," he replied, and the woman's gaze returned to the drawings and symbols.

"Intelligent enough to create a coded lexicon, but you don't understand our language..."

She closed the book, her expression shifting.

"Sorry, but all of our tutors are taken. We don't have the time to entertain another preten—"

Mid-sentence, she froze, sighing before handing the book back to Adam.

"Show me your ticket."

Adam complied, brandishing his wrist.

"Huh..." She hummed with interest, observing the symbol of the god on the slip. "Fascinating. You're the genuine article."

"Genuine article?" Adam raised a brow.

"Don't worry about it. A slot opened up, and the teacher is requesting to meet in person," the woman said, surprising Adam by her complete one-eighty shift in attitude.

"Oh. Okay! Let's go Adam!" Titania said, beckoning him along, yet she was stopped, a magical barrier barring her path.

"Just the child," the emerald-eyed woman said. With some reluctance, Titania stepped back.

Adam frowned, feeling a bit cautious. However, he still stepped forwards, crossing a threshold into the facility that immediately vaporized him.

Catpurr 44

Nunna Beifong

Adam blinked, finding himself somewhere completely different as he took a step forward. It soon became clear he had been deconstructed and then reconstructed, magically re-atomized in a new location.

Though initially surprised by the sudden teleportation, he recognized the signs of physical displacement as his body reconstituted itself.

The new location seemed to be a library, standing on a large mat surrounded by low-hanging glass partitions on either side, boxing him in.

At first, he thought he had been teleported into a cage or container, but a sign reading "**Please Aim Low**" caught his attention.

Confused, he wondered what that was about when, without warning, he started vomiting, unleashing rainbow-colored puke, painting the entire enclosure. "ARRRRRGH. UUUUUGH!"

This went on for some time, culminating in Adam crawling on all fours, heaving and pleading for the torture to end. This was new, *definitely* new. His constant vomiting was either a symptom of his altered form, or the caster's warped sense of humor. Whichever the case, he'd had enough.

Through his blurry, vomit-stained vision he looked up and spotted a pair of wheels attached to a chair, bare feet perched on a small ledge on the vehicle.

"H-Help... m-me..." he croaked.

Suddenly, the glass cage lit up, blue light spilling out all over, forcing him to close his eyes at the brightness.

A moment passed, then another, before he finally opened his eyes to find that the vomit had magically disappeared.

The glass door swung open, revealing a brunette woman on the wheeled chair.

"Hello, welcome to my library. I'm Librarian Nunna Beifong. Many apologies for the teleportation; some folks can't stomach being rematerialized. May I have your name, please?"

Adam looked up, his eyes focusing on the paraplegic woman wearing a white robe. Her slanted eyes were clear, with the telltale signs of retina deterioration.

She was blind.

"A-Adam," he replied, the strength in his body leaving him, as his cheek struck the enclosure's blue mat.

* * *

Upon waking again, Adam followed the woman into her study, passing rows of books and moss-covered walls. Along the way, various mush folk ran around, and as Adam walked, he noticed their curious gazes becoming panicked when he looked back at them.

A few covered their faces, following the old logic of 'if you can't see it—', while others simply ran away.

"So, you *can* see them."

Startled, the boy quickly turned.

"Yes," he replied, unsure how the woman could know, given her lack of eyesight.

"Then you aren't human."

He froze, realizing the cat was out of the bag.

"I have no idea what you're talking about," he lied through his fangs.

The librarian giggled. "Yes, because humans have rainbow-colored vomit and possess furry ears. The Mush have set up illusionary barriers that specifically prevent *humans* from spotting them,"

Adam reached up, tapping on his head to feel the familiar hood still covering his head.

"Just because I'm blind doesn't mean I don't see," Beifong explained. "The Mush folk here act as my eyes, and we share a special connection. Don't be afraid; your secret is safe. Unlike the Church and the growing Purist movement, we're one of the few safe havens for demi-folk."

As she spoke, a large, six-foot-tall mushroom walked by, interrupting them as it stomped across the tile floor.

"Are you... also?" Adam began to ask, peering closer, to glimpse any gold sparks rising off her form. Perhaps he could ask how she hid her features.

Beifong giggled. "No, I am not. Although I once had a friend that did a lot for me. So the Clocktower remains open to all species. Of course, in secret." Adam didn't fail to pick up on the carefully chosen word '*had*.'

"So, you need language courses? And I hear you have research material?" Beifong inquired, gesturing towards a wooden desk where a yellow Mush folk in a black butler suit stood. "May I see it?"

He handed the notebook to Beifong, who glanced down before shifting her attention back to him.

"On the table, please," she instructed, the yellow mushroom clamoring up her shoulder to perch on her head.

The woman opened the book, examining the symbols, creatures, and various notes he had jotted down.

"Interesting. I recognize some of these characters as Grandzellian."

At the continent's mention, Adam's ears twitched.

"Full Grandzellian. A complete language..." Beifong whispered, her brows furrowing as rapidly shifted through the pages. "I don't recognize these characters."

She turned the book towards him and pointed at a specific set of characters

"That spells fish," Adam explained. Beifong quickly returned to her examination. "How do you know about Grandzellian?"

"We have bits and pieces of this language. Scraps left over from the Elsinorian dark age. I assume you're from Grandzalia."

Adam blinked.

Dark age? Wait, does this mean there are other realm travelers who came from Grandzalia? Does this mean she can help me get back?!

Seeking answers, he responded truthfully, hoping that the woman could help him return to his realm.

"I am. Do you think it's possible for me to return?"

"Possibly. But I don't know. My parents were originally from a realm called Kiyoshi, and they never returned there."

"Wait. You're a realm traveler?!"

"No, my parents were Chosen of Yashwa and were dropped here. Anyway, we have few to no records regarding Grandzalia. The only remnants are a few preserved notes from the Hero Asland, a children's tale, and a couple of scattered notes about realm travelers," Beifong replied, deflating Adam's hopes. This wasn't the response he had wanted, but at least he now knew he wasn't alone. Others *had* come here before him.

"Interesting," Beifong mused. "I can pay you ten gold pieces for this. Additionally, five gold if you provide a translation key and the full alphabet."

He blinked, mentally calculating the money.

One hundred and eighty-five gold remaining. The boy paused, recalculating his debts before shifting priorities. "Are you certain there's nothing about any realm travelers returning?"

"Hmm? There might be notes on such a topic somewhere; you're free to look around provided you handle the materials with care."

Well, at least not everything is a bust. I can study this world, maybe see how people feel about necromancy. With those questions addressed, he decided to look into the main reason he had come here. "What about the language courses?"

"Oh. Yes, I suppose I could also handle that," the librarian said, now fully engrossed in the book. "May I see your abyssal ticket?"

Adam started to lift his wrist, then stopped.

"Ten gold."

"Pardon?"

"Ten gold pieces if you want to see it. It's a valuable item that I can't simply hand over to people."

"Hmm... Fine," Beifong agreed, waving her hand and casually dropping ten gold pieces on him, her gaze never leaving the notes.

He revealed his wrist, the butler mush hopping off the woman's head to inspect the ticket.

"Hmmm... Fascinating," Beifong remarked. "I've seen this symbol before."

At her words, Adam's eyes went wide, yet another revelation hitting him.

"But you probably aren't going to like what I know."

He sighed. *Of course not.*

Catpurr 45

On the Road and an Imminent Threat

Two days had passed since his visit to the Clocktower, and during that time, Adam diligently worked while perched on the back of a moving carriage. He went over his homework while reflecting on what Beifong had said.

Ouroboros, Jormungandr, Kundalini—the serpent of renewal, creation, or death, depending on which story he picked up.

However, it wasn't the serpent's mythology that proved intriguing; rather, it was the implications surrounding the mark itself.

His divine insignia bore the stigma of evil—at least, that's what the Purists and historians of this world believed. This was because it belonged to the antagonist of the Hero Asland's story—a children's fable based on events from ten thousand years ago that laid the foundations for the entire Empire.

This was the current subject of his study.

"Wow. You've been pretty engrossed in that book," Titania commented, peering over the boy's shoulder as he turned a page.

"Yes. I particularly enjoy the part where Hero Asland raised his blade and led the revolution that wiped out ninety percent of demi-humans in this world," Adam replied sardonically, flipping a page featuring an illustration of a man graced with golden wings.

"That was ten thousand years ago. A lot has changed," Titania cheerfully offered.

Without looking up, the nekoboy turned his head towards the woman, and pointed at his hood.

"Right. Well, not *everything*. But still a lot," Titania ceded, taking a seat across from him. "So, how are the language courses coming along?"

"Beifong is an excellent teacher," he replied, turning another page with a *flip*.

"Yes, you're quite fortunate to have the elusive tower master take a personal interest in you. Even more so to secure a personal contract from her," she said, smiling.

"Yup." *Flip.*

Titania, Sehn, and Adam were on a quest to collect vials of a special concoction from an apothecary.

He didn't know what the serum was for; he only knew that Beifong had arranged it, allowing him and his benefactors to receive the payment.

"We're a day out, so we're gonna set up camp here," Sehn announced, pulling the reins to halt the rented brown mules.

Adam sighed, closing his book before rising to help set up camp.

The process was relatively easy, completed within minutes thanks to their proximity to the main road and open field.

* * *

After securing the last pin to bind the wagon in place and ensuring it was fastened, Adam wiped his sweating brow. Wearing the cloak all the time was becoming annoying, especially in the summer heat.

"Lad! You all done there? Let's train a bit before dinner," Sehn called out, brandishing a wooden sword.

Adam sighed. *Right. It* is *about that time.*

For the past two days, Adam and Sehn had been training, to help the boy acclimate to his body and practice using his newfound skills.

Adam walked to the open field where Sehn stood, holding a wooden dagger in one hand and a wooden sword in the other, both weapons glowing with mana.

"Are you ready, kid? You gonna show me that new skill you got from the trial?"

"Not yet."

"Suit yourself. Are you ready?"

Adam huffed, closing his eyes briefly before reopening them.

"Yu—"

Before he could finish his sentence, the older man was before him, smashing down with his wooden sword, eyes focused. Adam's arms came up, the black robes he wore pulling back to reveal leather vambraces on each arm, softening the impact of the blow.

[-5HP]

He winced; the impact, though dulled by his armor, was still painful. Adam attempted to back away, yet Sehn wouldn't let him, doggedly pursuing him with a flurry of slashes, stabs, and thrusts with sword and dagger.

"Tsk!" In response to the onslaught, Adam's claws emerged, his hands enshrouded in mana as they slashed at the weapons, finally blocking Sehn's assault.

The two separated, the nekoboy's hands glowing blue as his mana circulated to his palms. Initially, he had wanted to spend his skill points on his skeleton, but considering he kept ending up naked with no tools or gear on his back, he finally caved and decided to keep an ace up his sleeves.

Or, well, fingers.

One point went to integrating his claws into his mana system, another for **Mana Claws**, while the last one was spent on **Mana Bolt**.

The nekoboy lifted his palm, a cat-shaped energy bolt spinning up almost instantly and firing, striking the dirt.

With its increased AoE from his **Explosive Renaissance** passive, coupled with projectile speed, the attack created a blast of dirt that forced Sehn back and obscured Adam's movements.

Adam shot forwards, using the dust to conceal his counter-attack before crouching low and striking at Sehn.

The man's eyes narrowed, tracking his opponent and slashing downwards, anticipating the claws. Yet, just before his weapon connected, the boy fired a **Mana Bolt** point-blank, aiming at Sehn's chin, forcing him to lean back and reflexively kick.

"Hulp!" Adam exclaimed as Sehn's boot planted itself into his solar plexus.

He flew, rolling across the ground several times before his claws came out, digging into the ground to halt his slide.

Sehn advanced as Adam stood up, the latter raising his palm, willing **Explosive Renaissance** to the maximum and spinning up a **Mana Bolt**.

He fired a volley. Sehn expertly dodged and even deflected a **Mana Bolt** with his wooden sword, slashing at Adam, who grew wide-eyed at the approaching weapon.

Crapbaskets!

Adam raised his hands to defend himself, bracing for the blow. Yet just before it could land, the warrior was suddenly buried into the ground.

"GO EASY!" Titania barked, standing atop her compatriot, who lay prone in the dirt. "How is he supposed to learn if you keep beating him up?!"

"Errrrgh," Sehn moaned, bleeding from his head, smoke rising from his wounds as Titania's boot ground down on his skull.

"Dinner is ready. Are you hungry?" she asked, leaning towards Adam with a gentle smile on her face.

Remind me not to make you angry, the boy thought to himself, nodding as Titania finally stepped off Sehn, who sputtered out a groan.

Suddenly, Adam felt a tingle, a familiar sensation he hadn't felt for a long while. His eyes went wide, his body tensing as a connection was re-established.

"Schrödinger..." he whispered, eyes quivering.

* * *

Elsewhere, in a distant realm.

"We've done it! By Voltrain's blessing, we've managed to isolate the tether!" a scribe in burned robes exclaimed.

Despite the *many* conflagrations caused by a fluffy white cat, a dozen priests scattered unconscious on the ground, and a woman on fire running in a panic, cheers broke out. The clergymen were ecstatic at their success.

Junith stood beside the scribe, hands on her hips, as the necromancer's monster thrashed against the barriers created by dozens of rotating priests to ensnare it.

Several pages approached, hauling away the unconscious priests who were drained of mana, while others stepped in to maintain the barrier.

"So. How long until we can trace it and send someone over?" Junith asked.

"With the relic, we can do so immediately. However, once we activate it, we won't get another shot at it for another year, and it can only send one person at a time," the scribe explained.

"Inform Lord Bishop Alexander," Junith declared, her voice resounding. "The sooner we find the heretic, the sooner we can end this debacle and return to spreading the word of Voltrain to the faithless."

"As you command, Sister." The scribe bowed before turning to the contraption beside the entrapped cat.

Junith gazed at the silver relic; it had come to her and her research team in a dream. Instructions, schematics to construct the contraption, and even the location of the relic—all bestowed by what must have been their benevolent lord personally blessing their crusade and endeavor to eradicate the heretic. Nothing short of divine intervention.

Their god watched over them, sanctifying their mission, and as servants to the primordial being, they would not fail.

"Who shall be chosen to fulfill the task?" Scribe Hayden asked, his singed brow furrowing.

Junith's gauntlet rested on her sword. "I shall go. This time, I *will not* fail to dispose of the coward."

Catpurr 46
Evolution

"Adam? Adam, are you okay?" Titania asked. The boy had suddenly frozen, gazing into the distance as if he'd been struck by some shocking news.

Adam furrowed his brow, body rendered mute. He had a feeling, a *very bad* feeling. For but a fleeting moment, he had sensed Schrödinger, but as swiftly as the feeling arrived, it inexplicably vanished. The feeling of his friend, lost once more.

His heart raced, worry etched on his face as he desperately struggled to focus on the feeling of his companion and what emotions yet lingered.

Fear, anger, and hunger.

Schrödinger was trapped somewhere, angry and starved.

His fists clenched, jaw tightening. Someone was holding his friend captive! And he had a pretty good idea who that someone was.

"Adam? Sweetie, are you alright? You're sweating," Titania asked, finally crouching in front of him. Her hands gently rested on his shoulders, pulling him out of his stupor.

"Huh? Yeah. Sorry, just lost in thought," he mumbled.

"Well, don't think so hard you get an aneurysm," Titania teased, patting the boy on the head.

The duo took a break for dinner, a simple potato stew mixed with carrots, green stalks, and other locally sourced vegetables.

After dinner, Adam approached the cart, using an oil lamp to continue reading and studying the lexicon. He continued well into the night, as Sehn and Titania lay fast asleep in their respective sleeping bags.

Thanks to the wagon's close proximity to the main highway leading out of the city, a modest stream of pedestrians and patrolling guards regularly traversed the road. This provided a level of safety, assuring the trio that their journey to the village was devoid of the usual concerns about monsters or highwaymen.

At least, that was what Sehn had told him.

Still, being cautious had never harmed anyone, especially with his sudden sense of foreboding. Adam just couldn't shake the feeling, and with his anxiety on the rise coupled with the uncertainties surrounding Schrödinger's condition, sleep became scarce.

So, he decided to take a stroll, both to clear his mind, and to use his gacha system.

Considering the past cesium incident, he thought it would be best to get some distance, just in case another explosive surprise awaited him.

Quietly slipping out of his wagon, Adam walked through the cool crisp night, traveling until he reached the treeline, shielded from anyone's prying eyes.

He summoned his interface, activating the gacha function, the jester icon appearing once again.

[Cicero's Gacha Coins x 01]
[Daily attempts left: x 03]
[Tier 1 Box Prize Pool: 24 items]
[View Pool]
—Ring of Holding Upgrade x1 (5/5 Available in Tier 1 Machine)
—Thunder Stone x1 (1/1 Available in Tier 1 Machine)
—Fire Stone x1 (1/1 Available in Tier 1 Machine)
—Shadow Stone x1 (1/1 Available in Tier 1 Machine)
—Divine Catnip x1 (1/1 Available in Tier 1 Machine)
—Evolution Point x1 (2/2 Available in Tier 1 Machine)
—EXP BOOSTER x1
—Cicero's Gacha Coin x2

—HP UP x1 (2/2) Available in Tier 1 Machine)

—MP UP (2/2) Available in Tier 1 Machine)

—Cicero's Gacha Coin x5

—Water Stone (1/1 Available in Tier 1 Machine)

—Flower Stone (1/1 Available in Tier 1 Machine)

—Cape of Shielding (1/1 Available in Tier 1 Machine)

—Pebble of Smiting x1 (1/1 Available in Tier 1 Machine)

—Amulet of Eli x1 (1/1 Available in Tier 1 Machine)

While looking over the contents, nothing stood out as particularly dangerous, except for the various elemental stones. Considering his recent streak of misfortune, he half-expected to receive a thunder stone and then immediately be struck by lightning, or a fire stone and instantly combust, or a water stone and immediately drown. The list was endless, and his distrust of the system grew exponentially with each encounter and quest he'd been forced onto.

However, there were also certain items in the 'machine' that caught Adam's attention, specifically the evolution point, the MP ups, the amulet, and the upgrade for the ring of holding. These were items that could be useful, particularly the MP ups when optimizing the range support strategy.

Once he was free of Sehn and Titania, he could have Skittles draw aggro while he focused on sniping enemies from afar. Given the increased firing speed and range of effect, what he *really* needed now was more MP, especially if his skeleton were to be destroyed mid-combat, or if he wished to summon his crab—a skill he still needed to test.

Though Sehn had asked him about his trial clear rewards, Adam felt it was better to keep at least one secret to himself. It wasn't that he didn't trust the man, but rather that he wanted to surprise him, and pay the warrior back for all the pain he had endured during their 'teachings.'

"Right, let's see what I get," he sighed, tapping the jester icon. Immediately, a floating translucent box materialized, showcasing items that rapidly changed with each half-second, each flicker displaying a new item, *TOUCH!* flashing brightly below.

Adam drew in the cool night air, holding it in his lungs for a moment before pressing the glowing red letters, a sense of dread and anxiety descending on him.

[DING!]
[Item obtained! Evolution Point x1! ½ Remaining within Tier One Machine!]
[Please select an Evolutionary upgrade!]

Adam blinked, his system proudly displaying the point.
Huh... It looks like the gods are finally smiling upon me, he thought, realizing he had actually gotten something useful as the options were displayed.

[Cat Tail Module]
[Enhanced Muscular Ligature]
[Reflex Sensitivity Tuning]
[Ocular Sharpening]
[Lightweight Body Optimization]
[Bone Density Upgrade]
[Healing Factor Boost]
[Sound Perception Tuning]
[Smell Refinement]
[SEALED UNTIL 0/5 Improvements are selected!]

"Interesting..." he hummed, realizing that the system granted him the ability to upgrade his body physically. That is... *evolve.*

He perused the list, noting **Healing Factor Boost, Reflex Sensitivity Tuning,** and **Ocular Sharpening** as the most significant choices. He wasn't quite sure what he would do with a tail, considering he already had impeccable balance when he wasn't being kicked around or abruptly teleported. Other options seemed to be more detrimental than helpful.

At least when it came to being able to explain any changes or new abilities to his companions.

From his brief stint at the Clocktower and conversations with Beifong, she had no knowledge of a gacha system, let alone who 'Cicero' was. This implied that his system was different from others, and had additional functions.

Hmm... This is probably going to hurt isn't it? he mused, making his choice.

[Reflex Sensitivity Tuning selected!]

Instantly, his muscles began to contract, sensory neurons firing off as his entire body emitted steam, cooking from the inside out.

Oh... This was a bad idea, he had the time to think before he screamed. His body aflame with pain, he collapsed to his knees, every fiber of his being *itching* as if he had been bitten a thousand times by bloatflies.

"Ha! HAHAHA!" Adam erupted into laughter, the pain transforming his screams of agony into twisted fits of deranged laughter, tears streaming from his eyes.

"Adam?! Adam!" Titania's voice called, but despite hearing them, he could only respond with another pained fit of laughter before crumpling onto the forest floor.

* * *

Elsewhere, in a distant realm.

"Are you ready, Sister?"

"I am," Junith replied solemnly, standing before Bishop Alexander as a large crowd watched reverently

"Then, by the ministry of Voltrain, by the will of the Primordial One, by the grace of the Most Luminous. Let us pray."

At the Bishop's words, the assembly of robed figures immediately knelt, ceremonial knights in white flanking the hall, clacking their weapons together. Junith knelt and began to pray.

"My faith is my blade. My faith is my armor. My faith is my soul. In your name, I shall know no corruption, I shall know no defeat. Lord Voltrain, I beg thee for grace. Teach this humble shell patience. Teach this shell humility. Teach this shell the knowledge of thine enemies, so that we may bring thy guiding light to the unilluminated. O lord, this I pray. Bless your servant," Junith finished, standing with her silver sword in hand as the scribes began to activate the relic, causing the creature they had entrapped to meow piteously.

"Go, child. You are blessed with strength, courage, and the spirit of our lord. But be warned, your foreign presence and strength may provoke a reaction in the planar field. Ensure you strike true and swift."

"I understand, your grace," Junith replied, tempering her soul.

"Good. We will bring you back in a year's time," Bishop Alexander said as he placed a hand on her chest and drew the symbol of Voltrain. "Go. Go now, and exterminate the heretical, the foul, and the unclean!"

A portal spun open. Junith squinted as mana fluctuations created sparks, striking at the cathedral walls with vicious fury, causing several enchantments to shatter.

The necromancer's cat let out a wail, breathing fire against its bubble as the relic spun and shot a beam of mana towards it, establishing a connection with the portal, and subsequently, their target.

Donning her white plumed helmet, Junith smiled, the visor descending as she walked towards the portal.

Catpurr 47

Agent 47

Adam awoke beneath an unfamiliar ceiling. His eyes fluttered, glancing around to see a room filled with flowers, incense, and various golden statuettes. Removing the soft, green blanket covering him, he stepped onto the cool, wooden floor.

Hmmm... We must have reached the village, he surmised, absorbing his surroundings while pulling on his leather boots. *Weird.*

His gaze fell on the statuettes—a pure bronze one of an obese man smiling, and another resembling a cat with an arm bobbing up and down via some clever internal mechanics.

Standing up, he walked towards the cat statue, eyes tracking the bobbing paw. The nekoboy raised his hand and tapped the statue's appendage repeatedly, making it bob faster.

This continued for a solid few seconds until a door slamming shut drew his attention, head rapidly turning towards the source of the sound.

Glancing back at the statue, he resisted the temptation to tap it again, managing to tear himself away. Beyond the bedroom door he found the foyer of a homely cabin.

"Hello?" he called out, tightening the hood around his head as he scanned the log cabin. The sharp scent of mint filled the air, plants and wooden furniture decorating the homey entryway.

With no response, Adam decided to investigate, exploring the kitchen, other vacant rooms, and an indoor outhouse before concluding that he was alone.

He sighed, dreading what needed to be done. With no other choice, he shuffled back to the main foyer, extending his hand.

Grimacing, he mustered his courage, clenching his jaw as he placed his hand on the doorknob and turned it, revealing harsh sunlight that immediately blinded his senses.

"ARRRRRGH!" Adam screeched, the scorching rays of light searing his retinas, making him cry out in overwhelming agony. "*WHY* MUST THE SUN KEEP RISING?!"

"Adam!" Titania's familiar voice called out, as Sehn beckoned, "Over here!" Beneath both voices was an elderly man's chuckling.

Adam shuffled across the dirt ground, blinking as he tried to adjust to the outside world and the sensation of people moving about in the village.

"Ohoho, not a morning person, are we?" an elderly man wearing a sunhat remarked, narrow eyes settling on the groaning boy making his way through the vineyard and trimmed hedges.

"Daylight was a mistake," he announced, sweltering from the sun's oppressive heat on his hood.

First thing I'm going to do when I can is find a cooling enchantment. Adam grimaced, gaze shifting to the man's rough and scarred hands squeezing citrus fruits into a pitcher.

"Ho, but without light, how would we be able to see the various wonders of the universe?" the old man countered.

"Dark Vision," Adam deadpanned, tugging at his tunic.

"Even Dark Vision requires light," the elder corrected, his tone still jovial but reminiscent of an instructor's. "The skill produces a tiny source of light on an infrared scale that allows us to see when our eyes are modified by the skill usage."

Adam squinted, immediately alarmed at the old man mixing powders and sugars into the large pitcher. He was intelligent and knowledgeable, far more than what one might initially perceive. Clearly someone to exercise caution around.

"So, did we get what we came for?" Adam asked, disinterested in the lesson and eager to return to the city to delve further into the Clocktower archives.

"You're watching the elder make the concoction now," Titania said, observing as the man poured the contents of his creation into three glass containers.

"Thank you, Elder Maxxson."

"Thanks."

Titania and Sehn spoke in unison, both turning to look at Adam.

"Oh. Right. Thanks?" he said as the elderly man handed him a glass of squeezed juice.

"Here's to a fresh crop," Elder Maxxson said, downing his own cup.

"To a fresh crop," echoed Titania and Sehn, drinking the cool beverage. Adam, not wanting to appear rude, went to follow suit but hesitated when the scent of the drink reached his nose.

Something was wrong, but he couldn't quite place it.

Examining the drink and then the ingredients, Adam realized that his innate senses were warning him of danger. The drink was citric, and from what he knew of cats, citrus was fatal to them.

Maybe it's fatal to me as well... Come to think of it, I felt something similar with the chocolate bar Arnold fed me...

Cautiously watching as the three downed their glasses with closed eyes and refreshed glee, Adam tossed the contents of his cup over his shoulder, directly into a nearby bush, to avoid arousing suspicion and everyone's ire.

"Wow, that's really good," Titania said, inspecting the yellow drink. "So, when do you think you'll have the rest of the cases by?"

"Tomorrow at best. Our juicer is an older industry model," Maxxson replied, taking Adam's cup. "Until then, you're free to look around our village, or stay another night in my residence. We have a number of new shops opening up, and an enchanter in town, if you're interested in magic gear."

Catlike ears twitched at the mention of an 'enchanter.'

"Thank you, Elder. We appreciate it," Titania said, bowing to the man as Sehn lazily dug in his ear. She elbowed him, making him clutch his side before thanking the man as well.

"Thank you," Adam chimed in, and the three walked off towards the bustling village.

* * *

Finding a small noodle shop nestled on the side of the road, Adam and his pair of chaperones were served by an elderly man named Ichiraku, donning a full white cook's outfit.

"So, are you okay?" Titania asked, turning to him as she placed several coppers on the table to cover their meal of hot noodles, called "ramen."

"Hey, what about my meal?" Sehn asked, noticing that the woman had paid enough for *two* meals, not three.

"You've got working hands and feet. Get a quest," Titania shot back, prompting her cohort to grumble about unfair treatment. "So how are you feeling? Are you okay? You had us worried when we heard you screaming, only to find you passed out."

"Oh... that?" Adam said, taking a moment to think. "I saw a bug."

"A bug?"

"Yes," he replied deadpan, doubling down on perhaps the worst lie he'd ever told. Not that it was *malicious* in any way, but because it was just... bad.

"Hmmm, okay," Titania replied, turning her attention back to her meal.

That's it? Okay? He had to take a moment to reconcile that the woman was either extremely naive, or just didn't care. Fortunately, she was neither, just patient, as the next words that came out her mouth lent credence to her virtue.

"You'll tell us the truth when you're ready," Titania added, still focusing on her food.

At her words, Adam's jaw subconsciously clenched. The trio ate in silence for a while, before the boy opened his mouth to mutter, "Thanks."

He wasn't particularly *happy* lying, but he could never be too careful. Plus, what they didn't know couldn't hurt them, in case anyone captured or tortured them for information. The Duke of Volbrook had once done such to several farmers who had given Adam shelter, after he'd dispersed a monster wave.

Of course, Adam had tracked the man down and turned him into a frog, although that had been *after* he lost his temper.

"Man, it's hot…" he sighed to himself, staring at his steaming soup. He got up from the table, setting down a couple of coppers Beifong had lent him for incidentals, before he turned and left.

"Hmm? Where're you going?"

"Out for a walk. I want to explore the town a bit," he said, walking off.

"W-Wait! We'll go with you!"

"No, I'm fine. I kinda want to be alone right now," he replied, hoping she'd take the hint. He at least wanted to check out the enchanter and maybe get a gift for the duo using the coins he had.

Sehn raised a hand, stopping Titania, who was leaning to stand up. "Sometimes a man needs his personal space. Besides, you can take care of yourself, can't ya, kid?"

"Yeah," Adam replied. "I'll meet you guys back at the elder's house before it gets too dark."

Titania pouted, relenting with sagging shoulders.

"Fine. But be careful," she said before leaning in to whisper, "and keep your ears covered."

"Yup, got it," Adam replied, walking off, much to the reluctance of a worried Titania.

* * *

Elsewhere, at the same time.

In the woods at the outskirts of the large village Adam had gone to explore, a spark appeared in the air. It grew to become a tear, that quickly transformed into a golden sphere of magical energy.

Out came a foot, then an armored hand, followed finally by a woman in gold-plated holy armor, brandishing a silver sword, unbridled fury in her eyes.

Catpurr 48

A Nice Thing

Walking through the village, Adam did his best to stick to the shade. By his estimate, it was roughly a hundred degrees, sunny, with little to no cloud coverage and scorching heat that made his leather armor cling to his body.

"Uuugh," he groaned, leaning against a nearby wooden building roofed with red shingles. "This sucks..."

He took a deep breath, before pressing on, occasionally stopping to ask for directions from people who gave him odd looks, clearly wondering why a child would be covered up with armor and a cloak in such hot weather. Their instructions frequently led to areas marred with craters in the ground, singed wood, and the occasional burned shell of a home.

It was only after the fourth attempt at asking for directions that Adam managed to pinpoint the enchanter's supposed location. However, what he learned filled him with deep apprehension.

"The enchanter? Oh... Did no one tell you?" a man answered, pity touching his expression when he heard the boy's query.

"Tell me what?"

"He was kicked out of the village this morning for blowing up another tree, and being a general nuisance."

Terribly inconvenient. And yet it *did* explain all the splinters and craters dotting the village...

"Well, do you know where he is? I kinda need his services," Adam asked. The man seemed apprehensive at first, but was much quicker to point him in the right direction once offered a silver coin.

Finally, after roughly an hour of trekking, Adam found what he was looking for at the edge of town—or rather, he heard it, first. A bearded man stood before a small, rickety cart, blowing random things up with explosion magic and fireballs.

The boy grimaced, observing the mage draped in a black robe, wearing a skull cap with what appeared to be goat horns affixed to either side of his temple.

At one point, the enchanter lifted his staff—a wooden totem with a glowing inscription that read "**Taste the sun**"—and shot a gout of flames from the head of his staff, smiling with glee as he observed his handiwork.

Okay, maybe I'll just get Titania and Sehn a nice pair of matching bird skulls or something, Adam mused, backing away from what looked like a potential catastrophe. His heart stopped when he turned to leave faster, and found himself face to face with the very man he had tried to flee.

"Greetings! Welcome to my shop, young adventurer! May I have the pleasure of knowing your name!" the enchanter proclaimed, all smiles despite the dagger in Adam's hand, now pressed against his throat.

"Adam," he replied, his eyes dilating as he focused on the threat in front of him. He hadn't seen the man move; Nyx, he hadn't even felt the telltale signs of teleportation! He was a threat, in more ways than one. Not just because of his manic pyromancy, but also because Adam had reacted before registering his movement.

"And you are?" he retorted, trying not to lose his nerve.

Maybe I shouldn't have come alone.

"Oh... There are some who call me..." The man paused, his crazed, orange eyes darting to the side as if he had forgotten his name, and was trying to think of a reply. "Tim."

"Tim?" Adam arched an eyebrow. The enchanter was still uncomfortably close, before abruptly spinning, nicking his neck in the process as he pointed his staff to a nearby rock.

"YES! TIM THE ENCHANTER!" Suddenly, a bolt of lightning struck the rock, pulverizing it into tiny fragments and causing Adam to flinch at the unexpected theatrics. "HERE FOR ALL YOUR ENCHANTMENT NEEDS!"

The boy took a step back, his lips pressed together as the man continued to laugh maniacally, despite bleeding profusely from the cut on his neck.

"I think… I'll just get a nice skull or something for my friends," he said, walking away while still keeping a wary eye on the man.

Suddenly, the man vanished, reappearing behind Adam with a skull in his hands.

"Skulls? I have skulls! Boar skulls, riddit skulls, felinoids, goblins, tryks, T-Rexes, and pixies!"

Adam's eyes widened as the man approached him with an armful of assorted skulls, a truly massive apex predator skull landing nearby with a *thud*.

"Uh… No thanks," he replied, shifting uncomfortably, only for the enchanter to materialize in front of him again.

"Not to your taste?! I have human skulls too!" Tim shouted, dropping the collection of bones and proudly displaying a human skull in his leathery, liver-spotted hands, still adorned with a protruding arrow. "Please! Please just buy something. I'm poor!" Tim pleaded, falling to his knees and clutching the hem of his reluctant customer's cloak, tears mingling with the green snot dribbling from his nose.

Adam pursed his lips. Even for *him* this was weird. Wisest thing to do was to walk away.

"I'll give you a discount!"

At the man's words, Adam froze.

"Why didn't you say so?" he said, brandishing a smile as he turned his head. "I'll be happy to buy something from you."

* * *

Standing before the enchanter's cart, Adam browsed through a catalog of items.

To his surprise, it was meticulously detailed, with hundreds, maybe even a thousand entries illustrated on each yellowed page. The only problem lay in the fact that most of the items seemed utterly useless.

Permanently soggy socks, a regenerating chew toy, a bag of moaning, blindfold of blinding—just a few of the offerings that served no purpose other than to be gimmicks.

"Remember, one item per person, per visit. But since you're here for three people and stacking the discount, I'll allow you to choose something for your friends," Tim reminded Adam, the nekoboy's brow furrowing slightly.

"Do you have anything that can help me maintain anonymity while regulating my body temperature?"

He grinned from behind the counter of his cart which, much to Adam's dismay, was black. Not the color, but literal, pitch darkness. The only visible thing behind the wagon was Tim himself.

"I might have something, though I'll have to ask if you can afford it."

"Tell me the price," Adam said, rubbing the ring that held his gold.

Tim's gaze briefly flickered down to the ring, a faint smirk playing on his lips—a gesture that immediately put Adam on edge.

Had he identified the ring? Did he recognize what it was? But the enchanter showed no interest in the item beyond his smile.

"Fifty gold for this," Tim stated, placing a black item on his counter. "It won't regulate body temperature, but it'll surely mask yourself."

Fifty?! Adam narrowed his eyes, scrutinizing the half-mask resting on the counter.

Inspect.

[The Trickster's Persona (SSR)]

[**Item Description:** *A half-mask once worn by a man falsely accused. With this mask, he brought corruption to light and helped to reform society for the better despite his unfair treatment. Unfortunately, a bus would strike him down, sending him to a distant realm. When worn, this mask changes in accordance with its bearer's persona, shifting to obscure the wearer by way of illusions and distorting perception to* alter *their face as needed.* **10 EGO Minimum Required, +3 EGO,** *Soul Bound Upon Equipped. Regalian Item. ???, ???*]

Regalian?

While this item didn't have cooling functions, it certainly seemed to fit his needs. However the mischievous smile on the pyromaniac's face, coupled with the hidden functions, made him wary. It felt almost as if he were bargaining with a devil.

"I can't afford this," Adam said, his expression souring.

"Ah, of course! A discount, then, for a first time buyer!" His smile widened, untrimmed beard parting to reveal unnaturally white teeth. "Twenty gold!"

A sixty percent discount.

Adam quickly did the math.

Unfortunately, that would still be most of his money. He sighed. While he wanted the item, he also had debts to repay, not to mention gifts for Titania and Sehn.

What's one more day of sweltering heat? he rationalized, lying to himself that he was okay. "Sorry, but it's still too much for me."

"Pity," the merchant remarked, a glint in his eye. "If you want it in the future, simply present this card to a man bearing a matching emblem."

He handed the boy a black card, adorned with a white handprint and the words 'Black Hand' inscribed across it.

Ah... A black market organization. Adam was quite familiar with such shady underworld organizations. After all, in his previous life, the black market had been his primary source of information, along with food and treats for Schrödinger.

Come to think of it, the agent who fed me the intel on the Eye of Eli was also from the black market.

Adam frowned, the memory still fresh in his mind. Then he reopened Tim the Enchanter's catalog with a sigh, this time searching for gifts suitable for Sehn and Titania.

Catpurr 49

Junith the Luminous Knight

Sweltering under the summer sun, Adam retraced his steps, balancing an armful of books, a cooling stone now wrapped against his forehead.

After buying two gifts for Sehn and Titania, at the low, low cost of *one* gold, Adam had wandered through the town, buying items that he thought could be helpful.

In his hands he held three books: a book on Rigellian history featuring a detailed map of the land, a monster bestiary, and a herbology book detailing various plants and their usages. Sadly, while Beifong was an excellent teacher, it was against Clocktower policy to allow research materials to leave the building. This meant that Adam had to buy his own books, if he wanted to study or take notes.

Navigating the streets lined with red-shingled, wooden buildings, Adam opened the history book. The world faded away as he walked and read, his focus completely on the book in his hand.

People hurried by, some shouting, others engaged in lively conversation, but he remained lost in his reading. Despite the increasing commotion, he remained oblivious to his surroundings, until—

"HIDING A HERETIC IS PUNISHABLE BY DEATH!"

He froze, his heart skipping a beat as the words, spoken in Grandzellian rather than Rigellian, jolted him back to reality.

Huh? Blinking in confusion, he looked up to see a paladin, covered in gore, brandishing a gleaming, silver blade at the growing crowd.

"You've..." The unexpected sight of Junith standing before him stunned him. She turned, her bloodshot eyes locking onto his.

For a moment, they simply stared in silence. Junith's expression twisted with confusion and disbelief, her jaw hanging agape.

But the moment passed swiftly. Recognition dawned on her face, quickly replaced by fury as flames flickered along the length of her blade.

Oh, shit.

Adam took off and ran.

Seriously?! Of all the people! He grimaced, darting into an alleyway and abandoning his books. His heart raced in his chest as a torrent of questions flooded his mind.

How did she get here? *Why* was she here? How would he deal with her without his powers?!

His mind raced as he sprinted, pushing aside his questions for the moment. Approaching the Apothecary's vineyard, he spotted Sehn and Titania engrossed in hand-to-hand combat, surrounded by cheering children.

"WE GOTTA GO! WE GOTTA GO!" Adam yelled, his panic evident as he flailed his arms wildly, his hood slipping off to reveal his distinctive ears.

Startled by their friend's frantic behavior, Sehn turned, only to be struck in the face by a glowing green fist.

"What's going on?!" Titania demanded, rushing towards Adam as Sehn staggered back, temporarily stunned.

Suddenly, a beam of energy broke the quiet peace of the village, accompanied by a familiar, bloodthirsty scream.

"AAAAAADDAAAAM!"

"We have to leave now!" Adam repeated urgently, his senses tingling as he spun around, only to be met by a gleaming blade.

Oh SHI—

CLANG!

The clash of metal echoed as Adam instinctively defended himself, the force of the collision sending him tumbling backwards, caught just in time by Titania.

They hit the ground, rolling to a stop as Adam opened his eyes, stunned by the unfolding chaos.

Sehn rose to his feet, blocking Junith's relentless attacks with his coffin. His feet dug trenches into the earth.

"HERETIC!" Junith's scream pierced the air as she propelled herself off the coffin, creating distance to unleash a torrent of golden mana blasting from her raised sword.

Sehn's eyes widened in anticipation of the impending attack. With a swift pivot, his coffin opened, revealing a metal sword that he deftly wielded, intercepting Junith's onslaught.

"GUH!" Sehn grunted under the strain, channeling all his strength to redirect the energy blast skyward.

Junith stood firm, her gaze fixed on Adam, sending shivers down his spine.

"Adam..." Titania's voice was tender as she briefly embraced him, before letting him go. "Run."

He ran.

"ADAAAM!" Junith's enraged cry echoed behind him, as she pursued relentlessly.

* * *

Shit. Sehn's breath came in ragged gasps as he tightly clenched his cracked blade. Turning to Titania, who nodded in silent understanding, he knew they couldn't let Junith harm their youngest guild member.

This was beyond absurd. Sehn had *never* encountered someone of Junith's caliber within the Purists' ranks. But one thing was clear—she was determined to kill his charge.

"Not on my watch," he muttered to himself, crouching low.

"MAAADA!" the paladin yelled, her power propelling her towards the fleeing Adam.

Sehn sprang into action, body radiating with energy as he intercepted the charging woman. Shining blade met shining blade in a clash of raw strength.

His sword shattered under the pressure of their clash, unable to endure the force of their combined mana. Yet, undeterred by the loss of his weapon, Sehn maintained his focus as the woman aimed another strike, this time targeting his throat.

With a deft movement backwards, he narrowly evaded the blade before launching into a series of agile dodges, barely avoiding the woman's expertly executed slashes and thrusts.

Sehn gritted his teeth. Every fiber of his being was focused on evading her onslaught. Thankfully, Titania was by his side, providing support with elemental blasts from her fists.

But the druid's attacks did nothing. The paladin spun, kicking Sehn away as she charged right for Titania.

"AH!" Titania cried as the paladin's blade sank into her shoulder—and kept going. Despite the pain, she fought back, pressing her glowing hands against the silver sword. She needed to stop it from severing her arm completely.

Seeing his companion bleeding, a red haze clouded Sehn's vision. It wasn't metaphorical—around his body, a crimson aura flared.

"TITANIA!" Sehn's roar echoed with primal rage as he propelled himself off the ground, summoning and hurling his coffin at the paladin. She casually knocked it away.

"BASTARD! AWAY FROM HER!" he bellowed, eyes ablaze with fury as he clashed with the paladin once more. With a resounding clap of his hands, a divine blessing appeared in the form of a glowing spear, the only weapon capable of withstanding the force behind the woman's relentless attacks.

"Uoy era desselb yb dog. Tub yna ohw dluow retlehs a citereh si a citereh, sevlesmeht," the woman said coldly, contrasting their fierce blows. Sparks crackled around Sehn's divine spear as it clashed against the woman's blade.

Tsk! What is that sword made of?! Sehn grimaced, a realization dawning on him. *Wait, I recognize that language!*

It was the same language Adam had been screaming when they found him. The warrior narrowed his eyes.

But Sehn didn't have time to dwell on his revelation. A sword filled his view, prompting him to spin his spear upwards in an attempt to skewer the woman's head.

She dodged with the agility of a seasoned veteran, her head leaning to the left, causing Sehn to frown as she closed the distance.

Drawing on his experience as a soldier, he expertly dodged her silver sword by mere millimeters, dispelling his spear as she darted inside his guard. He ducked, evading a sideways cleave before popping back, cracking the earth as he countered with a powerful punch.

"Oh, shit," Sehn muttered as his glowing uppercut landed, yet the impact only made the paladin take a single step back, glaring down at him with purple irises radiating power.

"Enogeb. I erit fo siht," she spat.

Sehn backed away, attempting to create distance between himself and the woman as he summoned his coffin. But his wrist was caught by her, followed by a sickening *crack* that made him yelp, even despite his high pain tolerance.

Sehn's wrist snapped, and as he moved to strike the paladin with his other hand, a blade pierced his gut.

"Ah, *shit*," he grunted, strength rapidly draining as the blade sapped his energy.

"SEHN!" he heard Adam cry.

Catpurr 50

Junith vs the Silver Swordsman

Adam ran, turning his back on his benefactors and fleeing for his life, knowing he was completely outmatched. But with every step he took, he clenched his teeth, feeling the weight of his heart dragging down his feet.

I have to go back.

He knew it was foolish, but he couldn't, not for the life of him, leave the pair to deal with his mess alone.

Fighting against every survival instinct he had, he turned back towards the sounds of clashes and blows.

Racing out of the bushes, he came face to face with Junith, her blade gore-slick, protruding from Sehn's gut.

"SEHN!" he cried out, panic coursing through his body. He watched helplessly as his benefactor tried to retaliate, only for his dagger to catch on Junith's inner armor. Her gaze shifted to Adam as the sound of his voice pierced the chaos. Carelessly her bloodied blade exited Sehn, before she shoved him aside, leaving him to crumple in a motionless heap.

Nonononononono! Adam's eyes dilated, absorbing the scene before him. Both Titania and Sehn lay bleeding out onto the gravel of the vineyard.

What have I done! What have I done?! His teeth ground together as his jaw clenched, fury surging through his veins as he did something incredibly foolish. He charged at the paladin.

"Cute," Junith remarked as Adam unleashed a barrage of energy bolts at her head, all of which she casually deflected with a smile. "But utterly futile."

[-50 HP]

"GAH!" he gasped, feeling the woman's boot slam into his tiny frame, sending him skidding across the ground. His chest squeaked involuntarily from the impact, as the gravel scored countless cuts and bruises across his body.

Finally landing on his stomach, he struggled to move, his entire being seizing from the pain, lungs struggling for air.

Rib. Maybe two. Three? Crack in solar plexus? Clavicle fracture? The diagnosis came automatically, even as his body lay racked with pain as he retched rainbow colored spew.

[Pain Tolerance Lvl 1 acquired! Reduce the effects of pain by 20%]

Immediate relief followed, too quickly cut short as the sudden crunch of boots drew his attention upwards. Above him loomed the paladin, smiling from ear to ear with glee as she held her sword to his Adam's apple.

"You have no idea how long I've waited for this," Junith said, kicking the nekoboy onto his back, slowly lifting the sword aloft. Adam mustered his strength, grabbing a handful of nearby sand and throwing it at the woman in a desperate bid to save himself. She only grinned in response. "Shame I can only kill you once. Any last words?"

This is the end, was his only thought as his vision grew hazy.

"Just... tell me one thing. Please," he choked. "Is Schrödinger okay?"

Junith furrowed her brow. "Who?"

"My... cat," Adam mumbled, every inhale stabbing needles into his damaged diaphragm

Junith blinked.

"Not for much longer. Once I deal with you, I'll return to deal with your abominable feline." She placed a foot on his chest, making him yelp.

"Take solace in the fact that very soon, you, and all others that follow you, will *burn* in the glory of Voltrain's light."

The blade rose, glinting in the sunlight. "Goodbye Adam."

"Hello. Would you—" Suddenly the old apothecary was standing beside Junith, tapping on her shoulder. She spun, interrupting the old man with a swing of her blade. Surprising both Adam and Junith, a thin rapier calmly turned it aside "—kindly refrain from damaging my gravel path? The nice Es'landers boy just finished setting it up."

The old man's squinted eyes opened slightly. "*While I'm asking nicely.*"

"DIE, SCUM!" Junith roared, her mouth opening to unleash a violent blast of golden mana that pulverized the earth. The apothecary leapt back, slashing the air and creating a barrier that dispersed the attack, before sucking in the ambient mana with a *whoosh*.

"How rude," the elder said, suddenly striking a pose, weapon held aloft, diagonally pointed towards Junith.

"ANY WHO WOULD HARBOR HERESY SHALL BE JUDGED UPON THINE ALTAR!" Junith shouted. She pushed off the ground with an eruption of power.

With the paladin distracted, Adam wasted no time. Despite the fervent wish of his every cell to lay down and die, he forced himself up, clambering to his feet. The strong taste of copper lingered in his mouth.

He rushed towards Sehn. The man was prone on his back with his hands on his stomach, billowing smoke.

"S-Sehn! I-I-I'm sorry!" Adam cried, immediately pressing down on the man's wounds, trying to staunch the bleeding.

"Kid, listen closely. Blade passed through, I'm bleeding badly, so I can't move my hands. Open my left breast pocket, and fetch the vials," Sehn instructed. Adam quickly did as told. Inside the pocket, he found small vials he recognized as health potions. Carefully he wiggled them out.

"Uncork one, drink it and use the other on Titania. Do it! Now!" Sehn barked.

"But what about yo—"

"Go, lad! *Go!*"

Adam downed the vial, immediately he felt his HP pool replenishing. Flesh knit back together and splintered bones reformed, wringing a yelp from his lips. But he didn't let that stop him. He pressed on, trudging towards the bleeding Titania as the fight raged on elsewhere.

He grimaced, frozen at the sight of Titania's bloody body. So much crimson seeped into the ground around her.

Major chest laceration, disconnected ligaments, multiple contusions. This wasn't good.

But despite the severity of her injuries, Titania was still breathing, albeit faintly. Encouraged by this, Adam took the vial and poured the contents on her wounds.

The reaction was immediate. Limbs spasmed slightly as smoke billowed from her gaping wound, the alchemical concoction guiding her flesh to stitch itself back together.

"A... dam?" Titania murmured, emerald eyes fluttering open to look at the boy.

"I'm so sorry. I never meant for this to happen!" he cried. A blast of golden energy set fire to the vineyard, and Adam flinched.

"WHO ARE YOU?! WHY DO YOU VERMIN IMPEDE VOLTRAIN'S HOLY JUSTICE!" Junith yelled, her weighty blade slamming against the rapier held in Elder Maxxson's frail hand.

"My, aren't you feisty? Would you *kindly* refrain from damaging my property any further?"

Much to Adam's dismay, the man held his ground. Skillfully he twisted his wrist along the blade and struck Junith's gauntlet. For a moment, nothing appeared to have happened.

Then the armor fell to the ground with a *clang*, revealing the leather straps securing it had been severed. Junith stepped away from the man, who until recently had appeared to be a simple apothecary and winemaker

"I asked politely. I won't be asking again," Maxxson said, raising his lightweight weapon once more. A fearsome aura emanated from him, taking the form of a massive, lizard-like creature. Countless translucent scales, serrated fangs, and scaly wings spoke to its draconic nature as it gained detail.

Junith's expression twisted. Her body released a golden-red aura that shifted into the visage of a glorious red bird, screeching triumphantly towards the heavens.

Maxxson's eyes widened, caught off guard by the emergence of an opponent of equal caliber.

She pounced, taking flight with wings of crimson flame, colliding with the old man's roaring dragon as her sword struck its throat

An explosion ensued. Adam dropped, draping himself over Titania as debris from the vineyard and shack, along with wrecked gardening tools, rained from above.

"We have to get out of here!" Adam yelled, mustering all his strength and dragging Titania. The druid was still weak from the blood lost.

Suddenly Sehn appeared, reaching down and grabbing the boy by the scruff of his neck, before lifting Titania up and draping her over his shoulder.

With Adam tucked under his arm and Titania on his shoulder he crouched low.

"Hold on!" Sehn barked, before rocketing forwards, becoming a blur that sent the trio racing through the vineyard. Behind them a silver rapier flew through the air, landing point-down in the scorched earth.

Catpurr 51

The Bite of '97

Sehn held onto Adam and Titania tightly as he darted through the woods, careful to avoid the roots and stones below. Only now did the druid begin to wake from her stupor.

"Holy crap, I'm alive!" she cried.

"Stop wiggling, or I'll drop you!" Sehn scolded, slowing down as the sounds of battle grew more and more distant. "Holy crap, kid, who did you piss off?!"

Suddenly a particularly loud explosion sounded. The trio froze in their tracks.

"Adam, Titania! Get out of here! I'll stall her!" Sehn yelled, dropping them.

"What? We can't!" Titania began, but was cut off by Sehn's glare.

"I'm not asking," Sehn said, a golden spear materializing in his hand. "Gah, I shouldn't have left my coffin behind."

Adam looked at Titania. Her expression reflected her warring emotions as she stared hard at her companion's back.

A moment passed, then another, until finally Titania stood beside Sehn, her hands and legs glowing with mana.

"Seriously, wom—"

"You don't get to tell me what to do," she snapped. "No one, especially you of all people, is going to be making a noble sacrifice today. I'd have the cloud of your death hanging over me forever if you up and died buying time for us to escape."

Sehn turned first to her, then Adam. The nekoboy grimaced, but shared the same sentiment.

"You staying too, lad?"

"If you can't take her, there's no chance *I* can. Might as well die fighting, I guess."

"That's the spirit lad," Sehn said before downing several colorful vials.

A heroic last stand would have been utterly futile. Even buying an hour's worth of time would not do much to stop a bloodhound like Junith. The woman was tenacious, more so than any creature alive.

On one previous occasion, Adam had lured her into a cursed labyrinth, thousands of miles below the ground. Every hour its serpentine passages would twist and shift, changing them entire layout. The paladin had not been waylaid for a second. She had dug mile upon mile until she reached the surface, using only her sword as a shovel.

He would have thought it impossible. But hearing her brag about it, he went to take a look himself. What he found was a hole that went on for near infinity.

The vibrations grew louder. Distant trees splintered and fell, a voice rising above the sounds of destruction.

"ADAAAAAAAAAAAAAAAAM! YOU CAN RUN, BUT YOU CAN'T HIDE, FILTH!"

"Alright. If anyone has any super special skills, now is the time to use them," Sehn said, sweeping his gaze over the others.

"I got something," Adam said, downing a vial of mana before standing resolutely alongside the others. With an unexpected air of confidence, he stretched out his hand. Both his benefactors watched with intrigue and wariness as he activated **Summon Morian Crab**.

A bubble of water suddenly materialized mid air, its crystal blue surface churning as all of Adam's energy culminated into this one, singular skill. The bubble spun, creating a floating vortex of blue liquid that raged violently, stirring up the surrounding air into a near-cyclone.

"Jeez, kid, you were going to use that on *me*?!" Sehn yelled, his voice nearly drowned out by the sound of raging water as his hair blew wildly.

COME FORTH! **MORIAN CRAB!** Adam intoned mentally, willing the skill to complete as he heard Junith begin to sing, her voice eerily echoing "*Adddddaaaam, Addddddddddaaaaaaam*" through the gloom of the woods.

Suddenly, he could feel it. His new companion. A beast that would give its life for him, gradually emerging from the portal to the heart of the raging sea. With the skill's completion came a sense of ecstasy. It couldn't stand up to Junith's might, but at least he'd see the skill he'd put so much effort into earning. The culmination of his efforts.

He smiled, as the tiny tip of the crab's claw barely peeked from the portal.

However, Adam's smile soon soured.

Of course. Because why would anything be easy?

Instead of the massive Morian Crab he had been expecting, like the adults he had seen, a tiny blue crustacean appeared, cat ears affixed to its shell.

It hopped out the portal, landing on the ground where it immediately began clacking its pincers. In Adam's head a high-pitched voice chanted, *FOR THE KING! FOR THE KING!*

Stunned, he could only watch as the tiny crab, barely the size of his palm, scurried up his trousers, crawling up his body to sit on his head, where it brandished its claws against any would-be attackers.

"Summoning snacks, are we?" Sehn asked. "Very impressive, kid. *Very* impressive."

Suddenly the crunch of boots drew their attention, all sets of eyes turning towards the paladin. The scuffle with Elder Maxxson had marred her armor, leaving a gaping hole over the unblemished skin of her left side. But otherwise, she appeared completely untouched.

"*Foun-d-chu,*" Junith sang before laughing, her body boiling with energy as holy flames licked form.

"Well, gang, it's been an honor," Sehn huffed as he downed even more vials and slapped his cheeks, taking in a deep breath as the woman stalked towards them, savoring the moment. "I really didn't want to have to use this…"

Adam gritted his teeth, staring at the paladin as she held her blade aloft, the surrounding mana churning and overflowing.

"*Luminous Light. Of Grand Salvation,*" Junith chanted, the wild energy suddenly focusing and condensing.

"Sehn!" Titania's eyes widened, panic in her irises as Junith's figure began to float.

"I SEE IT! REGALIA!" Sehn replied, taking a stance with the tip of his spear suddenly crackling with red energy.

"*Be judged! Let all darkness be burned away!*"

"*Ephemeral Grace of the Warlord, I, the pious, evoke your name,*" Sehn growled in a rushed whisper. Suddenly hidden tattoos of red energy pulsed across his skin. His hair stiffened and rose, burning with the same red energy, beating in time to some unknown tempo.

"Sehn!" Adam cried, as he saw blood leak from his mentor's eyes. He moved to stop him, yet was stopped himself as Titania thrust out a hand, her eyes never leaving her compatriot as he continued to chant.

"*By Voltrain's grace! Begone, heretic! Be judged! Turn into ash beneath his glorious light! Hear my plea, VOLTRAIN!*" Suddenly the world dissolved into an incandescent light upon Junith's scream. Her raging mana came together in the form of a flaming bird. Its massive wings spread from her body, illuminating every tree and lurking place

In response, Sehn stood tall, his body completely transformed. Muscles ripped and thickened, red hair cascaded down his back, and magic became radiant. Gone was the lanky man who had once stood, defending them with a coffin. In his place stood a tattooed God of War. He took aim, power twisting and pulsing down the length of his now-red javelin.

"Evoke your name to exterminate my enemies!" Sehn spoke. *"YASHWA!"*

Sehn's attack flew as Junith released her brilliant phoenix, the two attacks laced with divinity colliding in the space between the two parties.

The pressure of the attack was overwhelming. To stop himself from flying away, Adam hugged a tree, digging in his claws. His crab companion wasn't so lucky, vanishing from sight even as little beams of mana fired from its eyes.

"Just hang on!" Titania called out from where she hung onto her own tree, voice drowned out by the almighty detonation. Despite trying his best, Adam's grip failed, sending him flying away as Titania called his name.

Then, as suddenly as the attack began, it stopped. The winds, light, and even the overwhelming pressure abruptly disappeared as there came a sound of glass breaking.

Adam hit the ground and looked up, spying the source: a crack in the sky, like a shattered window or a tear in the fabric of the universe. Poking through was a massive claw. As quickly as it appeared, it was abruptly dragged back inside. From the other side of the crack in the sky came clear cries of anguish.

All Adam could do was shrink back at the terrible sight. What it could be was impossible to say, but he had little time to dwell on it—the sound of Sehn choking distracted him immediately.

The man was caught, his fearsome visage dispelled as a bleeding Junith held him aloft, at the same time pinning Titania beneath the heel of her boot.

With no mana and no tools, Adam charged. His instincts to protect were the only things moving his feet. A cry was ripped from his throat. "Let them go!" The injured paladin turned to him as he pounced at her, clamping down on her exposed, bleeding wrist.

"Seriously?" Junith said, laughing as she peeled Adam off with a grin.

"Why! Why are you like this?! What did I ever *do* to you!" he yelled, flailing.

"You are an abom—" Junith began, then stopped, eyes twitching as she unceremoniously released him.

The nekoboy scrambled back, getting away from the woman who had suddenly dropped to her knees. From her body rose strange black steam.

"AH! ARRRRGH!" Junith screamed. The earth cracked around her, shattered by her wild energy. Something was wrong, but what? The only thing clear was that Junith was in pain, screaming at the top of her lungs as her flames and magical energy were savagely snuffed out.

"ADAM!" Junith roared in hateful agony, before the entire world was bathed in white.

Catpurr 52

Junith's Fall From Grace

As the blinding light faded, Adam cautiously opened his eyes to find the surrounding area pulverized by Junith who was, oddly, nowhere to be found.

Where she had stood was now a large crater, her shards of white-hot armor embedded in the nearest trees.

He looked around frantically, scanning the surrounding area for the irate paladin. Was this a ploy? A sadistic game? Or maybe divine intervention? It was hard to be certain. But what *was* certain was that his friends were dying.

He rose to his feet, rushing towards his companions' last known location, only to see Sehn and Titania standing up and licking their wounds. As he watched them from the bushes, both called out for him.

The nekomancer hesitated. He wanted to run towards them, to ask if they were okay and do everything he could to help them. Yet standing there, his stomach felt heavy. His feet seemed chained to the ground, weighted by the knowledge that their injuries were the direct result of *his* past.

"Why is it that everyone that comes near me gets hurt?" he lamented, anger at his unjust life rising. Seeing his benefactors, so ready to give their lives for him, in this sorry state, Adam made a choice. Doing the one thing he could to protect them, he turned, and fled. Distantly he heard as Titania hugged Sehn and cried.

I'm sorry. Please forgive me.

***

In a cramped forest, Junith hobbled away. Even now, when she should have had nothing left to give, the paladin's body was still releasing waves of erratic golden energy. She struggled to remain upright.

"Bast… tard!" Junith huffed, leaning against a tree as she clutched her wrist. Her blood had failed to coagulate, and now her mana was endlessly leaking.

She hadn't meant to, but after that abomination's last-ditch attack, she had been teleported away. Apparently the nekoboy's bite contained some form of potent venom, which triggered one of her failsafe skills.

She grimaced, blood trickling from her mouth as a notification appeared.

[You have been infected with Felinthropy! Seek a source of gold or you will soon join the ranks of the Damned: *Progress: 30%***]**

Sticky black pus coated her hand from when she had tried to stem the bleeding. Immediately she flicked it away, then fumbled with the pouch at her waist until she found several gold coins.

She held them in her hand, leaning against the tree as she prayed. Yet nothing happened as she spit up blood, finally falling to her knees.

Damn it!

The coins spilled from her hand, scattering across the forest floor as Junith began coughing violently.

[Progress: *57%***]**

The infection was speeding up. Crawling along her arm with frightening speed were sickly black veins.

"Ugh! ARGH!" Junith cried, putting all her strength into summoning her sword. With one trembling hand she dragged it on the ground, struggling to lift it enough to sever her own arm. It was imperative to stop the infection's spread.

Her strength suddenly failed. On the interface, an alarming message appeared.

[REQUIREMENTS NOT MET TO WIELD THIS ITEM!]

What?

The blade fell from her hand, dissipating into golden light as Junith's eyes went wide. Her system began to glitch badly. *Error* messages crowded the screen as her stats rapidly dropped.

What is this?! NO! NO! NO!

Junith immediately lurched forwards, reaching for her coins, but her armor's weight, coupled with the burning agony crawling along her back only made her scream in pain.

Despite having **pain tolerance** to level five, this pain exceeded what she'd felt when she was a child, when she'd been flayed to strengthen her skills.

Suddenly it all clicked. Her skills were leaving, disappearing one by one. All her hard work, all she had been through, dissolving before her very eyes.

Junith panicked. What could she do? How could she stop this awful corruption, twisting and purging her very being? It seemed impossible, hopeless.

"ADAM!" Junith yelled, yet this proved to be another mistake.

[Progress: *82%*]

She hit the ground hard. Illusory ants seemed to march across her eyes, her ears, her entire body as it itched fiercely.

"*A—dam!*" Junith hissed again, her fury the only thing she could cling to.

Desperately, despite her body failing, she tried to drag herself along the ground, inching towards the gold coins using everything she had.

Please, Lord! Grant me strength!

[Blessing Corrupted! You have lost the Grace of your Patron!]

Junith's heart stopped, eyes widening as she read the system notification. Once. Twice. Thrice.

[Progress: *100%*]
[You have been claimed by a Follower of the Primordial Eli!]
[System Interface Updated!]

In that moment, time itself seemed to come to a standstill as Junith failed to process what she was reading.

"Th—This is a joke, right?" she choked out, voice cracking as her body shook with disbelief.

Suddenly she couldn't breathe. Her eyes burned, her skin crawled, and every bit of her felt weak as she lost all control of her muscles.

[Neko Conversion in progress! Please stand by...]

The alert blinked as her vision tunneled. She couldn't believe it. Her blessing! Her god!

A drop of rain fell.

Everything that made her who she was was evaporating, right before her eyes. She opened her mouth, desperate to protest and beg for her god, yet could do nothing as her vision faded to black.

Catpurr 53

I, Alone, Sleep in the Woods

Rain came down relentlessly, prompting the nekoboy to draw his robes tighter around himself as he cowered beneath a tree's canopy.

[Time Remaining until next Abyssal Trial: 543:42:02]

Adam sighed.

A day had passed since he'd fled from Titania and Sehn, disappearing into the forest as he waited for Junith to reappear.

Yet oddly, she hadn't come, leaving him clueless as to what had happened.

Maybe I shouldn't have left. The thought appeared, uninvited, as he shivered and pulled his boots away from the rising water.

Suddenly, he heard clacking. *"King! King! King!"* echoed in his head as his connection with his crab was re-established.

What? Adam looked at his full mana bar, then down at the crab, sailing through the water on a large leaf.

King! King!

Huh... Neat. By permanent, it seemed the skill wouldn't consume more mana after being summoned.

The crab clacked, its pincers waving as it hopped off the giant leaf and swam through the tiny puddle of water to its master.

"Well. At least I have you, Krabby," Adam sighed, picking up the crab and hugging it close to his chest as he closed his eyes and tried to sleep.

***

Waking to the morning dew, Adam found he was hungry. Still no sign of Junith. In her absence, the world seemed so much fresher. A clear morning sky greeted him, accompanied by an angelic chorus of birbs twirping. Adam indulged in a morning stretch, before finally exiting the tree trunk. As he did, he passed his crab, holding a lonely vigil.

His stomach churned. A sudden urge to eat the crab seized him, but he stopped as he eyed the crab's cat-eared headband.

The Nyx? He picked up the crab, its eye stalks turning to its master.

King? King?

He tried to remove the band, only for the crab to snap at his fingers.

Unhappy with this, the crab leapt off, landing on the ground with its pincers raised to protect its cat ears.

"Fine. I won't take your headband." Adam smiled, inspecting his summon more closely.

The crab had sharp pincers, apparently strong enough to snap tree limbs and pulverize stone. While its eye stalks possessed the same capability to fire bolts of mana as its predecessors, for the moment they were significantly less potent. But despite being tiny, it still packed quite a punch, cracking tree bark.

Suddenly, an idea came to Adam.

He summoned Skittles. The cat-shaped skeleton emerged from a portal to heed its master's call.

Adam placed the crab on Skittle's head, assuring he would not fall off with a piece of cloth torn from the hem of his cloak.

"My genius *never* ceases to amaze me," he said, smiling to himself as he combined his minions together.

* * *

Soon, Adam was chowing down on a breakfast, served up to him by the almighty prowess of the skelecrab combo.

With Skittles providing mobility and Krabby bringing its mana bolts, the duo swiftly became an apex predator of the forest, quickly hunting down rat-like rodents, birbs, and other creatures for Adam's breakfast feast.

Krabby's bolts weren't fatal, but they easily stunned small creatures, allowing Skittles to close the distance and pounce on its victims.

"Interesting," he said, studying the carcass of a rodent resembling a herbull from his home continent.

He summoned his journal, taking notes and sketching the various creatures laid out.

Then he stopped, one thumb idly rubbing the leather-bound book, a gift from Titania.

"It's better this way," he said aloud, suddenly feeling wistful. "I've always been alone, and it's better I stay that way."

[Follower gained!]

What?

There was a sudden tingling sensation, like a new connection between himself and another being. It was similar to his connection with Schrödinger, butthis was different, more distant, more...

"LET ME GO! I'LL KILL YOU, ALL YOU CRETINS!"

He jolted. Flashes assailed his mind, echoes of Junith screaming bloody murder towards unseen aggressors.

He winced. She was in danger, and oddly he could feel it—her panic, her distress, all these emotions flooding in all at once. Just like the bond he shared with Schrödinger.

And yet, despite the tidal wave of negative feelings assaulting his mind, Adam couldn't help but smile.

He shook his head, wondering what the Nyx was going on.

Who could be strong enough to capture Junith? Matter of fact, why is her irritating voice in my head? And what did it mean by 'follower'?

A myriad of questions buzzed in his mind. He pulled up his system and casually took a bite of a smoked rodent.

[Bonded: Junith Oatheart Lvl 1]

WHAT?!

If he'd had a drink, he would have spat it down. Instead, the bite of meat became stuck in his throat as he failed to make sense of those words.

"Ehk! EHHHK! ARGH!" Adam choked, standing up and hobbling around as he struggled to breathe.

I'm going to die. I'm going to die, and the last thing I hear is Junith screaming in pain.

He paused, blue in the face from a lack of oxygen.

Perhaps things weren't so bad after all.

Suddenly Skittles headbutted him in his chest, dislodging the meat caught in his windpipe.

"UGh!" he gasped, collapsing against a tree. Every fiber of his being sagged as he desperately gulped down air.

"Why do stupid things keep happening to me?" he lamented, bemoaning his miserable fate, before an idea struck him.

Catpurr 54

Plan of Action

"Well... That's unexpected, but not unwelcome... Hmmm, I sense trouble for me."

—A discussion between Eli and his faithful disciple Truck-kun, moments before interruption.

* * *

Tightly clutching the black card, the nekoboy slowly approached the scorched and pockmarked land. Only one organization could help in this time of need. A group which proved time and time again it could do what needed doing.

The Black Market.

"Adam! Welcome back to my shop! Can I interest you in a holy hand grenade or three?" Tim the Enchanter asked, standing on top of his cart as colorful fireballs orbited his palm.

"Uh, no thanks. I'm here because I need your help," Adam said, drawing his robes tighter around himself as he steeled his nerves. Hopefully, they would have information on Junith. He needed to track her down and understand this new system function.

"Certainly! My help is willingly given! At least, for a price. How may I be of service today?" Tim said, scratching his beard before abruptly disappearing. "Here to buy a skull? Maybe a drink? Or *purr*-haps a mask, to hide your ear-y features."

At the man's strange pronunciation of *perhaps,* Adam froze. The nekoboy's fears only grew more distinct as the enchanter loomed over him, clutching in his hands a familiar black half-mask. He quickly realized that the enchanter was not threatening him—he was merely an overzealous merchant with wares to sell.

"I can't afford this."

"On the house," Tim said, surprising him. "After all, I believe you and I will soon embark on a magnificent long-term business venture. Consider this a gift in good faith, provided you make it out alive, of course."

Adam pursed his lips. Something was up.

"Make it out alive?" he echoed, hand clenching. Within the bushes, Skittles prepared to pounce. The skelecat wouldn't do much, but it would buy time for his escape.

Hopefully.

"Consider this a freebie, as part of our budding business venture. The one you seek is on the road to Vilenciel," Tim said cryptically. Adam's brow furrowed.

"And *how* do you know what I seek?"

"I'm in the business of knowing!" Tim yelled, a ten-foot-tall wave of fire exploding from his staff. "As well as enchanting, procurement, and anything our clients need. Whether that be information, organs, or advice, the Black Hand offers it all."

"O... kay?"

Crapbaskets. I could have just headed back to Sehn and Titania, he sighed. It seemed his target would be further away than he realized, but that was only the least of his problems.

The implications of Tim's words weighed on him. He was being *watched.* Despite the chaos of the battle, someone had been alert and stealthy enough to track *both* Junith and Adam. That, or Tim was a seer of some kind, similar to Coco.

Whichever the case, Adam reassessed his impressions of the man. "But what do you mean by 'make it out alive'?"

The enchanter sashayed across the clearing with his hands behind his back and feet *quite clearly* a few inches above the ground. "Well, where she's going, most never see the light of day again," Tim replied, suddenly teleporting atop his cart again.

Crap. Crap! I need her! Adam grimaced. After seeing the notification that Junith was his new follower, his mind had endlessly churned, recalling all the things she'd said during their last encounter.

She had said *return*, meaning she had a way to go back to their realm. He needed to know more.

He took a moment and checked his system menu again, staring at the **Bonded** status and Junith's new level.

[Bonded: Junith Oatheart Lvl 1]
[Status: Incapacitated/Paralyzed]
[Information unavailable, distance too far!]

The implications alone were unsettling, but also gave him cause for hope. And considering he could still faintly feel her distress and fear, there was a good chance, too, she'd been depowered.

At least, that was his current theory. As a mega psycho fanatic of the Church, Junith would *never* be taken alive, even under extreme circumstances. Their encounter must have weakened her somehow, or injured her enough to be left helpless and paralyzed.

That, or a bigger fish had intervened.

The only thing certain was right now, she was vulnerable. This was perhaps the only chance he'd have to learn how to return home.

"And where, exactly, is she being taken?" he asked. The enchanter smiled and remained silent, until Adam finally sighed and set a gold coin upon his cart.

The coin was immediately consumed by a small explosion of flames, reappearing in Tim's hand. He placed the coin in his mouth, biting it.

"To the Duchess of Vilenciel, of course."

Of course... Adam racked his brain, recalling everything he knew about the Duchess. From what he had heard, she was the leader of the Purists, and mother to a daughter with an *unhealthy fascination* towards demi-humans. The same fascination that made demies dangerously unwelcome in Vilenciel.

"Who has her *right now?*"

Tim smiled.

"A couple of bandits found her when investigating the sound of crying, and are intending her as a gift for the Duchess' daughter. A pair of demi-humans such as yourselves are worth quite a bit. Especially unique realm travelers."

Girl? Not woman? Bandits?

Adam needed a moment to digest the overload of information Tim casually foisted upon him.

So, he knows I'm a realm traveler? The mystery of the Black Hand deepened—and made a friendship with them that much more valuable.

Wait, demi-human?

"Not to worry, though, I wouldn't sell you. Personally, I'm not a fan of the slave trade, although it *is* a highly lucrative business. I myself find it... *distasteful*, the bargaining of sentient lives," Tim added, mistaking his client's silence for worry. "Additionally, as an Abyss Diver, the organization feels we would benefit more from a... long term, *respectable* relationship."

"Demi... human?" Adam clarified, giving voice to his confusion.

What.

"You seem surprised. Is she *not* a demi-human?" the enchanter asked, giving the nekoboy a sideways glance. Adam opened his mouth but hesitated, instead holding out an open palm.

Tim smirked, revealing yellow teeth as he smiled wide. "Of course."

The magical merchant flicked a gold coin towards the boy, who snatched it gracefully.

"She isn't originally a demi-human," he said. It was important to offer information as a sign of mutual cooperation and respect, when building a business partnership.

"Fascinating," Tim said. He looked the nekoboy up and down with a discerning eye. "I assume you aren't, either."

Adam remained silent. The two stared at one another.

"How much would it cost to smuggle me into Vilencial?" he said, finally.

"For you? One gold coin."

"Good, I have a few things I'll need you to procure for me on the way there."

Catpurr 55
Path A or B

"Well, here we are," an agent of the Black Hand wearing a skintight suit declared. His name was Rolo. As the cart came to a stop, he unlatched the top of a wooden barrel within which Adam was sequestered.

The nekoboy blinked, clambering out of the container to come face to face with the vast, pitch black sky, beneath which lay the glowing landscape of Vilenciel sprawling out before him. Perched upon his hood, Krabby blinked with him.

According to the timer, it had only taken him a day to arrive in the capital city. Next he checked his interface, immediately pulling up Junith's information in the **Bonded** menu.

[Bonded: Junith Oatheart Lvl 1]
[Status: Incapacitated/Paralyzed]
[HP: 40/200]
[MP: 0/50][SEALED]

She was close, Adam could feel her. With each step towards Vilenciel City, the strength of her emotions only grew.

She was angry, very, *very* angry. Occasionally a spark of fear would flicker, only to be quickly swallowed up by an eruption of yet more rage.

"Three gold," Rolo grunted, expectantly holding out his white-gloved hand. In his other hand was a bag containing everything necessary for his mission.

Adam handed over the payment and accepted the bag, then took a moment to more closely observe his surroundings.

He was close to Twilight Plaza, close enough that he could see the various monuments and adventurers still flocking them even at this hour.

"How much would it cost to—" he began, turning to face the agent of the Hand, only to find empty air. "Well, so much for that."

He sighed, slinging the bag of tools over his shoulder as he turned his gaze to the decadent golden castle in the center of the city. It was time to get to work.

* * *

Now equipped with brand new gear, Adam scurried through the streets, walking with his hood pulled low through a cluster of buildings sitting just shy of a drawbridge. On the other side was his destination: the Vilenciel Estate.

Meandering through the candle-lit streets was a patrol of knights. Adam waited till they were out of sight, before he climbed on top of a roof using the building's rain gutters.

"Well, this brings me back," he grunted, exerting all of his strength to climb the three-story building, reminiscing on his days as an orphan thief.

Note to self. Add more points into strength, he grimaced, the weight of all his gear causing his muscles to scream.

Finally reaching the top of the slanted, black-shingled building, he removed the hook at his waist, stabbing it into the roof to secure himself, as he removed from his storage device his journal and a floorplan of the Vilenciel Estate.

Carefully he laid out the map, marking his location in the city's layout, then turning his attention to the floorplan.

Sewers or walls. Sewers or walls, he considered, determining which would be the best method of attack.

On a normal occasion, sewers made the most sense, but with the catsification curse, he'd almost certainly suffer the 20 percent stat reduction, something he really didn't need complicating a prison break.

He checked his newly acquired chronogear, a device for measuring time.

The bronze contraption's four hands were spaced out, pointing at different numbers that altogether told him it was roughly 0134, late at night, a time when most would still be asleep.

From the information he'd bought off Tim, there was a duct into the castle's underbelly, a secret compartment underneath the prison. However, the sewers connecting to it were infested with monsters—a rather convenient feature both for disposing of prisoners, and keeping the sewers sparkling.

Alternatively, he could enter by scaling the walls, but down that way lay a much higher risk of being caught. Yes, he had a schedule of the guard's shifts, but who could say what other traps and countermeasures existed. Not to mention, to enter the underbelly he would need to swipe a key from the duchess' daughter.

Man, this sucks.

Adam sucked air through his teeth, looking over the details. He had asked Tim if it were at all possible to hire someone else to rescue Junith, but he quickly discerned this was the Black Hand's test. And they wanted to see if he would sink or swim.

Not that he could hire anyone anyway, he only had ten gold to his name and no one wanted to piss off nobles.

Despite the Vilenciels not being system users, they held the King's ear, not to mention his purse. The family had roots that traced back to the founding of the Empire, with their hands in nearly every avenue of money.

In short, they controlled the economy so thoroughly no one bothered messing with them.

Fortunately, it was this same ego that made them arrogant, presenting Adam with an opportunity.

With the Duchess away at the capital accompanied by her most powerful guards, only two prominent system users remained in the estate.

Narbera and Sebastian. The Maid and Butler.

Two system users in service of the Vilenciel family, neither of whom were very fond of the eldest daughter. Resulting in them finding reasons to frequent areas of the estate avoided by her.

"Nothing ventured... nothing gained," he muttered, unhooking himself and making his choice.

Catpurr 56

Into the Thick of It

After bypassing several sentries and a group of drunken guards, Adam reached the moat's edge, rappelling down into the water quietly so as to not alert the guards. In the end, he chose the sewers, not only because he could kill monsters and earn experience, but because he wanted to establish an escape route. One that would make it hard for pursuers to follow him. Failing that, he could always make use of the bombs on his waist, to blow a hole in the wall or set the castle ablaze.

[CATSIFICATION CURSE ACTIVATED! YOU ARE WET! -20% to all stats!]

Slinking into the cool water, the familiar curse caused him to full-body shudder as he made his way towards the sewer duct under the cover of darkness. He neared the cylindrical bronze outcrop, the water nearby visibly stained by sludge and... other materials.

As he approached, the familiar stench of decay became overpowering, along with putrid feces.

Stopping just shy of the green crop of liquid flowing out, he downed a potion of **poison resistance,** a vial of **detoxify**, and a tincture of **body resistance**. The three most expensive items he'd gotten off Tim.

Nothing ventured...

Adam entered the duct. A sickly heat swept over him as he entered the toxin-filled sludge. Regardless he trudged forwards, only stopping when a rusted maintenance grate barred his path.

The cat burglar took out a set of picks. Certainly it would be quicker and easier to cut through with **Mana Claws**, but that would leave obvious evidence. Should someone come down to performance maintenance, he'd rather not give himself away immediately.

It took a few tries and several minutes, but eventually his diligence was rewarded with a click.

Heh. I still got it.

He pulled back the gate, entering and relocking it, finally taking a deep breath. While most would have vomited, or perhaps even quit from the smell alone, Adam was no stranger to the scent of decay. The same could not be said of Krabby. The creature refused to join its master as he made his way into the pipe.

So much for loyalty, he sighed, clenching his jaw as he took inventory one final time.

Club, check.

Potions, check.

Vials, check.

Daggers, check.

Rope, check.

Heat stone, check.

Glow stone, check.

And for good measure, the heat stone came equipped with a large wooden box to dry off in, for when he reached the dungeon.

Dredging through the green sludge, Adam made his way through the pipe, navigating the gloomy dark with the light of his glow stone. He walked for several minutes, up until the sludge submerged his thighs and began creeping towards his chest; a sign he was nearing one of the main pipes where the water would be the deepest. From there, he'd need to hold his breath and swim upwards.

Nothing ventured... He inwardly moaned as he clutched his pendant of the mermaid, the only reason this mission was at all possible. Without it, he'd have been forced to scale the walls. That wouldn't make this part any more pleasant, however. In order to reach the main area of the sewers, he was going to have to drown himself—as well as imbibe all the urine, acrid feces, and congealed matter that comprised the moist sludge around him.

"I need a break," he groaned. When he could delay it no longer he stepped forwards, allowing himself to be fully submerged with his mouth wide open.

He inhaled, the taste of the muck making him violently recoil, gagging as agonizingly slowly, the pendant began to activate.

* * *

After swimming for what felt like forever, Adam withdrew a stone slab in one hand and a glow stone in the other, using the latter to judge how far he had gone.

Just a few more meters, he told himself, and continued onwards. At last, *at last,* his head broke into the surface and he entered the dungeon below the prison.

Coughing and spitting up muck, he held his glow stone aloft, illuminating the area as he looked left and right, until he spotted the smooth black marble wall, wet with mold and ick.

His itchy eyes slowly adjusted to the gloom, his nekoboy nature allowing him to see more than most, despite the poor lighting conditions.

Paddling to the water's edge, Adam put his glow stone in his mouth and secured his grip on the slick stone floor, lifting himself out of the water slowly. He scanned the near pitch black darkness for possible threats.

*I should upgrade my eyes for **dark vision,*** he thought, adding it to the list of abilities to gain in the future.

Adam took a breath, taking a moment to rest before suddenly, his skin tingled. Every hair stood on end, his senses screaming.

Reflexively he dodged left, avoiding the *swish* of a projectile that splattered against the space he'd been standing. In response, he threw a potion in its direction, hearing a loud *ribbit*. Then he turned away and covered his ears. The vial smashed against the wall. It heralded first a brilliant light, then a deafening sound.

The nekoboy opened his eyes, pupils rapidly adjusting to the potion of **flash bang**, scanning for the enemy who dared ambush him.

Stumbling about was a slimy reptile of some kind—or perhaps it was more of a frog, if a frog could have spiked teeth and giant, bulbous eyes. Each eye protruded from either side of its slick, green head, and lolling out from behind its teeth hung a lumpy, reddish tongue.

The creature reeled, completely caught off guard by the sudden explosion of white light that blinded its eyes accustomed to the dark. With his prey stunned, he wasted no time and quickly crossed the black stone floor with a club in hand.

Putting everything he had into this swing, Adam smashed the creature on its head, caving in the creature's skull with a loud *SQUISH* as its eyestalks shuddered. Yet despite the sound of bone being pulverized and how the club grew slick with blue blood, he did not stop. He struck again, and again, bashing the monster's skull in. Only when he received a message with his new experience did he stop.

[+250 XP]

Thirty-three more of these and I'll be able to level up. Man, I'm tired, he thought.

Taking a moment to catch his breath, he put his hands on his knees, wiping his brow, already coated with monster blood and sweat.

"Ribbit."

Adam looked up, the fading ball of light from his flash bang illuminating the army of mutated frogs, peeking at him from the safety of the shadows.

"Oh... crapbaskets."

Catpurr 57
CATastrophe Averted

"Oh *my*. What a wonderful specimen. I haven't seen one of you before."

"Etib em!"

"Oh, and it *speaks*. Just not our tongue. Interesting, I've never heard that language before. Huhuhu. You're just *so adorable* with your angry face."

* * *

"Crap!" Adam barked, diving to the ground as several frogs spat acidic green ick at him.

He scrambled to his feet, avoiding a flurry of tongue lashings that pulverized the stone floor.

"Serpentine! Serpentine!" Adam mentally repeated over and over again. He fumbled with his glow stone as he ran, struggling to illuminate the winding and narrow path.

He turned a corner, racing down the sewer where suddenly a shadow lurched at him, forcing him to skid to a halt and lean back, reflexively activating **Mana Claws** and slicing through the creature.

[+100 EXP]

He glanced over his shoulder, glimpsing a splattering of green goop haloing a bisected crystal. No doubt the remains of the slime he'd just killed.

Sadly, he lacked the time to inspect his handiwork, as he raised his glow stone, illuminating dozens of slimes filling the cavern, coating nearly every inch of the tunnel.

"Oh... perfect," Adam groaned, as *ribbits* sounded nearby.

"Alright. Skittles! I choose you!" he barked, summoning his skelecat out of a cat-shaped portal.

The skeleton's bones clacked on the ground, chittering as its glowing spectral eyes stared down its master's foes.

Hunt!

The creature pounced. By Adam's estimate, Skittles would be more than capable of dealing with the slimes. Meanwhile its master turned, clutching his club in one hand as he prepared another **flash bang** potion.

He only had two left, but exhausted as he was from all the swimming, climbing, and running, he wouldn't last much longer without rest.

So Adam did what he did best. He went to work making corpses.

* * *

Huffing and covered in blue ooze, acid burns, and charred leather, he collapsed on the smooth wet floor, dropping his bloody club in the process. Sitting there, he ripped off the damaged pieces of his cloak and leather armor.

It had taken a while, but they'd killed everything. At least in this area and outer strata of the dungeon.

Adam eyed Skittles, the monster's feet clacking against the gore-covered floor as it held a red slime core in its mouth. It dropped the core at its master's feet, before nudging it with its skull.

"Thanks, buddy," he said, rubbing the skeleton's chin and causing it to chatter and shake, its body vibrating with joy. "At least someone is loyal, Krabby ran off first chance he got."

Skittles hopped into Adam's lap, cuddling him and making the boy smile.

"Well, you aren't Schrödinger, but you'll do for now, until I find my friend," he told it, petting the monster's boney spine.

Sighing, he opened up his interface, looking over everything while he had a moment to catch his breath.

BETA SYSTEM v1.03

TITLE: The Primordial Eli's Chosen (+20% Mana recovery, +5 Arcana. Undead Favorability)

NAME: Adam F. Glow

SPECIES: Nekoboy

LEVEL: 8

EXP BAR: 2950/8000

MAIN CLASS: Nekomancer

HP: 117/200(160)

MANA: 35/215(170)

EVOLUTION POINT: 0

Gacha Coins: 0

Free Points: 0

[Followers: 01]

[Bonded: Junith Oatheart LvL1]

Stats:

STR: 12 (10)

CON: 20 (16)

DEX: 12 (10)

ARC: 36(43)+5+2 **(EQ) (34)**

SEN: 10 (8)

EGO: 10 (8)

[RESISTANCES]: Fire (5%)

Buffs: Loved by Undead (unique), Blessing of Eli (unique), Eyes of a Predator V1, Corrupted Blessing of Nyx (unique), Adherent of Death V1, Explosive Renaissance V1, Pain Tolerance V1

Debuffs: Ha! You Sacrificed Your Stats for a Cat?! V1 (curse), Catsification V1 (curse), Wet (Catsification)

Skills: Animate Bone V1, Irritating Touch V1, Cat Claws V1, Identify V1

Summon Skeleton V1 (++), Mana Bolt V1 (++), Artificial, Linguistics {Rigellian}, Genocidal Aura, Summon Morian Crab, Mana Claws.

Adam huffed. Nearly halfway to leveling up.

Guard this area.

Immediately Skittles arose, performing the task as Adam rubbed his ring, eyeing his inventory. Inside, the box he'd bought for himself and the heat stone were both waiting for him.

He summoned the wooden box. It fell to the ground with a *thud* before he pushed off the thick top and climbed in. Here was a cozy pseudo-shelter that could shield him from the elements.

Little breathing holes were poked into the sides of the box, protected by grates. Four walls of heavy wood now surrounded him, allowing him a place to rest.

Using a cloth, he took his heat stone out, the item already radiating warmth that quickly filled the box, warming the curled-up nekoboy.

Tired, wet, and covered in blood, it only took a few moments, before he was out like a light.

* * *

[Level Up!]

Adam woke to a notification, and the dried stench of sewage on his body.

Seeing the level-up, he checked his mana, noting that Skittles was still active.

Huh...

Popping the hood of the box, he tossed his glow stone out. A moment later he peeked his head over the edge to survey the surrounding areas.

The once-drab area was now painted entirely in green. Not the green of sewage, but rather that of the decaying remains of monsters. Slimes, to be exact.

Everywhere he looked, Adam saw piles and piles of cores. Some shattered, some intact, a large pile left in front of his box, like an offering from Skittles to its master.

"Huh... Neat," he said, pulling up his system and spreading his stats out. His level-up had gifted him a skill point, too, but he saved it for later. Right now, he needed to move.

STR: 12 > 14

ARC: 36 > 38

SEN: 10 > 11

Adam crawled out his box, gazing at all the cores left by Skittles, as the skelecat batted one around like a ball of yarn.

Aww.

Idly, he wondered if the objects had a use as anything other than cat toys. He picked one up, identifying it.

[Dormant Core of the Slime [Recharging]]

[Item Description: *A core of a corrupted sewer slime, originally transplanted from a dungeon to serve as a sewer scrubber. After years on the job, this slime has become twisted, and its once-blue body has been filled with antiseptic, mutating it into a green bacteria super spreader. Thanks to their sublime nature, slimes naturally repel each other, however, on the rare occasion when multiple slime cores are in extreme proximity without their protective gel, there is an extremely rare chance for the cores to combine, forming a super slime. Can be used as an alchemical agent.*]

Adam's eyes went wide, reading the description before he looked down, eyeing the pile of intact cores Skittles had piled up together right below his feet. The pile twitched.

"Oh, you've gotta be—" An explosion of power sent him flying. He hit a wall, bouncing on the stone before landing on the ground as all the nearby green goo began to wiggle, snaking towards the pile of cores.

"OH NO, YOU DON'T!" He put his hand out, blasting the pile with mana and scattering them, just as the super slime was about to form.

Extremely rare, my ass.

He sighed, breathing in a sigh of relief at the catastrophe that was narrowly averted. A continuous *click-clack* drew his attention again.

"I thought you were on my team!" Adam hissed, turning towards his summon, still batting a slime core around.

Skittle paid him no mind. Instead, it began to wander around, moving without any input. Shaking his head, Adam returned to his box, about to place it back in his storage when he hesitated. Something underfoot crunched. Slowly he raised his foot, to find he had stepped on an intact slime core. Suddenly an idea came to him.

Catpurr 58

I Give You Peace.

Panting and utterly drenched in monster guts, Adam wrenched the metal gate shut and began the grueling march up the flight of stairs. He had only just fled a horde of sewer crocs, barely sealing the door shut behind him.

"Why... are there crocodiles... in a sewer? *Why-are-there-crocodiles-in-a-sewer?!*" he wheezed. He laid down on the stairs and curled up tightly, taking a moment to collect himself. Sadly, Skittles was no longer with him, as the crocodile had devoured his skelecat. Had it not been for Skittles' brave sacrifice, the crocodile that ambushed them would have gobbled the nekoboy up instead.

"Ugh... Why is life so hard?"

He took out a ration cube, munching on the tasteless item. A moment passed, then another, until his breathing returned to normal.

"Well... I'm not gonna get myself killed just sitting here," he groaned, finally working up the motivation to stand from the cool ground. He entered an area choked with dust and moss, and paused to scan the near infinite darkness.

Then he heard it. A creak, followed by a clack, a sound that was extremely familiar to Adam as his ears twitched.

Skeletons.

The nekomancer eyed the lanky bone being, as it lurked in the corner, looking down at him with its expressionless skull and dull, ghostly blue eyes.

On instinct Adam reacted, leaping away, club already raised to in preparation for a counterattack. Yet surprisingly, no attack ever came.

Instead it chattered its teeth, walking across the floor until it stopped in front of the boy, completely docile.

Huh... he thought, booping the skeleton on the skull as other skeletons of various shapes and sizes joined it, crowding around to watch Adam, who curiously peered back.

Then it hit him.

*My **Loved by Undead**!*

"Ha..." Adam let out, breaking into a low chuckle as he recalled his passive ability. "Haha... HAHAHAHAHAHAHAHA!"

Manic laughter soon resounded through the catacomb as Adam marched his way through the dungeon strata unimpeded. His only barrier now was the sheer abundance of skeletons crowding around him, boxing him in and making it difficult to move as they endlessly stared at him.

For any normal human it would have been extremely claustrophobic, but Adam didn't mind it. It was a far cry better than dodging acid balls, bacterial slime spikes, and ten foot tall sewer crocodiles that had *no business* being in a sewer.

There was just one thing that caused concern. Outside of a handful of animated human remains, the vast majority of the skeletons weren't human at all, but rather various races of demi-human.

It spoke to the scale of what lay ahead. Suddenly, he wasn't so jovial about the horde of skeletons surrounding him anymore.

*I should upgrade my own skills. Open **Summon Skeleton**.*

[Upgrade Summon Minor Skeleton]
[Available Upgrades]
—Upgrade skill to Summon Skeleton V1
—Increase Minion capacity+1
—Optimize Mana requirements (-20% REQ.)
—Strengthen Summon V1 (+10% To skeleton stats)

Optimize Mana Requirements is a no brainer, he concluded. Immediately upon selection his mana shot back up, the cost of the skill reduced from 100 to 80 mana.

Should be enough for two minions now, if I get minion capacity next upgrade, Adam thought to himself, smiling as he dreamed of spreading the gospel of undeath once more. A skeleton clacked loudly, jarring him from his fantasies.

He looked up at the bone beings staring at him.

"You guys have been through a lot, haven't you?" he mused, booping the skull of an armored skeleton carrying a rusted greatsword. Once, the weapon would've been a pristine beauty. Now it was little more than scrap metal.

It looked at its new master, its glowing blue eyes flickering in its skull, offering no response to the boy staring back at it. The nekomancer turned away, glancing at his vanguard composed of skeletons, zombies, and even a bone golem.

Pushing forward, Adam carefully inspected the area, wondering why there were so many undead in one area.

According to the floor plans and schematics, there were no catacombs or burial grounds attached to the estate. And yet every step, more and more showed up. Had he taken a wrong turn somehow?

But everything else seemed to match up with his research. And so, glow stone held aloft, h pressed on, accompanied only by the shuffling sounds of the undead, until another familiar sound rose above the clicks and clacks—the sound of rushing water. And with it, at last, was the answer to his skeletal mystery, too. Heaped haphazardly in a bend of the sewer was a mound of bones and corpses. It was massive, uncountable skeletal limbs and appendages piled to the ceiling, oozing pus and fluids. The result of dozens, no, *hundreds* of dead bodies just dumped into the sewer like refuse.

Adam's mind spun with questions. *How long has this been going on? How long have they been dumping bodies? How many victims have there been?*

This was no way to treat the dead. Even for *him* it was a bit much.

Once again his ankles were submerged in sewage as he approached the corpse pile radiating negative energy. He could feel it; their pain, their anguish. The fear they had experienced in their last moments of life.

It was almost always the same, the emotions felt at the end.

Typically, there were two ways undead may arise. Either a necromancer channeled mana through a corpse's dormant mana circuits, bending it to their will, or a corpse was revived by its lingering resentment, and what remained of its soul. Between battles, massacres, and unburied corpses, the latter was more common by far. It was only inevitable that such corpses would rise up.

It was a common occurrence, especially for souls not at rest. The stronger the resentment at death, the higher chance of rising. This was why proper burial rituals were critical.

It was something many didn't understand.

Adam reached for a potion on his chest, one he'd be intending to save for when he entered the castle proper. However, this was more important. The nekomancer uncorked the concoction, climbing the pile and pouring its contents all over the rotten mound of flesh, sinew, and bone.

Without his passive, this would have been utterly impossible.

Emptying the contents, he stood back, then with an unusual air of gravitas, took a deep breath and raised his hand.

"Mana Bolt."

The blast of energy spun up, striking the flammable concoction he'd doused all over the mound of flesh and setting it ablaze.

Familiar, vicious screams immediately rang in his ears, not dissimilar from tortured death throes. These were sounds Adam was all too familiar with, after a lifetime of roaming battlefields.

"I grant you peace from suffering."

He closed his eyes, absorbing the sound of hundreds of bones falling still, the victims around him released from their desecrated bodies. No longer animated.

[Level Up!]
[Level Up!]
[Level Up!]
[Level Up!]
[Level Up!]

The familiar sounds of notifications rang in his mind, yet despite the massive boost in levels... Adam wasn't happy. On the contrary, he was furious.

"You may have been discarded here. But I will ensure you find rest," he swore, fishing out a slime core he held in his pocket. Consequences be damned, he wouldn't stand for such villainy.

Catpurr 59

The Captive

"M-Madam Valentine!"

"You two have been avoiding me since returning."

"Whaaaaaaaat? *Noooo.* Why would we ever avoid you?"

"Are you sure? Are you sure you haven't been avoiding me because of *THIS MASSIVE BILL FOR REPAIR SERVICES FROM THE SILVER SWORD?!*"

"Hahahaha. We have *no* idea what you're talking about."

"Where is the boy?"

"He's, uh, running errands."

"I'll give you one opportunity to try that again."

"Choking! Choking! You're choking me!"

"We don't know!"

***

With five new levels under his belt, Adam continued through the sewers. Felling various slimes and frogs went twice as quick with Skittles-One and Skittles-Two, his newly acquired skelecat nicely bolstering his forces.

Between his enhanced dark vision and the 10 percent increase in Strength from the skeleton augment, the low level enemies became trivial.

Slime cores were also rapidly piling up. Each new one was added to the store in his storage ring, where they would be saved for a *special surprise.*

[Box of Slime Cores x68]

It didn't take long until Adam reached a duct leading upwards. Judging from the lack of water falling and the hill of bodies below rising up from the water, this was where he needed to go.

Shifting the soggy bodies out the water using his Skittles, Adam placed them to the side, laying them out on the stone and promising to come back for them later. Then he gazed up into the gloom of the duct.

The time, according to the chronogear, was 0231. Late at night. Odly, Junith was still wide awake, broadcasting her emotions clearly.

Time to get up there...

Standing on top of his skeletons, Adam put Skittles-One and Two to work, using their skulls as footholds to lift him up.

He clambered up, using his augmented strength and upper body to pull himself into the bronze pipe, before dispelling his Skittles.

Let's just hope no one tosses another body down here...

Climbing for what felt like an eternity, he finally pushed past a lid that led into a dark and bleak room.

There were beds, dozens of them, each bed housing either a body or bloodstains. No doubt they were the result of awful experimentation.

Satisfied that no one was around to see him, he crept through on little cat's feet, but not before gently shutting the disposal pipe's lid.

The room was populated by all sorts of humanoid bodies. Some with scales, some with fur, each in various stages of dissection.

Experimentation? Adam frowned, approaching a nearby vat filled with a red liquid. Its true nature quickly became apparent from the scent.

"B negative," he read aloud from the sign affixed to the vat. He did not dawdle there long, quickly continuing on his mission.

Each step he took intensified the feedback of emotions from Junith.

This had better be worth it. Hopefully, he had reached his goal. At the top of a long flight of stairs, the nekoboy pushed open a large, bulky door and entered a dank and empty prison.

Well, mostly empty. In the leftmost cell, strung up into the air by chains binding her neck, ankles, and arms, was a small blonde figure, clad in rags. Junith.

Despite her transformation, this was her. He could feel it.

Adam approached quickly, shuffling across the oddly sticky dungeon to stand in front of the now short-stacked woman.

"You! Necromancer!" Junith spat. Despite the dried blood staining her skin, she remained as feisty as ever. "WHAT DID YOU DO TO ME?!"

"And here I was worried you'd be too injured to talk." Her size wasn't the only thing that had changed. Now she was glaring from heterochromatic irises as he approached—one purple, one gold. *Fascinating.*

But even that wasn't what caught his attention. That privilege was reserved for the fluffy cat ears sat upon her head, and the furry black tail swishing viciously behind her.

Wait, why did she *get a tail?*

"TALK?! WHAT WOULD I HAVE TO TALK TO *YOU* ABOUT, BESIDES TEARING YOUR EYES OUT OF YOUR SKULL AND DANCING ON YOUR CORPSE, HERETIC?!"

"Go for it. I'd like to see you try," Adam replied, smirking at Junith. Her retort was to lunge at him. Chained up as she was, however, she only jerked uselessly in her chains.

"COWARDLY BASTARD! I'LL GUT YOU! *ILL GIT YUHK!*" Junith shouted. Bloody spittle flew from her mouth, as she bit her tongue in sheer rage.

Adam only laughed. "Sorry, would you mind screaming louder? I couldn't hear you from way over here, where I'm standing because *I'm* not the one in chains."

"Ish dish amusing to yu! Seething ME lok up! Bound in chains?!"

"Yes, actually," he replied. "This is just like Garjul, except *you're* the one in chains."

"I'LL KILL YOU!"

"You tried that already, and see what it got you? What do you think will happen the next time you try?" Only now did he realize the utter joy that could be found in someone else's suffering. How had it taken him this long?

"O'lord, grawt me sernity—" Junith suddenly began to pray as blood leaked from her mouth. "Grat me strenth. Gran me wishdom. Allow tee to bak in yur holey ligt, so tat I may do dewds in thy name and exterwminate the whicked, the shinner, and the heretik."

"Oh, great, and now she's praying to smite me." Adam rolled his eyes. "Listen, if you want out of there I need something from you."

"I woud raher die tan hep you!" she spat, first metaphorically, then literally. Calmly he sidestepped the glob of blood.

"Ya know at this point, that *can* be arranged. All I would need to do is preserve your body until I can raise it and then dominate your mind. I could even parade you around like a pack mule, or have you fight for me," the nekomancer explained. Junith's horrified expression quickly morphed back to complete wrath.

"My fath is my shield! Yew'll geht *nushing* from me!"

He shrugged. "Okay, welp, I tried."

He took out his lockpicks, and immediately tried to pick the lock on the heavy steel gate.

"Wha-Whah har you dewing?!"

"I'm unlocking the door, so I can drag your corpse out of here," was his response. "You are the only one that knows how I can return to my friend. And I *will* get my answer, one way or another."

Junith shrunk back, yelling obscenities at Adam to break his concentration, her fury belying her revulsion and fear as he tried to open the gate. Finally, with a click, the gate swung open. Just as the fallen paladin fell silent.

"Last chance," he said coldly, standing before the now-helpless girl who closed her eyes and began praying to her god. He took his dagger, placing it over Junith's heart. The cold steel made her flinch. Despite all the years of suffering under her thumb, Adam took little joy from giving her a painful death. On the contrary, he'd actually enjoyed their cat and mouse shenanigans. But when she took away Schrödinger she had crossed a line.

He placed a hand on her rough shoulder, holding her body in place, when suddenly a notification appeared.

[Follower Menu:]
[Pack Leader: Adam Glow Lvl 14]
[Bonded: Junith Oatheart Lvl 1]
[Geass: Not Set]
[Status: Fearful, Scared]
[HP: 53/200]
[MP: 0/50]
[SKILLS TAB]→

[Geass not set, would you like to input Follower command?]

Seeing a follower menu Adam hesitated. The dagger nicked her skin, just barely, but plunged no deeper. However, just before he could reply to the prompt, his skin prickled with the sensation of being watched. Slowly the nekoboy turned. Watching them from the cell's entrance was a woman in a lacey black dress, gazing at them with a predatory grin.

Catpurr 60
Lady Vilenciel

The nekoboy awoke slowly, tormented by the granddaddy of all headaches. He groaned, struggling to piece together what had come before, though the pain didn't make it easy. He had been moments from finishing off Junith, when he turned around and saw that wom— awareness returned to him. It quickly became apparent that he was chained up, and nude.

"AW, C'MON! WHY DOES *SHE* GET TO HAVE CLOTHES?!" Adam yelled. In the cell across from him, Junith sported a massive grin. He glared daggers back.

"The lord works in mysterious ways," was her self-righteous, insufferably smug retort. Both turned to look as the door swung open, the iron shackle around Adam's neck *clink*ing as he did so.

Entering the prison now was a heavily endowed, pale-skinned woman, no older than her twenties, clad in a black dress.

"Oh my, oh my." Her voice echoed gently against the moldering walls, as she approached the prison bars to gaze upon her newest captive. "My precious new boy is finally awake."

"Hello. I don't suppose I could pay you ten gold to let me go?" Adam offered, suppressing a frown.

The white-haired woman stepped daintily inside his cell, her finery a contrast to its miserable conditions. "You want to leave? But you just got here." Her wounded expression quickly became one of outright sorrow as she gently stroked the nekoboy's head, her well-manicured hands drifting up to rub his ears.

"You even speak our language…" she whispered with a similar fascination Adam had heard from himself, when he studied old ruins.

Okay. This woman is insane. His attempt to wiggle away was thwarted prematurely, when the woman suddenly grabbed his chin, forcing him to meet her eyes.

"I deluded myself into thinking I could be content with artificially creating my own neko," she whispered. Her breath on his skin was oddly warm, pupils shrunk to pin pricks, like a hawk that had just glimpsed dinner. "I even prayed every night and every day, hoping to find one of your kind, begging on my knees. And just when I'd given up hope, the gods deliver to me not one, but *two* of you."

The duchess' daughter stepped back, hugging herself as her face twisted with perverted glee, causing Adam to cringe under the scrutiny of her gaze.

How the Nyx did this woman sneak up on me?

"You're almost perfect… So close. So very, *very* close," she lamented, reverently running a hand across the small of his back as a tear slipped down her cheek. Suddenly her grip tightened. "WHY COULDN'T YOU BE PERFECT!"

Immediately Adam began weighing his options. Fortunately his ring was still on his finger. Either the woman couldn't get it off, or she had succeeded only for it to return. Either way, he was not *entirely* helpless.

As the woman rambled to herself about *neko supremacy*, Adam took stock of his situation and pulled up his system.

First and foremost, his mana was being siphoned, no doubt by the shackles that bound him. Secondly… No, actually that was it. He was just nude, out of mana, shackled, in full sight of his arch nemesis, while a madwoman rambled on about the perfect husband. That was all!

Wait, husband? His mind blanked for a moment, before he decided to unpack that later and return to planning an escape. The woman's ramblings faded back into white noise.

As he saw it, there were two options. If he didn't use his secret weapon to escape, he'd be completely screwed. But if he *did,* then he'd be dead.

An extra life would be very useful right now...

"I know! I have the answer!" the woman suddenly exclaimed, startling him from his thoughts. "It was so simple!"

Oh, no. He frowned as the duchess' daughter gently rubbed his cheek, sending a shiver down his spin.

"If you don't have a tail... I can just give you one!" She smiled, slowly turning to Junith, who visibly flinched.

"Oh! I CAN HARDLY WAIT! LET'S START RIGHT AWAY!" Trembling with delight, the woman practically skipped up the stairs, finally exiting the prison.

At last the door shut. Junith wasted no time, launching into a tirade, demanding to know *what* the hag was planning.

"How attached are you to your new tail?" Adam asked, swapping dialects.

"What? Why would I be attached to it! I WANT IT GONE!"

"Oh, then good news," he said, his tone causing Junith to pale drastically. "I believe that's being arranged as we speak."

"Wha-What?!"

"Our prison master just ran upstairs for a bit to grab her extra big knives and scalpels, to perform what I believe is a transplant."

"WHAT?!"

"On the bright side, she probably won't kill me. *You,* on the other hand..."

"HOW IS THAT BRIGHT?!"

He snorted. "I didn't say bright for *you.*"

"ARRRRRGH!"

"You being upset is also a plus."

"Of course a monster like you would revel in my suffering," Junith spat.

Adam's eye twitched. "Monster?" he echoed. "MONSTER?! You have unapologetically slaughtered thousands in your damn holy wars! How am *I* the monster?!"

"You wouldn't understand, you never served a higher power. They willingly gave their lives in service to the Lord," she sniffed.

"WILLINGLY?!" Adam snapped at Junith's brazen declaration. "Then what about the innocent villagers! The cooks! The farmers! The mothers, daughters, and sons that wanted nothing more than to live their lives?! Only to be abruptly destroyed by *your* pillaging! *Your* tithes, taxes, and conscriptions, all in pursuit of 'service' to sustain your god's ego!"

Junith's brow furrowed.

"Tsk! They should be privileged to sacrifice everything for Lord Voltrain! Their donations allow us to spread the holy luminous light of our Lord even further! We do what we must to save their souls. To save *all* souls! An unrepentant heretic such as yourself wouldn't—COULDN'T understand," she spat back.

"Save their souls?" His teeth ground together. "Is that what you're doing when your wars attract monster waves?"

"What?"

"When they arrive to feast on your dead, when they move on to attack the defenseless villagers who are left unprotected, thanks to your conscriptions?"

"What? You LIE! Everyone knows that the monster waves were *your* doing!"

"Mine..." For a moment he choked on his own fury. "MY DOING?! I WAS THE ONE DEALING WITH THEM, YOU DISGUSTING MEATBAG! While *you* were all fighting and killing each other to prove *whose god was best*, my teacher and I were busy cleaning up your messes! Every time you'd fight a battle, you'd leave hundreds, even *thousands* dead. The scent of meat and sinew attracted scavengers far and wide. Or did you not think that there were *consequences* for sacrificing so many lives?"

Was this why they had branded him? Why they had ostracized him and his teacher? Because they had blamed them for their own stupid mistakes? He scowled furiously, and Junith met his glare with equal intensity.

"Tsk. Enough of your lies, necromancer. I tire of your falsities," she sniffed, finally breaking from his gaze. But Adam couldn't let it go.

"If your god was so omnipotent and good, why would he abandon you here with me?"

At last, Junith seemed touched by his words. For a moment, she might have felt something other than hotheaded fury—but then she doubled down on her tirade.

"SILENCE, HERETIC! I WILL NOT ABANDON MY FAITH!" Junith yelled. "VOLTRAIN IS THY SHEPHERD AND BRIGHTENS EVEN THE DARKEST LIGHT!"

"Hmp. Why do I even bother." He shook his head. The sound of a door opening interrupted their debate.

The woman in the black dress reappeared, gliding towards Adam's cage with an odd look on her face.

"Tell me, husband of mine, what blood type are you?" she asked, rummaging in a leather bag.

"No clue," he lied. In truth, he was O negative, a universal donor that could only receive O negative blood. Though, perhaps his new species had changed that, too.

A syringe emerged from her bag, glinting in the dim light as she opened the door and approached the nekoboy.

She looked at him sadly, remorse on her face as she rubbed his forearm, looking for a vein.

"Be still, I don't want to hurt your precious skin," she cooed. Then she plunged it into his arm, and the syringe began to fill with red.

Adam sighed. He watched impassively as the woman extracted his life essence, stroking the glass implement with a sort of glee. Then she quickly scurried away, racing back up the stairs and slamming the door.

How the hell am I gonna get out of this, he wondered, head hung low. A strange sound reached his catlike ears—Junith was crying.

Catpurr 61

Precipice of Escape

Without the benefit of the sun and moon or any windows, it was impossible to be certain how much time had passed, but by Adam's best estimate, it had been around two days. Two days of being touched, prodded, and examined by a woman who painstakingly explored every inch of his body, delicate hands clad in uncomfortable rubber gloves.

It wasn't the worst medical examination he'd ever been on the receiving end of, but he thought men were supposed to wait until they were in their fifties to be violated.

Fortunately, the Duchess' daughter was at a loss when it came to Adam's blood test results. According to her, a new shipment of O negative blood for her captive's surgery would arrive in a week. This made her irate and furious. To assuage these emotions, she spent more time with her beloved future husband. Constantly asking him questions, hand feeding him, and even playing a board game with him, known as chess.

"Six, F. Checkmate," Adam said. She slid his white queen across the board, sealing her defeat.

"My, oh my. You're quite good at this game, Adam." She smiled lovingly, knocking over her own piece.

"You aren't so bad yourself... Alencia." Although he smiled back, it was just a false veneer put on to appease her and hide his true feelings.

The Lady of Vilenciel put away the glass chess board, carefully stowing the pieces into a leather bag before snapping her fingers, summoning her servant, Sebastian Cartwright.

The silver-haired butler appeared, carrying a folding wooden table in one white-gloved hand and balancing a plate in the other, which he quickly set up within the cage.

Judging by the man's expression and the way his brow occasionally furrowed, there was little love lost between the two. Sadly, he had ignored any subtle requests for aid when Adam was alone with him during the man's cleaning duties.

Soon candles were set up, and the butler brought out a violin.

"Din din time, darling," Lady Vilenciel chimed as she removed a silver cloche, revealing the dish below.

Immediately the scent of cooked fish, greens, and grains wafted in the musky dungeon, hitting the nekoboy's sensitive nose and causing his stomach to growl.

"Say *aaah*," she hummed, taking a spoon and beckoning for Adam to open his mouth.

He played along, hoping to appease her, and opened his mouth.

"I SAID, SAY *AAAAH!*" Alencia spat, grabbing his chin roughly.

He went limp, his jaw unhinging.

"Now, isn't that good?" Alencia smiled, setting down the spoon as a knight entered the dungeon.

"Milady! The Duchess has returned, and requests your presence post haste!"

"Tsk. Old crone." She smacked her lips, annoyance plain on her face. "I'm sorry, darling, we'll have to finish our dinner later."

She got up and left, taking with her the butler and the knight, and leaving behind the food cart.

Adam sighed, sagging his shoulders before turning to Junith. The starved paladin stared at him with a mix of envy and hatred.

"You must be happy. Being treated like a king. Hand fed and pampered," Junith spat.

"Yes, being locked in chains with *you* as the only thing to stare at all day has been my one and only dream—"

King! King! King!

He froze at the familiar telepathic voice.

Krabby?

King! King! KING!

From beneath the white cloth on the food cart scuttled a small crab with a familiar cat eared accessory. His companion had been biding its time to rescue Adam.

Did you get bigger?!

Immediately the crustacean crawled up his body, skittering across his chest and to his arm until it reached his shackles. With its enlarged pincers, it began pinching them fiercely.

"What the Nyx is that?" Junith asked, staring with a baffled expression at the sudden emergence of the enlarged crab.

"My friend."

"Of course you'd be friends with a crab..."

"At least I *have* friends. What do you have? That's right, nothing."

To Adam's surprise, the metal began to chip, and although Krabby couldn't seem to destroy the chains outright, the tiny chip in the metal was enough to marr its runic engraving, restoring its master's mana regeneration.

And here I was thinking I'd have to charm my way out. Or commit suicide. A door creaked open, alarming him. *Go! Hide!*

Krabby hopped off his arm, scurrying beneath the cart once more as Lady Vilenciel entered the dungeon.

"Oooooh, loverrrr. Let's continue our dinner."

Adam sighed. It was going to be a long night.

* * *

It took hours of drivel about Lady Vilenciel's dreams of making Adam her 'perfect' nekoboy husband, and her aspirations to create cat people, but *finally* the noblewoman had fallen asleep, curled up on the floor of his cell.

Adam quickly checked his system interface. His mana had regenerated just enough to allow him to fire a few mana bolts.

Those he would save. Killing the defenseless woman would be a simple matter, but her butler would be her soon, and immediately catch the culprit.

Like clockwork, the silver-haired and impeccably dressed man appeared, opening Adam's cell to enter and retrieving the lady's slumbering body.

But as he cradled her prone form, something seemed to catch his eye, as his eyes fixed on something to Adam's right. More precisely, his manacle—the manacle that Krabby had nicked, disrupting the siphoning rune.

Oh, crapbaskets!

Adam did his best to hide his panic, yet the man still noticed. His silver eyes darted between the boy and the shackle, as the nekoboy's heart pounded, wondering if now was the time to release the slime cores.

Surprisingly, the man blinked, turning as he carried the Lady of Vilenciel towards the stairs. The butler paused, just outside the metal bars. "Lady Alencia has sealed the sewers. If you intend to escape, go through the west wing. If you go east, I will have to stop you. Do not squander this chance. Your items are laid out in the room ahead." He quickly departed with the slumbering woman—leaving the gate unlocked.

The door to freedom closed. Adam wasted no time. Angling his right hand, he blasted first the chain connecting to his neck, then the one shackling his left hand. For a moment, a single chain held his entire body weight, putting painful pressure on that wrist. He winced, before blasting those chains too.

He hit the ground and began to repeat the process with his ankles.

Catpurr 62
Slight Cature

"Do it. Get it over with," Junith spat. Adam grimaced, before raising his free hand high, gathering mana within it. The blast severed the chains, and the ex-paladin fell to her knees. She hit the ground with a thud, much like Adam had. Before she could get her bearings, Adam grabbed her. He pressed a hand against her neck and the interface activated, displaying a follower menu.

"You will not attempt to kill me, you will obey my will and reasoning, and you will answer my questions. Do you understand?" he hissed, willing the geas function to activate.

Immediately Junith tried to pull away, but stopped as she again collapsed to her knees, screaming in pain.

Adam released her as a familiar glowing mark appeared upon her chest—one in the shape of a serpent devouring itself.

"I... understand," Junith hissed, though her eyes spoke of nothing but violence. "You won't... get away with this!"

"And yet, here I am. Getting away with it. Let's go. Keep your voice down and follow me," he ordered, heading out of the prison. For a time, he'd considered leaving Junith to her fate at the hands of the Lady of Vilenciel, but the nekogirl held knowledge he needed.

"YOU—" Junith began, but suddenly fell silent, furious scowl at odds with her strangely demure behavior.

Ha. I could get used to this, he laughed inwardly as he climbed the stairs and slowly pushed open the heavy wooden door.

His gear was laid out on a long, metal table, each item neatly arranged, from vials, to daggers, to his armor, and the tattered remains of his cloak arranged upon a mannequin. But something gave Adam pause as he went to collect his things—plastered to nearly every inch of the study were hundreds and hundreds of sketches of himself.

Oh, crapbaskets.

A shiver went down his spine as he looked left and right, stepping around the charcoal sketches of himself, each proving eerily accurate.

"By Voltrain's light..." Junith muttered. She made a point of kicking each page she came across out of her way, even stomping on several. Then a gleam of light caught her attention.

Wasting no time, Adam dressed quickly, as his reluctant companion ran off to another table bearing her shiny armor.

She eagerly tried to pick it up, but failed—as she was now, it was apparently much too heavy.

Junith began to tear up, desperately struggling with her armor. Yet no matter how hard she pulled, it wouldn't budge from the table.

At the pitiful sight, Adam reluctantly walked over, placing his hand on the metal. A notification blinked in the corner of his vision.

[Faith Stat too low! Unable to properly utilize Item!]

Adam frowned. *Faith stat?* This was the first he'd seen such a stat.

Probably because he never took an interest in anything religious.

He removed the abyssal ticket from the storage device, slapping it against his wrist. Then he pocketed Junith's gold armor, swapping the two items.

"MY ARMOR! UHK!" Junith's mark lit up, burning her. Tears gleamed in the corners of her eyes. "What are you doing with it! GIVE IT—*back!*"

Adam only shrugged.

"Taking it to sell for later, obviously."

"Wha—WHAT?! Y-You can't sell a priceless artifact!"

"Uh, sure I can?" He resumed dressing, nose twitching at the lingering stink of sewage.

"YOU—" She fell to one knee, spasming, as the mark activated again.

Frustrated, Junith began to tear up the Lady Vilenciel's drawings, new claws protruding from her hands. All the while a low, droning groan emanated from her throat.

Adam nearly chuckled, feeling her frustration through their bond, but kept silent. Rather, he moved to a table covered in diagrams and materials for some kind of machine. Its function appeared to be altering the body in some way, as nearby were images of various demi-humans.

He pocketed the notes, sticking them in his journal where they would be safe, cramming other jewels and items he picked up in his storage.

"What are you doing?!" Junith hissed, watching him pilfer everything shiny in the workspace.

"Recuperating my losses," came the response as he stuck a flask of unknown liquid in his belt. "Let's go."

Gritting her teeth, Junith followed. The two creeped together through the door and into what appeared to be a garden filled with stone statues.

The nekoboy scanned the moonlit courtyard, looking for any signs of threats or patrols before setting foot upon the stone path.

Suddenly something clanged to the ground. Adam's gaze snapped to Junith, who was clutching at her chest struggling to breathe. At her feet lay a gleaming silver knife.

"Did... you just try to backstab me?"

"Y-Yes," Junith growled.

"Wonderful. Make sure no one sneaks up on us," he ordered, before walking into the garden. At least he knew for certain the geas would work.

As the pair progressed, Adam carefully scrutinized each of the statues they passed.

A pattern quickly emerged. Demi-humans, all of them, arranged in various poses.

Some were talking, some appeared to be singing, while others were posed regally.

Each of them was uncannily lifelike. In the dim moonlight, a few could have been mistaken for living people—as if someone had simply frozen them and painted them stone-gray.

"What are you doing?" Junith hissed. Her tail lashed in anger. From a catwalk overhead, voices from a patrol echoed softly.

Adam reached out, touching the statue, only to immediately recoil as the familiar energy of the undead washed over him.

"What? What's wrong?" she asked, sensing his tumultuous emotions.

He grit his teeth. The noises of the patrol grew louder, and Junith dragged them both into the bushes behind a statue, where they hid as the patrol approached.

"The statues are bodies," Adam finally explained.

Her gaze sharpened, ears pricking upright. "How can you tell?"

"I'm a necromancer, undead are my specialty." His ears twitched, picking up as a voice hummed a familiar tune.

Lady Vilenciel.

Jeez, don't you ever sleep?! He found himself inching closer to Junith, who visibly winced.

"By Voltrain, you stink." Awkwardly, she leaned away from Adam's sticky armor.

"Sorry, that's what happens when you crawl through a sewer."

"Well, no one told you to do so!"

"I had to, in order to rescue you!" He jostled Junith as they argued, then quickly looked towards Alencia. Fortunately she had yet to notice them.

"And that's going swimmingly, isn't it."

"Is that all you're going to do, be annoying? I'm *trying* to save you."

"Only so you *can* use—MFHM!" Adam's hand clamped down on her mouth.

"Hush, you idiot!" Sharp teeth dug into his hand. "Ow!"

"I'm not an idiot, you heretic!"

"That's it!" he barked, lunging and grabbing the girl as he activated the follower menu. "From this moment on, you can't call me a heretic anymore!"

[Error! Geas already set]

What?

"Ha! Heretic! Heretic! Heretic!" Junith chanted. She shoved Adam into the dirt. "You filthy here—"

A gasp interrupted them, and both froze. Not far away stood a furious Lady Vilenciel, eyes locked onto the nekopair. *Oh, crapbask—*

"GUARDS!"

Catpurr 63

Welp, I Tried. Let's Die Together.

"Arnold…"

"Yes, dearie?"

"I sense something is wrong."

"Oh dear."

"Fetch Sehn and Titania, I'm fairly certain they're about to do something that's going to piss me off."

***

"GUARDS! GUARRRRRDS!"

"What's the plan!" Junith yelled as she followed Adam. The pair raced haphazardly through the ornate halls of the castle, the Lady Vilenciel's screams echoing down the decadent corridors.

"Me?!"

"Yes, you! Is there anyone else I could be speaking to, necromancer?!"

"I don't know! You spend a lot of time talking to your invisible friend, I just figured you were usually insane!" A guard lunged for the nekoboy and Adam leapt, just barely avoiding capture.

"Really? You're still being snarky with me?" The pair careened around a corner, only to stumble to a halt as a wall of knights appeared. They dashed down another corridor.

"Being snarky is really all I have at this point!" He fumbled with a potion. "I'd shove you into that woman's arms, but sadly I need you to return me home, so I can rescue my cat!"

"Cat *this!* Cat *that!* Is that all you can think about?!" A servant tried to grab at her—they received a dagger for their trouble. "We're in a life-or-death situation, being hunted by a madwoman trying to *cut me open!*"

"BIT IRONIC, DON'T YOU THINK!" He hurled a vial into the ceiling. Green goo splattered everywhere.

Immediately, the roof began to melt. Debris fell from above, cutting off the knights chasing them as they turned, fleeing east.

"WHAT'S—Uhk!—that supposed to mean?!"

"It means, HOW DOES IT FEEL TO HAVE A CRAZY LADY CHASING AFTER YOU?!"

"I'M NOT—UHK! *ARRRGH!* CRAZY! I'M NOT CRAZ-ZZzzzy!" Her retort became a scream as the mark blazed to life, zapping her with electricity. She stumbled, losing balance and falling face-first.

"Crapbaskets! I think we're heading east."

From every direction came the tromp of heavy footsteps, and the shouts of approaching knights.

"Ugggh. I'm. Not. Crazy." Drool dribbled from Junith's mouth, pooling on the luscious red carpet below her. Her breath was heavy, haggard, as she coughed into the carpet.

"Get up, we don't have time to waste."

"You filthy... necromancer..." The nekogirl went limp, eyes rolling up into her skull.

SERIOUSLY?!

"ARGH!" Adam had little choice but to hoist her up onto his back, and start to sprint.

"ADAM! COME BACK TO ME, DEAREST!" Lady Vilenciel yelled. A nearby window exploded, splintered glass flying everywhere as the woman of the house appeared.

Colorful shards embedded in her skin. She broke out into a savage grin, eyes wide with a predatory madness as she took off into a full sprint, trailing ribbons of blood.

"*ADAAAAAM!*"

The sight was ridiculous, like a rhinoceros chasing down a butterfly—Adam could only shake his head in disbelief at it all. Struggling to balance Junith's limp body, he uncorked a bottle of frothing white liquid, and tossed it at the noble lady. Still she ran, heedless of obstacles, chasing down her fleeing quarry.

"ADDAAAAAAAAAAAAAAAM!" Lady Vilenciel wailed like a banshee. "LET ME LOVE YOU!"

Where the hell do I go?! Closed doors surrounded them, obscuring the way forwards. Suddenly one opened, and a white-haired girl hastily beckoned them towards her. "Psssp! Come come!" she whispered. "I can help you!"

"GO, YOU IDIOTS! DON'T LET HIM ESCAPE! THEY TURNED DOWN THAT CORRIDOR! TO LULUCA'S ROOM! GO! SEIZE THEM! A THOUSAND GOLD TO ANYONE WHO CAPTURES HIM!" Lady Vilenciel yelled. The clanking of knightly armor was approaching from every direction.

"Screw it." The fugitive nekoboy dove into the lavish bedroom. The girl shut the door, already jerking her head towards the ornate, rose-wood closet.

Adam didn't need to be told twice. He flung Junith hard through the doors with a muffled *thud* before hopping in himself. It was a long shot, but he was out of options as he hid between expensive dresses. Junith lay crumpled in a small heap by his feet.

"Ssssh," the red-eyed girl whispered, closing the door.

Albino? Or is she a vampire?

"Lady Luluca! Lady Luluca!" A guard banged at the door. Adam instinctively tensed, rubbing the storage ring in preparation. Should a fight become inevitable, there was still a way to recover his mana, but winning would be impossible with Junith on his back. There also remained the slime cores...

The soft creak of a door silenced even his thoughts. Ears strained, waiting for whatever came next. Junith moaned. He slapped a hand on her mouth, muffling it.

"Yes? What is all the commotion?"

"Lady Luluca, we apologize for waking you, but we are in pursuit of dangerous fugitives that have broken free from our prison!"

"Oh, I see. Well, I have heard none come my way."

"Thank you, milady. Please, stay inside your room while we search for these ruffians."

"Thank you, Sir Gillian, I do hope you find what you seek."

The door closed. A sigh of relief escaped the closet's occupants.

One moment passed, then another. When nothing happened, Adam opened the door a crack, peering out into the room. However, its resident appeared to have vanished.

Where did she go?

The closet door fully opened, and the girl beckoned him to come out.

"Hello. I'm Luluca von Vilenciel, welcome to my bedroom." She curtsied, lifting the ends of her frilly purple dress. After spending the better part of the night hellbent on escape, *this* was what caused Adam's mind to blank. How was he supposed to reply?

"Adam," he finally introduced himself. Then he recalled the situation at hand.

Should I take her hostage? Use her to facilitate my escape? The thought crossed his mind, and it certainly was an option worth considering. He'd never hurt an innocent if he could help it, but the Vilenciel knights didn't need to know that. And the perfect hostage was standing before them now.

Suddenly a shiver went down his spine as he recalled a certain silver haired butler.

Only if I need to, the nekoboy decided he fished Junith out, still unconscious, and draped her over his shoulders.

"Sadly, I do not possess adequate food or beverages to accommodate you. I was not expecting guests," Luluca said, as if Adam had just popped in for afternoon tea and *wasn't* currently scanning her room, charting possible escape routes. "If you seek an exit, the only way out is through my door. Because of my condition, sadly, there are no windows."

According to the chronogear, dawn would be breaking soon. The light of day would only make a stealthy escape that much harder.

He sucked in air through his nose, racking his brain for options. A full-body chill suddenly seized him.

Danger.

A cold steel dagger was already against Luluca's neck by the time Sebastian emerged from the shadows. "Unhand her!" he barked, silver eyes radiating golden power as his muscles strained against the confines of his black butler's uniform.

Adam shook his head.

"I'm really sorry about this. But I can't, not if I want to get out of here alive."

"If you should harm one hair on Lady Luluca's head, I will personally exterminate your entire bloodline," came the cold response. Sebastian took a single step forwards. Adam instinctively took a step back.

Suddenly the door slammed open, revealing a powerful woman clad in heavy onyx armor, and dragging a four foot tall steel mace. Flanking her were dozens of guards.

"Crapbaskets," Adam muttered. He was grateful for his small size, because the crowd of armed soldiers forced him against the wall.

"RELEASE THE LADY, CRETIN!" the lady knight barked. Her crimson eyes flashed beneath her visor, as the helmet magnified her echoing voice.

"Is there any way we could talk about letting me go?"

The knight only sneered at this, as she and the butler readied their weapons.

"Okay. Well. I tried. Good luck, everybody."

With no other option, Adam opened his storage ring and released the slime cores.

Catpurr 64

Destroying a City... Oops!

"A... box?" a soldier muttered. The guards crowding the room glanced left and right, as others warily eyed the wooden box that had fallen from Adam's storage ring.

The earth trembled. Both the silver-eyed butler and the lady knight raised their weapons, preparing to surge forwards. Both were halted as Adam pressed his blade closer to their young mistress' throat.

"Not a step further!" the nekoboy barked. Despite how the world rumbled, he stood firm with a look of grim determination. Sweat poured down his back, as heat and light roiled in the air, churning around the wooden box. It shuddered and trembled as the slime cores fused within.

Seeing the storm of gathering mana, the soldiers in the room began to flee. Only Adam, Luluca, and her two servants remained, each tensed to move, carefully watching the others.

"Huwha?" Junith slowly roused, sputtering awake. With a dazed expression she attempted to rise. "ARE YOU TRYING TO KILLLLLLLLLLLL—"

The volatile energy quickly overwhelmed her. Within seconds she was unconscious, spasming on the floor again.

"Boy! Do you know what you are about to do!?" the silver-haired butler demanded, face scrunched up into a hateful scowl. Dust trickled from the ceiling as the entire castle rumbled.

"Well, I ASKED politely!" the boy in question yelled over the noise, "BUT *noooooooo*. Everyone wants to kill me just for being different, so now! We can *all* die here together!"

He was bluffing. He had no intention of dying here. The second an opportunity for escape presented itself, he'd be taking it.

CRACK!

A fissure split the floor, spewing a geyser of goo.

The two parties dispersed, Adam with Junith on his back and Luluca in his arms, while the butler and knight darted backwards. Debris fell everywhere as a tidal wave of slime surged towards the box.

Immediately the two servants sprang into action. Silver cutlery flew from Sebastian's sleeves. Beside him, the knight raised her visor, a stream of flame flowing towards the box of cores.

Neither attack connected. A wall of slime shielded the cores, spikes erupting from it and jabbing towards the servants.

Suddenly, a chill wind blew, pricking Adam's ears. Following it, he spied a crack in the bedroom wall, leading to freedom. With a system user's augmented strength, turning it into an impromptu door was trivial. He dove out, still clutching both Junith and Luluca close.

Luluca made a noise of distress.

Oh, crap.

This was a mistake. That was Adam's first thought, when he realized just how high up they were. The moat was far, *far* below them. Behind, a massive slime roared as it turned the castle into its plaything.

No going back now. Junith would have to serve as a makeshift cushion. He hugged Luluca tightly, angling his body to shield her from the rapidly approaching waters below.

Surrounded by brick and mortar, the trio hit the water. Immediately the catsification curse activated. Adam shuddered, but refused to let go. Kicking his legs, he broke the surface again, and dragged Luluca with him to the shore. She had remained oddly silent throughout the whole ordeal—the only noise she'd made was to suck in a breath of air.

Junith had been separated from them upon impacting the water. He spotted her floating upside down in the moat, slowly carried away by the waves.

Adam swam towards her, flipping her over as debris fell like rain from the castle. In the distance, the city was slowly beginning to wake up around them, and boy would *they* be in for a surprise. Fortunately, it turned out that Junith was rather naturally buoyant. She made for an excellent flotation device, which Adam used to swim towards a sewage pipe, away from the crumbling castle.

* * *

Elsewhere, in a distant realm.

"Well, your Adam is panning out to be much more of a troublemaker than I thought he'd be. Mind if I take him off your hands, Eli? As a favor to you, of course."

"Hmmm, yes, a *favor*. While tempting, I will have to forgo your generous offer."

"Hey, is it true he blew up Unidine's mother's temple?"

"That event is canon, yes."

"Oh, this just keeps getting better and better."

"You do understand that he used one of *your* artifacts to do so."

"...What?"

"Yes, I believe it was the multi-dex ring fashioned out of Pandora's box, that I won from you during a game of goldfish. The one with the randomization gimmick."

"You didn't..."

"Do you still want him?"

"Ehehehe... More than ever before."

* * *

Vilenciel City

"EMERGENCY! EMERGENCY! ALL FIRE USERS C TIER AND ABOVE, REPORT TO THE FRONT!" a crier called out. All around him, cacophonous bells rang and the entire city mobilized.

"MY GABBAGES! NOT AGAIN! WHY, FREYA! WHY!"

Eyeing the spectacle, a certain sopping-wet nekoboy pursed his lips, hooded, staring in mixed awe at his handiwork. Vilenciel City had been completely transformed.Everywhere he looked, the ground oozed slime. Some form of chain reaction from the super slime, if he had to guess. Hundreds of soldiers darted back and forth, carrying torches, as they desperately struggled to stem the lethal tide of goo.

"Oh, man... I am—" he turned, and was met with a blank-faced noble girl, equally drenched. "—in so much trouble."

At first, he was just going to leave the girl at the entrance of the sewer. That plan had been scrapped when a river of slimes burst forth from everywhere, forcing him to flee with Junith on his back and Luluca in his arms. Again. The whole debacle culminated in their return to the surface, whereupon they witnessed armies making a valiant attempt at slaying the newborn Slime God.

Making his way through the chaos, Adam headed in the direction of the church, where he hopefully still had an ally. Although his initial instinct was to return to the guild hall, he couldn't risk Luluca being found there, and getting his benefactors punished.

Not only was Coco the most well-informed regarding his situation, but she was part of a major organization that could shield her from consequences.

Hopefully.

It was also a safe place to leave Luluca.

"Sorry about destroying your home. And kidnapping you. And threatening you. Just know I didn't intend for any of this to happen," he said, as he checked for safe routes to the church.

"I understand," Luluca replied, the first time she'd spoken since their fall from the castle. "If it will assuage your concerns, this is my first experience beyond the castle walls. 'Tis quite exhilarating, verily so."

Surprised, Adam turned. Gleaming in Luluca's eyes was the same wide-eyed fascination that he had glimpsed in her sister's.

The Crazy must be hereditary, he decided.

In the distance, the titanic slime continued its rampage. Its roar shook the foundations of buildings, even this far away. The nekoboy wasted no time dodging patrols of guards, darting up the marble stairs, and entering the Rip-off Temple. Within, it was surprisingly absent of its typical templar complement.

"Hello?" he called, looking for any sign of, well... *anybody* within the temple. "I guess everyone *would* be busy..."

"Yooooooooohooooooooooooooooo!"

Adam spun. Perching in the eaves overhead was Coco, waving down at him. Sat atop her head were artificial cat ears.

"Hi hi! I see you've brought guests this time," Coco said, smiling as she leapt off the archway and landed gracefully in front of Adam and Luluca. "You must be Luluca."

The noble curtsied, bowing slightly to the shrine maiden. "That I am, voice of the gods."

"Hohoho, you're so cute. Oh! OH!" Coco's eyes went wide, fixating on Junith, precariously perched upon Adam's back. "FOR ME?! You shouldn't have, Adam!"

"Not now, Coco. I need your help to disappear." He batted Coco's grasping hands away from the nekogirl's tail.

"I take it you have something to do with the giga-slime currently assaulting Vilenciel," Coco said as a massive *boom* shook the world. A distant flash followed, forcing them all to close their eyes. Even this far away, the mana pressure was still palpable.

"What was that?" Adam asked, blinking his eyes as the light faded.

"Oh, don't worry about that. It's just the duchess trying to find the slime core by blowing everything up in a five mile radius around it," Coco laughed, patting Adam on the back as she leaned in. "What she doesn't know is that the core has already left the castle and is puppeteering all the slimes at a distance. Faaaaaar away from the city."

Right. The woman was blessed by clairvoyance.

"Don't worry too much, everything will sort itself out. Maybe." The priestess shrugged. "Now, as for you disappearing, I know just how to do that!"

"Really? How!?"

Coco giggled. "Simple! We'll just throw you into Trial Two!"

* * *

"CICERO! YOU FIENDISH BEING! I KNOW YOU TAMPERED WITH THOSE SLIME CORES! COME OUT!"

"Ehehehehehe."

Catpurr 65

Welcome to Trial Two

"What?" Adam frantically brought up his timer.

[474:22:05]

A little less than three weeks.

"You can just send me into another trial?"

Though sounds from the ongoing battle penetrated the temple's inner sanctum, things seemed a little more peaceful here, lit by the gently glowing floor.

"Sure I can!" Coco smiled. "The timer is just there to notify you when it officially starts, you can rush it at any time! Heck, you don't even need the abyss obelisk in the city square, you can just come here."

"Oh..." It made sense when he thought about it. After all, this *was* where he got the ticket. "Can't you just help smuggle me out of the city? Or let me take shelter here? My... Friend and I kinda need some time to prepare."

Another explosion rang out, closer. The floor below flickered and buzzed, briefly shining brighter.

"Nope! And nope! Only church personnel and those blessed by the gods may work here! Speaking of, somehow, you've managed to make three separate gods angry." She walked towards the pool as Adam racked his mind.

"Three?! What did I even do—besides accidentally blow up a temple?!" Coco gave him a pointed look. "Okay. Now that I'm saying it, I hear it. But that wasn't my fault!"

Coco shrugged. "I only know what I know, lol. Come along! We'll send you and your follower to your next trial."

Wait, what? He followed the priestess' gaze, finding it landed on Junith.

Suddenly another explosion of light broke out in the distance, interrupting their conversation. A holy presence caused Adam to full-body flinch.

"Vol... train?" Junith groaned, as the caress of her deity's energy roused her.

"Here we are!" Coco smiled, the water in the pool parting around an obelisk rising from its depths. "You best get going! You've made quite a few beings REALLY angry!"

"Does this mean Junith can come with me?" Adam sought clarification as Coco took Luluca aside, preventing the noble girl from following him.

"She's bonded to you. I don't see why not," the priestess said, eyes seeming to trace some unseen connection between them. "You're both tied together, so good luck!"

Great...

He turned, observing the obelisk as the city shook once more. He raised his arm, offering his ticket to the pillar. A soft light soon consumed it.

One way to deal with my problems is by not dealing with them at all, I s'pose.

[Do you wish to Enter the Abyssal Trials?]
[Time Remaining until next Abyssal Trial: 474:16:20]
[Yes← No]

Upon choosing yes, a familiar bone-lined portal manifested. Skeletal arms reached towards him and his new companion.

"Oh! One more thing!" Coco suddenly called out. "Voltrain says it's on sight! So watch out for the Voltrain familia!"

The Voltrain what?

"The Voltrain *what?*"

Before she could reply, the skeletal hands reached him and Junith both. The ex-paladin bolted upright, immediately screaming, when another shock of electricity sent her back into dreamland.

"WHAT DO YOU MEAN, ON SIGHT?!" Adam called out. But Coco only waved, as beside her Luluca curtsied.

He was pulled through.

* * *

In an instant, Adam was deposited into an entirely different location, landing on top of Junith. The much-abused nekogirl only groaned. Somehow, she had successfully retained consciousness for longer than half a minute. But perhaps it wasn't worth it, as now she laid upon her stomach, retching up rainbow puke.

Oh so that's what that looks like from—

Adam's train of thought was interrupted by a wave of nausea, as he vomited all over Junith.

"Eh? EH!" Junith went wide-eyed, freezing as she gazed upon the rancid, colorful vomit that coated her arms and face.

"Ah, sorry." Another wave of nausea passed over him.

"ARGH!"

[Inertia Resistance Lvl 1 obtained!]

[**Skill Description:** *You are a speed demon. Somehow, you've achieved warp speed and have been constantly subjected to G forces that should kill you. 10% Inertia resistance. You don't fly as far when thrown.*]

[CONCATULATIONS! QUEST COMPLETE!]

Oh?

[Rolling Rewards...]
[DING!]
[Minor Health Potion x 1 obtained!]

Fairy lights coalesced into a delicate vial, filled with glistening red liquid, almost like diamonds at night. Gently it floated down into his small hands, where Adam eyed it closely, tilting it this way and that. "Huh... Neat."

He fell to his knees and vomited.

* * *

Once they were no longer throwing up everywhere, it was easy to tell that this was a completely different world.

Sequestered between two high-rise buildings in a damp and refuse-ridden alley, Adam looked up, spying what appeared to be glass buildings that ascended well into the heavens, as large, white birds glided along the bright blue sky.

"Argh..." Junith moaned, crawling to her feet as Adam picked up a piece of papyrus off the smooth concrete floor to examine it.

"Of course..." he muttered.

It was just as he feared. An entirely different realm, judging from the incomprehensible characters scrawled across the paper, and the architecture that seemed to defy gravity and common sense.

But more than that, it was the *noise*, loud and obtrusive. Now that he had a moment to stop and listen, a headache was taking shape in his head. The constant *vrrr* of machinery, the overlapping hubbub of the crowds, the occasional *honk*s of some great beast—it was all too much.

Cautiously he approached the edge of alleyway, keeping to the shadows as he peered out at the impossible spectacle before him.

What?

Everywhere, crawling all over the place, were *humans.* Sat in colorful boxes crammed on stone roads, gazing at tiny boxes that emitted light and sound, walking here and there with cups and foodstuffs that assaulted his nostrils. Everywhere he looked, dizzying mobs of them.

[Welcome to Floor Two! The World That Devoured Itself.]
[This world is a mirage, one created to reflect the end of a civilization that fell to a great plague.]
[Mandatory quest given!]
[Main Quest: Survive The End of the World!]

Who what *now?*

Catpurr 66

Meeting the Administrator

[Main Quest: Survive The End of The World]

WHAT?!

[Survive for 28 days.]
[Hidden Scenarios x 4]
**[ERROR! The Trial has not begun yet! Please wait for a Trial
Administrator to contact you!]**

As Junith's eyes darted about, bewildered, Adam's gaze was fixed on
the blinking notification before him.

Administrator?

"You! What devilry is this?! Where are we?!" Junith demanded. After
many, *many* painful reminders, she appeared to have learned to restrain
her tone somewhat.

Before he could tell her to shut up, Adam was interrupted, as a chill
shock of mana bolted down his spine.

"A mirror marble designed by bored beings," answered a high-pitched
voice. The nekopair turned, to see a floating, rainbow-hued rock.
Attached to it were two googly eyes, and a scribble of a mouth not unlike
what a child might draw.

"The administrator, I take it?" Adam asked, brow raised at the child's
pet rock.

"Correct," the rainbow stone replied, its drawn mouth moving as it
spoke. "And you are quite early, Chosen."

"Hey! Where are we?!" Junith repeated. Adam ignored her, instead choosing to **Identify** the floating rock.

[**Title: Beloved Pet of Islandr**]
[**Name: Administrator of Realm Z-28DL**]
[**?????**]
[**Strengths: ?????**]
[**Weaknesses: ?????**]

Islandr? The image of the green-skinned shortstack who stole his hard-earned prize wandered across Adam's mind. *This is her pet? Why is her pet serving as an administrator?*

"Chosen, are you aware that it is quite rude to identify someone?" the rock said, prompting him to quickly apologize. "Just this once, I will forgive you, but subsequent attempts may make me reprimand you."

Despite the administrator's goofy appearance, it still radiated substantial power.

"HEY! I'm talking to you!" Junith suddenly shouted, waving her arms at Adam.

Fed up with waiting, she smacked him on the back of the head.

The nekoboy retaliated with an open-palmed smack of his own. She was sent reeling, as the wet *thwack!* echoed through the alley.

Dazed, Junith could only stare blankly at the brick wall beside her, before furrowing her brow and growling.

Oh no.

"RAWH!" the nekogirl lunged, tackling him. They rolled in the muck-stained alley scratching, biting, and pulling hair as they fought with each other. Refuse and other debris were knocked in a disarray as they grappled with each other.

"OW! OW! Stop biting my fingers, you idiot!" Adam yelled, his phalanges in Junith's mouth. Her canines ground against his skin.

"Stawp pullin mah hair, hereTIC! And git oHF meh!" she growled back, biting down even harder and drawing blood. She began to tremble as her shoulder glowed, the geas activating.

"OW!"

Instinctively she bit down harder, tearing skin.

"STOP! BITING!" Adam howled, releasing her hair and wrapping his free arm around her neck. In a desperate attempt to free his hand, he began to strangle her.

"Uhk! I'LL TAKE! I'LL TAKE yor flingers to ELL wit ME, HERETIC!" Blood dribbled from her mouth as she screamed.

"Go to sleep! Go to sleep! Go to sleep!" the nekoboy chanted, until finally his adversary went limp. He pried his bleeding fingers out from her jaw, clutching his hand. The floating rock was still patiently waiting.

"Trouble in paradise? Slaves are always hard to control if you don't geas them correctly," the rock said, causing Adam to frown.

"She's not my slave."

The administrator only laughed. "Yes, I suppose not. May I see your abyssal ticket, Chosen?" the rock asked. Mentally, Adam decided to dub the administrator *Rocky*.

He held up his wrist, brandishing the ticket for the rock's 'eyes' to see.

A moment passed, then another. What was Rocky looking for? His eyes shifted to check the ticket for anything strange.

"Fascinating."

"Problem?"

The corners of Rocky's scribble-mouth had perked up into a grin. "Nonononono. Not at all! In fact, I'm quite ecstatic that you are here!"

"Really?" He scrutinized the rock with suspicion as it bobbed up and down, as if nodding.

This... can't be good.

"OH, YES! It's been nearly twenty-four hundred thousand years since I last saw a follower of Eli!"

"You mean two *million* years?" That length of time was mind-boggling.

"Yes, yes, Chosen! Two ages, by my approximation!"

It wasn't so odd that there had been others before him, or even like him. He'd suspected as much previously. But he hadn't expected to find someone who was familiar with his divine patron.

"What happened to him?"

"*Her!* A feisty one!" Rocky proclaimed. "Sansa, I believe her name was. Or was it Sasha? Slanthra? Sanhasha? Anyway, she was incinerated by an aeroplane falling on her and exploding!"

His ears folded at the jubilance of the rock's casual proclamation. "Aeroplane?"

"Oh, yes, yes. If you direct your attention upwards, Chosen, you can spot white aeroplanes in the sky."

It must have meant the giant white birds.

So those are aeroplanes. Adam summoned his journal, sketching one such bird as it soared overhead, and making a note to watch out for their supposedly explosive nature.

"Oh, this is so exciting! The only form of entertainment I have is watching you Chosen fight each other, so having an extra participant is always a bonus!"

Wait, what?

"What do you mean by fighting each other? Are there other Chosen here?"

"Soon! Soon! You'll all get to meet, we're only waiting for a few others," Rocky proclaimed. Suddenly Adam felt something tugging him. His and Junith's bodies began to glow, as the tugging became more forceful, pulling him every which way.

Realizing what was about to happen, Adam opened his mouth to shout, but it was too late. He and Junith disintegrated.

Catpurr 67
The Contestants

Adam fell to all fours, dry heaving alongside Junith as the effects of teleportation struck their bodies.

There were two ways teleportation worked. One was by establishing a connection point between two spaces and swaddling the target in protective mana, before rocketing them to their chosen locations. Alternatively, the target would be disintegrated and reconstructed at the destination.

Adam hated both ways, as each method seemed to rack his body with convulsions that made him puke.

I miss my old body... he whined inwardly. Left exhausted and drained, he curled up on his side, struggling to catch his breath. Fortunately his stomach was already empty, so there was no more vomit, just some retching.

"Ha, hserf taem."

"Sdik?

"GMO! YEHT EVAH TAC SRAE!"

At the sounds of foreign language, Adam made an effort to scan their surroundings. This time the nekopair had been sent to a brightly lit, white-walled room.

So much for being the early one.

In the center of the room stood three humanoids.

A blonde human clad in a blue uniform, his belt crammed with various gadgets and a staff of some sort slung across his chest.

A human woman dressed in all pink, with a matching oversized coat, beret, and pants that cut off just above her upper thighs. Sticking out of her purse in comedic fashion was what looked like a sword.

And lastly, a bipedal, black-furred canine warrior of some kind, the pieces of bronze armor he wore not quite hiding his numerous scars.

The canine's red eyes locked onto Adam, drool leaking from his wolfish mouth.

Oh, crapbaskets.

Adam's own golden eyes immediately noticed the blood-stained axe strapped to the wolf's back.

"Hello?" the nekoboy offered. All three turned towards him, but only Pinky approached, a familiar look on her face.

Oh no. He'd seen that look before. It was somewhere between Coco's expression when she first saw him, and the horrific obsession of the Lady Vilenciel.

"ERA ROUY SRAE LAER??" The woman's hitch-pitched voice was like steel on steel, making him cringe as she reached out to touch his ears.

"Stop! What's with everyone trying to touch my ears?!" he barked, slapping away the woman's pink gloves.

She only smiled, not taking the hint. Again she reached out.

"Seriously?! What is your problem!"

"PLAY NICE, EVERYONE! Let's try and get along, shall we?" Rocky chimed in. The magical floating rock simply appeared in the middle of the group, as Adam grabbed at the woman's grasping hands.

"HO, ER'UOY GNORTS!

"Go away, woman!"

"EMMEL HCUOT MEHT!" Pinky cried, prompting Blue to shake his head and act. He hooked his arms around her armpits, dragging her away as she began throwing a fit. "Pots! Tel em—"

[SYSTEM LINGUAL TRANSLATOR TURNED ON VIA FLOOR ADMINISTRATOR COMMAND]

"—TOUCH THEM! HE'S SO CUTE!"

The woman's ravings began making sense—well, in that Adam now understood the language.

"Can you calm the hell down, woman! You can't just touch random children, that's how you get put on a registry!" Blue yelled, as his companion groaned.

"Whatever. If this was Earth, I could just buy him..." Pinky pouted, her attitude akin to that of a spoiled brat denied a toy.

"I'm going to pretend I didn't hear that. Sorry about that, kid," Blue said, releasing Pink. Junith had sat up by now, staring at Pinky and the ornate sword hilt poking out from her purse. Blue cautiously approached the pair, hands held up. "I'm Sergeant Redfield, a police officer with the NYPD and Chosen of Unidine." Redfield kneeled, offering a hand to shake.

On Redfield's palm was a symbol eerily similar to the one Adam had seen in Undine's temple. Cautiously, he accepted the hand.

"Adam," he replied, mind still on the symbol. *Undine and Unidine, perhaps they are related...*

"Just Adam?"

"Yep." Movement in the back of the room drew his attention as three more individuals stood. A dark-skinned human wrapped in bandages, a humanoid reptile of some kind, and finally, what looked to be an oversized gerbil, standing at ten feet tall with muscles bigger than Adam's torso.

If we're supposed to fight each other, how the Nyx am I going to fight that?!

Upon tracing Adam's line of sight, Redfield gave him a reassuring smile.

"Eh, don't worry about those guys. They aren't very chatty. If anyone gives you any trouble, just let me know," he offered, all smiles before he turned to Junith. "Hi, little girl, what's your name?"

"Piss off, heretic," Junith spat, eyeing the mark on his hand.

Redfield blinked, completely taken aback.

"Don't mind her, she's just an idiot," Adam cut in.

At his words, Junith's face scrunched.

"I'M! NOT! AN! IDIOT!" the nekogirl cried, body sparking wildly with each word as her geas flared.

Stubborn idiot. Adam shook his head, as the health bar on his follower menu steadily dropped.

"Whoa! Jeez!" Redfield exclaimed, backing away from Junith cautiously as the others stared at her.

Junith huffed, her hands balling into fists.

"Sit down and shut up," Adam said, turning to the man. He looked more closely at the metal wand on his chest, wondering at the red, cylindrical objects decorating it.

Weird. What kind of wand has a switch?

"Is your sister okay?" Redfield asked. Junith growled at his assumption.

"She's fine. Just gets worked up over nothing." Junith's growl became deeper, head snapping towards Adam now.

"Well, let's get along Adam, and uh—what's her name?" Redfield asked.

"Judgy."

"Right, Judgy," Redfield said, brandishing a too friendly smile.

Either the man was being overly nice, or he was plotting something. That, or he simply didn't know they would be fighting one another.

Outside of the canine, the only ones Adam was really worried about were the giant gerbil and the reptile. Both of them were fully grown demi-humans with natural armor, and very likely skills to match.

The gerbil appeared to be a brawler type, an easy guess from the bulging muscles beneath his fur, while the reptile was a spearman, a golden trident blatantly balancing on his shoulder.

Wait, am I going to have to kill these people?

"WELL! That's that! No more waiting, honorable Chosen!" Rocky suddenly exclaimed, its rainbow body visibly shaking. "It seems our last Chosen was sadly hit by a truck! How *un*fortunate!"

Truck? Briefly he wondered at what *that* was, before something else occurred to him. *Wait, why does this trial have an administrator? Why didn't the first one have one?*

That would have to be saved for later, however. For now, the rock was practically dancing—as much as one could without limbs.

"Thank you for all being patient! I know it took a few of you stragglers days to arrive, with others cutting it close to the deadline, but here we are!"

Wait a second. Something about Rocky's words didn't seem to be adding up.

"Excuse me." Adam waved his hand to get the rock's attention.

"Yes? Oh! A question?!"

"Uh, yeah, I thought you said I was early. Do we all have different times to be here by?"

"Oh, no no, you are all right on time, and share the same trial deadlines."

"Then how can I be early, while being right on time?" The timeline seemed almost paradoxical.

The rock bobbed a bit, as all eyes turned to Adam, clearly filled with confusion.

"Simple, when I teleported you, I merely kept you in a state of suspended animation until the trial began. Although the early bird gets the worm, it wouldn't be fair if you had a *twenty-day* head start, now would it?" Rock exclaimed, then turned its googly eyes to address the rest of the Chosen.

Wait. I've been out for TWENTY DAYS?! Adam paled. All the time lost! All the gains, exploration, and knowledge he could have been procuring! Not to mention, twenty more days he was separated from Schrödinger!

Any other questions he had intended to ask vanished from his mind, as he joined Junith in blankly staring into space, processing the information. From their shared bond, Adam could tell she was just as shocked.

"So! Without further ado! Here are the details of your trial!" Rocky continued.

[Mandatory Trial quest given!]

[Survive for 28 days in the Zombie Apocalypse!]

[A magical infection will descend soon in New Yor City, raising the undead and turning those that succumb to the infection into ravenous beings. You have 24 Hours before the outbreak begins.]

[Hidden Scenarios x 2]

[Sub Quests]

[Protect Survivors: 0]

[Quest Description: *The more humans that survive each day, the more points will be generated. Large numbers of points will be necessary to obtain better rewards.*]

[Kill Survivors: 0]

[Quest Description: *The more humans you kill, the more points will be generated. Large numbers of points will be necessary to obtain better rewards.*]

Catpurr 68

Discussing Zombies

[**Mandatory Trial quest given!**]

[**Survive for 28 days in the Zombie Apocalypse!**]

[**A magical infection will descend soon in New Yor City, raising the undead and turning those that succumb to the infection into ravenous beings. You have 24 Hours before the outbreak begins.**]

[**Hidden Scenarios x 2**]

[**Sub Quests**]

[**Protect Survivors: 0**]

[**Quest Description:** *The more humans that survive each day, the more points will be generated. Large numbers of points will be necessary to obtain better rewards.*]

[**Kill Survivors: 0**]

[**Quest Description:** *The more humans you kill, the more points will be generated. Large numbers of points will be necessary to obtain better rewards.*]

Undead?

A wide grin broke across Adam's face, as he doubled over laughing.

The contestants stared at the boy. Pinky and Blue quickly began whispering to each other.

"I wonder what's so funny?" Pinky asked. She seemed about to approach him, but Redfield put out an arm to stop her.

"Just leave it."

"But—"

"Do I have to tase you again?"

"Awww."

Adam ignored the pair, straightening up and more closely scrutinizing the quest and its requirements, including the contradictory objectives of the two conflicting subquests.

Is this what Rocky meant by conflict? Do they want to pit us against each other?

Though the presence of the undead put things in his favor, if everyone in this room decided to hunt down humans, things would quickly spiral out of control. It would not end well for him.

I'll have to play this by ear.

From the reactions of the various Chosen, it appeared they too came to the same conclusion.

Rocky did a lap around the room, circling everyone to corral their attention once more. In the walls of the room, clearly labeled doors began to appear.

Police Department.

Mall.

Community Center.

Hospital.

Apartment Complex.

Docked Cruise Ship.

After a moment, Adam realized that despite being perfectly legible, the signs were in an unfamiliar alphabet.

"If you direct your optical systems to the walls around you, Chosen, these are points of interest that have been picked as areas to spawn in. Once everyone is in, you'll have twenty-four hours to familiarize yourself with the area, before the trial begins," Rocky said, shaking left and right. "So, without further ado—"

The reptilian spearman raised his green scaly hand, interrupting the admin. His forked blue tongue darted in and out of his mouth.

"Yes, CHOSEN?" Rocky asked, eyes rolling towards the lizard.

"Are there ruless or sstipulationss? Limitss to what we are allowed to do?" the lizard croaked, its voice oddly feminine, with only a light lisp.

Ah, that's a good question.

"Nope! No limitations! No rules! Leave the city, drink expired milk, burn down orphanages, cure the zombie plague! Do whatever your heart wants, just survive for twenty-eight days!" Rocky chimed happily.

Cure the plague?

As Rocky finished speaking, the doors suddenly opened. Behind them swirled portals, each showing glimpses of a different vista.

The administrator disappeared with a popping sound. The remaining contestants warily eyed each other, as if sizing one another up.

The canine man moved first, immediately heading into the door labeled *Community Center*.

"Hey, wait! Where are you going?" Redfield called out. "We should stick together, if we want a better chance at surviving."

"Our truce was for Trial One. With your nature, you'll slow me down," the wolfman said, before disappearing into the portal.

"My... Nature?" Redfield blinked. "The hell is that supposed to mean?"

"Itsh meanss you're too nice," the lizard woman replied. Her tone was almost teasing.

They know each other.

"I just want us all to survive. Is that such a bad thing?" Redfield asked. Pinky giggled.

"Oh, you're so naive, cutey. If only you were a little older." Redfield shook his head at her words.

"We should figure out a plan. I recommend the police department. There'll be armories, cells, and a sturdy defensive structure with police officers like me," he said. Now it was Pinky's turn to disagree.

"Nope. Have you seen the movie *28 Hours Later*? Or any zombie film? Those places are the first to be overrun," she corrected, touching her pink lips. "Plus, we don't even know what kind of zombies they are."

"There are different kinds?" Redfield raised a brow as the gerbil and the dark-skinned man approached to listen in.

"Yeah, you got *Romeros, Biohazard, 28 Hours, Walking Teds, Voodoo, Dead Void*, there's a bunch of different kinds. There's even one where the infection spreads through fungus," Pinky explained, unbothered as all eyes focused on the cheery woman.

"Can you give me their characteristics?"

"Well, most spread the infection through bites, but others can infect with scratches or bodily fluids. Since the Trial is to survive twenty-eight days, I think what we'll be dealing with is angry, zoomy boys. Like, the ones that go all RAAARGH and chase you at full—"

"Enough babbling, Nursse. Sspit out the information," the lizard ordered, clearly annoyed.

"I told you, my name is Liza."

"No, you told me your name iss *Nurse* Liza. Ish it not common to be addresss by your firsst name?"

"Nurse is my title, *not*—"

"Focus!" Redfield cut in, hand on his tool belt. "As you were saying."

"Bites and body fluid. Two things we need to avoid. They can be stopped with enough damage to their bodies, but—"

"Brains is what we're aiming for," he finished, tapping his own skull. "See, I know a thing or two about zeds."

"My apologies. I am Jerbull. I am not aware of what a zed is but am hoping to learn," the gerbil said, his hulking frame towering over the other survivors.

"I am Abdullah, shinsu of sands and Chosen of Yashwa," the black-skinned man said, extending his scarred hand, wrapped in black bandages, to Redfield.

The blonde man took it.

"Redfield, Chosen of Unidine. A zed is an undead, or zombie. They can turn you into one of them too, if you aren't careful."

"Ah, so like a zilundas. Mindless, ravenous creatures, yes?"

"Uh, yeah."

Adam frowned, listening in. While there were types of undead that could propagate via the infection of their bites, this was the first he'd heard of so many variants.

Best to take notes.

"Okay, so to recap since we're doing introductions, these four would be—" Redfield pointed in turn "Liza of Voltrain, Sethiss of Freya, and Adam 'n Judgy."

Junith growled at the name. Beside her, Adam's eye twitched. He remembered well Coco's warning about the followers of Voltrain.

"Many moons to you," Abdullah said, shaking everyone's hands with a bright smile. When it was Adam's turn, the nekoboy hesitated.

Something was wrong.

Wedged between the man's bandages were little grains of sand, slowly flaking off. Some primal instinct was warning him against touching them.

Instead he refused the gesture, offering a simple "Hi." Fortunately the warrior seemed to approve, raising a brow and smirking as he replied.

"No harmful intentions," he assured.

I doubt that.

"Right. So, where do we all want to go?" Redfield asked, scratching his chin.

Adam reassessed the portals.

With his passive, he didn't have to worry about undead. In fact all he had to do was find a place to survive.

Junith, on the other hand...

Now that he thought about it, his new follower was unarmed, unarmored, skilless, and... well.

She was dead weight.

But until he got his answers, she was *his* dead weight.

In the meantime, he could probably use her like one of his skeletons, provided he leveled her up. Matter of fact, this could be a good opportunity to test some things.

Would his passives translate to her?

Did they share experience?

How would her being his follower affect—actually, when he thought about it, judging by how Junith was looking at Pinky, Voltrain *probably* wasn't happy one of his flock was now a nekomancer's follower.

"So. Are we all in agreement?"

Adam blinked, realizing he'd zoned out.

"Sssounds like a plan."

"Makes sense."

"I concur, we stand a better chance together."

"Adam, are you two with this?" Redfield asked.

Who what now? Redfield was beckoning the nekopair now, expecting an answer.

"Yeah, sure," Adam replied.

I'll just lose these guys, first chance I get.

"Alright then," Redfield sighed. "Apartments it is."

Catpurr 69

Not Nice

Beyond the blue portal, Adam and the other Chosen emerged in a narrow alley, flanked by red wooden fences.

A number of sensations blasted him all at once. The brightness of the sun's rays, the stink of trash, the overlapping sounds of honks, conversation, and distant machinery. The nekoboy scrunched his eyes shut, ears pressed flat against his head.

"Ugggh."

"What? Not a day person?" Redfield laughed, smacking him on the back.

"No," he replied deadpan. Behind them, Jerbull and Sethiss stepped down from the portal.

Not far away, a road was crammed with extremely heavy traffic, mostly consisting of those magic boxes. They crawled up and down the lanes at a snail's pace.

As they stepped out into the open, no one seemed to pay the odd group any mind—even when said group included a seven-foot tall gerbil, a humanoid lizard, a dark-skinned man in full bronze armor, and a woman in the most eye-catching pink.

"Ah! This is just like Earth!" Pinky waved. "Hello, people!"

That *did* catch the attention of a few people—who then began walking away faster.

"Stop! What are you doing?" Redfield exclaimed. "You're drawing attention to us."

I think we draw enough attention, Adam thought to himself, taking in their ragtag team, only to freeze.

In the reflection of a red box on wheels, he saw his cat ears were gone, his cloak replaced by a large, cat-eared black hoodie.

He reached up, touching his head. Despite what his eyes were telling him, he still felt his cat ears.

An illusion? Fascinating.

Reflected in a glass window beside him, Jerbull had become a tall muscular white man, in shorts and a tight T-shirt. Sethiss, a black-haired woman dressed in green snake-leather and high boots, her spear replaced with a pole. And finally, Abdullah. The man's wrappings and armor were instead a suit studded with gold buttons.

I guess Pinky and Blue are normal enough, Adam surmised. Not far away, one woman walked up to a still red box and entered. It seemed to activate, joining the congested river of other boxes.

Fascinating.

He summoned his journal, taking notes and drawing sketches of the various contraptions moving on the smooth, paved road.

Does everyone own one of these? Maybe I can find a manual.

"Watcha doing?" Pinky asked, looking over Adam's shoulder.

"Taking notes."

"Smart," Redfield said, walking down the pavement. "Looks like these are the apartments."

Above them were various large brick buildings, all lined with glass windows and surrounded by tall, black iron fences.

"Alright. We'll get in there and find a room. I'll see if I can find the superintendent," Redfield said, moving towards the entrance.

Why did they choose this?

Adam frowned. This was far from defensible, with so many openings.

Still, he took notes on the building, recording his findings to sell to Beifong and the Clocktower when he got back.

Actually... I wonder if everyone back home is doing okay.

***

Vilenciel City, three weeks ago.

"Report," ordered the tall, black-haired woman in rose-gold armor, folding her gauntleted arms. All in the room withered under the intensity of her silver-eyed glare.

Guild Master Valentine looked over at the people gathered in the remains of the Duchess' office. The roof of the stone room was gone. Strewn about the once-luxurious office were dozens of books, gold pieces, and other debris.

"The core has been found and neutralized, thanks to the adventurers' quick response," Lloyd the blond spymaster said, holding up a report that showed the details of the battle.

"Damages?"

"Roughly ten Goldsun coins," reported a bald man in dark robes, eyes peering from behind thick glasses at his ledger. "The damages range from the castle, all the way to Twilight Plaza. The noble district was hit the hardest, which is where much of our costs are coming from. There is also the issue of citizen displacement, with which the Temple has agreed to help."

"And where is Coco?"

"The Priestess is..." the bald man adjusted his circular glasses, "occupied. Something about cats."

Why do I get the feeling that boy is involved? Valentine frowned.

Duchess Vilenciel closed her eyes, taking in a deep breath before she opened them once more.

"And the guild?"

It was Valentine's turn to respond.

"A few hundred wounded and displaced, but no fatalities of note. My husband is taking care of the wounded as we speak. There was also an issue with undead, but they have been disposed of," Valentine reported dispassionately as she sat on Lunafreya's back, the maid desperately trying to hide her look of contentment at being used as a chair by Valentine amidst all the debris.

The Duchess nodded, rubbing her gorget.

"Good, you will be compensated for your assistance. Now." Duchess Vilenciel's gaze swept to the left, focusing on the overweight man hunkering into himself. An attempt at making himself smaller and unnoticed, ironically only drawing more attention to him.

"Iskar," Duchess Vilenciel said, tapping her fingers across her gold desk. "What happened to the dispersal and suppression fields? As well as the patrols sent to routinely clear out the sewers to prevent things like this from occurring?"

The portly man coughed, tugging at his collar as sweat visibly poured off his body.

"I-Ineffective, once the cores left the bounded area, your grace. As for the patrols..." The man trailed off, completely flustered.

"Spit it out!" Vilenciel barked, slamming her rose-gold gauntlet down and cracking her much-abused desk.

"We stopped because it was getting too dangerous!" Iskar blurted out, causing Valentine to shake her head. Behind the desk, the Duchess sighed and pinched her nose.

"You mean because you were too CHEAP!" she barked. A wave of mana radiated outwards, and even the hairs on Valentine's arm stood on end.

As a Chosen of Voltrain and a floor fifty contestant, Duchess Vilenciel was one of the strongest beings in the Empire, by virtue of her ability to harness an immense amount of mana. In fact, her armor was specially designed to dampen her natural mana. Without it, merely existing among regular and low-leveled system users may actively harm them. Unbound she was a flood of energy, a weapon of mass destruction, prohibited from fighting in wars unless another country preempted the attack, and even then there were stipulations.

After all, no one wanted to fracture their realm and summon a Judge.

"When you came to me with the proposal to use slimes to help sanitize our sewers, do you remember what you said about the possibility of a supercore fusion?"

"Y-Yes, Duchess."

"Pray tell, what was that probability again?"

"O-One in one b-billion."

"And yet, somehow, despite the failsafes, a cluster of not one, not two, but at least *a hundred* cores managed to go into fusion, sparked by some *boy!*" Suddenly the duchess raised her hand. A tendril of energy lashed out, lassoing around the man's neck. His feet lifted from the ground. "You utterly incompetent, corrupt PIG!"

The man squealed as the room grew brighter, the tendril of energy generating heat and burning him until the Duchess swiped with her hand. The man was thrown, screaming, out a gaping hole in the wall.

Duchess Vilenciel's head fell into her hands with a heavy sigh.

"I shouldn't have done that..." she muttered, before snapping her fingers. The distant scream became louder, as a large, flaming bird deposited the portly man back in the center of the room. "Thank you, Reslov."

The phoenix squawked, before disappearing in a flash of heat, leaving the panicking man to fumble on the ground.

"You are fortunate that I require your skills, Iskar." The noble smacked her lips as she folded her hands in front of her. "One more screw up, and I'll turn you into phoenix feed. Do I make myself clear?"

"Y-Yes, your grace! Your immanence! Your magnificent—"

"Cut that crap. I hate suck ups almost as much as I hate leeches. Sadly, you are both. Kell, take Iskar and get the budget balanced," Duchess Vilenciel ordered. The bald man with glasses quickly took his leave, practically dragging the flustered treasurer. Valentine watched them go, as they exited through the remains of a half broken door. The duchess rose from her seat. "As for the rest of you, I have orders. We are looking for a boy, a demi-human in particular, one that goes by the name Adam—"

Valentine's heart stopped.

Of. Fucking. Course.

"—who I'm led to believe is the source of this mess. Courtesy of my daughter, we already have images and fliers ready for use," the Duchess said, waving a hand at the aforementioned fliers in the remains of her desk.

Valentine frowned, accepting a hand-drawn flier as it was offered to her and eyeing the lifelike sketch of Adam, ears and all. Below the image was a reward of ten thousand gold coins for information leading to his arrest.

Oh... crap.

"Take a few stacks and distribute them. All across town, the guild hall, and even to the black market and any departing merchants. I want this boy found, immediately," the Duchess ordered. She picked her way through the debris and stopped, silhouetted in the gaping hole against the damaged skyline of Vilenciel City.

"As you command, your grace," Valentine said, standing up and taking Lunafreya with her, the latter of which was completely stone-faced at the news.

Catpurr 70
Hotwiring a Car

Adam closely observed his environment, taking note of the shabby building's derelict halls as he waited on Redfield. The man was engaged in a deep conversation with the building's inn keeper, the latter of which kept staring nervously at Redfield's golden emblem as he waved it around.

Hmm, police officers must have a higher station than I thought, the boy considered, nose scrunching at the superintendent's stink of distilled grass.

"Alright, we got a room," Redfield said, coaxing everyone to follow. Pinky had tried to pet Junith, but each time she snapped her canines at the woman.

"Feisty, hehe."

"Alright. We've got twenty-three hours until the event starts," Redfield began, drawing everyone's attention as they spread out across the spacious main room. "We'll use this place as our base of operations as we scout and look around. So, let's break out into teams, gather supplies, mark POIs, and meet back here at least two hours before the trial begins."

"OH! Oh! I pick the cute catboy and his sister!" Pinky cried, hopping up and down. She flashed what was clearly *meant* to be an endearing smile at the nekopair.

"No. Absolutely not," Adam replied seriously, crossing his arms in an X. Junith only growled.

"I'll go with the kid," Redfield said, firmly. "We'll attract a lot less attention with a cop watching over two kids."

"Tsk, you're all no fun," Pinky whined as Sethiss raised a hand.

"What iss a P-O-I?" the snek woman asked.

"Place of interest. Anything like food stores, gun shops, pharmacies, or even places that look interesting," Redfield explained. From his utility belt he removed a notepad and shiny, mechanical writing tool. Quickly he scratched something down.

"Mark them down and copy their addresses. We are on 41st and Main Street. Apartment 493, top floor. Remember this address. If you get lost, try and return here," he said, tearing off pieces of paper and handing them out to everyone.

Fascinating.

The mechanical tool did not hold charcoal, but actually blue ink! Adam gazed at the page with something akin to awe.

I need to get me one of those. Already the man was tucking the inking tool away into his belt. Adam salivated, imagining the nice, dark lines and detailed notes he could create.

I wonder what his other contraptions can do. Inevitably the nekopair would have to ditch the man, as well as the other contestants, but for now he seemed the most interesting. The group broke out into teams. Abdullah, Pinky, and snake woman were to head east, while Adam, Junith, Jerbull, and Redfield would head west. Both squads were on separate missions to document the land and find supplies.

* * *

Having already bid Pinky and her team farewell, Redfield walked with determination and purpose as he led his party away from the rundown apartment, gazing about almost as if he were looking for something specific, even as they simply stood on the sidewalk.

"Why did we choose this area again?" Adam asked, glancing around at the buildings. They all looked so similar to each other.

"Less populated, less chance of being overrun by civvies looking for aid, and usually by this time tomorrow most will be at work," Redfield replied, briefly distracted as the sun reflected brightly from glass windows.

Seeing an opportunity, Adam pilfered the man's shiny pen. It was eye-catching, the way the metal reflected the sunlight. Entranced, he pushed down the button at one end, creating a *click*ing noise that revealed a pointed metal edge.

Ooooh. So the ink is safeguarded by the sheath, and unveiled by this mechanism. A second click seemed to resheathe the ink blade.

"You want it?" Redfield asked, upon hearing the contraption's clicking noise.

"Really?"

"Yeah sure, it's just a pen," Redfield said as Jerbull approached.

Pen. Adam took out his notebook, excitedly going to work drawing the pen and spelling out the word.

"What is the plan?" Jerbull asked, lumbering in the background as Adam doodled and Junith scratched her ears.

"We need a set of wheels. Cover ground faster and see about grabbing supplies." Redfield took off, apparently spotting what he was looking for.

The group followed slowly as the man jogged to a red, L-shaped machine. Wheels were affixed to its back, not dissimilar to a wagon. Redfield wasted no time as he took out a stick, jamming it into the machine between the door and the glass pane.

"What are you doing?" Adam asked.

"Stealing us a car," Redfield replied. Abruptly he stopped, blinking, and turned to the boy with a smile. "Which is okay, because I'm a police officer. But which you should never do, because it's bad."

"I see," Adam replied. Redfield turned and went back to work. But the nekoboy's curiosity had not been sated. "So how does this *car* work exactly?"

"Uh... Something with gasoline, engines, and electricity."

"Electricity! Like a lightning bolt?"

"Uh, yeah. Something like that. Do they not have cars where you're from?"

"No." *Click* went the box on wheels as it popped open. Redfield paused, finally seeming to register the boy's leather armor.

"I suppose that makes sense," he said. "Do you come from some kind of fantasy world?"

"Fantasy world?"

"You know. Swords, shields, flying dragons?"

Adam's brows furrowed in thought. *Flying?*

"You mean drag-ons? I've never known them to fly," he said. The dragons he knew were overweight, scaly lizards that dragged themselves everywhere, hence the name, as he eagerly explained. Normally preferring to burrow underground and hibernate, they would only emerge to mate or catch prey.

"Wow," Redfield said, apparently disappointed by the description, even as he directed Adam and Junith into the leather seats inside the car. He unslung his staff and tossed it onto the floor. "That sounds super lame, kid. Dragons are supposed to be huge, massive lizards that fly and breathe fire, with giant teeth, and hoards of gold."

"That sounds absolutely terrifying." Some trial and error was necessary to make the nekopair fit. Unfortunately, Junith ended up squished sideways, Adam sitting on her knees. Such were the sacrifices that had to be made. "I think you're talking about dragonoids."

"Maybe." Redfield leaned underneath the wheel that jutted towards the car seat. The man strapped on black rubber gloves, then took out a knife, stabbing at a panel until it broke free, revealing several colorful threads. He began tinkering with them.

Adam leaned over, observing with fascination as the officer split a rubber thread, only to reveal the metal strings entwined within it.

"Adam, can you check in the glove compartment box for a user manual?"

"The what?"

"Ah, sorry. Pull the lever on the compartment, should be a car manual inside."

Adam peeled his eyes away from Redfield, spying the lever and pulling to reveal stacks of white envelopes and what appeared to be an instruction manual.

Fascinating. He opened the colorful pamphlet in his hand and began reading it. Below him, Junith had started banging her head against the side of the car out of boredom.

"What am I looking for?" he asked, trying to be helpful.

"Here, let me see." The officer held his gloved hand out for the manual, causing Adam to frown. "If this world is anything like mine, there should be a wire code somewhere in the instruction manual. Just need to make sure I'm handling the starter wire and battery."

Despite not wanting to part with the treasure trove of information at his fingertips, Adam handed the manual to the man. He quickly flipped through it until he found the page he was looking for.

"Alright," Redfield said, returning the manual to him. Upon trying to pocket it in the storage ring, the nekoboy found his inventory to be full. Thus Adam was reminded of its randomized item deposit.

Ah... crapbaskets. He pulled up the inventory list, displaying the new item that had replaced the box of slime cores he had left behind.

[Stielhandgranate x 01]

What? It was not a word he recognized, let alone one he could define. Sadly, he couldn't identify the item without taking it out, and the last time he had done so had resulted in him... Exploding.

Suddenly the metal chassis around Adam shuddered to life, almost purring, as Redfield cried out "AHA!"

"Hey! Big guy, get on back, we're going for a ride," Redfield called out to Jerbull. The entire car tilted to one side as the hulking mass of fur and muscle climbed into the attached flatbed.

Redfield closed the door, grabbing onto the steering wheel before he turned and helped Adam and Junith buckle in.

Junith hissed, but relented with a little coaxing from Adam, tenderly administered via a hand chop to the head.

"I hate you," was Junith's response. Then the car peeled off into the traffic, causing both nekos to tense at the movement.

"Alright. Let's see if we can find some guns and ammo." Redfield grinned, pressing down on one of the pedals, fully unaware that he and the others were being watched by a certain woman in pink.

Catpurr 71
Terrorist Plot?

"Seriously?" Redfield asked, watching as Junith trudged through the aisle of the bookstore, barely visible behind a stack of manuals, How-to books, and diagrams held in her arms as she reluctantly trailed Adam. "I said pick three items. That's more than three."

"Three? Three! How am I supposed to choose *three* within this treasure trove of information?!" Adam demanded, almost offended that the man was telling him to put anything back. "There's so much to learn here!"

"Well, unless you get a job and start earning money, three is all you can get, kid. My storage band can only hold so much."

Adam groaned, almost taking out the stielhandgranate to chuck to the side. The memory of his last incident stayed his hand.

"Fine." Adam deflated, slowly walking over to Junith and picking out three books. *A History of New Yor City*, *History of Firearms*, and *Automobiles 101*.

"Judgy, put everything else back," he ordered, shooing Junith away like he would one of his minions.

"DO IT YOURSELF, HER—UHK!" Junith snapped before catching herself, eyes twitching with visible fury. She spun, the massive stack disappearing behind the shelves of books.

Ha.

"That's the fifth time that's happened, is your sister okay?" Redfield asked.

"Hmm?" Adam peeled his attention away from a row of books beside him. "Oh, yeah. Judgy is just special, is all."

"ARRRRRRRRRGH!" sounded a shout, heralding the sound of shattering glass.

* * *

"Great. Are you happy? You got us kicked out," Adam spat, possessively clutching the three books he smuggled out of the shop before the owner made them leave.

"Screw you," was Junith's response as they approached the red truck parked in an alley of an area called a *strip mall.* Leaning against the flatbed as he organized items was Jerbull.

"Hey big guy. What, uh... Whatcha got there?" Redfield asked. Within the flatbed were several bulging bags.

Jerbull turned, clearly holding a clear cup of pink liquid in his titanic hand. "A smoothie."

"No, what I mean is *all this!*" Redfield asked, pointing at all the goods on the back of the truck.

"You said we needed supplies," said the ten-foot tall gerbil. "So I got everything that was requested on the list."

"And how did you do that without any money?" Redfield stepped up to the bags, opening one to reveal a jug of juice.

"Simple, human. I got money."

Uh oh. Adam didn't like where this was going.

Suddenly a loud *weee wooo weee wooo* echoed in the distance. As the obnoxious blaring grew louder, the nekoboy's ears twitched.

"Oh my God," Redfield sighed, pinching the bridge of his nose.

"Please. Please, explain to me, in depth, *how* you got enough money to afford all these supplies."

"Simple. I took it from humans."

The police officer closed his eyes, shoulders visibly sagging.

"Right. Okay, we're leaving! Right now. Everyone! Let's go! Let's go!" Redfield hurried, tone urgent as he opened the door and directed everyone inside.

Adam ordered his 'sister' in, much to her displeasure as she struggled to resist. Seeing Redfield's expression, Adam simply picked her up and chucked her inside. The vehicle lurched at the impact.

Junith snarled, preparing to pounce at the nekomancer, until—

"Sit!"

"You FUC—"

"And be quiet!" he added, climbing in, careful to avoid the stacks of ammo, snacks, and guns laid out across the floor. He and Redfield had pilfered from them various stores using the officer's storage band.

Speaking of, the man entered last, starting the car as the sounds of sirens grew ever-closer.

"Let's just hope no one saw him loading up the goods into our truck," the officer groaned, putting the car in reverse and taking off.

Or, at least he *tried* to.

Their escape was blocked off as several black cars flashing yellow and green lights suddenly appeared, their arrival heralded by the now-deafening sirens.

All around the vicinity, uniformed humans had begun swarming.

"Nonononono." Redfield's face grew paler and paler, as his eyes darted between his ill-gotten gains. "This is bad. This is *real* bad."

"SHUT OFF THE ENGINE AND GET OUT WITH YOUR HANDS UP!"

A voice bellowed from outside, as several humans dressed similarly to Redfield began to appear, each holding onto objects Adam came to learn were called 'guns'.

"Sonuvabitch," Redfield sighed, gripping the steering wheel tightly before releasing a groan and slamming his head on the steering wheel.

* * *

"Is he… going to be okay?" Adam asked. Redfield and Jerbull were being dragged away in chains. Despite some complaints from the officer about the cuffs being too tight, both seemed surprisingly calm.

The nekopair were left in the middle of a busy office space as blue-clad men and women buzzed about them. After *many* attempts at biting people, Junith had been left shackled and gagged for the better part of an hour, as people tried to question her companion.

"Him? He'll be fine. He's gonna get what he deserves for impersonating a police officer and abducting children for his terrorist cult," the woman sitting behind her desk wearing a red blazer said. Her attempt at a warm smile quickly became a grimace, as she caught sight of Redfield's retreating back and glared.

Okay. Well. I guess that's two less contestants I have to worry about, Adam thought, pulling up the event timer.

[Time Remaining until Event Start: 18:21:03]

Not even six hours, and we're already in trouble…

"Now, can you tell me your name? Where you live? Where your parents are?" the woman asked, filling out a piece of paper. From upside-down, Adam could barely make out the words *Child Services.*

"Like I told the other lady, I don't have any parents," he replied. The woman's shoulders sagged, before something seemed to catch her eyes. She straightened up again.

"Right. Well, looks like social services are here anyway." Adam twisted around, to see what was behind him.

Immediately his eyes widened.

"Hi! Detective Wong? We talked on the phone," spoke a familiar voice. Its owner then crouched down to address him. "And you must be

Adam and Bitey! I'm Liza Joy, a social worker with child protective services."

The owner of the voice was none other than Pinky.

The woman had gone through a complete makeover. Gone were her short shorts, her beret, pink hair, and pink outfit. Instead she wore a striped gray business suit, black heels, and a leather bag. Orange sunglasses perched upon the bridge of her nose.

"How are you doing today?"

"I'm ok..." Adam played along, when the detective's black box chimed. She sighed, staring at the object.

"Right. I'll leave you three to it. I've got a call with a mad scientist to take, so see you. Be careful with the girl, she's already bitten several of my men. Good luck, Adam," Detective Wong said, undoing Junith's bindings and taking off as Junith snapped at her, only to get bopped on the head by Adam.

"Behave," he whispered.

Pinky watched her go, waiting for the woman to leave through the office's double doors before turning to Adam and Junith with a smile.

"Shall we?"

* * *

It was late afternoon by the time Adam, Junith, and Pinky stepped out of the police precinct. Waiting for them was a white car marked with an emblem that clearly read *Social Services.*

Where did she get the car and outfit?

Pinky took off her wig, revealing her pink hair neatly tied up. She quickly released it, shaking it out.

"So! How was my performance?" she giggled, brandishing a smile as she opened the back door for Adam and Junith to get in.

Adam hesitated.

"What about Redfield and Jerbull?" he asked. Liza only shook her head.

"Abdullah and Snek are on it. Don't worry. Plus, if they wanted to, I'm pretty sure they could escape on their own," Liza said, her attitude more serious than usual. "Come on. Let's go, we've gotta get some more supplies, now that your truck was impounded and the gear seized."

"Oh, alright," Adam relented, stepping into the back seat alongside Junith.

Liza closed the door with a smile, opening the driver seat and getting in. She started the car and peeled out, a small trickle of what seemed to be blood trailing behind their vehicle.

Catpurr 72

Ice Cream and Psycho Nurses

"Wow! What is this marvelous item!" Adam exclaimed, licking the creamy, frozen treat held in his hands.

"It's called ice cream," Liza said as she, Adam, and Junith walked in tandem down the afternoon street, after exiting the ice cream peddler's shop.

"Fascinating. I'll have to see about replicating this." Yet another topic to add to his growing catalog of things to research. Beside him, Junith ate her ice cream in silence.

She had finally calmed down, not because she had grown tired or finally accepted her position, but rather because she was also appeased by the deliciousness of the sugary treat.

"So..." Liza said, the trio nearing the parked car. "Can you tell me about your god?"

Alarm bells rang in Adam's head. He froze. "Why do you want to know?"

"Well, you know I serve Voltrain, I figure it's only fair that you let me know yours as well." She smiled, as she opened the passenger side door. "C'mon, I bought you ice cream, after all, it's not like I want to *kill* you or anything."

Actually, that's a good point. Not the fact that she had bought him ice cream, but the fact that she had money at all. She *shouldn't* have any, not unless she took it, earned it, or by some miracle found it.

Judging by how much she could throw around so quickly, it was doubtful she had just earned it.

Something's wrong. Adam clenched his jaw, glancing over to Junith, who was also staring intently at Liza. She could feel his distress, just as he felt her suspicion.

Carefully he reached into his cloak, unsheathing his iron dagger.

"Do you want some beignets?" Liza asked, suddenly changing the subject.

"What's that?" Again and again, the warning from Coco echoed in his mind.

"A treat you and Junith will like, I promise. So come on, let's get!" Liza said joyfully, tapping on the roof of the car. It didn't stop Adam's eyes from drifting, as he spotted movement near the trunk of the car. Water appeared to be trickling out. On closer inspection, however, the water looked odd. Was it rust? No—Adam recognized the dark red of blood, crimson droplets staining the otherwise pristine white of the car, as they snaked down to the tarmac below.

"Hey..." His grip on his dagger tightened.

"What's up, buttercup?"

"How do you know Junith's name?"

Without missing a beat Liza cocked her head to the side, blinking once as she brandished a reassuring smile. "You told me, silly! Back when you introduced yourself!"

Adam locked eyes with the woman.

"No, I didn't."

He dropped his ice cream, hand going up as Liza's arm moved. Suddenly a knife was in Adam's shoulder, while Liza had ducked behind the cardoor, now an impromptu shield against his **mana bolt**.

"RUN! FOLLOW ME!" He grabbed Junith's wrist and sprinted away from the alley, firing bolt after bolt at Liza.

"My ice cream!" Junith wailed. Somewhere behind them, Liza cried out.

"ADAM, come back!" she yelled, as the duo ran into the afternoon street, barely ducking around several cars that stopped just shy of running them over.

The nurse gave chase, leaping over the dented metal door and rushing through the street, knocking people out of the way. Despite the nekopair's head start, she was catching up quite easily.

Curse these tiny legs!

Spotting several people nearby, an idea came to him.

"Help! Help! Kidnappers!" the boy yelled, drawing the attention of various passersby, some even spinning completely to see the commotion.

"HELP! She's trying to kidnap us! She's trying to kill me!" he yelled again, using his child-like appearance against the tall woman as she loomed above, a golden sword now drawn.

She lifted her hand, blade raised high as Adam turned his head, eyes wide at the woman about to slash him. Her blade came down, swishing through the air and aiming not for Adam, but Junith!

He yanked, pulling the unaware nekogirl close, his hands glowing. Just as the edge of the blade nicked his brow, he caught the attack in his claws.

"Why are you doing this?!" Adam yelled, wincing as blood dripped into his eye.

"Sorry! It's either you two or me!" Liza squawked, kicking Adam in the chest and sending him crashing into Junith.

"Ugh..." Still, he managed to stagger to his feet again.

"I'll make this painless. I promise," the woman said. She lifted her blade, the metal gleaming with an inner light. Before she could strike again, a man emerged from the crowd, tackling her to the ground. He wasn't the only one, as several other adults acted to subdue the seemingly mad woman.

"Get off! ADAM!" Liza screamed, kicking a grown man off her and into a street lamp as the two children raced away, turning down a corridor.

"ADDAAAAM!"

* * *

Leaning hard against a wooden fence, Adam gasped for breath, wiping his sweating brow as he assessed the knife in his shoulder. A regular iron dagger, one caught in his leather armor and trapped by the padding underneath. Luckily it missed his body by mere millimeters.

I need a new plan. Figure out a way to ambush her.

He removed the dagger, spending a few moments looking it over, before he sighed and merely dropped it to the ground. "Augh! Why does every woman I meet either try to kill me or hug me?!" he groaned, clutching his head as he slid down the wall. "Maybe I just need to stay... Away from them."

Junith snickered. Despite the exhaustion weighing her down, the nekogirl barely managed to remain upright. Even underleveled, disheveled, and completely out of breath, the girl had kept up, spurred on by her geas forcing her to run.

"You... Deserve everything... You get, scum," she huffed, braced against a nearby wooden wall.

"Do you ever give it a rest?"

"I won't. Not until every heretic is dismembered and burned at the holy altar of Voltrain."

"Wow. Okay, you do realize that she knew your name too, right?"

She kicked a can. "Okay? And? What's your point, scum?"

Adam grit his teeth. "My *point!* You idiot—"

"Grrr—"

"—is that I got this from protecting you!" He gestured at his head wound. Certainly, it had healed by now, but he thought the dried blood illustrated his point rather nicely. "She was after me *and* you!"

The argument came to a brief halt. Junith's jaw clenched, gears turning inside her head. While Adam couldn't say what was going on in her thick head, he was sure it'd be a problem for him. "You lie."

"Why..." He paused, wiping blood from his face. "Why would I lie?"

"Because you need me."

The nekoboy blinked, then nodded. "You're right. That's right... I do."

Junith gazed at him quizzically as he approached.

"Where is Schrödinger?"

The ex-paladin hesitated. When she remained silent for too long, the brand began to activate. Despite the pain, Junith gritted her teeth. "I won't! Tell you! ANYTHING!" she ground out.

Adam crouched as Junith fell to her knees. Her little body trembled.

"WHERE IS HE?!" He grabbed her face, keeping her from looking away. "Tell me. Tell me where my friend is."

A tear fell from Junith's wide eyes as she struggled against the brand. "Nev—"

"NOW!"

"In the Holy Sanctum of Voltrain located in Faith," she spat. Finally she was allowed to collapse upon the ground.

"Is he being fed? Watered?" Adam asked. The girl only growled.

"No."

Immediately Adam's hand found her throat, eyes wide as he bore down on her.

"What do you mean *no?*"

Junith shook at his icy tone. She had pursued the necromancer for a long time. Never before had she heard his voice go so cold.

"He keeps teleporting and doesn't require food, and when we tried to feed him food laced with sedatives, he shot a fireball at our scribes."

"What?"

Adam released Junith. The girl struck the ground face-first. But that came second to the implications of her statement.

Fireball? Teleport? Doesn't require food?

Schrödinger was Adam's best friend, and possessed an extended lifespan. But besides that, he was just a normal cat. He shouldn't have any special abilities. Then again...

Adam looked down at his own hand. On command, little claws extended from his fingers. His ears twitched. *Maybe he was changed as well...*

[Time Remaining until Event Start: 17:10:12]

Seventeen hours. Adam turned to the exhausted Junith. The nekogirl lay in an exhausted puddle, breathing heavily from the ordeal.

Time to see everything she knows... The nekomancer crouched down, and reached for the shivering, fallen paladin.

Catpurr 73
The Trial Begins

"Are you done?" Junith spat. The two had made camp within a small cave, somewhere within a nearby forest. The exhausted girl sat by as Adam stoked the flames of their campfire, by the entrance of their cave.

"No. You said you have a year until they come for you." He pried open a can of tuna with a can opener, both items he'd swiped from a convenience store on the way out of the city. "Tell me, how do they know where you are?"

The geas dragged the answer from her. "A portal locks onto my position, establishing a connection between my soul and the relic."

Well, now he *had* to keep Junith around.

"It won't matter, anyway. You and I aren't strong enough to survive the journey back."

"What?" He scooped out a handful of tuna, swallowing it. "Elaborate."

"The portal opens a tunnel through the aether realm. Allowing only those worthy enough to pass through. Those who fail are torn to shreds, consumed by void beings."

Void beings? Must have been that thing in the crack I saw when Junith and Sehn fought.

Through hearsay, Adam was aware of the existence of void beings, within the realm between realms. It was the first he'd heard of a device that could facilitate travel between realms, however.

This was also the first he'd heard of anyone from his original realm managing to travel to another. Meaning the Church had made this great breakthrough specifically to hunt *him* down.

It was almost flattering.

"Fascinating what we can achieve with hatred alone," Adam muttered, offering his can of tuna to Junith. She looked at it with disgust.

"Savage."

"Fine. Suit yourself." He shrugged. "See if I care if you die from starvation."

"Whatever."

Adam laid back, tossing several twigs into the fire as the scent of burning wood filled his nostrils.

A year, huh. Above them sprawled the starry sky. Would he even be able to survive that long?

Already, he'd died multiple times, and now he was out of lives. Absentmindedly he pinched a handful of dirt, feeling each grain as they slipped through his fingers.

A year to train and garner enough strength to rescue Schrödinger. One year.

There would be other obstacles, of course, like Liza. Killing her wouldn't be his preference, but she may not provide him with much choice. He had to stay alive—not just for his own sake, but for Schrödinger's, especially having heard how the Church was treating his friend.

[Time Remaining until Event Start: 13:03:42]

Thirteen hours left.

He sighed, glancing over to Junith. The ramifications of her transformation were... Interesting. It was clear that biting her had triggered the transformation, meaning that Adam had the ability to spread his curse. However, Junith kept landing on her face. While she had inherited the curse, she had *not* inherited its perks.

Hmmm... Maybe I can just bite Pinky. The amusing thought made him chortle, until one of her words struck him. *I'm just like one of the zombies she described.*

"What's so funny?"

"Nothing. Stay around me and get some rest," he ordered, kicking dirt and other refuse into the campfire to smother it. "We're going to have a long couple of weeks ahead of us."

"Hmp!" She turned on her heel and headed into the cave.

Adam folded his arms, leaning back against a tree outside the cave as he thought about everything that had transpired thus far.

"So much for properly planning..."

* * *

Beneath the canopy of leaves and above the cool grass and dirt, Adam and Junith slept soundly, each sticking to their chosen side of the camp.

Late into the night, the sound of rustling leaves roused Adam. His eyes snapped open, as he frantically scanned the foliage. He relaxed when it became apparent Junith was simply rummaging in his bag of supplies.

The nekogirl was gnawing at a can, having failed to open it with the can opener. After a few moments of this she paused, futilely banging it on the ground, snarling.

Were you always this stupid?

He considered saying something but decided against it, instead laying on the ground and pretending to sleep, as the sounds of her struggle reached him.

The leaves rustled again and she froze. Her gaze darted towards Adam. She scrambled, hastily putting everything back in the rucksack before scurrying away.

"If you're hungry, you can just ask," he said aloud, eyes still closed. "I know the only thing you've eaten in days is ice cream."

"As if I'd accept help from you."

"Fine, suit yourself."

* * *

In the early hours of the morning, the leaves rustled again. This time, it was not Junith—as Adam opened his eyes again, he was greeted by a dark-skinned man.

"Many moons to you," Abdullah smirked, silhouetted by the rising sun.

Adam's hand snaked to his dagger. "How did you find me?"

"You are mistaken that I track you with sands. This is not true. The moment you let me near, this one marked you with his skills."

"Perfect. So, are you here to kill me, too?" With a thought, his system appeared, the tab for tracking status effects already open.

It was blank.

Abdullah laughed. "Believe me, friend, if this one desired you dead, you would already be a cool corpse beneath the sands."

"Is that so..." Their eyes met, gold to dark brown. "So, what do you want?"

"A partnership," Abdullah said, surprising Adam. "I have borne witness to your feats against the pink one, and you are the only one to sense my magical sands. I believe we would work well together."

So he saw that, huh... I wonder how long he'd been tracking us...

"I smell the stench of a warrior on you. Unlike the rest, only the canine possesses the air of death. And if we are to survive, this one believes we would do so together."

The stench of death? Abdullah must have meant either Adam's class as a nekomancer, or his passive from **Adherent of Death**.

"Where is the snake woman that was with you?" Behind Abdullah, Junith was slowly approaching, clutching a rock.

"We came to a mutual agreement to go our separate ways," Abdullah said.

"Is that so?"

"I do not speak falsities. She has found love with an item called, *motorcycle.*"

A moment passed, then another. Each waited for the other to break the silence first.

"No thanks," Adam sighed. Abdullah's eyes widened in surprise. Clearly this wasn't the answer he'd been expecting.

But for Adam, it was a no brainer. Having an extra with him would slow down his plans. Not to mention, this man was a stranger, and his previous partners had been nothing but trouble.

Fool him once, shame on them.

Twice, shame on him.

But thrice?

No way. He'd had enough shenanigans.

"May this one ask why?"

"I work alone," he said. Abdullah turned to look at Juuith. "*Mostly.* I think we'd hinder each other more than help."

"You wound my soul, young one. But, if this is what you wish, This one understands, kytah. I shall leave you alone. However, if you wish, if sands willing our paths cross, the offer shall persist."

"Thank you." As he watched the bronze warrior take his leave, something occurred to him. "Hey!"

"Yes, kytah?"

"You won't tell Pinky where I am?"

Abdullah smiled.

"Of course not, I have no love for the bright one."

The man disappeared into the bushes, leaving Adam second guessing his decision to turn down the offer.

Crap... Maybe I should have used him to fight Liza.

He pulled up the timer.

[Time Remaining until Event Start: 04:31:09]

Four hours until the trial starts.

Adam stood up, carefully approaching Junith, then held something out to her. "Here." She scowled at his outstretched hand, examining the dagger offered to her with suspicion. "Abdullah has a point, if we're gonna survive, we stand a better chance together."

The ex-paladin took the dagger, eyeing it for a moment. Then she thrust towards Adam's throat. It froze, mere inches away.

"Really?" He could only raise a brow at that.

"Damn! You! ARGGH!"

To add insult to injury, Adam patted her head, chuckling. Junith's cheeks grew redder and redder, steam rising from her ears, until she collapsed in the ground. Passed out from sheer anger alone.

"Ah. Crapbaskets."

It took an hour for Junith to reawaken. The first thing she did was glare at Adam, hatred in her eyes.

"Are you done?" he asked, having taken the time to knight leaves, vines, and other bits of foliage into a net. The nekogirl only hissed at him. "Good. Get up, we've got work to do."

Before the apocalypse began, he wanted to survey the forest, establish a camp and an area to return to, as well as set up a hideaway using the cave.

"What are you doing?" Junith asked, looking at the net Adam dragged over.

"Camouflage. How do you think I avoided you for so long?" he said, draping the cover over the entrance of the cave.

"By luck."

"Yeah, *luck.*"

She frowned, watching for a moment before her eyes drifted to two camouflaged skeletal cats as they appeared from the bushes. Immediately

Junith leapt back, eyes wide at the leaf-covered abominations, clutching at her new dagger.

"Relax. Skittles One and Skittles Two, meet Junith." He waved his hand casually as they deposited bundles of twigs and sticks.

"A-Ah-Ahbomolinations!"

"Yes, yes, get it all out of your system." By now he was completely ignoring her, affixing the netting to the cave's ceiling with a stone. "Get used to them, as you'll be seeing a lot of them from here on out."

"Disgusting. How could you rely on such things?" she spat, shaking her head.

"Well, I obviously can't rely on you, so I make do." He crouched down, petting the skeletal cats and cooing. "I didn't mean that, my babies, of course you're better than her."

Both skeletons chattered, rubbing up against their master.

"How could you hate such cuteness?" Adam asked, rubbing the chin of a skellie-cat.

"Absolutely heretical, how dare you play with the dead as if they were toys." She clutched her dagger like a child's blanket. "Making them pretend to be cats to reinforce your delusions!"

"Pretend?" he echoed, opening his mouth to respond, when a blinking alarm appeared before him.

[Anomaly! Due to the actions of another, fate has been twisted, the event has begun!]
[Trial Two! Survive the End of the World!]
[The countdown has begun!]

Catpurr 74

Undead Safari

"Oh... Neat. Everything is on fire," was Adam's first observation, upon climbing up a tree to observe the carnage of the city from the safety of the woods. Yet another aeroplane fell from the sky, crashing into a skyscraper quite dramatically. "Second time today. Must not be very stable."

Four days had passed since the event had begun, and to say the zombie infection had spread like wildfire was purrhaps an understatement.

Within the city, the streets seemed congested by cars, burning debris, and the remnants of various aerial craft. It was quite inconvenient for the government as they tried to get a handle on the outbreak.

Occasionally a few of the metal craft, adorned with giant windmills sticking out perpendicular, would land, dropping off people in camouflage outfits and black masks. These people would go on to use guns to combat the undead.

For the first few days, they appeared to be making great strides, easily dispatching multitudes of infected humanoids running at them with bursts of fire, establishing safe zones and order. But as other types of undead began to appear, the camouflage people were quickly overrun, their own biomass eventually joining the rest of the raging horde.

Now, though, it seemed as though they were searching for something, rather than trying to hunt the undead or stem the infection.

"Fascinating," he muttered to himself, eyeing a large hulking zombie with inflamed muscles dwarfing its body. This forced the monstrosity to use its arms to propel itself forwards through the dilapidated, decrepit streets, knocking various cars and debris out of its way in search of more victims.

While the things he'd seen throughout the last few days were certainly a horrific tragedy, as a mirror realm that existed solely for the trial, Adam didn't particularly feel guilty about the citizens and people dying to the undead. After all, none of this was real, but it did prove a source of bountiful ideas. And he would be taking copious notes.

"Hey!" Junith called out from the bottom of the tall pine tree, tail swishing. "I'm hungry!"

"So eat something!" The nekoboy's eyes remained fixated upon the titanic undead, not even looking down as he sketched its form and bulging muscles, adding the creature to his growing list of notes.

"The can opener is broken!"

He sighed, before yelling, "Is it broken, or did you break it?!"

"It's stupid!"

He pinched his nose. *How can an inanimate object be stupid?*

He went to call Junith an idiot, but froze as she kicked one of his skeletal cats as it tried to brush up on her.

Seeing this, Adam grabbed a pine cone, pelting the nekogirl in the head and making her snarl.

"Don't kick my cats! What the Nyx is wrong with you?!"

"What's wrong with me?! WHAT'S WRONG WITH YOU, PERVERT?!"

Junith screamed, grabbing a pinecone and throwing it back at Adam.

"Animating the undead to do your bidding! Using them to rub up on me!"

"AS IF I'D EVER! BE INTERESTED IN YOU!" The projectile sailed past his head. He grabbed another and launched it straight at Junith's head, this time at full force.

"AHK!" She fell, sprawling into the leaf-covered dirt as the pinecone bounced off her head.

Nostrils flaring, the fallen paladin struggled back to her feet, but a quick "Stay!" from Adam made her starfish out onto the ground.

"YOU SUCK!"

"NO, YOU!" Another cone rained down on her. "And now! You're going to stay there with no food, until you apologize to Skittles!"

As if to rub salt on the wound, Skittles One clambered up Junith, clattering and curling up on her chest despite her pleas and protests, much to the latter's dismay.

"ARGH! I HATE YOU! I HATE YOU! YOU SICK SCUM!"

"Shut up! Do you have no self preservation skills?! You're gonna attract all the zombies here, you idiot! Then you'll get eaten!"

"YOU'RE YELLING TOO YOU DIMWI—DI—OW!" This time a cone landed in her mouth, lodging between her canines. "MWWWRGH!"

Adam turned, looking back towards the city. The hulking monstrosity had disappeared, replaced instead by several shamblers that came out to pick at its leftovers.

"Tsk, I didn't finish sketching it." Giving up on research for the day, Adam finally climbed down to join Junith, who was being mercilessly bopped on the head by Skittles Two.

"Get up and go into the cave. Skittles One, protect her, let's go, Two," he said, giving out orders as he donned protective gear in the form of gloves, goggles, and a face mask in preparation to venture out into the city.

Groaning as she usually did, Junith got up, heading into the safety of the cave, Skittles One trailing at her heels

* * *

On the edge of town, two undead fought over a human arm, near an abandoned police car. The pair stopped as Adam approached, only to take off running, nearly colliding with him. But at the last second, they stopped to stand beside him.

The zombified man and woman leaned over Adam, both staring with milky eyes as he looked at them, observing their clothes, torn flesh, and the bits of blood caking them.

The blonde woman wore a black hoodie, ironically with the words *BITE ME* scribbled across it. Below her shorts, a bite wound festered. Beside her, the man wore a white shirt, a belt oddly hung around his neck, standing in his gray underwear. His bite wound was on his hand.

Two unfortunate victims of the apocalypse. Two victims that would be accompanying the boy on his journey. At least for a little while.

This first test of his passive had been extremely jarring, but fortunately, his **Loved by Undead** still applied, allowing him to walk completely unharmed amongst the sprinting zombies.

Instead they, much like the skeletons underneath Vilenciel Castle, followed him around, aimlessly shuffling behind him unless disturbed by something like a survivor or a loud noise.

The streets were filled with smoke, viscera, and garbage as Adam drifted through them, a sight that wasn't that much different than the battlefields back home.

"Now, where did you run off to?" The monstrosity's tracks should have been simple to follow. Right now, he wasn't seeing any of them—only several ransacked stores on either side of the street.

He opened his notebook, looking through all of the infected he'd documented thus far.

Obviously, there were the zombie dogs, the fast canines which occasionally ran down survivors in the streets. They were jittery creatures that didn't particularly like sitting in one area. Beyond their speed, though, they were rather unremarkable.

Next, there were the humanoid lickers, with their long, serrated tongues. They lurked in shadows, pouncing from one area to the next with enhanced agility, taking out soldiers with bone claws protruding from their wrists and joints.

Then the spitters. As the name would imply, they spat bile and other viscous substances at their prey, attempting to infect or blind would-be survivors with sticky acidic bile that stunk and attracted other infected. Adam had witnessed such a scene only yesterday. Nearly a hundred infected had shown up, tearing the victim to pieces.

A pretty horrific scene, but one that provided lots of data on the nature of the infection and the evolutionary ability of the undead to deal with survivors.

And lastly, perhaps the most deadly of the undead so far, the alphas. These appeared mostly human, albeit with more muscular bodies, blackened, cracked skin akin to carbon, and tentacle-like, fleshy growths protruding from their arms. These growths could be removed to infect others.

Things referred to as *bullets* proved highly ineffective against their blackened skin. Indeed, their skin seemed to act almost as armor, a form of body hardening brought on by the infection to create a chitin-like carapace.

Another note of interest was how the alphas acted as commanders, often staying back while the lesser undead assaulted survivor holdouts. Additionally, unlike the other undead that would follow him around, the alphas were rather uninterested in Adam, choosing instead to wander away from him if he kept poking and prodding them for examination.

All fascinating in the nekomancer's eyes as he looked at his notes. Judging from the way the plague kept adapting, there had to be a key hive or controller directing the mutations. Possibly an overlord that could be the key to ending the trial early.

If only it were easy. He sighed, closing his book as one of his newly acquired zombified admirers began drooling blood, almost staining his notebook. At the last second, he snatched it away.

"Hey! Shoo! Stop that!" He ordered, poking the undead girl on the nose with his glove. In response, the zombie girl let out a moan before patting Adam on the head with a gray hand, ruffling his hood.

Seriously?

Now he was tracking the latest in a string of mutations, the bulky *titan,* as he dubbed it, a creature apparently designed to combat the survivors' portable cannons and defenses with its unparalleled strength and size.

"How is it possible I lost him? Cheeky bugger," he wondered, continuing his safari down into the destroyed city and scouring alleyways, holes in buildings, even climbing up onto a roof of a red brick building, a car stuck halfway up its wall, to survey the area for the titan.

Then, Adam spotted something that caught him off guard: two undead grappling with each other.

What is that? Adam took out his salvaged binoculars, more closely scrutinizing the two undead. Both seemed rather unremarkable, but something about one of them caught his eye—it was wearing cat ears.

What.

He dropped his binoculars, the shock of the scene causing all thoughts to cease.

Fortunately the sound of his binoculars cracking jolted him from his stupor, making him curse.

"Aw, crapbaskets!" The lenses were cracked, which was terribly disappointing, until he remembered what had shocked him so.

I gotta get down there!

Adam descended from the roof of the convenience store, hopping onto the hood of the car embedded in it, to join his two zombie friends as they waited for him. Skittles rode shotgun on the shoulder of the zombie girl.

He rapidly approached, climbing over a pile up of burnt-out car wrecks just in time to see the zombified nekoman chomp down on a regular zombie as it returned the favor, the two attempting to eat one another.

Suddenly Adam was pushed to the side, his two honorguard zombies racing forwards, attacking the nekonized zombie.

"Wha—"

The three zombies quickly overwhelmed the nekoman, feasting on the decayed body as he stood to the side watching with a mix of emotions.

Suddenly, the original zombie that had been locked in battle with the neko began to spasm, hitting the ground and convulsing.

Adam blinked several times in disbelief, watching in horror as within seconds, the zombie had been transformed, sprouting cat ears and a tail. Neck Belt and Hoodie swiftly turned, attacking their former comrade.

"What the Nyx?" In the desecrated remains of the original zombified nekoman's corpse, something shiny glinted.

Shoving passed the two undead devouring their friend, Adam reached down, grabbing the metal emblem, emblazoned with the letters *NYPD*.

Ah, crapbaskets.

Catpurr 75

Choosing a Class For My Arch Nemesis

"What the hell is that?!" Junith screamed, jumping away from the snarling zombie. The undead lurched forwards, frothing, restrained only by the belt around its neck.

"A zombie," came Adam's casual response, slowly marching in the newest addition to his cat-eared army. It had been a pain getting him here, but with the belt around its neck, the nekoman zombie could be guided away from the hordes of others and into the cave.

"I CAN SEE THAT!" The still-living nekogirl pressed against the furthest cave wall, until she was practically flat. "BUT WHY IS IT IN HERE!"

"Judgy, meet Neckbelt, Neckbelt, Judgy."

"STOP CALLING ME THAT!" The zombie snapped and bit the air, as she skirted just beyond its reach.

"Hey, I think he likes you."

"NOT FUNNY! WHY DOES IT HAVE CAT EARS?!"

"I don't know, why don't you tell me?" With his free hand, he flashed the NYPD badge.

Junith glanced at the metal badge, shaking her head lightly as her mouth twisted into a confused frown.

"Is that supposed to mean something to me?!"

His eyes darted from the girl, to the badge, and back. Seemed he'd have to be more direct. "How many people did you bite?"

"What?"

"At the police station. How. Many. People. Did you bite?" He dropped a dagger at her feet, punctuating the final words.

The ex-paladin finally seemed to realize just what she had done, as her eyes went wide as saucers.

"Two?" She snapped up the dagger, pointing the tip at the zombie as she held it at arm's length.

"And you didn't get a follower menu or anything?"

"No, I did not."

Interesting. It seems her bite has a similar transformative ability like mine, but not quite the same. This would require more testing.

"Kill it," he suddenly ordered. Junith did not waste a single second. The dagger plunged into the zombie's skull.

[Follower has Leveled Up!]
[Please select a Starting Vocation!]

A context menu appeared before Adam as the undead's body went limp, cementing his theory that Junith could still level up. The ability to select a class for her, however, came as a complete surprise.

Both Adam and Junith were shown the same screen, it appeared, but only Adam was capable of making a selection. This came as a shock to the both of them.

[Available Vocations based on criteria!]
[Squire: *Must be a servant.*]
[Vassal: *Must be a servant under one who has commanded an army.*]
[Priestess: *Must possess Faith.*]
[Clergy: *Must possess Faith.*]
[Marionette: *Must be under the control of another with autonomy restricted.*]
[Berserker: *Must possess Boiling Rage and disregard for self.*]
[Gladiator: *Must be a servant and have killed on orders.*]
[Singer: *Must possess the ability to sing.*]

[**Warrior:** *Must possess proficiency with a martial weapon.*]

The list went on, numbering over two dozen different vocations. Speaking of...

Vocations... Not classes? He rubbed his chin, looking at the list and pondering the possibilities.

"Fascinating," he said. This could allow him to mold the ex-paladin into whatever he wanted.

"MY CLASSES! MY SKILLS!" Suddenly he was being shaken by a screaming nekogirl. "Please! If you have ANY DECENCY, YOU'LL AT LEAST PICK—"

"Hush, I'm thinking." Junith was chided with a bop on the head, as he looked at the clergy and priestess. Was there a difference between those classes?

For a trial centered around undead, it wouldn't hurt to have a holy class that could **Turn Undead**. Not that *he* needed it, but if Junith came under attack, she'd need some way to defend herself. All the better if healing came as part of the package, too.

The other classes could work. If Junith had a weapon or more physical strength, berserker could have had some real potential, but judging from the various types of special infected, she'd most likely lose in any direct confrontation.

The best defense is avoidance, Adam determined, reminiscing on all undead Junith had turned to ash with just her paladin skills alone.

Actually, could **Cure Disease** *cure the infection? Might need testing. Preferably on a live or recently bitten subject.*

From what could be observed, it wasn't the bite that turned people, but rather the infectious disease that killed, *then* reanimated the corpse. At that point, the victim's biomass was added to the rest of the horde.

After pondering it a little longer, Adam made his choice. Priestess seemed the most useful class to assign Junith.

Immediately the nekogirl's body was enveloped in a light, illuminating the nooks and crannies of the cavern.

What the Nyx? Adam blinked, then looked away to avoid being blinded by the brilliant light.

[Vocation selected!]
[Mark of Eli recognized! Vocation augmented to Priestess of Eli!]

The light suddenly warped, becoming purplish in hue, before it died down. He looked up to see a shocked Junith, now emanating a familiar energy. One he'd become quite well versed in.

Death.

"No…" Her voice was small, in a way he'd not heard from her before. Slowly she raised her shaking hands to stare at them. Her lips quivered, her body shook, every part of her being quaked as her mind failed to process what she'd become.

Upon her hand, clearly visible, was the mark of a serpent.

"NO. NO! NOOOO!" she screamed, clutching her head as she fell to her knees. Tears fell from her eyes in fat, hot globs as she began shaking her head, her composure completely shattered. Despite their long rivalry, there were many things Adam had never known about Junith. One of those things was how she viewed her class—as her *salvation*. A chance to show her piety to her patron. A chance to continue serving him, just as when she'd been a Sister at the chantry. "VOLTRAIN! PLEASE!" Junith implored. But it was no use. She curled into the fetal position, sobbing, as the last vestiges of her god's grace evaporated from her body.

[Corrupted Blessing of Voltrain has been extinguished by the Blessing of Eli]

Even corrupted, the faint power of her patron had given her comfort, gave her strength in the face of what was *surely* a trial to test her resolve.

Now the light and warmth of Voltrain was gone, completely. In its place was cold, the foreign touch of undeath upon her soul. She could only shiver.

Adam watched all this, oblivious to Junith's crisis of faith. He scratched his neck as she wailed her god's name again and again, prayers muffled by her choking sobs.

"Riiiiiight." Slowly he backed out of the cave. "Don't, uh... Don't hurt yourself, or whatever. I'll be back."

He grabbed the ankles of the corpse at his feet, dragging the body out of the cave towards a spot where a shovel lay.

"Well, buddy, time to get to work." From somewhere behind him, he tuned out the sounds of Junith's hopes and dreams shattering.

Catpurr 76

Calm Before the War

"Another jellybean?" Redfield asked, offering the bag of candy to Liza.

"Got any pink ones?" The disheveled, pink-haired woman looked quite casual as she sat in her jail cell in a sports bra, slouched against the pole she'd been chained to.

Redfield peered into the depths of the half-empty bag. "Mmmmmh, nope." For the past few days, the diminishing bag of candy had been their main source of sustenance. "Couple of reds, a few blues. Do you want purple? I don't really care for the purple ones."

Liza sighed, glancing over to the crowd of cat-eared zombies sticking their decaying hands through the bars, struggling to reach one of them.

"Yeah... I'll take the purple ones." Redfield picked out several purple beans, depositing them in her outstretched palm.

"So... Wanna run it by me again, how you failed to kill a ten-year-old?" He swished around the contents of a half-empty water bottle.

"I told you, he ain't what he looks like. The kid is sharp," Liza replied, eyeing the quest objective for perhaps the thousandth time. "Probably isn't even a kid."

[Mandatory Quest: Kill the Chosen of Eli, 'Adam']
[Rewards: Blessing of Voltrain, SSR-Grade Artifact, Divinity Point]
[Failure: DEATH.]

"Is that so? Just checking your story, bad habit." Redfield placed the bag of candy on the ground, instead checking the magazine of a handgun. It had been tossed into the cell by another cop, shortly before that man was transformed, screaming, into yet another nekoman.

The cat outbreak had happened quickly and unexpectedly. One cat-eared man had suddenly barged in and began attacking an officer. It didn't take long for one to become two to become all. As if that weren't bad enough, zombies also appeared soon after, also infecting the nekofolk, only to be converted themselves to their ear-and-tail club. The station that had echoed with growls was now filled by a chorus of undead moans.

"What about you? You said you had the same quest," Liza said. "Why didn't you take him out when you had a chance?"

Redfield sighed, eyeing the various zombies groping through the cell walls.

"Not in the business of killing kids, I s'pose," was his answer, as he picked a crumpled box of cigarettes up off the floor. "Some lines you just don't cross. Besides, even if he isn't a kid, he hasn't done anything to me."

Liza's brow rose, staring at Redfield.

"And here I thought after floor one you'd wisened up, hehe," Liza giggled before she sighed. "Guess it won't matter anyway, then."

"Guess not."

"How many shots you got in there?"

"Not enough."

"Sucks."

"Yup."

The two sat there for a bit, staring at their captors, neither saying a word.

"Wanna make out?" Liza asked suddenly.

"What?"

"Just trying to pass the time. At some point we're gonna have to get out of here. Can't live off jellybeans forever."

"Yeah, I know," Redfield said, slamming the magazine into the handgun and racking the slide.

* * *

"Diggy diggy hole, digging a hole," Adam hummed, putting the finishing touches on a grave he had dug. He paused, tossing the shovel out of the hole before climbing up, joining Junith who was doing the same.

"Alright, grab her legs, I'll hold onto her arms," he instructed. Together they hauled the body of Hoodie by her arms, heaving the deceased zombie over to the grave. Quickly they deposited the corpse within the hole.

"Why are we doing this individually, instead of just burying them all in one mass grave?" Junith complained, as she wiped her sweating brow. For the past two days, she'd spent much of her time sulking, but her demeanor now was a far cry from that. "This takes forever."

"It's about respect, and giving peace to the souls that have passed on. They deserve a burial," Adam replied, climbing out of the hole. "Mass graves are disrespectful. The only basis they have is for sterilization."

She grunted.

"Says the hypocritical necromancer using heretical magic to raise them up to become pawns." She took up a shovel, beginning the process of burying Hoodie.

"I won't deny my use of undead. However, the undead I use aren't powered by souls," Skittles One clattered nearby, but paused long enough to accept a scratch below the chin, "usually. How do you think you and your band of idiots were able to catch me? You think if I was summoning dullahans and unboxing tombs, your army of half-wits would be able to capture me so easily?"

Junith's face twisted, unaware that he wasn't being egotistical, but truly sincere. With the power he formerly possessed, if he had bent souls to his will and summoned forth the most powerful undead he could muster, he could have easily created a bloodbath.

Yet he refrained. After all, there were already enough souls being reaped by the various religious nutjobs. He didn't need to contribute to the number.

"Tsk, whatever." She spat onto the ground, falling silent as they worked.

Once the woman was fully buried, Adam turned to the plot of earth. "I lay your body to rest so your soul may be at peace," he recited. Although he would have preferred to cremate the remains, he couldn't risk a fire attracting zombies, or worse.

Survivors.

Despite the administrator's words and the quest's description of the mirror world, this realm *felt* real. Probably a ploy to ease the contestants' minds, amidst the chaos unfolding. However, Adam knew he was in no position to help others, much less go looking for survivors. Taking care of Junith was annoying enough. He shuddered at the thought of adding randos to the mix.

He had his doubts about the whole trial. But looking at the graves surrounding him, he knew they would change nothing.

The pair had been busy terminating the undead. Using Neckbelt's belt as a noose and leash, Adam would lead zombies one by one into the forest, back to the camp where Junith would dispatch them for experience points.

This went on for a full day, by the end of which, Junith had reached level three, with a wealth of new skills to boot. Most notable amongst them were **Heal** and **Eldritch Blast**, the latter being something unique for the priestess of Eli class. Neither neko recalled the skill as being part of the healer vocation.

Unfortunately, unlike Adam, Junith didn't have the luxury of choosing what skills to unlock, so now the two had to do it the hard way as he power leveled her.

"Satisfied?" she asked, patting the dirt before looking out into the evening. Smoke still rose from the distant city.

"Yeah, that works." The nekomancer inspected the ground, smoothing out the dirt, before placing several stones in the formation of a cairn on Hoodie's grave.

Then he gazed upwards.

"It'll be dark soon, let's get in for dinner." Surprisingly, there was no complaint from Junith at the command. The duo passed through the leaves that camouflaged their hidden lair, now filled with books, metals, bags, and anything Adam found interesting; mostly shiny things.

"Tuna, spam, something called 'romen noodles,' and a can of beef stew," he rattled out, as he retrieved dinner options from his canvas bag. "Hmm, might have to run out and look for more food."

Junith stabbed the shovel into the ground beside the entrance. "Tuna."

"Tuna what?" he said, shaking the silver can.

Junith frowned, black tail swishing widely as her face twitched.

"I'm not saying it."

"C'mon."

"No."

"*C'mooonn.*"

"I'm *not* saying it."

"If you want food, just say the magic word."

"I'm not saying *please.*"

"You just did."

"Shut up," Junith growled.

Eventually the can of tuna was opened, and Junith brought it to her skulking corner.

She looked down at the can, before blinking and looking away. "Thanks."

"Hmm?" Adam's ears twitched as he went to light a candle."What?"

She turned away, sitting with her back to him and staring past the camouflage leaves to the area outside.

Whatever.

He turned his attention to his makeshift bed, presently consisting of a pile of scavenged blankets, pillows, and linens.

[Quest: Survive the End of the World]
[Time Remaining: 453:12:09]

Adam sighed, looking over to Junith as she quietly ate from her can. Finally he laid down, taking advantage of the calm to rest his strained muscles until finally, unintentionally falling asleep, blissfully unaware of what was soon to occur.

Catpurr 77

Administrative Meeting of Disgruntled Workers

Elsewhere, within the Administrative Realm...

Floating amidst an endless void of stars and motes of light were dozens of sentient beings. Each was unique in their own way, ranging from mythical golden dragons to twenty foot tall pandas. There was even a tiny pet rock with googly eyes stuck to its face.

"Greetings everyone, and thank you to all who were able to make time between their duties managing their realms to be here today," said a pink figurine donning a top hat, floating within a snowglobe. It turned gracefully to address all the gathered admins.

"Today, I would like to discuss an anomaly that has appeared within Realm Z-28DL. As some of you may have heard, he is a Chosen of Eli, which we have not seen in millions of years, an eon before during the Great Schism." Tophat spun, dusting the fake snow off her suit as she announced the topic of the meeting.

At her words, several admins turned to one another, whispering, some even groaning at the news. Soon the whispering became murmurs, then words spoken aloud, culminating in a shouting match.

"Yes! Yes! I'm well aware of the shared sentiment within the realms!" Tophat yelled, raising her plastic hands to quiet everyone down. "Now, the issue at hand is, what are we going to do about it?"

"This is! *Preposterous!*" a bow tie-wearing, purple T-rex with a green belly shouted, raising its stubby, scaly arm in a fist. "It's hard enough managing trials for six primordial beings, but now Eli is causing trouble again?! We are overworked! Underpaid, and *tired* of procedures not being followed! I SAY! WE KILL HIM!"

"YEAH!" several admins cheered at Rex's statement. Tophat pinched her nose in exasperation.

"We can't! LET ME BE VERY CLEAR! We can *NOT kill CHOSEN!* Once they've made it past their first trial," she reprimanded, met by a chorus of groans from the managerial staff.

"Hey! That's a good point! Whose realm did he pass through, anyway?! It's their fault we can't smite him!" a voice yelled, followed by multiple complaints and discontented gripes.

"He went through Undine's Temple," Tophat reported, pulling up a sapphire-blue marble. Within was a world covered with oceans, marred only by a small spot where the ruins of Undine's Temple lay, floating in the water. "An abandoned realm. Eli artificially created a trial to circumvent us smiting him."

"THAT'S UNFAIR! HOW ARE WE SUPPOSED TO WORK, IF WE CAN'T KILL THE TROUBLESOME ONES BEFORE THEY BECOME TROUBLESOME!" Rex yelled as various supporters voiced their assent.

"Okay, focus everyone! Let's remove killing him from the table for now, and instead focus on how we are going to handle the Seventh Primordial's Chosen," Tophat said, clapping her hands rhythmically.

"Well, I for one like his chaos, and think we should treat him as we would any Chosen," Pebble said. The pet rock administrator of Z-28DL chirped happily amidst the simmering discontent clouding the realm.

"Easy for you to say! You're the pet of a war god! Look at the chaos he's caused in your realm! *And* all the other realms he's been to!" barked a white and brown canine laying atop an Earth rocket.

"You should live a little, Laika, excitement is good for breaking up the monotony of our day-to-day operations," Pebble countered as Rex pulled up several spheres, enlarging them up to display for all of the administrators. Each showed a realm Adam had visited or been to.

"Destruction of a Goddess' Temple, untold swaths of destruction in waypoint realm-VV9S, not to mention the Morian Crab infestation and civil war ongoing in that realm, and now we have this!" the T-Rex bellowed as a sphere swirled to showcase realm Z-28DL, a survival trial where the undead were meant to wipe out every sentient being.

Instead, what was being shown were two massive armies of undead fighting each other, various decomposing monstrosities clashing against their cat-eared counterparts, each tearing one another apart, rather than hunting down the remaining human survivors, thus slowing the process down tremendously. "We are on a timetable here! We can't afford to let this anomaly cause chaos like this, when we need to focus on the power flow and distribution of Chosen!"

"Rules are rules. Even the gods—OUR bosses—have rules." Tophat sighed as she prepared to deliver the bombshell that would quiet everyone down, for better or for worse. "So, no smiting of the Chosen. Unless you want your existence annihilated. Eli has made it clear he will exterminate *any* guardian or administrator that negatively tries to influence his Chosen."

At Tophat's words a series of murmurs broke out, multiple admins tensing up as the revelation of what was said settled on the crowd.

"He... said that?" T-Rex said, his voice trembling slightly.

"Yes..." Tophat said, eyeing the giant purple lizard. As immortal beings, the only thing that could kill an administrator was either void taint, or a god. For a being such as an admin, however, such a death did not signify the end. Sooner or later, they would simply be reconstituted. However, there was one way for this process to be halted, for their revival to be stopped, and that was if a Primordial stepped in, striking them down and in the process erasing their very existence.

No revivals. No soul transfers. Just the void and deletion.

A fear that all admins possessed, ensuring they would work tirelessly to conduct the trials for the gods.

"So..." Tophat said. "With that in mind, how are we going to handle the Third Chosen of Eli, Adam Glow?"

Catpurr 78

Sure Sounds Like a Not My Problem

"Hey! Wake up!"

"Uuuugh," Adam groaned.

"Hey! Wake up!"

"Five more minutes…"

"HEY! WAKE UP!" Junith screamed, stomping on him with her dirt-covered, bare foot.

"UHK! WHAT! WHAT?!" He sprung from his bed, fury in his eyes as Junith stood over him, a bloody dagger in her hand. He squinted at the weapon, face contorting as he shook his head. "Great. Look, can you give it a rest already? You should know by now that you can't kill me."

"What? No, you heretic, we have a problem!"

"What? Did you break the can opener again?" Adam said, clutching his head from the headache. Slowly he leaned back, shutting his eyes again as Skittles One curled up in his lap.

Suddenly, he was grabbed by his shoulders, pulled up by Junith who began screaming at him.

"WE HAVE A PROB—"

A titanic roar interrupted her, jolting Adam from his grogginess. The nekoboy immediately sprinted towards the exit of the cave and into the sunrise, where he was met with the sight of something that made his head spin, mouth falling agape.

"Well… That does seem like a problem," he agreed, staring out in the distance at the sight of hundreds of dots in the sky.

Adam took out his salvaged binoculars, blinking once, then twice as he marveled at the spectacle. Crowding the air were what appeared to be flying cat-eared zombies, borne aloft on translucent wings similar to an oversized waspknight's.

"They fly now?!" Furiously he rubbed away spots of dust on the binoculars and checked again. Indeed, they flew now.

The zombies were locked in an aerial battle, zed against cat-eared zed, the two forces clashing in the skies as swarms of undead ran amok upon the earth below, engaging each other en masse.

Sat upon the rooftops were alphas, the commanders directing their army against a woman perched atop a cat-eared titan, guarded by several zombie lions.

Detective Wong? Adam frowned. The cat-eared alpha wore a familiar red blazer as she directed the feline horde, gesturing with what seemed to be a fire axe.

As the two forces clashed against each other, the city around them took the brunt of the damage.

Welp, there goes the food store. An orange, fur-covered catsified titan slammed another titan through the roof of the building Adam had been scavenging food from.

A number of zombie dogs appeared, encircling and pouncing upon a titan. *Hmm, I wonder how Abdullah and the others are doing.*

"What are we going to do?" Junith asked, standing beside him as the masses of undead spread out, waging their war even in the woods.

"Well, you were right, it is a problem," he agreed, handing her the binoculars and walking back to the cave with a yawn. "Just not for me."

"What? Where are you going?!"

"Back to sleep. Let me know when they're done killing each other or something." The nekoboy splooted out on the pile of blankets and pillows. However, as he laid there, attempting to go back to sleep, the sounds of Junith skulking and pacing kept him from it.

Maybe if I just keep my eyes closed, she'll leave me alone.

A moment passed, then another. Finally he opened his eyes, to spot Junith staring down at him once more.

"*What?*"

"You're squandering an opportunity."

"What?" he said, confused.

"You should be out there, killing zombies and earning experience, not laying here wasting time. Especially since there's so many of them, and none of them react to you," Junith said, hands on her hips as she coaxed Adam with a dirty toe. The girl had been walking around barefoot since their dungeon escape, he abruptly realized.

He opened his mouth to reply with a sarcastic remark, but stopped himself. Junith *did* have a point. However, with his luck, he'd probably get smooshed by fallen debris, or have a titan fall atop him.

Yeah, no thanks.

He folded his arms, rolling over as Junith scrunched her face.

"I'll get to grinding experience when everything dies down. Until then, I'm not gonna risk getting flattened by a falling building or hit by a stray aeroplane. Besides, every zombie is only, like, 400 experience, and with you leeching my experience, that's only, like, 200 per. And why do you care, anyway? Aren't you actively rooting for my downfall?"

A massive detonation seemed to punctuate his words. The earth trembled, leaving the nekoboy to sit blinking, until it quieted down.

"See? I'm just going to go back to sleep. Too much trouble going on right now." Whatever was going on was a future-him problem; right now, he was still too tired.

Suddenly, another boom sounded out, followed by crashing, and then the roar of something he didn't recognize.

"It's too early for all this crap," he sighed, finally getting up and heading towards the exit. Above were what appeared to be aeroplanes, at least a dozen of them flying in tight formation. But unlike the massive ones he'd seen crashing repeatedly, these were small, at least one-tenth the size of the regular birds, and moving swiftly.

Immediately he produced his sketchbook, watching as the metal creatures began producing a *BBBBBRRRRRRRRRRRRRRRRT* sound, heralding hundreds of flying undead falling from the sky.

Next, something detached from one of the birds, flying towards a massive clump of undead fighting in the city before erupting into a large inferno that spread light so bright, he winced from the sight and sound alone.

More tubes fell from the aeroplanes. He turned to Junith, backlit by a steady light of a city completely engulfed in crimson flames.

"So, you were saying?" Adam said, the smugness of his expression contrasted by her horrified disbelief.

"Duck."

"Duck?"

"DUCK!" She ran, leaving Adam to spin around, just in time to see a massive fireball careening towards them.

Eyes wide, he dove to the ground, narrowly avoiding the smoldering remains of a car as it flew by, smashing into trees and depositing several flaming zombies in the process.

Adam stood up, dusting the dirt off his knees and cloak. The flaming undead rose with him, completely oblivious to the fire consuming them. They quickly moved, heading towards the one and only thing here they were attracted to.

Junith.

"PISS OFF, YOU UNDEAD FREAK!" she screamed, bloodlust in her eyes as she whacked a zombie on the head with a shovel, sending it to the ground. Immediately she began stomping on its skull. "DIE, SCUM! DIE! DIE! DIE! BE CLEANSED, HERETIC!"

Ah, crapbaskets. Her outburst was attracting the attention of yet more zombies.

He unsheathed his dagger, preparing to strike, but froze as screeching from above sounded out.

One moment Junith was there, and the next she wasn't, a black shadow moving so quickly the only thing Adam could make out was the girl's scream of "*HHHHHWWWWWWWAAAAH!*" as she was carried away by something too fast to even see.

What... WHAT?!

It took a moment for him to process what had happened, but then he sprang into action, chasing after Junith as she spewed swear words, body flailing madly in the air as something with black wings carried her away.

"AH CRAPBASKETS! YOU IDIOT! WHY COULDN'T YOU JUST LET ME SLEEP?!" he yelled. Desperately he struggled to keep up with the zombified bird of prey, and the nekogirl clutched in its talons, as the fire consumed the entire forest around them.

Catpurr 79
Totally Not the Mansion From Biohazard... Totally...

"I see the humans have begun a counter attack. Marvelous, isn't it?! Look at him go!"

"Eh, change the channel, I'd rather see what the wolfman and Castellian are doing rather than Adam."

—Unknown

* * *

"Idiot! Idiot! Idiot!" Adam yelled, chasing after Junith for nearly twenty minutes through the woods choked with flames, as the metal birds spewed fire nonstop, laying waste to the city and countryside.

"WHY DOES EVERYTHING HAVE TO BE ON FIRE?!" he demanded, shaking his fist at an aeroplane above. As if sensing his frustration, the metal bird released its payload, dropping a canister right on to the nekoboy's head.

In the last few seconds shortly before it exploded, he could only wonder once more, *But why?*

* * *

Covered in soot, panting, and out of breath, Adam leaned on a tree, wheezing as he came to stand in front of an old mansion, silhouetted by a curtain of raging flames.

Eyes swept across the field, searching for any traces of Junith, which he quickly found in the form of a carcass.

A corpse, one of the mutated variety, in the shape of a black-winged humanoid, laying impaled on the rusted fence that surrounded the manor. "Crapbaskets," he muttered, inspecting the monster. Jammed into the creature's beaked face was a dagger—the same one he'd given to her, which he could now retrieve.

From his estimate, the stab wound was a nonfatal attack, but one that would have steadily bled for some time. Eventually, the monster must have lost strength, crashing into the gates below.

Just as I suspected, the infection isn't magical in nature. With enough bodily damage, the creatures could be taken out. It was a theory he'd had for some time now, but out of respect for the dead had refrained from actually testing.

After all, that was just *rude*.

Decorating the iron bars were droplets of blood, forming a trail to the decrepit, red-shingled structure nearby.

Adam narrowed his eyes, pulling up his follower menu.

[Pack Leader: Adam Glow Lvl 14]
[Bonded: Junith Oatheart Lvl 4]
[Geas: Not set]
[Status: Wounded]
[HP: 190/350]
[MP: 60/100]

*Looks like she's used one **Heal** and leveled up,* he surmised, closing the menu as he clambered over the fence and into the courtyard. Spiky bushes and overgrown roses dominated the fenced-in area, some climbing up the walls of the building.

At the end of the courtyard was a door left ajar, leaking darkness that seemed to beckon him forwards.

"Nothing ventured, Adam... Nothing ventured..." he repeated, until a horrendous scream froze him where he stood. "Ah, perfect. I wonder what untold horrors await me."

He ran in, daggers brandished as he used his position as pack leader to locate Junith. The dim light of the main foyer was no match for his feline eyes, darting wildly around the massive room adorned with a singular large stairway, a balcony overlooking the first floor.

Populating the once-grandiose entryway were the dead bodies. Corpses of zombies were scattered all about, fresh, judging from the blood stains and viscera.

He leaned down, inspecting the claw marks on the skull of one of the zombies.

"Ah, you idiot. You better not have gotten bitten." Blood speckled the zombie's molars. Judging from the lack of wounds inside its mouth, the blood had come from a victim, and rather recently.

"JUNITH! YOU IDIOT, ARE YOU ALIVE?!" Adam yelled, voice echoing through the mansion.

"I'M NOT AN IDIOT!" a voice screamed back.

Of course. Why did I know that would work? He sighed, shoulders sagging as he headed up the stairs towards the direction of her voice.

"STAY RIGHT WHERE YOU ARE! I'M COMIN—"

[Junith Oatheart]
[HP: 190 → 112]

The sight of her plummeting HP froze him—just as an explosion rocked the mansion.

"JUNITH!" he charged up the stairs, bursting through the rickety red door and entering a hallway, where he began following the trail of blood, running down the hall as her screams sounded out.

CRAPCRAPCRAPCRAPCRAP!

"GET OFF ME!" she screamed, followed by a loud snarl reverberating through the halls.

"You better not get eaten, I swear to Nyx!"

He turned a corridor, entering a hallway filled with windows. Finally at the end he spotted Junith, a canine and a twitching licker nearby.

The licker was still alive and crawling on its sharp arms, the gaping hole in its chest still smoking from a blast of eldritch.

Adam ignored the creature, focusing instead on where Junith was pinned to the ground, a zombified canine atop her as she struggled against the snarling mutt.

"JUNITH!"

Immediately Adam's dagger was in his hand, ready to be used, yet just as he prepared to do so, the window beside him suddenly shattered. The nekoboy flinched as shards of glass embedded in his skin.

A zombie dog hit the wall beside him, the mutt disoriented but immediately thrown again as Junith kicked her attacker off her and ran.

Crap.

"GET DOWN!" he ordered, his palm raising, firing a cat-shaped blast of mana.

[+25 EXP!]

[+25 EXP!]

[+350 EXP!]

The resulting explosion consumed the dogs and licker, shattering the rest of the windows and kicking up smoke that clouded everything.

"Are you okay?!" he yelled, opening his eyes to see that the rickety hallway had collapsed from his attack.

Crap, I shoulda held back.

"I'M FINE!" Junith yelled back. Despite everything he sighed in relief, which the dust transformed into a coughing fit.

"Are you bit?!"

The nekogirl took a moment to reply. "No."

"Alright! Stay there, I'll come to you!"

"I can't do that!" she yelled, just as inhumane snarls echoed from within the dust.

"Just stay alive! Are there any windows beside you?!" There was one beside him. Immediately he struggled to pry it open.

"Yes!" Junith's voice yelled. It became fainter as her footsteps retreated.

Of course the window is locked where I can't reach it! At the very top of the pane were a lock and bolt.

Hard way it is!

Adam grabbed a piece of debris from the pile beside him, flinging it at the window and shattering the glass. He wrapped his cloak around his arm, clearing away the remaining shards before perching on the sill.

Wind immediately hit his face upon sticking his head out.

"Of course," he groaned, realizing he was now on a cliff, overlooking a hundred foot drop into the sea below.

How the Nyx did that dog get in here?

A question for later, as he looked to his left, spotting the adjacent window.

"Easy enough." Adam crouched low, steeling himself within the square outcrop as he prepared to jump.

"I swear, if I die from this I'll come back from the grave and haunt you." He leaped, straining his little arms. One hand brushed the sill, barely grasping it.

"Hulp! Easy... enough..." Now came the hard part—climbing up. With the momentum he'd gathered, he reached with his free hand to swing himself up.

There was a sudden, sharp crack.

Oh.

Then another, followed by a creaking sound. His ears twitched, as the wooden panel he'd gripped began to snap and break.

Crap crapcrapcrap!

"No! Nonono. C'mon you, dastard, just hold long enough for me to climb!" A spiderweb of cracks raced across the board, even as Adam strained with his free hand. Never before had he missed his grappling hook so much.

"Please?"

A last ditch attempt, just in case the mansion was magical in nature or a god was messing with him. Unfortunately, his plea fell on deaf ears as the wooden sill snapped and sent him spiraling into the abyss below.

Catpurr 80

Into the Manor

"Assassin Actual, you've got the clear. Operation is green. Exterminate all infected, and locate the source of the infection."

"Understood, Overlord. Assassin on the move."

—Great Britannian Army commander, shortly before moving in with his regiment on New Yor city.

***

Hundreds of meters below, white waves crashed upon a sheer cliff face. Adam struggled not to look, as he dangled by his claws, clinging to the side of the mansion, chanting, "Idiot, idiot, idiot. I shoulda let her die!"

Pain jolted through his fingers, as they slipped slightly. With a wince and a furrowed brow, he flexed his free hand, and sighed. "Time to get up there."

Through **Mana Claws**, handholds were now created where there had previously been smooth wooden walls. Supporting his own weight quickly became much easier.

"Stupid Junith. Stupid gods."

Slowly the nekoboy scaled the old manor's crumbling walls.

"Stupid trials. Stupid manor."

One hand after another, methodical.

"Stupid aeroplanes!" With a spiteful cry he leapt onto the cracked window frame, only to find it blocked by plaster and debris.

He sighed.

"Of course..."

****

The next window he came across was *not* blocked. Upon shattering the glass, Adam slipped into the dimly lit hallway.

"Holy crapbaskets...

Corpses as far as the eye could see, the heads of each pulverized. Presumably a certain hotheaded nekogirl had left them, while painting the dreary, black hallway a much more exciting shade of red.

Adam swallowed, eyeing a dead shambler with a picture frame buried in its skull. Forced in, by the looks of it.

"Note to self, never give Junith the opportunity to receive the berserker class." He reached down, removing the frame and closing the undead's eyes, before he continued on.

"JUNITH!"

No response.

[**Bonded: Junith Oatheart Lvl 4**]
[**Geas: Not set**]
[**Status: Wounded**]
[**HP:** 120/350]
[**MP:** 20/100]

According to the follower menu, Junith had already used her final **heal**.

Damn idiot, where the hell are you?

At the end of the hall was a door left ajar, light spilling out from behind it. Past it lay what looked to be a machine of some kind, covered in levers, each marked with numbers and letters. The machine was mounted in the skull of a collapsed, undead man, a stained page of paper attached to both.

Adam picked his way through the carnage, approaching the body of the man in a white coat. It brought him closer to the page.

"Itchy... Tasty?" He looked down. This undead had been felled recently. Junith had definitely been here.

"How hard is it to stay in one place?" It seemed there was nothing else of interest here. He was about to leave, when something within the open closet caught his attention.

He leaned in closer to investigate, face unconsciously twisting into a devious smile. Oh, yes. *This* would be useful.

* * *

Junith huffed. The paladin-turned-nekogirl priestess panted, clutching at her bleeding collarbone. One of those infected—the type Adam had dubbed a licker—had slashed her there.

The wound had been bleeding profusely, and she couldn't get it to stop. It didn't stop her from staggering down a flight of stairs, though— just made her movements especially painful.

A zombie lurched at her, the shambling abomination climbing towards her and opening its gray maw, attempting to strip the flesh from her bones.

Junith had other plans.

She lifted her makeshift club—a bloody piece of debris pillaged from Adam's explosive endeavor—and slammed it into the zombie's maw, ripping out its jaw in a single motion. The zed splattered against a nearby wall, twitching. She struck it again, now aiming for its temple.

It crumpled, dying quickly as she broke the monster's skull and kicked it down the stairs.

"Damn it. Lord Voltrain... why do you forsake me in this godless abyss?" Even now, even here, her gaze drifted upwards. "Is this some test? Was I not pious enough? Not faithful to your whim and reason? Why, lord?"

She leaned on a wall, a trail of blood following her as she muttered her endless mantra. Still, her prayers went unanswered. Still she suffered. And now, she could no longer feel her god's presence, no longer hear or feel his warmth. She was cold... so unbearably cold.

Just like the orphanage...

She paused at the base of the stairs, leaning on a nearby pole, as her eyes fixed upon the stony floor beneath her dirty and worn feet.

Why?

"Auuuuugh."

"Why..."

"Uuuuuhgh."

"WHY?!" Junith snapped, swinging her club, bashing the approaching zombie. "CAN'T YOU SEE I'M HAVING A MOMENT OF CRISIS?!"

She roared, her fury driving her club into the downed zombie and bashing its head in, once, twice, three times. She kept hitting the zombie, smashing down with righteous indignation until the floor beneath the corpse cracked. The undead's skull was left an unidentifiable pile of mush.

"ARRRRRGH!"

Her screams of rage echoed , drawing out the zombies that permeated the underground cavern.

"COME ON! FIGHT ME! DIE! BE CLEANSED, FILTH!" Junith roared, her claws unintentionally erupting out as her hairs stood on end. Every fiber of her being was consumed by incandescent rage, rage at being abandoned, for being enslaved, at the situation she found herself in. Hatred cascaded from every pore of her body.

Despite the blood flowing from her shoulder, Junith went to work doing the thing she was trained her whole life to do.

Destroy monsters.

She pulverized, she crushed. With inhuman strength, she tore through undead around her. With her club, with her bare hands. Their skulls were all dashed upon the floor in the end. None were safe, as she made her way through, hunting down the undead abominations that dared to exist in the presence of one chosen by—

She stopped. Her bloodied club was raised for a coup-de-grâce. There, upon her hand, was that serpentine symbol.

The splintered remains of her weapon fell from her bloody hands, knees buckling as the strength left her body. That white-hot fury was smothered by the numbing reality of her situation.

She was alone. Abandoned by her god, in the dank basement of a foreign home where she would no doubt die alone, her HP dropping swiftly as her own actions ripped open her barely healed wounds.

"Why..." For a moment, she eyed the shard of wood, the promise crossing her mind, if only briefly, of a way out.

But this... was a cardinal sin.

Maybe it'd be better to die, than to live as a slave...

Something slithered in the shadows, scales of some kind. Junith's survival instincts and training overpowered her self-loathing.

She scanned the room, transformed irises penetrating the unnatural darkness.

Then she grabbed her splinter, clutching it tight as *something* in the darkness uncoiled.

A snake.

A giant undead reptile, exposing its deadly fangs as it yawned.

"I... I..." Junith began, unsure how to react as it bore down on her, its blistered tongue spilling corrosive pus as it flicked back and forth wildly in delight.

"GET DOWN!" Adam yelled, suddenly appearing nearby and wielding what appeared to be a shotgun, the same item Redfield had slung across his chest upon their first meeting.

She didn't need to be told twice. Compelled by Adam's geas, she dove, hitting the cold stony ground as the snake struck, attempting to swallow her whole.

BOOM!

A massive blast echoed, and snake viscera rained down, covering Junith as Adam was sent flying through a wall.

Catpurr 81

And I Crashed Into You, and Went Up in Flames

[+2000 EXP!]

"HA!" At last, Adam triumphantly emerged from his hole, wielding his shotgun. "COULD YOU IMAGINE AN ARMY OF SKELETONS EQUIPPED WITH THESE!"

Despite the sharp pain of a broken rib or two, the glorious vision of an undead army made unstoppable with this weaponry filled him with ecstasy.

He looked over to Junith. The nekogirl didn't seem quite so enthused. Instead she sat unmoving on the cold floor, dripping viscera as she breathed heavily.

Ah, crap.

Adam dropped his shotgun, letting it dangle on the sling across his chest as he quickly rushed over. The sudden movement made the pain in his ribs flare, but that didn't matter—not when his ticket home was in danger.

"Hey! Hey!" Getting closer, he could now see Junith's injuries—on her chest near her clavicle was a visible laceration, bleeding profusely. The skin around it appeared deformed and swollen.

[30/350]

Crapbaskets!

On the follower menu, the girl's HP dropped further with every passing second.

"Ah, crapcrapcrapcrap." Desperately he patted around his body for any vials that could be useful. Finding none, he tore his cloak and began packing her wound. It wasn't the most sterile, but it was what he had. The priority right now was stopping the bleeding.

Oddly, she didn't make a peep, showing no reaction as Adam pressed down on her gashes.

"Junith," he said, pushing the girl's chin up so her dull golden eyes could meet his. "I need you to put pressure on your wound. Now."

"Okay," she whispered hollowly, doing as instructed.

"Okay." What next? How was he to stop the priestess from succumbing from her wounds? As he racked his brain he glanced around the room, noticing the carnage she had caused. No doubt the reason her wounds hadn't healed. "You idiot."

"I'm... not an idiot..." Even as she said so, her eyelids fluttered weakly.

"Of course you respond to that." He made to remove something from his storage ring, hesitating only a moment. "Tsk. I didn't even get a chance to try and synthesize this..."

Out came a purple vial; a mana potion that could fully recover one's MP.

Oh... the things I do for love...

Immediately he uncorked the vial, shoving the contents into Junith's mouth and ordering her to swallow.

"Heal yourself."

She complied, activating the skill, as he took over applying pressure. "Ugh..." Immediately her complexion grew a little livelier.

Moans interrupted the nekopair, as zombies stumbled up the stairs and out of the shadows, heading towards the fresh source of meat.

That complicated matters, especially with Junith already injured.

If only I could dominate them... He sighed, briefly mourning the loss of potential underlings.

"Go."

At his command, a blue light gently illuminated the room. Two cat-shaped portals appeared and deposited his skelecats, which clattered about before immediately pouncing into action, leaping at the gathering of undead.

"Junith," he said, drawing the girl's attention. "I need you to focus on not making the wound worse. Hold the cloth close, and keep pressure on the wound."

"Okay."

Tsk. The Nyx is wrong with her? Her hotheaded tendencies were annoying before, seeing her without them was simply unnerving.

And we were making such good progress.

Adam helped her to her feet, dusting the snake guts off and walking her back up the stairs as his skeletons made short work of the undead.

* * *

The pair back-tracked, returning to the room with the mysterious machine.

Once there, Adam began rifling through the closet, pushing away the boxes of ammunition and pulling out clean clothes, as well as a small red box that read *first aid*.

Aid.

It had to be something useful. Within it were bandages, adhesive, scissors, and something labeled *alcohol wipes*.

"Kills 99.9 percent of bacteria..." he read aloud. "Is this some kind of salve?"

He gathered all the supplies, placing them beside Junith, before freezing. His hands were horribly dirty, spattered with grime, dust, and blood. He ordered his summons to him, the two skeleton cats appearing a moment later, covered in undead viscera.

"Protect her, I need to find a bathroom."

It didn't take long for him to return, this time with a metal bowl and clean water, his hands cleaned as he kneeled over Junith to inspect her wound.

'HP' was not a simple representation of one's overall health. Really it was the measure of a special regenerative energy all system users possessed, as well as overall durability. It was possible for a User to survive to be okay, even with an HP of 0. But what was more likely was that they would die, or enter system shock: a comatose state where their body would shut down as the system prioritized survival above all else.

Both options were a danger to Junith right now.

Fortunately, Adam was a healer—or at least had the necessary knowledge. His master had believed that in order to understand death, one must also understand life. Heal as well as harm, and to use his knowledge of the corpses he'd dissected to better comprehend the inner workings of the human body.

So, he learned how to heal, mend flesh, reforge bodies, and aid in their recovery, even to the point of putting his knitting skills to use in stitching his own wounds.

When Junith bled through her makeshift bandage, he put another cloth on top, pressing down as he leaned her body against the nearby wall. He waited, eyeing her HP bar until the bleeding seemed to slow, no longer flowing through the fresh cloth.

Adam removed the cloth, quickly inspecting the flesh as it mended itself back together. The process was slow going, and the girl's breathing was shallow.

Rinse, disinfect, then bandage, he recited to himself as he used the scissors from the kit to gently cut away her rags, exposing her torso. Idly he noted it had tufts of black fur, similar to his own. With the bowl of water, he began the process of cleaning out the wound. It wasn't just deep, but long, extending from the clavicle down to the belly button. Fortunately there it grew shallow. He wouldn't have to worry about holding in her guts.

When he was sure there was no debris lodged in her, he grabbed the alcohol wipes. The scent of antiseptic hit his nose immediately upon opening it, confirming its intended usage.

He went to work cleaning the girl's wound, dabbing gently with the pieces of cloth until they were saturated with blood. Next came the process of bandaging.

"Ah. Done."

Adam wiped his brow, observing his hard work before he went to ransack the closet again, retrieving an adult-sized, polka-dotted shirt, which he draped over her. Then he turned his attention to the undead body, dragging it out into the hallway.

How much more of this? With little better to do than wait, Adam checked his system, only to realize he was on the cusp of leveling up.

BETA SYSTEM v1.03
TITLE: The Primordial Eli's Chosen (+20% Mana recovery, +5 Arcana. Undead Favorability)
NAME: Adam F. Glow
SPECIES: Nekoboy
LEVEL: 14
EXP BAR: 6650/9000
MAIN CLASS: Nekomancer
HP: 268/300
MANA: 35/235
EVOLUTION POINT: 0
Gacha Coins: 0
Free Points: 0
[Followers: 01]
[Bonded: Junith Oatheart Lvl 4]

Stats:
STR: 15
CON: 30
DEX: 15
ARC: 40(47)+5+2 (**EQ**)
SEN: 13
EGO: 13
[**RESISTANCES**]: Fire (5%) Inertia 10%

He sighed, leaning on the wall and dropping to the ground.

Maybe Junith is right, I should probably focus on leveling up. His head turned towards the girl's sleeping form. *If I clean out the undead, it would be safer for her as well, I suppose.*

He sighed again, using his shotgun as leverage to stand and go hunting. However, as he opened the door, the entire building began to shake, the vibrating floorboards knocking him off-balance. He reached out, grabbing the door frame. An explosion sounded throughout the manor, as something underground had collapsed.

The vibration suddenly ceased. Adam's eyes darted back and forth as he tried to make sense of what just occurred. It felt like someone had crashed into the manor, or, at the very least had hit it, causing it to jostle. Whichever the case, he had the feeling that something was wrong.

* * *

Wayne Manor, same time.

"Is everyone okay?!" Redfield yelled through wheezing coughs, picking himself up off the floor of the subway cart as he waved the cloud of dust and debris out of his face.

"Fine! We're okay!" Liza yelled. From the next cart down, Abdullah sounded off as well.

Redfield looked around, clutching his automatic rifle as he began walking down the tram cart, checking in on the families and civilians onboard. It was a very good thing that the emergency brakes still worked on their tram.

"Alright! I need a perimeter! Right now! Secure the area and check up on any wounded!" Redfield barked, using his strength as a system user to pry open the broken subway door. From there he ordered the cops and armed civilians out into the brightly lit terminal they had crashed into. "Abdullah, how's our prisoners?"

"Fine like geonsion sand. A little coarse, but okay, this one thinks," the warrior in gold reported, entering from the rear cart where Sethis and the wolfman named Lyke were bound and chained. "This one still believes we would be safer if we—"

"I'm not executing them," Redfield cut in, grabbing a bag of supplies from an overhead compartment. He tossed it to the bronze warrior, who perked up.

"Ah! But then I—"

"No. *WE* aren't murdering anyone," Redfield said, before turning to Liza. The nurse was fixing her makeup, using the subway tram's cracked window as a makeshift mirror. "Same goes for you."

"You really aren't any fun, you know that?" Liza said, puckering her now pink lips before brushing past him and exiting the cart, heading off to join the rest of the survivors that they had managed to save.

Redfield furrowed his brow, before turning to his prisoners. The two were cuffed, chained together, and muzzled in the next tram over, watched by two armed officers.

"Atkins, Forest, keep an eye on these two. If they attempt anything, shoot them in the legs," Redfield instructed as he locked eyes with the glaring snake lady and the indifferent canine.

The two officers nodded as Redfield turned and exited the tram, joining the rest of the survivors to inspect the spacious underground cavern, more akin to a basement than a subway station.

"Alright, now, time to figure out where the hell we are," Redfield said as he clutched his assault rifle.

Catpurr 82

Catflict of Interest

"Head count," Redfield ordered, standing amidst the wreckage of the subway car. With it, he and the other survivors had narrowly escaped the city, before the bombs fell.

"Twelve wounded, minor injuries, nothing serious, all accounted for. Forty in, forty out. Al says the train is unusable now, though," reported a young man named Marvin in camo fatigues. Previously a platoon had striven to protect the civilians in the subway station, making use of IEDs, tripwires, and DIY traps to slow the infected. Of that platoon, only six soldiers still survived. Martin was one of them.

"Ammo?"

"Only what we packaged last minute and had onboard. Few boxes of 7.62, couple of bags of 10mm, and a box of grenades. Oh, and the shotguns we managed to grab from the raid on the police station," Marvin reported as he looked over to Liza, humming to herself.

Because the subway survivors had been running low on ammo, they had dispatched a team, a raiding party accompanied by Abdullah, that had entered the 99th Police Precinct. Inside they encountered Liza and Redfield, who had finally retrieved the prison cell keys from a zombie, with the help of a baton.

"Alright, lock it down, secure the area. I want guns posted at every point of ingress and egress, while I take a team to scout this building," Redfield said, pointing to three uniforms and beckoning them over.

Despite being a newcomer, his enhanced strength and ability to manipulate water into potent ice walls made Redfield a reliable fighter and leader, especially against the swarm of undead.

He quickly earned the others' trust, and worked tirelessly to aid the survivors in fortifying and scavenging for supplies, alongside Liza. The survivors easily trusted him, thanks to his commanding presence and how he put an swift end to Lyke and Sethis' murderous rampages.

"I don't think it's wise for you to leave us," Marvin said, his eyes worriedly glancing over to the families spread out amidst the structural pillars. "Especially with the... two rogue magic people in custody."

"Abdullah and Liza will be here, should anything go wrong. Outside of their strength, a bullet will put them down like it would anyone," Redfield said, as the three cops joined him.

"What, uh... What if they start using magic and stuff?"

"Center mass, if you must. But only if you *must*," Redfield replied, as a man tossed him a bag filled with ammo. He didn't want to kill them, for fear of invoking a god's wrath, or becoming marked by other followers like Adam. Instead, he planned on keeping them tied up until the trial was over.

"With their hands bound and mouths shut, they can't activate their skills. Just make sure to keep an eye on them." Redfield pointedly looked at the silver subway car, containing Sethis. From within, she gazed back.

"Yes, sir. We'll get it done, just be careful," Marvin said, before getting to work organizing the defenders, as Redfield walked towards a door left slightly ajar.

* * *

The final zombie fell to the floor with an "Ukh!" as Adam removed his dagger from the undead's chin.

"Sorry." The nekomancer repeated his ritual of shutting the dead's eyes, before dragging them to the side of the hallway, to sit with the rest of the victims of his cleaning. Some time had passed since the massive boom. For about an hour Adam had waited, before curiosity and hunger took over, propelling his feet around the mansion.

So far, he had found some green and red plants, a shiny ruby, a sapphire, and a golden medallion in the shape of an eagle. Besides the plants, none of them were edible, but at least he had some new, shiny objects.

"Tsk. Why are there so many people in this mansion?" he complained, throwing his dagger and impaling another white-coated zombie in the head as it shuffled towards him. "And how is it there are two kitchens! But *no food?!*"

He rubbed his temples, attempting to suppress his headache as a zombie leaned over him and reassuringly patted his head.

"I just want to go home and hug my cat..." He sighed, dispatching the unfortunate soul with a quick knife to the chin. The zombie sagged against his leather pauldron.

"Sorry."

Adam continued his journey. Occasionally he would run into special infected, like a licker or a spitter, all of which paid him no mind, allowing him to dispatch the creatures easily with a quick stab through the skull.

"Almost to level fifteen..." His journey hadn't been completely unfruitful, he was close to leveling up. Two thousand four hundred experience points away from it, to be exact, even with Junith siphoning a portion of his experience he was still—

BANG! BANG! BANG!

The sound of gunshots echoing throughout the manor caused his body to tense up.

Shouts and screams chorused, followed by a roar as a battle of some kind erupted elsewhere in the mansion.

"Great..." he muttered, pinching the bridge of his nose. "Survivors."

It was bad enough that he couldn't find any supplies, but now he'd have to share what supplies he *did* find.

"Unless they don't find me," he realized, as the sounds of battle approached.

Hmmm, if I leave them alone, maybe they'll get themselves all killed and I can loot them for some food.

Adam closed his eyes and pinched his nose, shaking his head as all the remaining zombies in the hallway began shuffling off, drawn by the sound of commotion.

"Uuuuugh," he moaned, not unlike the undead, as he debated what to do.

"Nyx below... Why am I like this," he sighed, finally falling in line with the zombies as he shuffled along, rather unenthusiastically. His knife flicked out, diminishing their number where he could, as a decision was reached.

Catpurr 83

Run-in With an Abomination

"It got Sullivan!" a cop screamed. With trembling hands, he pointed his cobalt pistol at a ten-foot-tall monstrosity, currently impaling a man through the chest with a fleshy tentacle. The man jerked unsteadily, struggling to point the barrel of his own gun at the pus-riddled undead, yet his dying body failed him as his strength faded and fled.

"Get back!" Redfield barked, yanking the officer away. An overgrown appendage armored in chitin came down where the cop had just stood, leaving only cratered earth.

"Keep your distance! Range is the only thing we've got against that thing!" Redfield ordered, backing away to the far end of the manor library and opening fire with his assault rifle at the creature that still held his ally.

The trio's combined bullets riddled the creature's flesh with holes. Despite everything, the abomination wasn't even bothered.

"Shit," Redfield murmured. The creature turned away, impervious to their gunfire as it lifted the carcass of the now-dead officer.

The bipedal monster's bulbous head split open, revealing mandibles inlaid with row upon row of sharp teeth. They latched onto the dead man's face and pulled, easily stripping away the flesh.

"Ah, no. Ah, hell no!" the young officer, Theo, yelped, immediately fleeing towards the hidden entrance in a blind panic at the gory spectacle.

This was a mistake.

Seeing the man's rapid movement the monster lashed out, its arm sending out a tentacle that flew low and flew fast. Redfield reacted on instinct, catching the slimy tentacle with his gloved hand, preventing it from skewering his comrade.

Time seemed to freeze. Redfield's eyes widened with shock. *Hells bells, I can't believe that I actually*—"SHIT!"

The tentacle curled around his arm, drawing him into the monster's embrace. Its hungry maw blossomed like a meaty red flower.

"NO! NO! NO!"

"Hold on!" the last cop yelled, opening fire. The monster's remaining arm immediately sent him flying.

"Peralta!" Redfield yelled, planting his feet into the ground as he lifted his free hand up, emptying the magazine of his gun.

It did nothing.

"AH, COME ON!" Redfield dropped his gun, instead taking out his engraved revolver, the weapon he'd brought from his home realm. It unleashed a monstrous roar as he pointed the barrel at the abomination.

The monster reeled, stumbling from the force of a forty four full metal jacket entering its face and tearing away one of its mandibles.

"Take that, you freak! Good ol' American craftsmanship!" Redfield yelled, before firing twice more at the monster's arm. Finally he wiggled free of its tentacled grip.

Three shots left.

He grit his teeth, gaining distance and aiming the nose of his barrel as the monster shrieked with fury.

BANG! BANG! BANG

Redfield let loose, emptying his silver revolver in rapid succession as Peralta got up. The officer grabbed one of the many scattered books and threw it. It bounced off the monster's face as he frantically scoured the messy floor for his pistol.

"Keep up the pressure!" Redfield opened his revolver, dumping the casings and placing a speed loader in, quickly reloading his weapon as Peralta kept the monster's attention on him, hurling books into its open mouth.

The abomination shrieked again, the frills on its neck visibly vibrating before it spat a blast of green bile at Peralta. The cop dove behind a bookshelf, as the bile corroded the floor where he'd stood.

"Hey! Ugly!" Redfield yelled, firing his revolver once more as his free hand activated his skill, **Water Spear**.

The putrid creature turned, flexing its remaining mandibles as Redfield used **Cold Manipulation**, freezing his **Water Spear** and forging a jagged hunk of living winter.

He fired his gun, six rapid yet accurate shots in its muscular torso that pierced and cracked its chitinous armor. Then he launched his spear.

The skill connected, burying itself in the creature's chest and spilling blood, causing the abomination to stumble back.

"Seriously? What the hell does it take for you to die?" Redfield spat, quickly dumping his casings and reloading as the monster roared.

"Redfield! We've got more zombies!" Peralta yelled, directing Redfield's attention to the banging from the adjacent doors, leading into the library.

"Retreat! Get out of here!" Redfield yelled, turning and running back into the hidden entrance nestled between two bookshelves as the doors were thrown open and zombies flooded the space.

* * *

"Oh! Shiny!" Adam said, as the gleam of moonlight on metal caught his attention.

"Hmmm. Neat, a can of... oranges?" he read aloud, mood shifting as he examined the tin a zombie had just been holding. "Of course it's citric."

The nekoboy sighed, dropping the shiny object as more gunshots sounded out. He walked forwards, eyeing the gaggle of undead congregating around the exit at the end of the hallway.

"Move, please, thank you," he said, shoving a pair of moaning zombies to the side to reach the decrepit brown door. At the front of the crowd, an armless zombie was banging its head against the door.

Adam tapped the zombie in a bloodsoaked white coat, drawing its attention. It stared at the nekomancer, motionless with uncomprehending eyes.

He sighed. "Look, if you all keep banging on the door, then I can't open it. Can you *please*! Just step back... I'm asking nicely."

"Uuuugh?" was the zombie's eloquent retort.

"Why am I talking to you as if you understand me?"

The trio of zombies paused, looking down at him before they collectively reached out, patting his head.

The nekomancer closed his eyes, a sigh from deep within his soul escaping as the group of undead continued patting and rubbing his ears. Fondling him as if he were a pet. Well, two of them. The third zombie was armless, though it made a rather valiant attempt.

Nyx below, what did I do to deserve this?

Suddenly the house shook, another roar sounding out, this time so close Adam felt its vibrations in his bones.

He pushed the three zombies back, before grabbing the bronze door knob, throwing it open to dart inside, ahead of the undead crowd.

Immediately he was frozen at the sight of an abomination that looked like the monstrous offspring of an alpha, a titan, and... *something*. The monster had a meaty, bulbous head, titanic muscles protected by chitinous armor, pus bubbles pocketing its body, and for extra grossness, red, meaty tentacles wiggling on its arms.

"Fascinating," he murmured. Amidst a sea of blood and dismembered corpses he took out his notebook and began to sketch. Right now the creature was quite distracted by banging on several bookshelves—a secret passageway, if Adam guessed right.

"Hey!" he called out, causing the creature to almost jolt with surprise before it shifted its hulking body to face the sound of his yell. "Yes, you, stay right there so I can draw you for notes."

The monster's head tilted sideways, gazing almost dubiously at him with its single bulbous eye, before it slowly began to approach. This close Adam could see the numerous injuries on its chest, including a massive ice spike, lodged where its solar plexus should be.

He furrowed his brow. Something seemed off as the monster approached to tower over him, head opening up to reveal rows of sharp teeth and the slimy drool leaking from its abyssal maw.

"Oh, great, are you going to pet my ears too?" Menacingly, the creature raised its arms. "What is with you all and my ears?!"

Adam sighed, shaking his head as the monster did, indeed, want to pet his ears.

Catpurr 84

Why Is There So Much Math Involved? No, Seriously!

[Level Up!]

The familiar message appeared as Adam sat atop the gargantuan monstrosity, his hand deep within the chest cavity of the now-dead creature.

"Hmmm, that was definitely important. Oops." The nekomancer had simply been rummaging around the fleshy cavern, until his hand grasped something bulbous.

Now he blinked away the notification, returning to the task at hand: dissecting the fascinating specimen.

"Ah... there you are." The arm soaked with blood and other viscous fluids retreated, now replaced with a dagger as he set to prying open the chest cavity for a clearer line of sight of the monster's nucleus.

Slowly filing away the chitinous material with his dagger, Adam was able to slice the flesh open and peel back part of the rib cage, exposing the heart, which he quickly retrieved and placed in his storage ring for preservation.

[CONCA*TULATIONS! Level 15 Reached!]
[Skill Points Available: 5]
[Bonus stats awarded for Level 15]

He paused upon seeing the notification, caught off guard by the bonus level and skills.

BETA SYSTEM v1.04
TITLE: The Primordial Eli's Chosen (+20% Mana Recovery, +5 Arcana. Undead Favorability)
NAME: Adam F. Glow
SPECIES: Nekoboy
LEVEL: 15
EXP BAR: 300/18000
MAIN CLASS: Nekomancer
HP: 289/300
MANA: 45/235
EVOLUTION POINT: 0
Gacha Coins: 0
Free Points: 10
[Followers: 01]
[Bonded: Junith Oatheart Lvl 5]
Stats:
STR: 15
CON: 30
DEX: 15
ARC: 40(47)+5+2 (EQ)
SEN: 13
EGO: 13
[RESISTANCES]: Fire (5%) Inertia 10%

While getting twice as many free points was a welcome surprise, the massive leap in experience for the next level was less so. That was a disappointment.

Then again, I have been leveling up rather quickly.

Adam rubbed his chin, smearing blood on his face unintentionally.

[Please Select a Skill from the Nekomancer Skill Tree!]
[Upgrade Summon Minor Skeleton [Upgrades available 5]
—Locate Bones
—Drain Mana
[Upgrade Mana Bolt [Upgrades available 7]
[Upgrade Mana Claws [Upgrades available 4]
—Double Jump
—Mana Dash
[Upgrade Cat Claws [Upgrades available 8]
[Upgrade Eyes of the Predator [Upgrades available 4]
—Emit Mana
—Necro Heal
—Bone Armor

"Holy crap." Now he had to lay down on the grotesque monster. It seemed there had been a notable quality of life update improving the system, not to mention all the new skill upgrades he could choose from.

"Why does it feel like I'm being used as a test subject for a system?" he muttered aloud. before he pulled up his follower menu. Fortunately, Junith seemed fine. It was safe to focus on the task at hand.

Maybe it's time I upgrade my skeletons, he thought to himself, immediately dumping all ten stat points into Arcana.

ARCANA 40 → 50
[Arcana Requirement Met!]
[Natural Mana Recovery increased!]
[3 MP per Hour!]

His body abruptly tensed as his internal circuits reconfigured themselves for the intake of mana. There was a sensation of expansion, almost as if he was ballooning, until finally, release, as new energy flooded his veins.

He let out a sigh, relaxing. Now it was time for stronger undead.

[Upgrade Summon Minor Skeleton]
[Available Upgrades]
—Upgrade skill to Summon Skeleton V1
—Increase Minion Capacity+1
—Optimize Mana Requirements V2 (—10% REQ.)
—Strengthen Summon V1 (+10% To skeleton stats)

If I upgrade **Summon Skeleton, Loved by Undead** *should upgrade it further,* he rationalized, before opening the other skill upgrade lists to see various potential upgrades. From **Flame Claws,** to infusing **Mana Bolt** with darkness energy, the list went on. Adam had to whistle at the sheer number of options. It seemed by meeting level requirements, he could infuse or specialize into different skill types. even his **Eyes of the Predator** could be upgraded to fire **Mana Bolt,** a notion that seemed absurd, but did inspire some ideas.

[Summon Minor Skeleton, Promoted to Summon Skeleton.]
[!Loved By Undead Detected!]
[Summon Skeleton Promoted to Summon Greater Skeleton!]

"Yes!"

[Mana Requirements not met! Dispelling summons!]

"NO!" Adam clutched his head, running his bloody fingers down his face as he groaned.

"Uuuuugh." Upon pulling up the skill again, it became apparent the requirements had leaped exponentially, from 80MP to 240MP. And that was *with* his efficiency upgrade, meaning it was 300 MP *alone* to summon a skeleton. "Why can't anything be easy for once?"

Fortunately, he could downgrade the skill, allowing him to summon his minions. *Un*fortunately, he still needed a vast amount of mana to sustain more than one summon.

Unless he optimized.

[Optimize Mana Requirements V2 Selected] -10% REQ.
[Optimize Mana Requirements V3 Selected] -10% REQ.
[Optimize Mana Requirements V4 Selected] -5% REQ.

He kept tapping his screen, not stopping until he realized the optimization had lowered.

Hmm... Twenty five percent plus twenty, forty five. One hundred and thirty five mana for one greater skeleton. At two eighty five mana, I can summon two greater skeletons, leaving me with fifteen. Enough for **Mana Claws**.

One skill point remained for him to do with as he pleased. "Hmmm, if I upgraded capacity, I could get up to *five* tier one skelecats."

He discredited the basic **Summon Skeleton**, as they needed his constant input, something he had no time to do. Instead he snapped his fingers, looking over the list.

[Drain Mana selected!]
[Skill Description: *Requires physical contact with an object or being that is in possession of mana. Slowly drains target at 1MP per 30 seconds, dependent on* **EGO**. *Target must pass an* **EGO** *check in order to resist being siphoned —*
0MP]

Well, that takes care of mana, still need to increase my capacity. The nekoboy stretched as he stood, balancing atop the monster's carcass.

"I should get back to Junith," Adam muttered, turning to head back the way he came, when suddenly a voice called out, stopping him.

"Adam?"

There by the wrecked bookshelves stood Redfield and Abdullah, along with several humans carrying guns. They spilled into the library from the tiny passage in the wall, each with stunned looks on their faces as they eyed the nekoboy covered head to toe in gore and viscera.

Capturr 85
Catlateral Damage

He had *known* the survivors were going to be more trouble than they were worth. Already, their repeated questions were growing tiresome. "For the last time, undead don't bother me."

"So, what? You've just been sitting here in this infested mansion? Alone? The entire time?" Redfield asked, hands on his hips as Adam submersed himself in the pages of a blood-spattered book, struggling to ignore the humans busying themselves with inspecting the corpse of the monster and surveying the area.

"Eh, mostly just in a cave in the woods." Finally he stuck the book in his coat, replacing it with a new book from the floor. "But pretty much."

Then Adam hopped up onto the deceased abomination, oblivious to the wide stares of the others as he casually used it as a foothold to reach a particularly high shelf.

"What are you looking for?" Redfield asked, tamping down his desire to ask the boy if he had anything to do with the nekofolk running around. Unlike the other humans in the room, as a trial participant, he could see Adam clearly for what he was: a cat-eared child.

When we're alone, Redfield said to himself.

"Reading material, mostly, we still have two weeks of the trial left." Adam grabbed a book titled *Chemistry 101.* "Got to make the time pass somehow."

"Hah. *Reading material,* he says. We're out here fighting for our lives, and he's just strolling around," Redfield scoffed, shaking his head with a sigh of resignation. "Where's your sister?"

Adam paused, realizing Redfield was asking about Junith. "Dealing with the consequences of being... well, herself. A terrible illness, if you ask me, but she's fine if that's what you're asking. Whatever happened to, uh... Jer... bull?"

"I honestly can't say. He was put in a different cell, and I haven't seen him since the outbreak began," Redfield said, as Abdullah peered over Adam's shoulder, glancing over the book the boy had opened. "Say... could you do me a favor?"

"Depends on the favor."

Redfield smirked. "Nothing bad, I swear. Look, I've got a number of people downstairs, they're hungry, injured, and have been cooped up together in an enclosed space for too long."

"Ooook?" Adam replied, uncertain where the man was going with this. Abdullah seemed to find something interesting, disappearing behind several bookshelves.

"So, I need to know if this place is safe. How many zeds are ahead, and where we can get food, water, and other amenities."

"Ha!" Adam snorted, going back to the book. He'd just come across a particularly interesting passage about nitroglycerin. "Good luck on the food front. I've been up and down this decrepit place, nothing here besides zombies, zombies, and more zombies."

"Shit," Redfield swore. Adam raised a brow before turning away. "Well, can you give me a headcount, maybe—"

"Yooo hooo!"

Adam froze, body tensing up as the familiar bubbly voice echoed out of the hidden passage.

"What's going on up there? Are you guys all dead? You gotta tell me if you're dead! BUT! If you're undead, can you just stay up there?"

Emerging from the hidden passageway was none other than Liza. As she and Adam caught sight of each other both froze, locking eyes.

The room seemed to hold its breath. Redfield quickly stepped between the two, lifting his hands.

"Now, let's just take a moment!" Redfield barked. All eyes turned to him as Adam lifted his palm and Liza pointed a handgun. Both seemed determined to kill each other, Redfield the only thing stopping them. "Easy! Easy. Eaaaasy."

"She tried to kill me!" Adam spat.

"It's nothing personal," Liza replied immediately. They circled each other in the library like two lions about to pounce, gleaming eyes intent for any weak point. Redfield scooted around them, blocking their line of fire with his body.

"Look, I know you two have your differences, but—"

"Differences?! Trying to murder me is a bit more than just differences!" Adam cut him off. The boy wanted nothing more than to blast the crazy woman to cinders, but Redfield's interference prevented him. He had no quarrel with the man, even if he was annoying.

"I understand that! But killing each other isn't going to help us survive! Right now, we need to work together. *Regardless* of past and current circumstances. Right now, we *need* each other," Redfield reasoned as the other humans began to spread out, weapons raised at Liza. At a signal from Redfield, they all lowered them again.

"She tried to murder me. And not just me, but Junith too!" Adam spat, more angry that the woman had nearly taken out his ticket home. "She even put a knife! IN! MY! SHOULDER!"

At Adam's words Redfield turned, brow furrowed in disapproval. Liza only scoffed.

"Like I said, kid, it's not personal. I just have a quest, and it's either you or it's me," she hissed, eyes narrowing. Adam struggled to process the bombshell she had dropped.

A quest. A quest to kill me? Is this what Coco meant? A mark for death?!

"And I choose *me*."

Distracted by the implications, Adam was slow, too slow, not fast enough to react as Liza pulled her trigger. From her firearm flew a bullet, intended for the boy.

Adam was too slow... but Redfield wasn't.

The cop dove, immediately shielding Adam with his body, the bullet diverted into Adam's face. He staggered back.

"What the hell?!" Immediately the other officers sprang into action, but Liza turned, firing on them as Redfield's body collapsed across Adam.

"Red?" he muttered, half his vision gone as he lay beneath the cop. He quickly shifted Redfield's heavy body off him, inspecting the man's wounds. Liza fled, racing back down the stairs as she traded gunfire with the officers.

"Red?" Adam said again, feeling for a pulse on the man. He only stared up blankly at the ceiling, mouth ajar, blood oozing from his head.

"Red?" he repeated again. Compared to his shock at the figure lying limp and prone, the pain in his left eye had gone numb, even as it bled profusely.

Redfield was dead. Just like that, he was gone. No pulse, no dying breath, just gone. His whole existence, a mere whimper in the wind.

Adam's jaw clenched. He was no stranger to death, no stranger to mankind's cruelty and irrational behavior, but this... this was new. He'd never had someone die defending him. A stranger at best, someone he disregarded, and yet...

His fist balled up, arms shaking as his face twisted, his jaw clenching so hard his mouth flooded with the metallic taste of blood as it leaked from his lips.

Something clicked in Adam, like a match being struck, igniting something inside buried beneath layers of repressed emotions and self control.

Fury.

Catpurr 86
Short Hunt

Sounds of gunfire rent the air, chased by screams and vibrations as Liza battled the regular humans in the space below Adam's feet.

He let out a breath of air, frowning as he rose from Redfield's body.

"Come to me," Adam whispered. Space was torn to make way for a large, cat-shaped portal, as something skeletal answered his call.

It was a skelecat, but completely unlike his usual summons. No, what appeared this time was a skeleton three times as tall. Its bony legs were like tree trunks, from its maw spouted two gargantuan tusks, and a set of glowing blue orbs swiveled within its eye sockets. Its jaw clacked, massive mandibles releasing a *click*ing noise as it growled, despite the absence of necessary organs.

"Go. Fetch me her soul," the nekomancer whispered gently. "But leave her alive."

The creature became a blur, racing towards the sounds of battle.

Adam closed his remaining eye, calming himself as he clutched at his trembling fist.

Finally, when the trembling stopped, he opened his eye and advanced. At the end of the passage he came upon a metal door left ajar. Behind it were two parties, engaged in a shootout.

The wolfman and the snake woman both hid in the wreckage of a long metal box, trading gunfire with the human survivors cowering behind pillars and debris.

No sign of Liza...

The chaos was irrelevant. Adam only took notice when he spotted one of the men who had been in the room when Redfield was shot, clad in camouflage clothes and barking orders to the gathered humans.

"Flank! Flank! Keep them suppressed! Burst fire to conserve ammo!" the man yelled. When he noticed the young boy apparently appear beside him, he opened his mouth to address Adam. "You need—"

"Where did the woman go?"

The man halted, eyes tracing from Adam's one good, glaring eye, to the dagger in his hand. "So you *are* one of them after all..."

"Focus. The woman, where did she go?"

"That way." The man pointed to an entrance at the far side of the room, its doors laying busted off the hinges. "Giant sabertooth in tow."

"Good." Adam turned away, leaving behind the chaos as he entered into a corridor, descending further into the abyss. Fresh droplets of blood created a trail, painting the walls with ribbons and splotches of crimson.

* * *

It didn't take long before Adam caught up to his summoned minion, the bones created in the form of a sabertooth prowling back and forth before a dented metal door.

"Is she behind this?" The massive skeleton turned its feline skull towards Adam. Its face was now marred by black streaks; no doubt damage from gunfire.

Its jaw opened, sharp bloodied teeth clacking as if to respond to its master.

"Good." Adam patted the skeletal feline on its skull, rubbing its chin as he eyed the security door. The bloody trail vanished underneath it. "Knock it down." The monster's bones seemed to flex before it lifted its snout, releasing a loud roar as it charged at the door, denting the already-rent metal fixture.

One bang, two bang, three bang, four.

Death's visage waited beside the door.

Finally the metal busted apart, revealing a lightless hole. A wrathful scream emanated from within, followed by gunshots. The loud bangs quickly gave way to repeated faint clicks.

Beneath the noises of his sabercat mauling the metal structure, Adam carefully listened to the noises within the room.

Like a prey animal, she breathed frantically, ragged breaths coming in quick and shallow, each laced with terror.

He snapped his fingers. The cat stopped and stepped aside, allowing him to peer into the hole.

There was Liza. The woman's back was to a glowing wall. Her face twisted with shock as she glimpsed Adam.

"Any last words?" the nekomancer asked gently, his tone monotonous. Liza could only stare at him with dumb confusion. "Last requests or wishes?"

"Piss off!"

Liza took her empty gun, throwing it through the hole. Adam merely sidestepped, catching the impromptu projectile. "Suit yourself."

He snapped his fingers, sending his summon once more to work, until finally, the creature itself entered the vault. It was greeted by the screams of its prey.

"Nononononono!" she shrieked, falling to the floor as the skeleton bore down on her, pinning her arms as she flailed madly around, attempting desperately to escape. "NO! NO! NO!"

Her cries were lost beneath the sabercat's roar.

When Adam entered he crouched down beside the prone woman, lightly poking her fear-ridden face with his dagger, right on the nose.

"What happens next depends solely on the answers you provide." Liza's eyes darted frantically, quivering as the ice-cold tip of the dagger dragged along her cheek. "You killed a man to get to me... Why?"

"YOU HAVE TO UNDERSTAND! I HAD NO CHOICE!" Liza spat, her fear erupting into fury as she struggled. A yawn from the sabertooth froze her again.

"Why, pray tell? Did you not have a choice?" he asked, cocking his head to the side.

"I have a quest! Either I do it, or I die!" she yelled, shrinking away from the teeth bearing down on her. "I didn't have a choice!"

That was as good as confirmation of his suspicions. *So it IS a mark for death... I'll have to be wary of all Voltrain followers from here on out.*

"So you killed him to save yourself."

"Don't look at me that way. He wouldn't get out of the way!" Liza spat. "What would you do in my position?!"

"*Not* harm an innocent to get what I want."

"But you'd still kill me to save yourself."

"Of course," Adam replied, zero hesitation.

"See! We're the same!"

"No. We aren't. And the reason why you can't see that... is the reason why you have to go away."

At the words "*go away,*" Liza shuddered, eyes wide as it at last fully sank in that she wouldn't be getting out alive.

"You're the one responsible for the rabid nekofolk outbreak, weren't you?" she asked, before turning her eyes to face the skeletal cat. "Probably started the undead apocalypse too, huh? So what? What are you going to do to me? Turn me into a zombie? Make me a rabid cat freak? Just do it! Get it over with, you freak!"

Listening to the pink haired woman's rant, an idea came to him, one he hadn't considered before as he removed his dagger.

"No. I think I have a better idea," he said, as he grabbed her slender wrist, bringing it to his mouth as she violently thrashed and struggled.

Catpurr 87

Build-a-Nekogirl

Time to see how this works.

Adam bit down, sinking his fangs into the woman's thin wrist.

Hmmm... Salty. The nekomancer was careful to bite Liza in the same way he'd bitten Junith. After all, any good experiment required a control. That didn't stop a sudden feeling of hunger from surging.

Immediately Liza began thrashing around. The pink haired follower of Voltrain struggled to break free, yet all this did was tear the wound further open, flooding his mouth with blood.

"You! YOU!" Liza screamed until she froze, eyes fixed on something unseen. Panic engraved itself upon her face. "GOLD! GOLD! I NEED! GOLD! GE!

"GAAAAAH!"

"Gold?" Adam released her wrist, spitting out her blood as she thrashed wildly, despite being pinned down by the skeletal sabercat.

"Now why would you need gold?" His golden eyes glinted with fascination. "Is it perhaps tied to the transformation?"

"AAAAAAGH! AAAAAAAAAAAAAAAAAAAGH!" From the bite mark stretched black veins, slowly marching up her arm.

"Fascinating..." He gave little response to Liza's agonized screams. Instead, as fur sprouted from around her neck, he merely retrieved his sketchbook to take notes.

"AHK! NO! NO!" the pink haired woman screamed. Steam curled around her body as her frame began to contort. In jerking fits and starts her body was made smaller, as if crushed by some greater force.

So, it seems my bite will revert my target to a childlike appearance, he surmised. Her wails rose in pitch as her flattened chest blazed with light, a familiar symbol branding itself on her body.

The Ouroborus, the symbol of Eli.

Tsk.

"MY BOOBS!"

Adam gazed impassively at the profile of his new follower.

[Bonded: Eh'Liza Oktober Lvl 1]
[HP: 60/70]
[MP: 10/10]
[Fearful]

Once satisfied, he willed it away, instead turning to eye the now-nekonized Liza, drowning in oversized clothes.

Her hair remained pink, but her frightened eyes became bright gold, matching his. Sticking out from her tiny, gasping body were little bits of pink fur.

"Y-you... What did you—"

Before she could finish her sentence, Adam reached out with a hand, grabbing her face by the temples and wrenching it around to look him in the eye.

"Your penance is this! For however much life you have left, you will never harm an innocent again. You will dedicate your life to the betterment of... all sentient life, and follow my orders," Adam said, picking his words carefully. "You will not harm me or those in my employ, you will not bite or infect another, and if asked for help, you will render aid whenever possible to those in need."

Liza's eyes flooded with confusion.

"DO YOU UNDERSTAND?!"

[Geas set!]

The serpent seemed to visibly wiggle and coil as the brand burned with a green-violet light. The newly formed nekogirl twisted and screamed.

Adam released her, ordering his sabercat off. The beast complied, albeit with one final growl.

Some attitude on this one.

He stood, leaving through the wrecked door.

Truthfully, he didn't know all the consequences of biting her, or if she would even live or die. But as a demi-human now geased to atone for her sin, he'd leave her to her penance. Wherever *that* took her.

"Wait! Where... Where are you going?!" she called out weakly. "Are you going to—"

"Leave you here? Yes. Do whatever you want. You aren't my problem anymore." Liza was left speechless as he simply left.

Killing her was too easy, and he lacked the skills as of now to raise her as a zombie. And so, if Voltrain wanted to urinate on his week, then he would do so with one less follower. At least until her quest failure activated and she died.

In a way, Liza was also a victim, but it didn't excuse what she had done.

A truly devious thought wandered across Adam's mind, lightening his dark mood as he smirked.

Maybe I can convert all of Voltrain's followers... Well. It was certainly a goal to consider.

* * *

Elsewhere, in a distant realm...

An ornate temple sat in the midst of a meadow, its gilded walls and ivory towers providing a magnificent backdrop to the God of Light. Every morning, he would sip from the rarest and most delectable teas known to mankind. Today, seated at a one-of-a-kind diamond table perfectly situated to behold the temple's beauty, delectably nuanced flavors still lingered on his tongue, even as he choked and spat the tea all over the desktop.

"WHAT?!" Voltrain sputtered, eyes wide with fury as he drove his fist down, much-abused diamond table, scattering his minifigures and even leaving a smoldering crater in the ground below.

This attack would have even greater consequences as the earth trembled, great swaths of his magnificently constructed temple all but disintegrating.

"Eli! ELI?!" Voltrain yelled, his green irises consumed by golden power. "Damn that filthy necromancer! ANOTHER ONE?!"

"Sir," spoke a woman in a flowing white gown, descending upon wings of silvery light. Her beatific features sat in contrast to her visibly strained smile. "I hope you realize that if you keep having outbursts, we'll never finish construction of the pylon on time."

Voltrain took a breath, calming his emotions before swiping back his golden hair, pausing for a moment as ichor began to leak out of his mouth and eyes.

"Yes. I am aware, Brunhilda," Voltrain replied, sighing as the Valkyrie dabbed his mouth with a delicate silken cloth, removing the blood and blue paint staining the god's face.

"Shall I bring a new host?" the woman asked, her icy blue eyes glaring down at the God of Light as he reclined in a gold-wrought chaise.

Voltrain raised his palm, the inner side of his hand crackling with energy spilling out from within.

"No, this one's time isn't up just yet," Voltrain said, narrowed eyes flickering with light.

Looks like no more painting for some time...

"Well. If you're feeling up to it, Unidine is looking for you with a few choice words," she reported, reaching down to gather the scattered half painted figurines.

"I assume regarding the—"

"The death of one of her Chosen, yes," Brunhilda finished.

"Not quite sure why she'd be so angry, when the mortal clearly ignored her orders."

"Be that as it may, Unidine claims he was a noble soul."

"If he was so noble, I don't see why she can't send him to Atlantis, then."

"She would have, but according to her, Eli intercepted the soul, calling her Chosen to his domain."

Voltrain froze, eyes wide. He blinked.

This was definitely a first. The aging god wasn't known to interfere with others and their Chosen, not directly, at least. In fact, a lot of incidents that had been occurring as of late were completely unprecedented. The elder's careless fumbling was proving a headache for Voltrain.

Voltrain's shoulders sagged as he sighed.

"If she wishes to see me, she can schedule an appointment with Skul or Sigrun. Whichever of the Valkyries are on duty this year. Otherwise, just tell her I'm too busy."

"Busy with painting minifigures and destroying months of hard work?" The Valkyrie planted her hands on her hips, as if she were speaking with a child.

"Don't talk to me as if I were still a petulant squire learning from Odin. It's *therapeutic*. Between fighting the void spawn, dealing with administration, and trying to keep a leash on Eli, this is one of the few pastimes I have," Voltrain retorted, picking up the blue figure of a knight, a Greek Omega painstakingly painted on its pauldron.

"Yes. So you've said. In any case, I feel that scheduling an appointment may not be a priority of Unidine's," Brunhilda replied. In the distance a sapphire geyser erupted, engulfing what remained of the palace and surrounding meadow.

Voltrain sighed, the familiar wash of his sister's power sweeping over him as the explosion mushroomed into the atmosphere. "Oh, dear God. I'm going to have to kill another one of her hosts."

Brunhilda placed a slender hand to her mouth as she giggled.

"What? What's so funny now?" Voltrain demanded as he summoned a box, gently placing all his minifigures within.

"Nothing. Just after all these years, it's adorable that you still cry out to yourself."

Voltrain rolled his eyes.

"Yes. Yes. I'm God now. Very funny, we're all laughing. Now, if you will excuse me, I suppose it's time for this *god* to fulfill his *godly duties* and kill his baby sister again." As Voltrain rose from his seat, wings burning with holy fire unfurled from his back, and a similarly burning sword manifested within his clenched hand.

Catpurr 88

Discussion of Faith

Now alone with an unconscious Junith, Adam sat, reading a book titled *Firearms, Bacteria, and Steel,* by the light of a glass sphere set upon a bronze stick.

Fascinating, he said to himself, turning the page as he read a section about how this world's colonists had used a stratagem of disease-riddled gifts of clothes and fabric to decimate the original inhabitants.

Although crafty in his eye, the move was too callous, too indiscriminate, as the disease targeted *anyone* it could come in contact with, wiping out entire populations.

He picked up the silver handgun on his desk, admiring the craftsmanship, one of the few things he was able to retrieve from Redfield's body shortly before it glimmered away.

"Wouldn't it be nice if I could create a disease that targeted only Voltrain's followers. Infect them with my... condition?" he sighed, distracted from his speculation as the sound of nearby rustling drew his attention.

The firearm disappeared, safe within his storage ring.

"Huwha?" Junith groaned, eyes wide as she sat up, clutching the oversized shirt draped over her nude upper body.

"Mornin," Adam greeted her as his follower collected her bearings.

"Y-You! What did you do to me?! Did you! You—" Junith's brow furrowed, anger in her eyes as her voice rose in pitch. "—have your way with me?!"

He blinked, his expression sullen and slackened.

"Ew."

Junith reeled, caught off guard by the reply. "Ew?"

"Yes. Ew, meatbag, as if anyone would ever want to sleep with you, much less *touch* you."

"Are you calling me ugly?!"

"No," he replied coolly. "I'm calling you disgusting, both inside and out. The idea of sexual intercourse with you actually makes me physically ill."

Her eye twitched. "WELL, I'M GLAD THE FEELING IS MUTUAL, THEN!"

The nekogirl leaned against the wall, sliding down as she clutched her head, muttering incoherent musings.

"Tell me, Junith. How does your god work?" He adjusted the torn fabric bandaging his left eye, and returned to the book.

It took her a moment to respond, seeming to watch Adam carefully in that time.

"Voltrain... is the God of Light, Life, and Creation. Through us, his work is carried out. What happened to your eye?"

"Yes, yes, I've heard this from your blubbering mouth a thousand times," he replied, ignoring Junith's attempt at changing the subject. "No, what I mean is, how does your god *work?* His powers, his—"

There was a knock at the door.

"Hello?" a voice called. It took a moment for Adam to remember its owner was Marvin, the soldier he'd briefly encountered.

"Come in," Adam said.

"HEY! NO! I'M NAKED!" Junith screamed as the door creaked open. At her outcry it slammed again.

Adam rolled his eye, electing to simply join Marvin in the hall. He found two others standing with the soldier.

"Sorry... Were we disturbing you two?" Marvin asked cautiously, clutching his gun close.

"What?" Adam asked, confused.

"Ehem. Nevermind."

"Is there something you need? I asked not to be disturbed." Frankly, Adam wanted nothing to do with the survivors. Unfortunately, the survivors had other ideas.

"I know, but we need your help."

"I have my skeletons patrolling the grounds, hunting down every undead in the vicinity. What more could you need?"

"Food. Water. Materials we can't acquire. You said it yourself, the undead don't bother you," Marvin said.

Ah... crapbaskets. "And you don't find that suspicious?" raising a brow.

"We work with what we have. And right now, I have forty men, women, and children in the basement of this mansion that are in desperate need of food, water, and medical supplies. Not to mention, the rogue magic people that are God-knows-where," Marvin said. "So, regardless of my own suspicions, right now you're our only hope. Redfield stuck his neck out for you, I'm hoping you'll do the same for us."

Adam took a deep breath. As much as he wanted to separate himself from the survivors, they did have a point. They wouldn't survive without food and water, an issue which also plagued him.

"Oh, if only I had a ring of sustenance," he muttered.

"What was that?"

"Nothing. I'll see what I can do." Adam paused. "You said medical supplies... Do you have injured?"

"Yes, a few. It's not a high priority, but I'd rather not have people dying from infection and blood loss."

"Judgy! Get out here." From within the room came sounds of grumbling discontent, meandering closer to the door. It slammed open.

"What?!" Junith hissed, the nekogirl now swaddled in only an oversized, button-up shirt patterned with palm trees.

"Go with them, tend to their wounded. I'm sure you know how to perform basic aid?"

"Tsk, of *course* I know. I'm a paladin of Voltrain, we…" Her words quickly died in her throat. "Let's go."

She then scampered down the hall, leaving Adam and the officers behind.

"Wrong way, idiot." He pointed in the opposite direction.

"I knew that!" she growled, stomping her way back. This time, Marvin and the others followed behind. "AND I'M NOT AN IDIOT!"

"Mmhm."

Adam watched them go, casting his eyes down as he frowned.

Just a few more days.

* * *

Over the next few days, the city streets would be stalked by skelecats, scavenging on behalf of the survivors as Adam conducted research on their world and technology.

The mansion contained an impressive library, holding a vast collection of poetry, research, and notes on the history of this realm and its technology, all of which he greedily devoured.

Now, he found himself enraptured by a book on chemistry, when he found his reading time interrupted.

"A scholar *and* a warrior," came the smooth voice of Abdullah, as the warrior entered the study. "You continue to surprise me, kytah."

"Hello, Abdullah. Shouldn't you be hunting the others?" Adam asked, relaxing upon realizing who it was. He looked up from the textbook to see the man was dripping with blood. In one hand he gingerly held a pouch.

Abdullah chuckled.

"Yes. The hunt has been partially fruitful." He brandished the bloody bag. "Would you like to bear witness to this one's trophy?"

"Uh… No thanks," Adam replied. While he was interested in who Abdullah had hunted, he didn't want to contaminate the room of books and notes any further. "I'll take your word for it. Who was your target?"

"The serpent!" Abdullah announced, before his voice shifted from jubilance to sadness. "Slippery woman, this one only managed to take her tail..."

Adam shuddered, reminded of the Daughter of Vilenciel and her plan for a transplant.

Heh. Perhaps I should pay a visit to her. This time with a bite or two.

"What do you find amusing, kytah?" the bronze warrior asked, peering over Adam's shoulder at the page he was reading.

"Just plotting," was his reply before returning to his book.

"Ah, dangerous is the warrior who plans." A formula on the page seemed to catch his eye. "Hmm? Studying black powder?"

"You know of it?"

"Yes. We, like this world, have weapons that make use of it, called boomtubes. Not as fast or quick as this realm, but still very deadly."

"Fascinating," Adam replied, realizing he had a chance to inquire more about the man's world. "Would you tell me more about your world? Perhaps about your god as well?"

Abdullah's expression lit up, joy on his face at the prospect of sharing his world and culture.

"Of course, kytah!" Abdullah replied as Adam found a seat on a wooden chair, taking out his sketchbook as the bronze warrior joined him.

"I come from the sea of sands, a realm of three moons and a sun that sets once every three days," Abdullah began, before he regaled Adam with a tale of his culture and his tribe, who were known as the Li'hiken. "We have fought a thousand conflicts, and we will fight a thousand more! Ahaha!"

"All that bloodshed for Yashwa?" Adam asked, recalling the item descriptions he'd seen back at the temple of Undine.

"Yes! Yashwa is the primordial being of War, Conquest, Courage, and Honor!" Abdullah replied, his bronze bangles jangling as he slammed an arm on the table. "And through our offerings, his grace gives us strength!"

He gestured to the bloody bag oozing red onto the table.

Grace gives us strength... He'd heard the same phrase before, from Junith.

Adam leaned forwards, folding his fingers together. "Tell me, Abdullah, how does one measure the strength of their... strength, from their god?"

"Through Faith, of course," Abdullah replied, his expression shifting. "You are a Chosen, no? Do you not possess Faith?"

"I've never been much for reliance on a higher power, no."

"Ah... so you are an infidel," Abdullah replied solemnly, stroking his chin. A screen appeared between Adam and the warrior.

WARRIOR'S SYSTEM
TITLE: The Butcher of Arka
NAME: Abdullah Tel'svi'norri Li'hiken
CLASS: Geomancer
SPECIES: Human
LEVEL: 13
HP: 720/800
MANA: 35/75
FOCUS: 20/150
STR: 23
CON: 40 (x2)
DEX: 17
ARC: 15
FAI: 30
SEN: 20
EGO: 19

Surprising, that the other man would be so quick to share his information. Still, Adam wouldn't waste this opportunity.

Huh... tangible rewards. Of particular interest to the nekomancer was the Faith stat and Focus bar. *Explains why they are so fervent.*

"Through penance, worship, and valor, does Yashwa grant me strength," Abdullah explained. "You would be wise to reconsider your stance on the gods, kytah. For beings that are capable of such wonders, they are also capable of great wrath and anger."

"Hmmm... Thank you, Abdullah, this has been very... insightful."

The warrior rose from his seat. "The pleasure is all mine, kytah. Rare is it to find a fellow who values conflict as well as knowledge." Abdullah bowed, hand over heart as he eyed a skeletal cat perched above them.

"Where are you off to now?"

"To hunt, of course!"

"Of course," Adam replied as he returned to his books. Somehow, speaking with the man had left him feeling... refreshed.

[WARNING: Follower HP is low!]
[Bonded: Eh'Liza Oktober LvL 2]
[HP: 10/80]
[MP: 20/20]
[Fearful]

"Huh?" Through his bond, sensations of fear and pain abruptly overflowed. But what surprised him was not that these emotions came from Junith, no—according to the follower menu, they were coming from Liza.

Just as he was about to return to his books, another stab of pain distracted him. Now Junith's HP dropped.

Oh, great. What is that idiot up to now? he sighed, standing up. Why had he decided to leave the crazed zealot alone without supervision, again?

Catpurr 89

Interacting With the Locals

"Stop! I said stop! Back away!" shrieked Junith's voice, echoing through the walls and greeting Adam as he approached the basement, skeletal cat in tow.

Upon opening the door, he was met with a strange sight. Junith stood before the crumpled and bleeding form of Liza, brandishing fangs and a dagger in defense of the injured nekogirl. Around them churned a clearly displeased crowd.

"Move, girly!" yelled an irate man, covered in tattoos. In his own hands he aimed a gun. Junith seemed blasé towards the firebrand, merely glaring with defiance. "Move, or I'll blow your head off!"

Marvin was nowhere to be seen.

"COME ON, THEN! If that's how you repay me for healing you, then do it!" The man flinched at Junith's snarling outburst. Then he kicked her, forcing the priestess onto the ground as she scrambled to shield Liza with her body.

"OK! ENOUGH!" Adam clapped his hands, drawing everyone's attention. Then he pointed to Junith ordering her back by his side.

She resisted, spasming as she struggled to shield Liza.

"Great! Another one of the voodoo folk," the man spat, turning to face Adam. His face sat glued in a mask of rage.

"Yes, yes, we're quite magical. Now, can you please explain to me why you're waving a firearm like a lunatic and kicking one of my tools around?"

Junith shot him a glare, clearly not delighted at being called a tool.

"Francis, put the gun down," coaxed a woman with red hair, placing a hand on the man's forearm. "Remember what Marvin said? Leave them alone, Redfield wouldn't want—"

"I don't give a damn what Marvin said! Who made him leader, anyway?! Bill is dead, and the only reason we followed Redfield was because he looked like he knew what he was doing." The man known as Francis spun, jabbing the redhead in the chest. "Now he's dead—"

"I'm only going to ask you *once* to put the gun down," interrupted Adam, before yawning.

"Oh? And why should I answer to you?" Now the gun spun towards him. The nekoboy did nothing, as one of the Skittles brushed up against his ankles, hissing at the enraged man.

Adam's eyes swept across the room. Most of the supplies he'd scavenged were being stockpiled here, it seemed, filling the once-empty space.

"Simple. Because if you seek comfort in the protection I provide, the food you eat, and the amenities you enjoy, you'll do as I say. Otherwise, I have no qualms leaving you to fend for yourselves."

The redhead once again approached Francis. "Please, Francis, put it down. I know you're hurting. I am too. But we need their help."

"This isn't right!" Francis spat, before pointing at Liza. "Because of that bitch freeing the other voodoo people, we lost six guys! We lost Louis! And I'm supposed to be okay with her flouncing around, offerin' aid like nothing happened?!"

It hadn't occurred to Adam that, while Liza had failed to kill him, she might have *succeeded* in killing others, nor had he wondered before now who had released Sethis and the wolfman.

Ah... crapbaskets.

"Killing her won't bring them back. Please, don't do anything rash," said the redhead. Finally Francis shut his eyes, expression openly pained.

"It would be wise of you to listen to her," Adam said, as more skeletal cats appeared from the shadows, responding to his emotions. "While I'm being merciful."

Adam felt for the survivors, he really did. But he also couldn't risk Junith being killed, when she was his only ticket home, to his one true friend, the only thing that truly mattered to him.

The skelecats approached, rattling their bones. Francis and the others seemed unnerved at their appearance, unconsciously clumping closer together.

Maybe I should try a different approach.

"I sympathize with your losses. Had I known she was responsible, I would not have been so callous with my orders," Adam said. He gestured for Junith to bring Liza nearer as he spoke. "To clear up the confusion, as a means to stay her execution, this woman is currently my prisoner, serving a life sentence of repentance."

Junith picked up the unconscious Liza, bringing the beaten girl to Adam, escorted by a pair of skelecats who carved a path through the sea of frightened survivors.

Yet more dead weight in his quest wasn't appealing to Adam at all. But at the very least, he didn't want Liza dying so quickly, either. Not when she had a lifetime to repent, or, well, however much time she had left before she failed her quest. But a lifetime didn't have to be long, did it?

The bubbly nurse he had previously met was now broken and beaten, cradled in Junith's arms. After all she had done by her own will, however, he couldn't help but find her appearance fitting.

Not that he took much joy from her current state. If anything, it was a shame she wouldn't be very useful. Not in the ways he first envisioned, anyway.

Adam sighed. This was the *problem* when interacting with others. His plans and ideas always seemed to backfire in some way.

The nekotrio left, followed by a small parade of skelecats. While heading up the stairs they passed by Marvin and a group of officers, just returning from a patrol.

"The hell happened?!" Marvin demanded. Adam merely waved.

"The issue's been settled. Don't worry about it." Now, he was *really* going to leave the humans to their own devices.

* * *

While Junith cared for the unconscious Liza, Adam whittled away the free time with his books, by this point simply waiting for the trial to finally end.

"So... what's the deal with this one?" Junith asked, cleaning the bloodied scrape on Liza's shoulder. "Why did you convert her?"

"To test a few theories."

"Why? What do you plan on doing with her?"

"Nothing," Adam replied. "She has a quest from Voltrain to kill us both. I reckon once she fails, she'll be smited. Smote? Smitten? Anyways, I want to see what that looks like. In the meantime, I was planning to get some free labor out of her."

There were several moments of silence, before Junith finally found a reply to that. "You're sick."

"Sick for passively observing the demise of another, who actively wishes you and I dead?" he intoned. "Not much different than you standing over my injured body and savoring the act of killing me. Or the public executions your church hosts for heretics. Didn't you guys burn someone on a spike at one point?"

Junith frowned, her brow furrowing at Adam's words.

"Come to think of it, if you had just stabbed me with your sword instead of ranting like your lot always does, you wouldn't be in this predicament," he continued, rubbing more salt in Junith's proverbial wounds as he returned to his book.

"Tsk!" she spat, clenching the wet rag in her hand until dirty water and blood trickled from her hands. "The church has its faults, I can admit that. But it is *not* without purpose or gain. What do you stand to gain from this?" Adam blinked, not expecting the paladin's reply.

A moment passed, then another, before he opened his mouth.

"What it means to fail a quest. All knowledge, no matter how slight, can be useful. There can be nothing gained if nothing is—"

"Ventured," Junith finished, meeting Adam's good eye.

They remained that way for several seconds.

"Funny how closely our lives mirror our predecessors," he remarked. Junith broke eye contact, turning away. "Do you think they'd be proud of what we've done with our lives? That we've continued their feud in their absence?"

No response. Not that he was expecting one.

Adam went back to reading, as Junith continued taking care of Liza. Uninterrupted silence reigned, until something began scratching at the door.

"Great," Adam muttered, closing his book. "Why is it that *everyone* wishes to disturb me while I'm working?"

It was one of his skeletons, a cat posted in the hallway to alert him of approaching humans.

Adam got up, exiting into the hallway. Once outside glimpsed Francis, escorted by Marvin and two other officers. He shut the door behind him a little more forcefully than he really needed to.

What now...

"I heard about what happened," Marvin said, standing in front of Adam. Occasionally he peered out of the corner of his eyes towards the tattooed man. "And I believe Francis has something he'd like to say."

The man grumbled before fully opening his mouth, however before he could speak, Adam raised his tiny hand.

"Stop. I don't care. Bygones be bygones. No one was hurt that didn't deserve it, and quite frankly, I'm not interested in apologies." He paused, then trying to more carefully moderate his tone, began again. "Although, I do appreciate the sentiment. Now, was there something you needed? I am *quite* busy."

Marvin looked to the cop beside him as Francis shook his head, and scoffed. The quartet seemed caught off guard by Adam's reply, and were struggling to formulate a response.

"Fine. If you two won't spit it out, I will," Francis huffed. "We need your help, kid."

"With?"

Marvin opened his mouth, finally deciding to voice his request.

"We want to bring more survivors here," Marvin said. "We found a working communications room below the subway, where we can contact other holdouts, other enclaves, let them know of the safe haven here."

They must have meant the room he opened up. The one Liza had tried taking refuge in. *Where are they going with this?*

"Okay? I fail to see what this has to do with me?" His gaze drifted along the rickety ceiling and floor. The men may call this place a safe haven, but it looked fit for demolition.

"Outside these walls, there are still zombies around, lots of them skulking about that survived the bombing," Francis said.

"Enough to pose a big threat," Marvin added. "If people start moving here, they will need protection. A guide."

Wait.

"Protection you can provide."

No. No, no, no.

"We want you to use your skeletons to help locate survivors and bring them here, acting as guides and guardians to people needing aid. Maybe even lead them here yourself."

The nekoboy released a long and drawn-out groan, as if the weight of the world were on his shoulders. The men exchanged odd looks.

"Why can't I just finish a book," Adam muttered to himself as he turned on his heel, marching back into the library.

"Is that a no?" Marvin called out, tone tinged with worry as Adam reached for the door.

"I'll see what I can do." And the door shut once more.

Catpurr 90
Here Be Safety

"Run! Don't stop! We're almost there!" Frank yelled. Spotting a crying little girl who had fallen on the sidewalk, he scooped her up before the infected could reach her. Now the zeds slammed against the metal fence that blocked their path, barring them from the survivors in the alley. "Go! Go! Go!"

"Aw, man! Good thing they can't open door knobs!" Ramos laughed, jostling the camera around his neck, before a shriek interrupted him. A familiar cry, belonging to a very memorable type of zombie. Ramos' laughter instantly died.

Damn hunters, Frank thought, desperately scouring the shadows on the rooftops above. He hugged the shivering girl close, frowning as she soaked his expensive shirt with snot and tears.

The group of five survivors exited the alley, escaping into the bombed-out street cluttered with destroyed cars, craters, and debris.

"Crap, man! Was this 81st street or 82nd?!" Ramos yelled, clutching his sledgehammer tight as more infected shambled down the road.

"Don't you own a mechanic shop here?! I thought you knew the layout of the city?!" retorted Chuck as he checked the magazine of his assault rifle and slammed the magazine back in. Gunfire lit up the night as he fired on the encroaching hoard.

"Yeah! But not when it's all bombed out, dude! Everything is different!" the mechanic replied, slamming his hammer down on a shambler.

"Focus, people! Focus! The broadcast said we just need to get to the subway. We find the entrance and then, presto! We're out of here!"

Rebecca said, straining to remain calm, even as she emptied the magazine of her pistol at a licker. It tried to spear her with its long tongue, but Frank deflected the strike with a metal chair.

"Swapping mag!" Rebecca cried as she slammed in a new magazine and resumed fire.

"There!" Frank yelled, throwing the foldable chair at a zombie before pointing. There hung a tattered cloth, upon which was written *Here be safety!*

The group took off, pelting down the underground stairwell, even as undead crowded around it.

"Almost there!" Ramos yelled, when a nearby explosion sent him flying. Debris showered down upon all as a titan emerged from the clearing smoke.

"Greasemonkey!" Rebecca called, running over to the injured Ramos as zombies began to swarm him.

"Oh, fug!" Frank spat, stumbling back as he held the girl in his arms, frozen by the titan blocking his path.

Chuck opened fire, shooting at the hulking monster as it roared, bellowing its hatred. With its decomposing fists it slammed on the ground and beat its chest.

"Crapcrapcrap. Damn it!" Chuck yelled, his gunfire becoming useless *clicks*. Without missing a beat he struck an approaching zombie across the head with the empty firearm, but it wasn't much help now—the titan and the rest of the crowd were boxing them in.

"Mister E-East. I-I'm scared. I want my mommy," the little girl in Frank's arms whimpered as he set her down, taking out his revolver from his waistband.

Six shots. Enough for everyone here... Well, it was worth a shot...

Frank looked up from his gun, smiling at the girl as he prepared himself for what he was about to do.

"It'll be okay. Just close your eyes, sweetie," Frank said, brushing the gore and dust out of the girl's black hair back.

She did as told, as Frank took one look around, assessing the situation.

This was it. After surviving the apocalypse in the bunker of a library, living off of expired rations, they would finally meet their end. Originally a group of twenty, their numbers had dwindled drastically as people left, died, or just succumbed to starvation.

That was the final straw, the man dying from starvation.

With supplies next to nil, the survivors had been forced from their shelter.

Which, of course, resulted in more losses. Now they had pinned their hopes on one final hurrah, one final plan to seek safety from starvation and the hungry dead.

The broadcast.

"Goodnight, kid," Frank said, knuckles whitening around his pistol, steeling himself to do the unthinkable as the girl closed her eyes. "You'll see your parents so—"

A cloud of sand rose around them, striking the zombies and constricting the roaring titan. It was a strange enough sight to freeze Frank in his tracks.

The monster was tied down, its arms pinned to the ground as sand buried the monster. From the subway, skeletal cats began to pounce upon the zombies, which strangely made no attempt at all to fight back.

"What the hell...?"

"Ahoy! Many moons to you!" a voice called out, as a black skinned bald man in a fancy gilded suit strode out from the subway, smiling.

Frank gripped his gun as the man calmly strolled forwards, ignoring the titan even as a trio of skeletal cats ripped it to shreds.

"You... Who the hell are you?" Chuck asked incredulously, as Frank aimed his gun at the man.

"Ah, friends. I am merely a hunter in service to Yashwa. But you may call this one Abdullah," he said in an odd accent, bowing as he gestured to the abyss of the subway. "Shall we go? Safety awaits you, my friends."

Chuck turned to Frank, who then turned to Rebecca. The police officer was helping a limping Ramos over to the others, as they stood in bewilderment. In plain shock, they watched the skeletons chase off any remaining undead.

One of the skelecats approached the group, clacking, but making no hostile movements, even as Rebecca aimed her gun at the creature. In reply, it merely rubbed up against her boot.

Frank let out a low laugh.

"Sure. Why not, can't be any worse than what was about to happen," Frank said, as he picked up the little girl in his arms and led the way into the subway.

****

"Hmmm... Maybe I should have thought things through."

High up on the mansion's roof, Adam sat, observing the new groups of humans stumbling from the forest to form ragged lines before the gate. There, a man named Peralta proceeded to screen them, alongside other soldiers.

Two days had passed since he agreed to lend his skeletons to help the denizens of this realm, and in those two days, survivors began to arrive in droves.

*Good thing I have **Loved by Undead**...*

Now the mansion was bustling with survivors, more than Adam expected. And still Marvin's offer for shelter and protection kept going out, rallying yet more to the manor.

"Oh well, what's done is done, I suppose." All he could hope for was that this turn of events wouldn't bite him in the rear later. He returned to his pad, sketching the scene below as survivors were escorted to a tent to strip, their items laid out for inspection and collection.

Once finished, he turned to observe the garden behind the manor. There, Liza and Junith stood, digging holes.

"Hey. We're ready," Marvin said, emerging from a hatch on the roof.

Adam closed his book, then rose and stretched. After sitting hunched for so long, his back ached something fierce. The officer led him through the manor now crawling with men, women, and children moving to and fro, bringing the dreary place to life with sound, music, light, and even laughter.

Watching them, Adam smiled to himself, if only slightly. Although it was cramped, it was a pleasant sight seeing so many that his skeletons had saved.

Tangible results, right in front of his own eyes.

"As requested," Marvin said as he brought Adam to a room that smelled of something familiar. Outside, several men stood, clad in gloves and facemasks. The nekomancer poked his head inside the door.

Herein lay the victims of the apocalypse. Within the room scores of bodies were laid out, the air thick with the stench of decay. Francis and Marvin had wanted to bury them in a mass grave for convenience, but Adam had refused, instead putting his followers to work digging individual graves.

"Let's get to work," he said, strapping on a pair of rubber gloves.

Catpurr 91

Sudden Teleportation

"And so, we lay to rest the departed. In the grace of the goddess, may she watch over their souls." The priest shut his black book and bowed his bandaged head. "Let us observe this moment of silence."

The crowd gathered around him fell silent, standing amongst the freshly dug graves of the courtyard. The night was a bright one tonight, as the garden was lit by bright beams.

Adam observed the ritual. It was quite similar to those from his home of Grandzalia, albeit with some minor changes. One of those most notable was that here, coins were to be placed on the eyes of the dead to serve as the Ferryman's toll. The Ferryman seemed to be a prominent figure, a psychopomp responsible for guiding the souls of the dead.

One of the skelecats approached the priest, dragging a burlap bag. It fell to the ground with a *clink,* as some bright coins spilled from its mouth.

The priest clad in black and green garments nodded in gratitude to Adam, who returned the gesture. Slowly the coins were distributed amidst the mourners.

Because of the less-than-sterile conditions and risk of infection, Adam advised that physical contact not be made with the deceased. Instead the decision was made to bury the coins alongside the corpses, only after they'd been wrapped, lowering the risk of contamination.

So, in accordance with their traditions, the group spread out, placing coins into the disturbed soil that marked each grave.

The crunch of boots on gravel drew the nekoboy's attention away from the crowd.

"Thank you for this," Marvin said, standing beside him with folded arms. "This might be the first step to normalcy we've taken in a long time. If you ever need anything—"

"Don't mention it." He turned back to the crowd, observing as several kids crowded a skelecat, completely unafraid as the creature batted at a yoyo a kid was using to tease it. "I've already gotten my reward. Besides, there's nothing you have that I want. Let me know if there's anything you need, I'll be up in my..."

He paused. "Office. Studying."

"Alright then," Marvin said. He remained behind with the mourners, as Adam retired inside the mansion, walking the now-lit corridors.

"Adam."

"Abdullah," he greeted as sand rose and parted, revealing the familiar bronze-clad warrior, weapon in hand. "How goes the hunt?"

The man chuckled, gripping the bloody axe. Adam immediately recognized it as the property of the canine.

"Very vexing. The wolfman is a shrewd and cunning warrior. This one must admit, I have been humbled in my pursuit," Abdullah replied, falling in step beside Adam as they ascended the stairwell, its handrail still undergoing repairs.

The boy turned to Abdullah to reply, only to realize the man was injured.

"You're bleeding." All along his bicep were visible claw marks.

"A trifle. Much like the kytah, the wolf has claws." Abdullah smiled as Adam stopped one of the manor's denizens, asking him to fetch Junith. "How is your eye?"

"It's healing. Slowly. My Constitution isn't exactly *high*."

Within moments, Junith joined them, a dirtied Liza in tow. While Junith wore her trademark scowl, Liza's expression was more downcast and sullen.

"**Heal** this man," he ordered. Junith complied, with a dour expression but few complaints.

Abdullah extended his arm, lowering himself as he allowed the nekogirl to examine it.

"Thank you, Judgy." Abdullah bowed.

"It's Junith," she growled. "Not Judgy! Junith!"

"Ah, my apologies," Abdullah said, almost reaching out and ruffling her hair, but stopping himself as he eyed Liza. "You know, Adam, one day, this one would like an explanation of your transformative abilities, and the god who has chosen you for his work."

Adam sighed, pressing against a wall as several survivors dragged a table down the walkways.

"Perhaps once I learn more. I hardly understand it myself. Don't even know who Eli is or what his goals are, really. Only that he seems intent on making my life difficult," he grumbled, watching as a woman in a police uniform hugged another female cop attempting to move supplies.

"Rebecca! Rebecca, I can't believe you're alive!" the woman said, tears in her eyes as she hugged the cop. "How did you survive?!"

"Oh! You should have been there! We were outnumbered a hundred to one! Dead on all sides, greasemonkey—this is greasemonkey, by the way—got grabbed after a hulk smashed through a building, and just when we were about to die!" Rebecca yelled, turning from her task to gesture wildly. "A bunch of cat skeletons appear! Jumping around, attacking zombies left and right! Saving greasemonkey!"

"My name is Ramos, ya know..." a man in gray overalls whispered.

Adam turned, feeling odd.

Junith took notice. "Are you blushing?"

"What? No—"

"Ah, that's the man with the sand. That guy, right there!" the cop yelled.

Oh boy.

"Thank you! Thank you so much!" the woman said, approaching Abdullah and leaping at him, only to be pushed back by a sudden wave of sand.

"This one appreciates the gesture," Abdullah said, waving his hand. "But no touching."

Man, I need to get me a skill like that... Adam shook his head as he left Abdullah be, resolving to return to his books.

[Hidden Objective complete! Cure the Zombex Plague! Completed by Chosen of Mimir, Jerbull Gehell]
[Trial Ended!]

What?

Adam froze, narrowing his eyes as he turned to Abdullah. The bronze warrior wore a similarly stunned expression.

[Prepare to be teleported!]

"No—" Adam said, the only word to escape his mouth before the world changed.

Catpurr 92

Am I the Baddie?

"—wait! MY BOOKS!" Adam looked about wildly, taking in his surroundings. He was in a void of some kind, purple infinity stretching as far as the eye could see.

Oh. Oh no.

Deep within, something familiar was churning and roiling.

Why? Why?!

"YOU!" hissed a woman's familiar voice, as a face he hadn't seen in some time came into view.

Sethis.

The disheveled snake woman charged. Adam tensed, raising his hands in preparation for a fight.

Suddenly laughter erupted from Adam's side, as a figure in bronze shrouded in sand raced forwards, wielding an axe in one hand and a scimitar in the other.

"MY PREY!" Abdullah bellowed joyously, clashing against the woman's spear. Sparks flew from their weapons as he laughed again.

"I'LL MAKE YOU PAY FOR TAKING MY TAIL!" the tailless Sethis screamed as a red light flared from somewhere nearby.

Abdullah leapt back and Adam pulled his cloak tightly, shielding himself from the blast as something inhuman snarled.

It was the wolfman, red-hot embers spilling from his angry maw as Sethis hissed and prepared to attack

Adam was left dumbfounded. *HE SPITS FIRE?!*

"Watch where you're pointing that muzzle of yourss!" Sethis yelled, twirling her spear as the canine's hackles rose.

"Then stay out of my way," the wolf spat. Both leapt back back as several spikes of sand nearly impaled the pair.

"Tsk!"

"*Hisssss!*"

Sethis and Wolfy both whirled towards Abdullah, as the warrior openly thanked his god for the opportunity to offer up worthy foes in his name.

The three squared off, hissing and snarling at one another, each prepared to kill the others.

"Come, Adam! Will you join me in this hunt?" Abdullah called, as sand swirled around his two weapons.

"Uh..." The familiar taste of foul eggs tinged the inside of Adam's mouth. "O-one... One moment!"

With practiced grace Abdullah deflected Sethis' spear, shooting the nekoboy a questioning look.

"Just! *HUHLK Huhk! Haaa.*"

Adam threw up, his rainbow colored spew flying everywhere. The canine summoned a barrier, narrowly avoiding being drenched. His serpentine companion was not so lucky, as his barrier bounced rainbow goo into her eyes.

"*Hissssss!* WHAT FOUL DEVILRY!"

"VERY NICE, KYTAH!" Abdullah laughed, charging as the canine man moved to intercept the mad bronze warrior.

The two raced at each other, eager to tear one another apart, but suddenly stopped. Dozens of portals opened, from which emerged chains of light, binding both warriors.

"Oh, nonononono! This simply won't do! You will cease! You will cease this at once, Chosen!" A ball of light coalesced, and a certain googly eyed rock appeared, hovering amidst the chaos.

Adam took a step back, bumping into Junith and Liza as rectangular, see-through walls of light materialized, separating the contestants.

"After all! The best part of the trial is about to happen!" Rocky announced, the purple void exploding with celebratory sounds as a massive *CONGRATULATIONS!* appeared. Below the words a podium appeared, upon which stood a giant furry creature, chowing down on a giant seed.

"Jerbull?" Adam muttered, brow raised as he wiped away his rainbow-hued vomit.

The furball warrior paid them no heed, instead happily munching on his reward as blips and screens blinked into existence all around the void.

"Congratulations to the Chosen of Mimir, Jerbull! For ending the trial a day early!" Rocky exclaimed, eyes shaking uncontrollably as its gray body bobbed up and down with excitement.

"Now! Without further ado, let's get to the rewards!"

As Rocky shouted, the screens began to change. The information and rankings of each contestant scrolled along the screen, as a little crown materialized atop Jerbull's head.

[Hidden Scenario Cleared!]
1st [Jerbull]
[Quest Objective! Survive for 28 Days!]
[Failed!]
1st [Jerbull]
1st [Abdullah Tel'svi'norri Li'hiken]
1st [Adam Glow +2]
1st [Sethis Gorgana]
1st [Lyke]
1st [Leo Redfield]

A strange emotion stirred in Adam's chest, seeing the man's full name. He turned to Liza, several questions buzzing in his mind as he realized she was no longer on the list of contestants.

[Secondary Quest Rankings]
[Sub Quest 1: Protect Survivors]
1st [Jerbull: 3,442,345,221]
2nd [Abdullah: 99]
3rd [Adam Glow: 69]

[Sub Quest 2: Kill Survivors]
1st [Adam Glow: 423,099,969]
2nd [Lyke: 489]
3rd [Sethis Gorgana: 23]
4th [Abdullah: 3]
5th [Jerbull: 0]

What...? Approximately sixteen eyes turned to gaze at Adam with shock. Even Abdullah couldn't disguise his surprise, as the canine snarled. *WHAT?*

"I... h-how?" was all Adam could say as he stared at the scoreboard.

"Good question, Chosen!" Rocky exclaimed excitedly, shortly before several screens swapped to images of feral nekofolk, running, leaping, and hounding down survivors. One of them boarded an aeroplane—at any other time, he would be delighted to learn it was not a beast of burden, but a mechanical vehicle built and controlled by humans.

Now, however, he could only focus on the image before him, watching with horrified fascination as the man rubbed his bandaged bite mark, taking a seat in between several passengers. Within an hour he'd become a nekofolk. It wouldn't be long before the rest of the passengers followed suit.

Dozens, no, *hundreds* of screens, each moving picture showing hordes of cat folk, leaping from building to building and chasing down survivors.

All of this, starting from one bite. A bite from Junith.

Adam turned, looking at the former paladin of Voltrain, who stared mortified at her actions. Watching as *her* infection tore people to bits, before turning their fangs and claws to the zombie hordes that began to crop up.

"Kudos to you for ingenuity! I actually had to start the trial a day early, because of you lot!" Rocky congratulated, its cheery tone contrasting Adam and Junith's horrified expressions. "Don't be so glum, chum! It's time for *reeeeewards!*"

In front of the images of mass destruction appeared new screens, showing each contestant their rewards from the trial.

[Title Obtained! Mass Murderer!]

[Title Description: You have reaped the lives of thousands without care. +10 Ego +5 Arc. All sentient species will be wary of you.]

But I...

[Title Obtained! Enemy of Humanity]

*[Title Description: You have culled a significant percentage of the human population, ensuring that your deeds will be recorded in the annals of a realm's history. All humans will instinctively view you with fear while this title is active, and must make an **Ego** check to resist. +30 Ego, +20 Arc, +10 Con, +300% Damage to Humans]*

I didn't...

[Title Obtained! Patient Zero]

*[Title Description: Through your deeds, you have spread sickness and death that has touched thousands. A walking pestilence, even the Goddess of Plagues is impressed by the virulency of your capabilities. **+200% Infectiousness for all infectious abilities.**]*

Adam read the list of his new titles, again and again.

Am I...

[Kill Counter Conversion: 423,099,969/100
= 4,230,999.69 EXP]
/2 Followers
1,410,333.23 EXP]

A villian?

[Level Up!]
[Level Up!]
[Level Up!]
[Level Up!]
[Level Up!]
[Level Up!]
[Level Up!]

A flood of level up notifications played, as Adam's level skyrocketed. Somewhere, Rocky was singing to lighten the mood, something about having done a good job, but it all felt distant, muted. Numb.

[CONCATULATIONS! Level 20 Achieved!]
[Bonus!] +5 Skill Points!
+2 Ability Points!
[Subclass selection unlocked!]
[CONCATULATIONS! Level 30 Achieved!]
[Bonus!] +1 Skill Points!
+2 Ability Points!
[CONCATULATIONS! Level 40 Achieved!]
[Bonus!] +2 Skill Points!

+2 Ability Points!
[Level 43]

Beside him, Junith fell to her knees. For once the nekopair understood each other perfectly, equally astounded by the turn of events.

The nekoboy's face grew ghost-pale. He had been aware, to some extent, of the risk Junith's bite carried. But he had *never* imagined it would be so far-reaching. So catastrophic.

He looked up at the images that swirled, each a reflection of the realm they had left behind.

I...

[Trial Two: The World That Devoured Itself]
[Cleared!]

He couldn't do it any more, couldn't keep watching, as his empty stomach churned. Adam looked away, instead watching as the other Chosen busily examined their new items and rewards.

Abdullah held a shield, Sethis a bow, while the wolfman got a sturdy black stick of some kind, which it was holding in its mouth.

Sethis glared at Abdullah, but with the barrier separating them, there was no way for her to attack the man as he grinned, taunting her with her bloody missing appengage.

Why?

[Calculating Trial Contributions...]
[Calculating...]
[Calculating...]

His gaze returned to the blue screen, numbly watching as it calculated rewards.

[Your Contributions have netted you a significant reward!] [Cicero's Gacha Coin x 20]
[Please select an—ERROR! Selection Overridden!]

Without any inpoint an item materialized, a glowing yellow page that floated out of his interface.

Adam grabbed it, eyeing the golden page as it emitted light. It felt so soft, so comforting.

[Unique Rarity Skill: Summon Red-Eyed Death Knight of The Bronx!]
[Mana Cost: 1000]
[Skill Description: *Once a day, channel mana to call forth a unique undead Knight of the Abyss. Stats scale proportionate to Faith. This Knight is an indestructible noble soul, one that gave its life so that another may live. As a being tethered to the infinite abyss, it can never be spiritually destroyed. If felled in combat, it will mark its target for vengeance.* **Upgradable]**

"Y-You! You!" Junith began. Adam could only glare at her. He could see the accusation already in her eyes, her confusion, the need to shift blame, the words on her tongue about to be unleashed.

"Be quiet and sit still," he commanded. Behind her Liza cowered, staring at him as she would a slavering beast.

Tsk. Adam winced. *Those eyes.* Those damn, fearful eyes. Her gaze was the same one he'd seen so many times before.

It's not fair…

While everyone else around him was caught up in their rewards, no care in the world about the effect they had on the realm they left, he clenched his jaw, a fury rising inside him.

It's not fair…

Eye shut, fists balling. Thoughts and possibilities swirled within his mind. Actions he could have taken beforehand, paths he could have walked... if *only* he didn't waste time with Redfield going to stores, if *only* he'd tested Junith's capabilities more thoroughly, if *only*....

Yet none of them mattered. What was done was done.

Adam accepted this.

He *had* to. He was an accomplice in the deaths of millions, and now was being rewarded for his role in their demise.

These gods... He could only feel disgust. Not only with himself, but also for the beings who gleefully rewarded such titles and items. Who allowed such misery. Who planned for, *encouraged,* such an eventuality.

The recordings displayed the carnage from so many angles, preserving it for all time. Hours of perverted entertainment, that Rocky showed off like it was something to be proud of.

What the Nyx is the purpose of these trials?

His gaze fell to his palm, his claws. More research was necessary. There *had* to be a purpose. Some rhyme or reason, some rational explanation as to why such chaos was permitted.

"What's done is done," he said aloud as Junith looked away from him, not realizing he was affirming it to himself, rather than her. He said it again. "What's done is done." But it didn't mean he had to be happy about it. No, if anything, now he had a mission. Something to strive for. A target.

The very gods themselves.

"Congratulations, Chosen, for surviving your trials! And good luck on surviving trial three!" Rocky concluded, as it began to glow, synchronizing with the blue embers wafting off of everyone's bodies. "Until we meet again! Thank you for visiting my realm!"

Adam grit his teeth, then sighed as he was teleported away.

Catpurr 93
Arguing in a Field of Reeds

Surrounded by an open field of lilies and reeds, Adam stood, staring at the azure expanse of sky above, a familiar golden city visible in the distance.

They were back in Rigellia.

"You! You! YOU!" Junith cried over and over again, stuttering as she struggled to process what had transpired.

"Use your words," he told her.

"YOU MADE ME! YOU—"

"I did not *make* you do anything!" he snapped. The nekogirl flinched as he jabbed her hard enough to force her back. She stumbled, then growled, balling her fists to strike Adam, who merely glared down at her.

"What? Are you going to hit me? Attack me? Go ahead. Do it," he coaxed, gaze unwavering. They stood closely together, noses almost touching. "No one told you to bite anyone, no one told you to act like an animal, no one *told* you to be a petulant child. If you want anyone to blame, then blame yourself, and the gods who made it possible for such an event to occur. Blame *Voltrain*."

"You! You dare blaspheme God!"

"*News flash, Junith!* Your god abandoned you!" he roared. "Abandoned you *to me!* Your foe! Your archnemesis! The very being that you were supposed to smite! The person you traveled realms to kill!"

He pointed at Liza.

"*And SHE!* She was ordered to kill me! To kill *you!* And yet she failed, because of me! So where is your god now, Junith?! WHERE IS HE?!"

His fingers dug into the scruff of her oversized white shirt, raising her off the ground. She grappled with him, failing to free herself as she spat and hissed.

"You lie," she said.

"DO I? DO I? YOU!" Adam pointed at Liza who flinched, not expecting to be called on as she sat in the dirt. "WHAT QUEST DID YOU RECEIVE FROM VOLTRAIN?!"

Slowly her gaze passed from Adam, to Junith, and back again. "ANSWER ME!"

"To... eliminate the followers of Eli. Adam. And Junith."

His head snapped back to Junith with a pointed, bitter look.

"I'll tell you where your god is. He's up above, looking down and watching us like playthings for his amusement. He's pissed off because not only has he failed to kill me once, now he's failed twice. You worship a so-called omnipotent being, who can't even kill one measly man."

"Shut up."

"Voltrain doesn't care about you. He never has, all the lives you've reaped, all the sweat, blood, and tears that you've shed in his name was meaningless. You were only a puppet—"

"ENOUGH! UNHAND ME!" Junith yelled, digging her claws into his skin.

"No. NO! You will listen to me!" Adam barked, ignoring the pain as Junith drew blood. "Your god doesn't care about you! He never has! And it's time you accept that fact! Voltrain has abandoned you, and wants you dead."

Her expression relaxed, brows smoothing out, as her pupils shrunk to pinpricks. She released his wrists, gaze dropping to the serpent mark on her hand.

"I... I..." Junith whimpered, her voice breaking as her eyes grew moist, fresh tears streaming down her face as it contorted under his words.

Damn it.

"Tsk!" Adam dropped her in a nearby bed of lilies, unable to stomach looking at her crying face any longer.

[Time Remaining until next Abyssal Trial: 719:59:57]

It was then that a familiar notification appeared, distracting him. *Thirty days.* Then he properly noticed Liza. The girl was still alive, having avoided a smiting from her god. *And now with more baggage.*

Adam sighed, considering his next course of action. In the distance, Vilenciel lay, but he wasn't quite sure how he was going to explain his sudden disappearance or re-appearance, accompanied by two additional nekofolk.

"Ah, crapbaskets." He'd been in such a hurry to leave, and now had no idea how to deal with the mess he'd left behind. It wasn't just Madam Valentine, but also the mess in the city square, and—*Wait a minute.*

He removed a very special item from his storage ring.

[The Trickster's Persona (SSR)]
[Item Description: *A half-mask once worn by a man falsely accused. With this mask, he brought corruption to light, and helped to reform society for the better, despite his unfair treatment. Unfortunately, he would one day be hit by a bus, teleporting him to a distant realm. When worn, this mask changes in accordance to its bearer's personality, shifting to obscure the wearer by way of illusions and distorting perception to shift their face as needed.* **10 EGO Minimum Required, +3 EGO,** *Soul Bound Upon Equipped. Regalian Item. ???, ???]*

Adam sighed. Sadly he only had one of these, and a child running around with a mask would be suspicious no matter what.
Hmmm.

BETA SYSTEM v1.04

TITLE: The Primordial Eli's Chosen (+20% Mana recovery, +5 Arcana. Undead Favorability)

NAME: Adam F. Glow

SPECIES: Nekoboy

LEVEL: 43

EXP BAR: 300/18000

MAIN CLASS: Nekomancer

Sub Class:

HP: 300/300

MANA: 15/285

EVOLUTION POINT: 0

Gacha Coins: x 20

Free Points: x 146

[Followers: 01]

[Bonded: Junith Oatheart Lvl Maxed]

[Evolution Available!]

Stats:

STR: 15

CON: 30

DEX: 15

ARC: 50(47)+5+2 **(EQ)**

SEN: 13

EGO: 13

[RESISTANCES]: Fire (5%) Inertia 10%

Buffs: Loved by Undead (unique), Blessing of Eli (unique), Eyes of a Predator V1, Corrupted Blessing of Nyx (unique), Adherent of Death V1, Explosive Renaissance V1, Pain Tolerance V1

Debuffs: Ha! You Sacrificed Your Stats for a Cat?! V1 (curse), Catsification V1 (curse), Wet (Catsification)

Skills: Animate Bone V1, Irritating Touch V1, Cat Claws V1, Identify V1, Summon Greater Skeleton V1 (++), Mana Bolt V1 (++), Artificial Linguistics {Rigellian}, Genocidal Aura, Summon Morian Crab, Mana Claws, Summon Red-Eyed Death Knight of The Bronx
Skill Points: 36

Well, there was some good news: all the level ups had boosted his stats appropriately, and he had plenty of points to spare.

Might as well just get this out of the way.

ARC 50 → 150

"HULP!"

With no hesitation, Adam dumped a hundred points immediately into Arcana.

Oh no.

Unfortunately, however, this abrupt and sudden spike of mana capacity caused his body to spasm. Every muscle seized up.

[Arcana Requirement Met!] (75)
[Natural Mana Recovery increased!]
[5MP per Hour]
[Arcana Requirement Met!] (100)
[Natural Mana Recovery increased!]
[15MP per Hour]
[Arcana Requirement Met!] (125)
[Natural Mana Recovery increased!]
[20MP Per Hour]
[Arcana Requirement Met!] (150)
[Natural Mana Recovery increased!]
[30MP Per Hour]

"Hep," he croaked. "Huuhlk. Halp."

Liza and Junith turned to stare at him, both wondering what was going on as he spasmed, completely losing control of his body. It twitched and jerked his limbs suddenly stiff and uncooperative. Speaking felt like doing so with a mouth full of marbles.

"Heaaaaa. Gizzalsnlaslk. Skllkksnlcnacaw."

"Is... he okay?" Liza asked, whispering to Junith as she leaned over.

Junith said nothing, running her claws over her serpent tattoo.

"Heha. Huuuuuuugggggggg. Haaalp meeeeeeek," Adam croaked, his eyes twitching and his face contorted. Within his body, mana circuits sparked and overloaded, causing steam to rise into the air. "Hwah hwah hwaaaaaa hwab bwha bwah."

"I think something is wrong with him."

Pooft.

Liza blinked. "Did... did he just... did he just fart glitter?"

Junith remained silent and impassive as the nekomancer foamed at the mouth. His foot caught on a rock as he went sprawling into a bed of reeds, eating dirt.

Why? Why does... ev...vry...thing.

He let out a low moan, before finally passing out, blissful unconsciousness accompanied by one more bout of glittery flatulence.

* * *

Elsewhere, in a distant realm...

Sitting in his pink bathrobe, Eli sat before an orb of cerulean flame, hung in the center of his chambers. Within the fire was a floating image of Adam, which his eyes remained fixed upon.

His worn and scuffed skeletal hand hovered over a series of buttons on a black contraption, balanced upon his throne of obsidian and bone.

Eli's jaw cracked, as the primordial skeleton wracked his memory vortex, struggling to recall which button caused which effect. Some of them had been determined not by him, but by certain meddlesome visitors. At last, he pressed one.

The empty underground chamber was suddenly filled by the echoes of ringing bells, bouncing off the stalagmites.

"Meow?" the voice of a cat answered.

"Bastet, please."

"Meow meow, meow meow, meow."

"This is Eli."

"Meow meow, meow?"

"Yes, I see. Yes, I am available to hold."

"Meow."

Upbeat music blared from the line, a tone that echoed throughout his chambers, as the Primordial God of Death sat in silence.

An indiscernible amount of time passed, the tone looping over and over again until finally, Eli raised his skeletal hand, conjuring a floating blue orb that displayed on a familiar orange-haired woman with cat ears.

She was in battle, the Goddess of Fertility and War, fighting against a horde of voidspawn alongside hundreds of panthers, lions, and jaguars in a realm overrun by monsters.

As the woman prepared to strike a purple monstrosity composed of thorny vines, he raised his hand. The goddess blinked out of existence, reappearing before Eli.

"RAWWW!" Bastet screamed, driving her fist into the smooth onyx floor of Eli's home. A violent impact traveled across the ground, creating fissures in the floor and walls.

The woman froze, noticing the sudden change in environment. "ELI?!"

"Hello, Bastet."

"ELI?! What am I doing here?! Why did you teleport me?!" the goddess screamed, slanted pupils shaking as her hackles rose.

"Yes, yes, calm down. I have to ask, why did you make my Chosen flatulate glitter?"

"What?!"

"Why did you—"

"I know what you said! Send me back, right this moment! RIGHT NOW!"

"Yes, after—"

"BECAUSE IT WAS FUNNY. NOW SEND ME BACK!" Bastet roared. Eli raised his body fingers, complying with the catwoman's wishes.

"Funny, hmmm," he mused, returning to the scrying portal, just as Adam's companions began covering his unconscious body with twigs and leaves

Catpurr 94
Truce

Some time later, the sound of laughter roused Adam. The scent of cooked meat filled his nostrils and he tried to sit up, only to find his entire body sore, steam still curling from his skin.

"Ow." Above him was a canopy of leaves, held together by sticks and knotted vines.

Carefully, he managed to shift, eyes peering out of the little hole of his makeshift canopy which shielded his whole body, more or less, from the elements. The one exception was his legs, which plainly stuck out, clear as day.

Or, well. Night, seeing as some time had passed.

Seriously? E for effort, at least...

Adam shuffled, crawling out from under the pyramid of leaves. The light of a campfire nearby immediately drew his attention.

Sitting around it were Liza and Junith, laughing as they shared a meal of cooked rodent.

A rustling caught their attention, both nekogirls turning towards the bleary-eyed nekomancer. The mood was swiftly extinguished.

They stared at him, saying nothing.

Oh... great.

"Evening," Adam croaked as he sat up, clutching his head. "Any left for me?"

The pair's disgust became more apparent as he approached, but they said nothing. The nekoboy chose a patch of earth opposite them to sit.

"Get your own," Junith growled finally, as Liza glared at him.

Are they teaming up against me?

"You know. I could just order you to give me your food," he said, glancing thoughtfully at the pair and their meal.

The nekotrio stared at one another until Junith frowned, reluctantly holding out the charred leg of a small creature.

"Thank you," he said, eyeing the meat but not taking it.

"Not that we have a choice," Junith spat.

Adam scoffed. "Of course you do. You could choose to not hand me a piece. Then I could choose to order you to hand me a piece."

Their traditional staring contest commenced.

"Not much of a choice, is that?" Junith spat.

"But it's still a choice. Even if coerced or under duress." A skeletal cat appeared by Adam's side as he continued eying the piece of rodent, before waving it away.

Junith blinked, retracting her hand and placing the meat on a nearby construct of tied-up twigs and leaves, some kind of pseudo-tray.

For some time there was only the almost sarcastically merry crackling of the campfire. No one said a word as the moon beamed its light onto the trio in the woods.

"Believe it or not..." Adam began, eyeing the skeletal cat in his lap, "I'm not your enemy, Junith. In some ways, we want the same thing."

"Oh, yeah? And what is it I want?"

"Empowerment of humanity, of course," he said, folding his arms. "Isn't that one of the tenets of Voltrain? The Golden God of Light, the Champion of Humanity, the Primordial Being of Light and Life? The Pure—"

"Is there a tavern between here and the point you're trying to make?" she growled.

"The point, Junith Oatheart, is that I'm extending an olive branch." His golden eyes gleamed in the firelight, trying to catch her gaze. "I'm not a fool. We will be spending nearly a year together, a year where we'll have to watch each other's backs, in a world hostile to our presence. And the way I see it, this plays out a number of ways."

"Oh?" Her face scrunched. "Please do tell me how you envision my enslavement to you."

Adam scoffed. "Please, you're hardly my slave."

"Says the master holding the leash."

"Look, Junith, I'm trying to be diplomatic."

"And that's going swimmingly, isn't it."

"If you shut up and let me talk, then maybe I could make some progress with your stupid, bigheaded—"

"STUPID?! YOU'RE THE ONE WHO ASSASSINATED OUR KING!"

Adam rolled his eyes, sighing. "It's been like a year, are you still on this? I apologized like *seven times!*"

"AN APOLOGY! Doesn't cut it when you commit *regicide* using heretical magics!"

"Well, excuse me for punishing someone harassing a woman."

"THAT SOMEONE WAS THE KING! AND SHE WAS HIS CONCUBINE! THAT'S HER *JOB!*" The nekogirl leapt to her feet, gesturing as if she'd rather be wringing Adam's neck.

"TO BE RAPED?!"

"TO BREED AN HEIR FOR THE IMPERIAL CHURCH!"

The argument quickly escalated, both shouting at each other as Liza shrank back, nibbling on her meat.

"You're insufferable!" Junith screamed.

"And you're an idiot."

"I! AMM NOTH AM IDIOT!"

"Says the idiot that just bit her tongue, like a dumbass."

"AM NOT DUMB! AM NOT DUM!" Junith shrieked, blood leaking from her mouth.

"Dumdum dumdum!" Adam sang, giving into his childish urges, as he pointed at Junith whose face suddenly contorted.

Oh—

"RAWWWWRGH!"

His follower lunged, tackling him. The two rolled in the dirt, clawing, pulling hair, and grappling each other. Somehow Junith emerged with the upper hand.

WHAT?!

She straddled him, pinning Adam to the grassy ground by his shoulders as he tried to fight her off.

"The Nyx?!" he cried. Suddenly Junith possessed a strength disproportionate to her tiny size and stature.

[Follower Menu]
[Junith Oatheart]
[HP: 900]
[MP: 230]
[Vocation: Priestess of Eli Lvl 20 (MAX)]
[Vocation Evolution Available!]

CRAP.

"GET OFF ME!" he bellowed. The serpent symbol blazed, almost responding to his emotions.

Its bearer spasmed, immediately gritting her teeth as her hands shifted to hover around his neck.

"GAAAH! GAAH! I HATE YOU! I HATE YOU!" she yelled in frustration, unable to close her fingers. Adam prepared to dump all his free points into Strength, resolving to yeet his archnemesis.

"Can you guys bang already?"

The pair stopped, turning to Liza in eerie unison. Adam's newest follower seemed entirely unimpressed, chewing on her meat while watching the spectacle.

"What?" Liza shrugged, unbothered by their twin glares. "I'm just saying, there's a *lot* of tension that could be settled if you two just banged."

"Ew."

"Disgusting."

They turned back to one another, disdain on both their faces.

"At least we agree on one thing," Adam said as Junith spit in his face. He pursed his lips as she stood up, stalking to the boundary of their camp, where the shadows were thickest.

"Really? Was that really called for?" Adam said.

"Ya know, in some places that's someone's kink. People would pay money for you to do that to them," Liza added, drawing a look of disgust from Junith as Adam sat up, calmly wiping the bloody sticky spittle off his face. By now his expression was touched by more annoyance than anger.

"You're such a child," he murmured.

"And you're insufferable."

"And you're an idiot."

"And you're—"

The two verbally circled each other, about to begin their dance of insults once more before Liza suddenly cleared her throat.

"This is fun and all watching... whatever this is. But what do you plan on doing with me? I know your plans don't exactly include my presence," Liza asked, her eyes focused on Adam.

[Follower Menu]
[Eh'Liza Oktober Lvl 5 (MAX)]
[Progression halted until Vocation Selection!]
[HP:70/70]
[MP:10/10]

Huh... He looked at the girl. The ex-Chosen was surprisingly calm and collected despite, considering her situation.

Honestly, Adam had no clue what to do with Liza. He wasn't exactly keen on slavery, nor was he looking for companions, and whatever she could do an undead could already do better. Not to mention, he'd have to provide her clothes, food, and shelter, on top of dealing with Junith.

"Do whatever you want," he said. The proclamation seemed to shock Liza. "As long as you follow the tenets I laid out, I don't particularly care what you do. Just don't harm the innocent or undeserving."

"I... see." Liza gazed at the sky, displaying a look Adam knew all too well.

For the first time, she was staring at an alien starscape.

Adam pulled up the follower list, eyeing the classes the woman had available.

[Available Vocations Based on criteria!]
[Squire: *Must be a servant*]
[Vassal: *Must be a servant under someone who has commanded an army*]
[Rogue: *Must possess innate talent and have stolen something*]
[Assassin: *Must possess Cold Blooded and have committed premeditated murder*]
[Marionette: *Must be under the control of another with autonomy restricted.*]
[Enchantress: *Must have charmed another for self gain and possess Arcana*]
[{Unique} Penitent of Adam: *Commit a crime and be judged by Adam, Chosen of Eli*]

I made a class?

Just by looking at the classes available, Adam could get a pretty good feel for her life. Assassin and enchantress both led him to believe she wasn't the most morally sound, so far as people went.

Might as well choose the unique one. He couldn't say much about the penitent's skills or abilities, but it was undoubtedly suitable for the girl. A permanent stain that would remain with her forever.

[Vocation selected!]

Liza blinked, looking away from the stars to stare at Adam, expression unreadable.

[Follower Menu]
[Eh'Liza Oktober Lvl 36]
[HP:70/1500]
[MP:50/500]

Light and steam enveloped her body as the sudden influx of energy transformed her to her very core.

Liza let out a groan, doubling over. Tendrils branched out from the crest of the serpent, covering her body, coating her arms, legs, and even her face. Odd runic symbols winked into existence, shimmering with violet light.

"What are you doing to her?!" Junith demanded, only for Adam to lift a hand to silence her. The light flared brighter, leaving searing after-images on both their eyelids. "Don't—"

"Hush!" he repeated, narrowing his eyes. Now the light began to fade, revealing the silhouette of a taller, humanoid form.

Liza stumbled out, her body shedding skin as if she were molting, bits of her fading away as her new form emerged.

Her hands seemed to catch her attention, bigger than usual. As the rest of the light faded, her new form was revealed. The nekogirl had grown taller, thicker. Now her body seemed to be that of a teenager, rather than that of a child.

Did... did she just grow?! Adam turned to Junith, wondering if the same thing could happen to either of them. *Maybe I won't be cursed to suffer this form forever.*

"I'm... a teenager again?" Liza whispered, expression confused as Adam approached her. Clinically he scanned her body, gaze finally landing on the serpentine mark.

"Fascinating... Perhaps I could use you after all..." he muttered, an idea forming in his mind as he looked down at the trickster's persona, still clutched in one hand.

Liza was left speechless as the nekopair observed her.

"Listen, Junith," he finally said, peeling his eye away from his follower's new form. "I'm not asking us to be friends. I'm not asking you to like me. Nyx below, I'm not even asking you to *protect* me. All I'm asking for is a truce. At least until we can go home. I only want to hold my cat again, to make sure he's safe. That's *all* I ask."

Junith seemed to actually hear his words, as she fell into a thoughtful silence.

"Maybe along the way, uncover more about the gods and these *Trials*. Maybe even find a cure to our condition," he said, drawing an odd expression from the former paladin of Voltrain. "You have to be curious, aren't you? About the gods and their schemes. About the curse that affects us both?"

Junith narrowed her eyes. "My place isn't to question Voltrain. Same as it isn't—"

"But you *are* curious," Adam interjected. "Curious as to who could defy Voltrain? Who could wield power enough to snuff out the Golden God's light? Think of it as research, in the name of understanding your god's archfoe."

***

Elsewhere, at the same time.

"Aakh-*KCHOO!*"

Voltrain blinked, narrowing his host's brown eyes as he looked down at his spilled ultramarine blue paint and figurines ruined by his sneeze.

"Tsk."

* * *

Junith inhaled, debating her options.

"I'm only asking for a truce. Once we're home and I have my cat, you can join the rest of your church to hunt me, for all I care," Adam said. "Can you do that? For one year? Help me learn more about the gods and watch each other's backs. One year, that's all I ask."

He held his hand out, extended for a shake.

She scrutinized that hand as if it were a venomous serpent, eyes darting between it and Adam's unwavering golden gaze.

Adam held his breath as she grit her teeth, muscles tensing as he considered the possibility of another fight.

But what happened next caught him entirely off-guard.

"Tsk, fine. I can settle for a truce," she spat, and she clasped his hand.

As they shook, he inwardly grinned, already making plans for the future. In his free hand he held the trickster's persona, as he turned to grin at a stupefied Liza.

Side Chapter 1

Schrödinger's New Bed

POV: Schrödinger

Meow. Meow. Meow meow. Meow meow. Meow. Meow meow meow meow. Meow meow meow meow meow meow meow. Meow meow meow meow meow meow meow. Meow meow meow meow meow meow meow meow meow meow meow meow meow meow meow meow meow meow meow meow meow meow meow meow meow meow meow meow meow meow meow meow meow meow meow meow meow meow meow meow meow meow meow meow meow meow meow meow meow meow meow meow meow meow meow meow meow meow meow meow meow meow meow meow meow meow meow meow meow meow meow meow meow meow meow meow quack meow meow meow meow meow meow meow meow meow meow meow meow meow meow meow meow meow meow meow meow meow. Meow meow meow meow meow meow meow. Meow. Meow meow meow.

* * *

In the Holy Sanctum of Voltrain, a pure ball of fluff with glowing red eyes reclined upon a fallen statue of a god, perched in decadent repose on its cracked marble body as it gazed upon its minions and servants.

Of course, scribes and nuns of Voltrain weren't really Schrödinger's servants, but that was only because they did not yet recognize the true god which they should be serving.

"Meow," Schrödinger intoned, the cat's very voice creating a vibrating pulse. The building shuddered with the earth, causing the clergy clad in black and white to tremble with it.

[Targets affected by Fear: 21]

The text blinked in front of Schrödinger. It batted at the words, scattering the church's denizens with a swipe of its mighty paw.

"ABOMINATION! FOUL ACCURSED BEEEEEEING!" a voice screamed. Schrödinger's gaze, bright with righteous indignation, towards the man in shining armor, radiating a light so bright Schrödinger's eyes dilated. The man sashayed through the pews with nigh-on hubristic confidence.

Immediately the chaos ceased, the panicked scribes turning to their savior with starstruck eyes. "Sir von Chesty!"

"It's the Blade!"

"The one blessed by the Holy Queen herself!"

"They said when he was two, he exterminated an entire village of heretics using only his feet, and dance moves blessed by Voltrain himself!"

"No, no! I heard he once had a breakdance battle that lasted three days and three nights with the Necromancer Adam over the souls of an entire kingdom!"

* * *

Elsewhere—Adam

"ACHOO! Why do I feel like someone's spreading lies about me?"

* * *

"Did he win?"

"Of course!"

"SIR CHESTY, WE LOVE YOU!"

"Please sign my head!"

[Fear effect dispelled!]

"Fear not, my fellow worshippers! I, sir Dominic von Chesty le Blanc, Blade of the Church, holiest of Voltrain's knights, champion of a million battles—" The wide-chinned man unsheathed a blade of gold from his silver scabbard, brandishing it as runes blazed to life, engraved across every inch of its surface. "—SHALL LAY TO REST THIS FOUL CORRUPTION!" he cried, triumphantly.

"SIR CHESTY, LET ME HAVE YOUR BABIES!"

"Dude, how would that even work? You're a guy."

"LOVE FINDS A WAY!"

The armored knight laughed, gesturing his free hand at the church servants-turned-fangirls, who immediately squeed. "Yes, yes. Voltrain's light be with you, my fellow worshippers!"

"He called me a fellow! A fellow!" one scribe screamed.

"Meow?" Schrödinger demanded, as the crowd became enraptured by the shiny weapon in the knight's hand.

"Today, the taint left behind by your corruptive master fades away as I! Dominic von Chesty le Blanc, Greatest of all Swordsmen! Holiest of all soldiers of Voltrain! Man blessed in the holy waters of Viliskapor! Slayer of Wingelum the Tyrant Penguin! Man of a thousand women! Stand before you, with the sword of Akelum!"

"Meow," Schrödinger considered, its eyes tracking the glittering blade as the man tossed it first to one hand, then the other. The glamorous weapon went spinning, and twirling as the very air began to hum with energy, and the crowd of servants cheered.

"NOW! RECEIVE THIS BLOW!" The man swung, bringing down the full wrath of his attack upon the cat.

Bonk.

"Huh?"

[Attack Nullified!]

The Holy Sword bounced off Schrödinger's head, having zero effect on the fluffy animal.

Chesty blinked, the effects of his attack catching him off guard.

Bonk.

[Attack Nullified!]

He gave the sword a quick polish and tried again.

BONK!

[Attack Nullified!]

BONK!

[Attack Nullified!]

BONK!

[Attack Nullified!]

"Meow," Schrödinger replied, affronted, its fluffy tail swishing as its eyes tracked the weapon. By now, the knight was sweating. He staggered backwards as the cat booped him in the face.

"SIR CHESTY!"

"FOUL BEING!"

"KILL IT!"

"NOT HIS PERFECT JAWLINE!"

The servants each began to scream in turn, crying out, rushing to their champion, only for von Chesty to raise his hand up.

"Stay back! Its chaotic devilish magic is bound not by the laws of our realm!" the paladin bellowed, sending the congregation back. "But fear not, fellow scribes! I! Dominic von Chesty le Blanc! The most handsome man of our time! The Blade Maestro! The swordsman of a thous—"

Schrödinger pounced.

"What?! Hey! HEY! I WAS MONOLOGUING!" Sir Chesty yelled, attempting to yank the sword away from the cat. Now that the feline's jaws had closed around its new toy, it was quickly proving a futile endeavor.

"IT'S ATTACKED, SIR CHESTY!"

"KILL IT!"

"GO! TELL THE BISHOP WE NEED CATAPULTS!"

The scribes began to panic, running in every direction as von Chesty struggled to wrestle the sword away from the cat.

"HOW ARE YOU SO STRONG?! WHAT DO THEY FEED YOU, PURE PROTEIN?!" von Chesty screamed.

In response, Schrödinger growled, its eyes burning red as mana began to accumulate in them.

"Oh, no."

VROOM!

Suddenly the entire interior of the massive cathedral was dyed red as Schrödinger released his attack, an almighty noise that seemed to wash away everything in existence in a sea of red energy. Every enchantment surrounding the church broke, every person within a mile shuddered, the fearsome power of Schrödinger made manifest inspiring the denizens of Faith to flee in a blind panic.

A moment passed, then another, until finally, the light died down. Sir Chesty and the congregation were left stark naked, without any hair remaining on their bodies. In the cathedral's ceiling was a massive hole.

"Oh my stars!" a scribe swooned at the majesty of von Chesty's glutes, immediately passing out.

"It has the sword! It has the sword of Akelum!" a scribe called out, voice quivering with fear, as von Chesty stood with his jaw agape.

Meow.

Schrödinger sprawled upon the flaming weapon, the warmth of the holy blade making for a most enviable bed.

"Foul being! If you do not hand me! Dominic von Chesty le Blanc, his sword back! I shall be forced to resort to more brutish methods!" von Chesty proclaimed with his fist raised, immediately approaching Schrödinger. The feline hissed, eyes glowing red once more as molten lava began dripping out its mouth. Von Chesty shrank back, reassessing his approach. "Hmmm... Yes. Perhaps you have a point."

The knight backed off, hands raised in surrender before pushing through the crowd and running away, stark naked.

"Sir Chesty?"

"Where are you going?"

"Wait for us, Sir Chesty!"

The naked congregation ran off, chasing after their star, leaving Schrödinger alone with its thoughts.

"Meow..." Schrödinger moaned, a low, sad meow as it watched the scribes go. While their antics kept it entertained, nothing helped to fill the emptiness inside that had been there since the day it lost its master.

"Meow..." Schrödinger cried piteously, eyes closing as it cuddled the holy weapon, a feeling of drowsiness overcoming it as it began to think of Adam, and the days they spent together.

Soon. Soon he'll be back, Schrödinger said to itself, mind quieting as it began to dream of its master.

Side Chapter 2
Battle of Brothers

In the underbelly of Vilenciel City, two creatures, both of similar stature and power, squared off, each prepared to give their life for their respective cause.

"Sebastian!" Krabby crowed, using his claws to transmit his message via clacks.

"Traitor!" Sebastian returned, the once-great Guardian of Undine's Temple now but a shadow of his former self. "You dare show yourself to me, after siding with the very being that desecrated our home! Slew so many of us?!"

"I answered the great calling, brother. One that you, yourself, would be wise to answer," Krabby said. The two crabs circled each other in the toxic green water, pincers raised, as if in an *en garde* position.

"Great calling? What greater call is there than to serve and protect our home, Eugene?!" Sebastian clacked back, using Krabby's original name. "Look at you! The once-great Eugene, now reduced to a tier one servant!"

"I no longer answer to that name. I am Krabby now, first crab knight of Lord Glow, devout follower and attendant, with a form I gladly accepted!" Krabby replied, using his eight legs to propel himself backwards as a blast of mana shot out of Sebastian's eyes.

"Traitor!" Sebastian accused, fury in his clacks as he raised his pincer high and slammed down, attempting to bludgeon Krabby. But the other crab caught Sebastian's claw in his own!

The two locked pincers, both struggling, but neither gaining the upper hand. Both seemed equally matched.

"You serve a dead god, a being who can no longer protect or give blessings to our kind. A being that has long abandoned us," Krabby reasoned, shifting sideways as a claw skidded off his carapace, nearly nipping his cat-eared headband, if not for the last second maneuver. "It is time to carve a new path, a new oath, brother! One that will set us on the path of glory once more!"

"Glory? GLORY?! What glory is there, in serving the Bane of all Crabkind?!" Sebastian shot back, his entire body beginning to glow. "To be a servant! To be a slave to the very being that destroyed our Lady of the Sea's home! Have you no shame?!"

The two continued their brutal dance, both attempting to hack the other's arms off in order to gain the upper claw.

"Said the crab who remains a slave to the past!" Krabby retorted, his eye stalks blazing red, intercepting a mana blast from Sebastian with his own. A small explosion sparked to life between them, as their mana blasts collided.

"A crab's past is his legacy! His history! To deny our past is to deny oneselves!" Sebastian roared, leaping through the smoke to engage Krabby.

The two traded blows, slash for slash, mana blast for mana blast, neither crab backing down as each tried to force his ideals on the other.

"What use is the past if you never learn from it?! If you do not use the lessons of our history for the future?!" Krabby screamed, another slash marring his armored shell, nearly taking his eye stalk. "You are a fool! A fool blinded by bygone legacies!"

Sebastian let out a roar, a skill that made the air vibrate and sent Krabby flying, almost landing into the green sludge. But at the last second, the crab fired his mana blast at a wall, the force propelling him back to safety.

Krabby landed and skidded across the smooth sewer floor, pincers raised once more for the second round against the crab he once called brother.

"Eugene..." Sebastian spat, as the Abyssal Crab glowed with energy. "You have sullied the name of our great clan. Tarnished our goddess and abandoned your oath. To protect our honor, to protect our Queen's

LEGACY! *You* must be the stepping stone to return us to our former glory."

Krabby's legs tensed up, bracing for the attack that was about to come.

"Fine," Krabby spat. "If you will not bend the knee for Lord Glow, then you, like all his foes, must perish."

And Krabby glowed too, his body emitting mana, clashing against the energy released off Sebastian.

"EUGENE!"

"SEBASTIAN!"

The two crabs screamed simultaneously before blasting each other with their strongest attacks.

Side Chapter 3
The Albino Adventurer

"Lady Vilenciel! Please! Please, hold on!" Sebastian, the silver-haired butler now dressed in a silver cuirass, begged, catching up to the little girl with pale skin and red eyes. She was clad in appropriately sized enchanted armor, a lacey parasol in her hands.

"My, it's a wonderful day isn't it, Sebas?" Luluca said, smiling as she breathed in the fresh pine scent of the forest.

"Please, do not run off without alerting me, milady! The outside world is a dangerous and harsh place to one as delicate as yourself!" Sebastian said, dabbing at his sweating head with a cloth.

"The danger is part of the excitement, Sebas." Luluca smiled. "I wish to take it all in, the highs, the lows. It's such a big world out here, with realms we could never fathom!"

"Please, milady, how about we return to the castle? Return home? Your mother and sister—"

"—don't care about me," Luluca finished, her mood souring. "Besides, as gilded as it may be, the castle was never a home, only a cage. I'm glad to see it destroyed."

Sebastian sighed at the little girl's response, docilely following behind Luluca as she continued forwards, walking through the woods and inspecting the local flora.

She reached out, attempting to touch a crimson-petaled flower that had caught her attention, when she found a pristinely gloved hand catching her own.

"If you're going to touch unknown flowers, I *must* insist you wear gloves, milady," Sebastian said, reaching into his cuirass and revealing a pair of white rubber gloves. "We never know what is poisonous and what is not, without close inspection and cautious behavior."

"Thank you, Sebas. I suppose my rashness should only extend so far," Luluca replied, donning the gloves and going to work inspecting the flowers.

As his liege became entranced by the local flora, her mind lost in thought, Sebastian's gaze shifted, scanning the nearby surroundings.

They were being watched.

Sebastian quickly picked up on their scent, ever aware of the spies that had been tracking the pair since their departure from Vilenciel.

Judging from the fact they hadn't identified themselves to him, it was a safe assumption that they weren't servants of Vilenciel.

Amateurs...

"Lady Vilenciel," Sebastian said, his face breaking out into a gentle smile. "Dreadfully sorry, I'm feeling quite parched, how about I fetch us some water?"

"Huh? Oh. Certainly," Luluca replied absentmindedly as she plucked the seeds from the flower's stalk, depositing them into a vial.

Sebastian turned around, his expression morphing from an old man's gentle smile, to one of a savage hunter, his grin suddenly much sharper, toothier, as fury glowed within his eyes.

Go. Bring them to me, Sebastian said to himself, activating his skills as dozens of shadows lurched.

* * *

Simultaneously, not too far from where Luluca was cultivating an interest in botany, several masked and hooded individuals watched her, their intent seemingly anything but pure as the old man walked off.

"Paw print..." a woman in leathers whispered, calling down to her elven cohort from atop a tree branch. "Paw print... PAW PRINT!"

"What?!"

"Why aren't you answering me?!"

"Because I told you, that's a stupid code name!" Locke spat, pointing his dagger at the rogue named Rochester. "Why can't I get a cool name, like Dragon, or Canine?"

"Are you still upset? It was your idea for masks and to ask the nomad what our codenames should be, I'm just using what YOU paid for," Rochester hissed back.

"Get to the chase, humie. What do you want?!"

"What are we eating for dinner?"

"Wait, are you seriously bothering me with such a mundane question?" Locke waved a dagger at the woman, his eyes narrowing.

Rochester scoffed, almost offended. "Dinner time is the most—"

"Please," Hyde interjected, sighing with exasperation. "Please, can you two shut up and focus on the task at hand? We need to keep an eye on them."

"What's there to focus on? The girl and the geezer have been doing nothing but staring at plants," Rochester replied, waving her hands dismissively. While it was true that after their unfortunate *incident* with a feral boy in the woods they became low on money, it wasn't exactly like they were starving.

"That *girl* should be addressed as Lady Vilenciel, please and thank you."

The trio froze, only now noticing the silver-haired man in their midst, standing primly on the very branch Rochester crouched upon.

Of them all, Rochester was the most disturbed by his appearance—she hadn't even felt him touch the tree, much less appear beside her.

"SCAT—"

Immediately the trio attempted to move, to flee, yet were stopped as shadowy hands rose up, gripping their ankles, arms, and mouths to prevent them from screaming or running away.

Rochester tried to resist, tried to pull away, as the fox mask was peeled off her face and her hood lowered by shadowy hands.

"My, how rude of me. Allow me to introduce myself," the butler said, his voice sending a chill down the trio's spines as they were gripped tightly by the shadows.

"Hello, and salutations. I am Sebastian Igneel White. Ex-dragon slayer, butler to the Vilenciel Familia, and current holder of the title 'The Fourth Horsemen,'" the butler said, bowing as if he were welcoming guests into his home. "Now that I have introduced myself, I believe it is time you state your business with the Lady of Vilenciel."

Suddenly the shadows morphed, twisting shape and form until they became clones of the butler who stood smiling at them with friendly expressions.

Rochester looked over to Locke. The three had been gathered together, side by side at the butler's mercy, their hoods down and their faces revealed.

"An elf? What a rarity. If you were closer to Vilenciel City, you'd be hunted for sport," the butler commented.

Rochester narrowed her eyes, her companions looking towards her as she began blinking in rapid succession.

Locke blinked twice, yes to the plan, as Hyde blinked thrice for no.

"Do or die." Rochester blinked.

"He'll get pissed!" Hyde blinked back.

"Interesting plan," Sebastian cut in, as Rochester's blood ran cold. "I can assure you that it would, as your companion so eloquently put it, indeed piss me off. I'd advise against it."

Fennec, he can read blips... Rochester cursed, her teeth grinding the magical capsule nuzzled between her molars.

A failsafe, one that would temporarily disable all mana manipulation in a small radius. As a non-system user, this was one of the few surefire methods regular folk had to combat the cheaters.

"Please do reconsider." Sebastian sighed. "I could just kill you here."

That was true, but Rochester couldn't risk being tortured. After all, it didn't seem like Sebastian was the kind of man to take the first, second, or even third confession seriously before he was convinced.

Screw it. Rochester bit down, activating the pill. A wave of blue energy flooded out from Rochester.

The shadows disappeared, even what appeared to be the real butler melting away, revealing that it was just another doppelganger.

"Go! SCATTER!" Rochester yelled, her companions taking off in different directions. But it was too late. Her entire world faded to black as a gloved hand suddenly filled her view, seizing her face in a death-grip.

Acknowledgements

First and foremost, I would like to thank Keanu Reeves for being a national treasure. Without handsome vampires like him, this world would be a darker place.

Thank you for reading a MoonQuill original novel. More exciting stories can be found on our website, www.moonquill.com.

We would greatly appreciate it if you could take a moment to leave a review. Every review helps the author and supports their ability to continue writing fantastic books for everyone to enjoy!

Additionally, we're looking for dedicated ARC reviewers and experienced readers to join our beta reader team. To learn more, drop us an email at info@moonquill.com or stop by our Discord.